THE COMPLETE SERIES

Whispering Cove

CATHRYN FOX

———————————

———————————

ISBN 978-1-928056-64-5

WET

In Whispering Cove

"I'll be seeing your bet." Harold Adair slammed a dollar bill in the middle of the table making a loud booming sound. "And raise you another fifty cents."

With three deuces and two face cards in his hand, he tossed two more coins into the pot. Inhaling the salty sea air wafting through the open window, he waited for the two men sitting around his kitchen table to respond. The soft breeze stirred the curtains and he glanced at the photo that sat below the windowsill. The pretty little redhead made him smile.

Stubborn and willful, she be just like her father.

The thought of his son brought a tear to Harold's weathered eyes. He coughed into his hand trying to mask the emotion tightening his throat. Of course, if his pain was still raw after all this time, he could only imagine how Andrea felt losing both her parents in that dreadful boat accident.

He raked trembling fingers through his thick gray hair. His numerous requests for the lass to return home had failed. Even dangling her ten-year class reunion did not encourage her to bury the memories and come back to visit old friends and her only living relative.

"You listening, you bloated, barnacle plucking ol' goat?" Errol Wilson's scratchy voice cut through Harold's woolgathering.

Harold's bushy brows shot upward as he pinned the aging man with a steely glare. "Bloated?" Laying his cards down, he placed his laced fingers on his extended belly and cocked his head. "Barnacle plucking ol' goat, ye say?" He slid his narrow gaze toward Byron Mitchell, another dear friend, and then winked. "I'll 'ave ye know 'tis better than bein' a pond suckin', baldin' beachcomber, who hasn't seen the bottom of a boat in over a decade."

Errol's whiskered jaw dropped and he scowled. Slowly, he reached up to touch the sliver of thin hair plastered across the top of his shiny head. For a moment, silence reigned. Then the tall, slender man patted his head before his frown dissolved and he burst into laughter. "I'll be damned if he isn't right."

Harold and Byron joined him, their deep guffawing filling the room.

When their chuckling died, Harold glanced back and forth between his friends and retrieved his cards. "So where are we?"

Byron, with his arthritic fingers gnarled and knobby, laid his cards before him. "I fold." He looked up at Harold, sympathy softening his cloudy blue eyes. "It's Andie, isn't it?"

Harold quietly nodded. "Short of me heart stop beatin', the lass may never return to Whispering Cove."

Byron cleared his throat. "You know, it's not a bad idea."

Errol's eyes widened. "*Byron!*" He tossed his cards on the table with something akin to disgust furrowing his forehead. "I can't believe you said that."

Byron waved a shaky hand, dismissing Errol. "Braydon

wasn't coming home either, until I dropped a few hints that I was having health problems."

The pit of Harold's stomach knotted. The three of them had been friends since he had left Ireland and arrived on the rocky shores of Maine. Fear almost caused him not to ask, but in the end he did. "You okay?"

Byron raised a hand before him. "If not for this rheumatoid, I'd be fit as a fiddle, but my grandson doesn't need to know that." Lowering his arm to the table, he continued. "My wife refuses to play along. Ruth says, 'I shouldn't get involved.' But the boy is almost twenty-nine, unmarried. He needs to settle down."

"The hell you say?" Errol pursed his lips, nodding his head. "My Katy is unmarried, as well."

Harold didn't need to say it, but marriage had eluded Andie too. Before she left town she had been engaged to a young man who had later become Whispering Cove's sheriff. Their relationship was a storybook romance, until the accident. Then his loving granddaughter had moved away, disassociating herself with anyone from the past. Yes, she wrote on occasions, but he missed her, wanted her back where she belonged.

A big Cheshire grin spread across Byron's face. "Braydon arrives next week, and I have just the right woman picked out for him."

"Why ye conniving old windbag," Harold barked, unable to stifle his surprise.

"What?" If innocence was what Byron was fishing for, he was casting without bait.

"You know, every time my granddaughter writes home she asks about Trent Parker." The gleam in Errol's eyes brightened. "He's never married." He thrummed his fingers on the table several times and then they stilled. "Maybe we should try our hand at matchmaking."

Without a word, Byron reached into his pocket and extracted a twenty dollar bill. He slapped it in the middle of the table, turning his attention to Errol. His chin rose in challenge. "Bet I can get Braydon to the altar before your Katy."

Errol reach for his wallet sitting next to the half empty bottle of rum he had brought to share. "You're on." Digging out two tens, he put them atop Byron's twenty, before he began to pour each of them a shot of the dark liquor. "How about you, Harold?"

"I'll take that bet, but only if I can get the lass home for the reunion." Harold raised his shot glass into the air before him. "Here's to marriage, family, and great-grandchildren."

1

Katy Wilson shifted restlessly in the spacious leather seat of her rental and stifled a yawn as she peered into the night. The bright headlights on the SUV sliced though the dark and illuminated the quiet, seaside streets. Towering oak trees lined the deserted sidewalks like Coast Guard Cadets, protecting the inhabitants who slumbered inside the quaint fishing village. Her heart lurched with longing as her gaze panned the neighborhood, noting that very little had changed since she moved away some ten years ago, turning her back on everyone and everything she loved.

The invitation requesting her presence had arrived by email, but she hadn't made any summer plans to return home to Whispering Cove, Maine, to attend her high-school reunion. At least not until her granddaddy had sent a rather lengthy letter explaining how business was down at the Seafarer, the famous East coast lobster house owned by her folks—a restaurant where Katy had learned her way around a kitchen.

"Damn economy," he'd explained. "Tourists ain't coming

like they used to." Oddly enough, Granddaddy Errol had insisted she keep her folks' financial woes to herself and had sworn her to secrecy. "They're too proud to ask for help, lassie," he'd warned.

Maybe so, but if her parents needed help, then she'd do whatever it took to help them, even if that meant braving her past and spending the summer in Maine. So here she was, back on the very street she used to cruise as a teen and hadn't spent much time on since. She'd returned home over the years, of course, but those visits had always been brief. Travelling during off hours, and cruising like a wind-propelled vessel, she'd sailed out of town as quietly as she'd sailed in, never hanging around long enough to see *him*.

Him, as in Trent Parker.

The boy she'd grown up with, climbed trees and scraped knees with, and more importantly, the boy she'd shared her first kiss with. The same boy who'd grown into a respectable firefighter and had every right to hate her.

God, what would it be like to face him after all these years?

As Katy thought about him, and the reason for their premature break-up, need prowled through her veins and a lump pushed into her throat. The last ten years hadn't been all they were cracked up to be. She'd left the quiet, unhurried streets of Whispering Cove behind and made her way to Chicago where her exceptional culinary skills had landed her a much coveted spot on daytime TV hosting her very own cooking show. Fame and fortune found her, but the hordes of fans who hustled along the bloated streets and stopped her didn't know the real Katy Wilson, the girl who played with fire trucks instead of dolls, and preferred sneakers to heels. No, those people only know her TV persona, Kathleen Wilson, celebrity chef extraordinaire.

The empty feeling in the pit of her stomach mushroomed

like a soufflé. The sobering reality of it all was that even in a big city like Chicago, Katy had found herself alone in the crowd more times than not. And she hated to admit to the people she turned her back on that her life wasn't all glitz and glamour. Deep down she longed to be home.

Now, with her contract up for renewal and her show on hiatus for eight long weeks, she had one hell of a big decision to make, because when it came right down to it, she knew life in the fast lane wasn't for her. Then again, with waning viewership, she wasn't even sure the network would want to renew her for next season. Despite all that, she yearned to be surrounded by caring, down-home folk—the kind only found in Whispering Cove. Behind her, Katy heard the roar of the ocean, the sound wrapping around her like an old familiar sweater, cocooning her in a blanket of warmth and safety.

Why had it taken her so long to appreciate the beauty and comfort in her own backyard?

She fiddled with the radio station and smiled when she came upon an old favorite. Taking the turn down her parents' private lane, she took note of the colorful flowers and trimmed hedges. She smiled. If Martha Stewart had a green thumb, her mother had a green hand. As Katy rolled her window down to inhale the sweet summer fragrances, it occurred to her just how much she ached to be back, to have things return to the way they were.

But if there was one thing Katy's gut kept telling her, it was that the past was the past and things could never go back to the way they were. Specifically when it came to Trent, the sweet, kind boy she'd walked away from. The boy who'd kissed her goodbye, but couldn't hide the sadness in his eyes. Never looking back, she'd tossed him away like an undersized catch, all for a chance to experience life in the big city. He'd let her go because all he'd ever wanted was what was best for her. She didn't deserve him, and the reason she'd never faced him over the last ten years was because she hated to see melancholy haunting his gaze, hated that she'd put it there.

She inched into her folks' driveway and watched the light in the upstairs room flick on. As Katy glanced up at the widow's peak, the glass turret overlooking the bountiful Atlantic Ocean lit up in the dark night, and she knew she'd awoken her parents. She knew how fast word of her arrival would spread, and in no time at all she'd be bombarded with questions about her future—mainly ones concerning her marital status. She also knew how complicated those answers would be. She couldn't tell anyone what her future held when she herself didn't know.

As she thought about the uncertainty of things to come, of how Trent would receive her after all this time, her heart crashed harder than the waves at Dresden Bluff. The rocky cliff was a place she and Trent had visited often, the same place she'd eagerly given up her virginity to him.

She patted the brakes, and as she tried to quiet her erratic heartbeat, wondered, for the hundredth time since she boarding the plane in Chicago, if she was making a big mistake by returning to her childhood home and facing her past, especially since her body and heart still ached to be back in the arms of the man who undoubtedly would rather run into a blazing building than rekindle their relationship's fiery embers.

2

Trent Parker didn't want to think about the plates of half-eaten food sitting on the long oaken table before him. Nor did he want to think about the pot of congealed spaghetti sauce waiting to be scrubbed. And he certainly didn't want to think about the suspicious fire up at Dresden Bluff that had caused them all to bolt from the firehouse late last night without finishing the meal he'd spent hours preparing.

But what he really, really didn't want to think about was that Katy Wilson was back in town, or the fact that he'd spotted her coming in under the cover of darkness, hoping to avoid any sort of run-in with him, he presumed.

A scraping sound behind him pulled his attention, and when he turned to see Adam Collins, his best friend and Whispering Cove's most sought-after bachelor, push open the swinging door and step into the kitchen, he shook his head to clear it.

"Hey, Trent, did you hear Katy's back in town?" Adam asked, as he sauntered across the room to grab a soda from the fridge.

Trent rolled his shoulder, hoping for casual, but the hitch in his voice belied his emotions when he said, "Yeah. So?"

Never one to be subtle, Adam added, "I hear she looks as good as ever."

Adam heard wrong. Katy didn't look as good as ever. She looked better than ever. He'd gotten a good look at her when she'd stopped her SUV at the corner of Main and Little. He was on the sidewalk next to the vehicle, and the overhead lamppost gave sufficient light for him to see her big blue eyes, dark wavy hair, creamy skin and plump lips that had his cock rising up for a front-row seat.

"I wouldn't know, and don't much care."

"So you think she's back for the reunion?"

"What part of *I wouldn't know, and don't much care* didn't you get?"

"The *don't much care* part." Adam tossed him a wry grin, and it pissed Trent off that his childhood friend and fellow firefighter could read him like an open book. Adam was as quick as a brush fire sweeping through the white pines. His bright intelligence, good looks and dazzling charm attracted women quicker than a shiny lure attracted fish.

"Is that right?" Adam probed. "You really don't care?"

"Yeah, that's right."

Adam twisted the cap off his soda and leaned against the table. He got quiet for a moment, a rarity for him since he always had an opinion on everything, then said, "I wonder if I can get her autograph."

Trent shrugged and walked to the sink, turning his back to his friend and their conversation, not wanting to talk or even think about Katy anymore. He flicked on the chrome tap and poured a generous amount of soap into the basin.

"You think she'll give it to me?" Adam pressed, refusing to give up on the subject.

"I'm sure she'll give it to you if you just ask," Trent finally said, hoping to put an end to the discussion. He gestured with a nod. "Grab a cloth and dry."

Adam didn't move. Instead he said, "I wonder what else she'll give up if I just ask…"

Trent spun around. Fire rushed through his bloodstream and raised his anger from simmer to boil, but when he caught the cocky, knowing grin on his friend's face and realized Adam was simply baiting him, he grinned back and shook his head. "Fuck off, Adam."

Adam pushed off the table and clapped Trent on the back. "Come on, Trent. You want her now as much as you always have. Admit it."

"I don't want her." Trent thought about all the girls he'd bedded down with since Katy had left. "I moved on, remember?"

"What I remember is that you fucked nearly every single woman in town after Katy kicked your ass to the curb, yet here you are still pining over her like some lovesick school-boy. It's pathetic, pal. Just pathetic."

"Adam—"

"Look, why don't you try fucking *her*? Fucking all those other girls didn't help so maybe fucking Katy Wilson is the only way you're going to get her out of your system once and for all."

"Unlike you, I don't think fucking solves everything."

Adam grinned. "Well it doesn't hurt."

Trent gave an impatient sigh. "Look, I'm not going to fuck her, Adam. I'm not going to do anything with her. I probably won't even see her or talk to her when she's here, so drop it, okay?"

"Fine, if you don't want to fuck her, I will."

"Like hell you will." The words flew from his mouth before he could stop them.

Adam laughed and gave a slow shake of his head. "Yeah,

Trent. It's real clear that you've moved on."

Trent was about to open his mouth to voice an argument, but the fire alarm went off. They both dropped everything and bolted to the garage where they found the others already suited up.

Less than five minutes later they were rushing through town and heading back to Dresden Bluff. It was the second time within twenty-four hours someone had lit a fire on the hill. Trent knew the kids were antsy this summer, especially with the unusually high temperatures, and according to his friend, Sheriff Brody McGrath, teens seemed to be getting into more and more mischief lately, but rarely would they return to the scene of a crime and risk getting caught. Whoever was lighting these fires was brazen and it didn't bode well.

But something else was gnawing at him, something about the fact that the fires were set on Dresden Bluff, as if they'd been deliberately ignited at the location he and Katy used to go to make love.

Trent hadn't been back to the bluff in ten years and returning to the site now was simply a reminder of what he'd loved and lost.

They parked at the foot of the bluff and Trent and Adam ran to the top with the hose. Once the small fire was extinguished, Trent moved into the thick brush. He pushed low-hanging branches from his path and sifted through the pine needles looking for hot spots. The fire had been contained near the rocks and he was pleased to see that very little damage had been done.

As the trees closed around him, blocking him from the others, he couldn't help but think about Katy. Being so close to the spot they'd made love unlocked all those buried memories and had him reminiscing about what it felt like to hold her, kiss her, bring her to orgasm beneath the stars as they listened to the waves crash against the rocks. He thought about the way she gave herself over to him, the way she trusted him with her body, her pleasure, her heart. He thought about her unique, arousing scent—honeyed vanilla and sweeter than candy—and the way it always seeped under his skin and filled him with longing.

Jesus, it was so perfect. She was so perfect.

Then she'd left.

"Fuck!"

Trent turned back around and shelved those thoughts to the recesses of his mind, not wanting to travel too far down memory lane. Christ, Adam was right. He was pathetic. Totally fucking pathetic.

Maybe Adam was right about fucking her, too.

The truth was, he'd never gotten over Katy and loved her now as much as he had back then, which was why he hadn't begged her to stay when she said she wanted to move on to bigger and better. It cut to his core when she left, but he couldn't fault her for wanting to experience life outside Whispering Cove. Not everyone was cracked up for small-town living. He knew that truth firsthand.

Right after high school, his mother had gotten pregnant. Some said she trapped his father, but Trent didn't like to believe it. His father had gotten a scholarship upstate, but with a child on the way, he never had the chance to go. Instead, he'd ended up working the fishing vessels like his father before him. His dreams of pursuing a career in engineering were flushed out to sea. Resentment ran deep, and his dad had ended up searching for happiness in the bottom of a bottle. He'd never found it. Instead he found his way to an early grave, his mother not too far behind.

Trent swallowed down the lump in his throat as old, painful memories rose to the surface like air bubbles. Jesus, he never wanted Katy to resent him the way his dad had resented his wife and son. He knew Katy belonged in Whispering Cove, it was in her blood, but if she had to go away to find herself, to forget who she really was and take on the persona of big-city-girl Kathleen Wilson until she came to that conclusion herself, then who was he to stop her? But deep down he'd thought she'd be back. Thought she'd come home. To him.

He'd thought wrong.

So maybe Adam *was* right and it was finally time to do something to get over her.

Something drastic.

3

Every single time the bell over the restaurant's door chimed, Katy jumped out of her skin, half expecting to see Trent sauntering into the Seafarer, and half hoping he wouldn't. She'd been home only two days now and the town was abuzz with her return, abuzz with the return of all those who'd come back for the reunion, in fact. But a lot of attention had been directed at her, and the notable fact that both she and Trent were still single.

She turned in time to see Doctor Danica Kent, Braydon Mitchell and his granddad Byron walk in and felt equal measures of relief and disappointment. Her folks had told her Trent and the rest of the boys from station 415 always gathered at the restaurant on Friday, and as of yet, every other member of his team had come except him.

Seemed Trent wasn't so keen on seeing her. Not that she could blame him. After all, hadn't she gone out of her way to avoid him for the last ten years? But she was in town for eight weeks and sooner or later they were bound to come face-to-face. A nervous sensation grew in her belly just thinking about it.

Katy grabbed her notepad and stuffed it into her apron, then smoothed down the skirt on her bright pink, fifties-style uniform. She couldn't believe her parents had kept her old uniform for all these years, or that she actually still fit into it. Although she had to admit that her hips were a little wider, her breasts a little fuller and she filled the uniform out in ways she never could as a teen. It felt a little sexy, a little daring, a step away from her usual professional television attire, and she kind of liked it.

Katy crossed the wide expanse of floor as even more people came through the main door and sat themselves in mismatched captains' chairs and boat benches turned into seats. To one corner, a large gathering of tourists were laughing loudly and tossing their shells into the recessed holes in the middle of the table while taking bets on who had the best shots. A few children sat to one end and were using crayons to draw on the draping sheet of white paper that doubled as a tablecloth. As she took in the crowd, a few more people she recognized from high school found their way inside. The sight of her old classmates had her thinking of Andie Adair, her long-lost best friend. Katy somehow doubted Andie would be back for the reunion. Andie and Katy had been tight, but Andie had pulled away from everyone and everything after her folks had died.

Katy wiped the frown from her face when she reached Braydon's table. She nudged him with her hip, and with a huge smile on his handsome face, he jumped up to greet her. They hugged and exchanged a few pleasantries as well as a few teasing jibes before she took their order. Just as she was about to leave, she thought about how good Danica looked and turned back to ask where she had her hair done, thinking her own could use a new style. However, the television station didn't like for her to do anything too drastic without their permission. Thinking of the station soured her smile and reminded her that she still had a huge decision to make. But it was a decision she couldn't make until she faced Trent.

Not wanting to dwell on it right now, she went to work on filling orders.

"Katy, order up," her mother, Annette Wilson, called from the kitchen.

Katy hurried to the back room, and when her mom with her pretty silver hair cut to frame her oval face gave her a warm smile, her bright blue eyes glistening in delight, Katy's heart turned over. It was clear how happy her mother was, having all three of the Wilsons back working together in the kitchen, just like old times.

Katy wanted to ask about business, but she also remembered her promise, so instead she decided to ease into the conversation naturally. "Mom, the place is packed and you're run off your feet." Despite that, Katy thought her mother looked fit and completely happy to be hustling about. Actually, she seemed to thrive on it today as much as she had when Katy was younger. "Maybe you should hire extra help," she suggested, giving her mother an opening to talk about her finances.

Her dad, Pete, left the grill, and came up behind her mother. His gray hair might be thinning, and his eyes might have more lines framing the edges, but he was still just as strong and robust as ever. He patted his wife on the backside and winked. "Cooking keeps her young. Just look at her, she's as beautiful today as the day I met her."

Her mom went up on her toes and gave him a kiss. Katy rolled her eyes as she watched them, but deep down she knew she wanted the same thing. A loving marriage with a guy who, after thirty years, still looked at her with love in his eyes. "Do you two ever stop?"

"Oh Katy, you're such a fuddie duddie," her mother said and waved a dismissive hand.

Katy laughed, and grabbed the order. "Fuddie duddie? Now that's something I haven't been called in quite a while." When Katy left the kitchen, she spotted Andie and Brody and just about dropped her tray as she rushed across the room to see them.

After seeing her best friend, and making her swear they'd get together soon, the rest of the afternoon had flown by. As she thought about making an evening appointment at Whispering Salon, a place where she was bound to get the best gossip in town, the bell above the door chimed.

Katy shot a glance around the kitchen and noted she was all alone. Where had everyone gone? The dinner staff would be coming in soon, but where had her folks disappeared to? She'd been so busy playing with new menu ideas, hoping the addition of a few gourmet dishes would help draw in new patrons, that she hadn't paid any attention to her surroundings. Not that the restaurant had room for more patrons, she mused. They were at peak tourist season and the place was packed tighter than a tin of sardines. She alone must have rung in at least two thousand dollars in sales that afternoon. Had her grandfather been completely honest about her parents' financial troubles? But since he'd sworn her to secrecy, she couldn't ask. She could only observe. Maybe she'd try to get a look at the books later.

She heard a noise in the other room, and heavy boots scraping over the old plank floor heralded someone's approach.

"I'll be with you in a moment," she called out over her shoulder, and wiped the sticky flour from her hands. She caught her reflection in the glass refrigerator door as she hurried to the dining area. Good God, she had flour on her face, and strands of hair, once neatly piled on the top of her head, had fallen out and were jutting out in all directions. Cripes, she looked like she'd styled her hair with an egg beater.

Concentrating on trying to stick the wayward locks back into place, she rushed through the swinging door and, not looking where she was going, collided with a solid brick wall. Air rushed from her lungs with a whoosh, and she stumbled backwards. Strong hands slipped around her waist to right her, and she glanced up only to discover that the brick wall was none other than Trent Parker.

Oh God…

"Hey," he said, as capable arms packaged her tight against his body. Dark, intense eyes met hers and they exchanged a long, heated look, one that spoke of want and desire. One that nearly shut down her brain. A tremble moved through her as delicious warmth spread over her skin.

"Hey yourself," was all she managed to get out as his hands slipped from her back to rest on the sides of her hips. His touch was shockingly intimate and did the most naughty things to her libido. He splayed his hands wider, and the feeling was so sensual, so damn erotic, her skin flushed hotly and she had to remind herself to breathe.

Trent continued to hold her to him, chest to chest, stomach to stomach, and groin to groin. A low breathy moan sounded in her throat and there wasn't a damn thing she could do to stifle it.

His glance raced over her and he placed his mouth so close to hers she could taste the sweetness of his breath. "You okay?" The tenderness and genuine concern in his voice produced a familiar fullness in her chest, right around the vicinity of her heart.

"Yes. No. I don't know," she answered.

Good God, with the way he was meshing their bodies together, she could barely breathe, let alone think. But the one thing she did know was that she was *not* okay. How could she be? The man she left ten years ago, the same man who was staring down at her with equal measures of disdain and desire, held her so intimately and so possessively it was all she could do not to tear her uniform off and beg him to take her right there on the restaurant floor.

A shiver of need ran through her as she carefully extricated herself from his arms. She stood back and took a moment to gather her composure, no easy task considering Trent was standing in front of her looking like sex incarnate. Her knees wobbled and she grabbed the edge of the counter for balance.

Trent took a step closer. "Well, which is it? Are you okay, or are you not okay?"

She fussed with her hair and wiped the flour from her face as her glance devoured him. Dear God, the boy from her past had grown into one hell of a handsome man, dark eyes, short brown hair, rugged features, sun-kissed skin and a beautiful mouth she instantly longed to kiss. Her pulse leapt as she breathed in his familiar earthy scent, and when she detected the clean smell of his favorite soap beneath the surface, warm and wicked sensations stirred her libido.

She cleared her throat and prayed her voice wouldn't fail her. "I'm okay," she lied. "But how about you?" Her question sounded rushed and breathless, even to herself. "I crashed into you pretty hard, and I'm not a lightweight anymore," she teased, trying to lighten the mood.

Looking sexier than ever, he grinned down at her, but didn't answer. Instead he took a measured step back and stared at her with dark, sensual eyes that made her blood burn in a way it had never burned before. After a long, lingering look, he drove his hands into his jean pockets, pushing them lower on his hips. Katy's glance dropped to his sexy oblique muscles, which were peeking out from beneath his untucked shirt, and tried not to think about the way her fingers itched to trace each sinewy striation.

He made a noise and her gaze darted back to his face in time to see the sadness in his eyes when they clashed with hers.

He quickly blinked it away, but his voice was a little low, a little rough with emotion when he asked, "How are you, Katy? Or should I say *Kathleen*?"

Katy swallowed, and felt the sting of his words all the way to her core. She couldn't fault him for his comment, but it didn't make it hurt any less. She stiffened and adjusted her apron, understanding how things were going to be between them, and wondering how she could possibly make it right again.

"You can call me whatever you want to call me." Desperate to put some well-needed distance between them, she positioned herself behind the counter and noted the way his gaze tracked her every movement. "Did you want to place an order or did you come here to glare at me?"

"I didn't think you'd be here."

"An order it is then. What can I get you, T?"

With that he took a small step back, stumbling slightly. His shoulders tensed and his jaw flexed. Raw emotions flitted across his face as undisguised need entered his eyes.

"What?" Katy asked.

He shook his head, and she watched his Adam's apple bob as he swallowed. "Nothing," he said. "It's nothing."

Katy knew it wasn't *nothing*. She took a moment to think about what she said, and then realized she'd made a horrendous slip. She'd called him T, her private nickname for him. The same name she called him whenever they'd made make love. She resisted the urge to slap her forehead. How could she have been so stupid?

"I'm sorry. I didn't mean to call you that." She braced her hands on the counter and said, "It was just a silly slip."

He visibly relaxed. "It's okay."

"No, it's not." Feeling completely flustered, and wanting to make things right, she rushed out, "Let me make it up to you."

"You don't—"

She raised her hand to stop him and said, "Your meal is on me."

Once again he tensed, and it occurred to her that she'd just made slip number two. God, what was wrong with her? She caught the look in Trent's eyes and knew he was thinking the same thing as her. Thinking about all the fun they had with food, drizzling each other with warm chocolate, or spraying each other with whip cream and languidly licking it off. Even though he hated her—the darkness in his eyes told her so—sexual tension still hung heavy. The fiery sparks arcing between them could very well set the restaurant ablaze.

"I mean..." When she caught the gleam in his eye, her voice fell off.

His mouth curved, and he leaned against the countertop. "Go on."

Before she could answer, the bell above the door chimed and four customers walked in.

Trent straightened, and there was a hardness in his tone that wasn't there before when he asked, "How long are you in town?"

She drew a shaky breath. "The summer."

"That long, huh?"

"Yeah. I'm on an eight-week hiatus."

"I guess I'll see you around then." With that he drove his hands deeper into his pockets and turned to go.

"What about your meal?"

"I'll take a rain check." He turned back to her, and warmth moved into his eyes when he said in a low voice meant for her ears only, "Oh, and if it's okay with you, I'd like to call you Katy."

Katy's heart raced as she stood there and watched him leave. He didn't go straight for the door, however. Instead, he stopped at the corner booth, her granddaddy Errol's favorite seat, and grabbed his cane. Her granddaddy must have left it there after lunch. Normally he sat with Byron and Harold, but today Byron was lunching with his grandson and Harold was home resting. Katy had enjoyed a bowl of chowder with her granddaddy on her break, and she remembered seeing the cane. She also remembered thinking it was new. He'd been walking perfectly fine for the last two days, and when she asked about it, he brushed her off. But she had to wonder why Trent was there picking it up for him. Jeez, she hoped Errol hadn't called the fire department claiming an emergency because he'd left it behind at the restaurant. Of course, she wouldn't put it past him.

As Katy watched Trent step through the door, taking pleasure in the sight of his perfect, firm backside, she ran through their entire encounter and wasn't exactly sure what had happened. One second Trent seemed to hate her, the next he seemed to want her, and Katy couldn't help but wonder if there was anything she could ever do to get him to love her again.

Desire was the first thing Trent had felt when she'd fallen into his arms.

Anger was the second.

It was the anger that had caused him to strike out at her, intending to hurt her as much as she'd hurt him. His actions were juvenile, he knew, and he was being a prick. A total fucking prick. But he couldn't seem to help himself. The second he'd felt her body next to his, his entire being ached for her in ways that ripped a hole in his armor. But the fact that she didn't want him the way he wanted her tore at his guts and had him acting out of character.

He'd seen the hurt in her eyes, and he hated himself for putting it there. He didn't want to hurt Katy. It was just that when she'd left she'd taken his heart with him, and in ten long years she'd yet to bring it back.

Then she'd called him T, and every memory of their time together came crashing back. Memories of the way she felt beneath his body, the way her hands had touched him with aroused eagerness, and the way she'd called his name during lovemaking.

As the world around him tilted on its axis, it was all he could do to stop himself from bending her over the counter and taking her, hard and fast. To remind her how good they were together. How good they could still be together.

Fuck, how he wanted her. And she wanted him too.

Physically, anyway.

He felt the way her body had reacted to his touch, and the look in her eyes spoke of physical want, and goddammit, he wanted to be the guy to satiate that want. The second he caught a whiff of her sweet, honeyed scent, he ached to bury himself in her again, to kiss her mouth, her breasts, between her legs.

But the question was, would fucking her help get her out of his system once and for all, or would it shatter the last vestige of his control when she sailed out of town for another ten years?

Maybe it was time to find out.

4

Wind whistled through the open window in Katy's beachside rental house, and she let loose a slow, relaxing breath, thinking she'd made the right choice when she'd picked out her summer accommodations. Naturally her parents had wanted her to stay with them in their big old Victorian house, but Katy had wanted her privacy, insisting they also needed theirs.

In other words, every time she turned around she didn't want to be bombarded with questions about work, marriage, children. Trent.

She loved her parents dearly. Working together every day was one thing, but living under the same roof with them for eight weeks was seven weeks too long.

Katy stepped up to the window and inhaled the salty sea breeze. A wave of warmth and familiarity moved through her as she hugged herself and looked out over the water. Off in the distance sail boats bobbed under the setting sun as white caps crashed against the sandy shore. Her mind drifted and she couldn't help but smile as she thought about the times she and Trent had jumped those waves as children. By mid-teens they were body surfing, and by the time they'd approached their twenties, they were running off to find a private cove where the cool spray would wash over them as they made love. The ocean was a part of her life and she missed it. She also missed making love with Trent.

Katy gulped, her smile falling from her face as she pushed away from the window. Just thinking about making love to Trent had her body reacting with urgent need. Pushing those thoughts aside and not wanting to dwell on the way she'd salivated over him earlier that day at the Seafarer, she walked through the quaint rental with its pine wood furniture, planked floors and light, ocean blue fabrics—designed to give it a seaside cottage ambiance—and focused on the new recipes she'd like to try out down at the restaurant. As her mind raced with new ideas, she stripped off her work clothes and hopped into the shower. Once clean and refreshed, and deciding that she'd be staying in for the night, she dressed in a silk nightie. With no air conditioning in the rental, she'd need something light to sleep in.

Nighttime had fallen over the fishing village as she settled into her recliner with her notepad. As she jotted down meal ideas for the restaurant, she heard a noise outside. She stiffened and glanced around, but relaxed a little when she realized she was no longer in the big city where the crime rate was rising at an alarming rate. She was in Whispering Cove, where apparently the biggest crime was that she and Trent hadn't married and produced a school of kids. Still though, that noise had startled her. She waited a moment longer to see if she could pinpoint the location, but after a few minutes of silence she passed it off as nothing. Probably just the dock creaking under the pounding waves. She went back to creating a menu plan, but when something smashed against the side of her cottage, she practically jumped out of her skin.

Katy dropped her notepad and padded softly to her door to listen. She heard something, something that sounded like shuffling, and glanced at her phone, thinking she might put a call in to Sheriff Brody McGrath. Jeez, it was so odd to think her childhood friend had become a sheriff. He'd raised more hell around town than any of them. But she didn't want to disturb Brody. He seemed completely caught up in Andie, and they had enough on their plates right now.

She flicked her outside light on, inched her door open and peered into the night. When a cloud of smoke drifted by her face and the pungent aroma reached her nostrils, she flung her door open wider and rushed outside. She hurried around the corner of her rental and stopped short when she spotted Trent. He stood with his back to her, dousing the flames in her garbage can with a garden hose.

"Trent?" she asked hesitantly.

Startled and still holding the hose, he spun around, and Katy jumped back as he gave her an icy-cold bath.

"Oh Jesus, Katy. I'm sorry." Trent dropped the hose and rushed to her.

Water dripped down her face, and she sputtered as she pulled her drenched nightie away from her skin. "What the hell is going on?"

"There was a fire...in...your...garbage." His gaze kept going from the can behind him to her dripping wet nightie, which now settled nicely against her body and clung to her flesh like a second skin.

"Yeah, but why are you here?"

He grabbed his cell from his pocket, and shook it, as if that explained everything. When she continued to stare at him, he said, "I was on my way to the pub, and someone called and told me about the fire." He jerked his thumb. "I could see the can burning from the street."

"They called your cell? Not the department?" Beneath the

exterior light, Katy scrutinized him, but that scrutiny quickly turned into a heated inspection as she took pleasure in his fine-tuned body. Her gaze flickered over his navy T-shirt and low-riding jeans that exposed tight muscles and hewn thighs —rock-hard thighs she'd love to feel wrapped around her.

Warm moisture dripped between her legs and she was pretty sure it had nothing to do with getting doused by that hose. Arousal punched into her gut and her nipples tightened painfully under the sensual assault.

Trent swallowed so hard the sound carried in the still night. "Yeah, I know how it sounds..." His voice fell off, and she could only guess why. His gaze dropped to her chest, and her sex fluttered as desire flitted over his face. "I...uh... someone is toying with me, Katy. I don't know what's going on but I damn well plan on getting to the bottom of it."

It took a moment for Katy to find her voice. "How is someone toying with you?"

"I put out two fires at Dresden Bluff." He frowned, and the worry lines deepened around his mouth. "And I didn't even know you were staying here until the phone call brought me here to the fire...to you."

At the mention of Dresden Bluff, Katy's mind raced and fire pitched through her body. As Trent stood before her, staring down at her with those smoldering eyes of his, she did not want to think about Dresden Bluff, all the times they'd gone there, or the intimacies they'd shared.

"Oh," she managed to say through chattering teeth as she wrapped her arms around herself to stave off a shiver.

Trent's expression changed to one of tenderness as he stepped close and put his hands on her arms. He rubbed quickly, creating heat with friction. His voice dropped an octave when he said, "Look at you. You're all wet."

Oh God, he had no idea.

"Well, you've got pretty good aim with your hose," she

said, then realized how sexual that sounded. Jesus, Freud would have a field day with her.

He grinned, and let his glance race over her body, which was naked and exposed through her wet nightie. He fell quiet for a moment, but she didn't miss the want in his eyes. As a hush settled over them, they exchanged a long, heated look, one that slid through her like a warm aphrodisiac and had her thoughts careening in an erotic direction.

Sexual tension grew heavy, thicker than the fog moving in over the ocean. Trent sucked in a breath and appeared to be waging some internal war. For a brief moment, conflicting emotions flickered over his face. When she spotted something dark, something remorseful in the depths of his eyes, she wondered what he was thinking. A frown touched his forehead as his glance trailed her curves one more time.

He exhaled slowly, shook his head as if to clear it, and broke the quiet by saying, "Let's get you inside before you catch your death of cold."

Katy gave a breathy laugh and felt some of the tension drain. "You sound like Grandma Margaret."

At the mention of her late grandmother, Granddaddy Errol's wife, the lines on his forehead deepened.

"What is it?" Katy asked.

"There was just something about that person on the other end of the line. Whoever called about the fire had been disguising their voice, but there was something familiar about it."

Katy's head jerked back with a start. "You think it was my late grandma?" She stared at him and wondered what he'd been smoking. Or worse, maybe he'd inhaled too much creosote over the years and the extended exposure was slowly killing off brain cells.

Trent laughed. "No, I don't. It's just that sometimes Errol rolls his Rs. So did the caller."

She crinkled her nose. "You think Granddaddy started the fire? Why would he do something like that?"

She took a moment to think about Granddaddy Errol and her heart lurched. He'd aged so much over the last few years, especially since he'd lost Grandma Margaret. His cloudy blue eyes had lost some of the shine except, Katy noticed, when they met hers. Since she'd come home, the wicked gleam that spoke of love and life had returned. She pushed back the guilt. God, she hadn't meant to hurt her granddaddy when she'd left, and knew how much he wanted her to return home and have a family of her own, one that he could enjoy and watch over.

"No. No, of course not." Trent shook his head.

Katy stepped in front of him to open the door. "Because I don't think he'd put me in danger and—"

Trent cut her off, leaned forward and put his mouth close to her ear. "Yeah, but maybe he knows as long as I'm around you'll never be in danger, Katy."

His warm breath trickled along her spine and the heat in his voice when he spoke her name had her spinning around to face him. "I...I still don't think he'd do something like this."

He dipped his head lower, and his lips were so close to hers she was sure he was going to kiss her. "No. You're probably right.' His voice was so deep, so full of desire, it seeped under her skin and brought on a shiver.

From the top of her head to the tips of her toes, her entire body trembled. She was about to say something, but he touched her nightie and rolled the material between his fingers. Oh God, those fingers. She remembered how they touched her, how they felt caressing her body, how they felt inside her.

"We need to get you out of this," he murmured low.

"Mmmm, yeah, good idea..." Katy's mind drifted off, filling with erotic visions of Trent peeling the slip of material from her body and kissing a lazy path over her flesh until he reached the spot that needed his tongue the most. In her mind's eye she envisioned him burying his mouth between her legs while he pushed two thick fingers inside her and brought her to orgasm. Another shiver wracked her body.

When his warm chuckle reached her ears, her mind snapped back to reality. She blinked her eyes into focus, and when she caught the sexy, crooked grin on Trent's mouth, she said, "Wait. What? Why?"

Trent moistened his lips and she damn near orgasmed then and there. "It's wet, remember?"

Oh yeah, she remembered.

"You're shivering and we don't want you to catch..."

She cut him off, and realized he'd mistaken her shiver. "I know, I know. My death of cold."

His earlier words hit like a cold, wet facecloth. Trent was a nice guy, a sweet caring man who didn't want her to get sick. He was not making a pass at her, no matter how much she wanted him to. And he was not at her house because he wanted to see her. He was there because someone was toying with him. Probably an old school chum back in town for the reunion.

Speaking of toying...

His enticing scent played havoc with her senses as he reached past her and pushed open the door. "After you."

Katy slid her arms over her chest to hide the telltale hardening of her nipples as she slipped inside and made a beeline for her bedroom.

Trent was a gentleman. A firefighter. Simply doing what good firefighters do. Helping victims of a fire, no matter how big or small said fire was. Yeah, there were sparks between them, but he did not want to sleep with her. He still hated her for leaving. She needed to get that through her skull.

Flustered, she tore off her nightie, grabbed her housecoat,

and in her haste she somehow tangled the belt around her arms. A noise behind her had her spinning around, only to come face-to-face with Trent.

He stood in her doorway, leaning against the jamb with his hands deep in his pockets. His hot glance raked over her naked body and she had to lock her knees to keep upright.

"Hey," he murmured, and she heard the raw ache of lust in that one word.

Katy swallowed. "Hey yourself."

A long pause, then he pushed off the doorjamb and took a predatory step toward her. "Looks like you might need a hand."

Katy sucked in a breath as her body pulsed. Okay, so maybe he did want to sleep with her.

5

Trent's gaze raced over Katy's shapely contours as he took two long strides toward her and quickly closed the distance between them. The sight of her beautiful, naked body evoked a myriad of sinful thoughts and bombarded him with primal hunger. It was that raw hunger that threatened his last vestige of control. But he needed that control. Without it, he'd never be able to fuck her and get her out of his system.

As he hovered over her, his cock ached and pressed so hard against his jeans he was certain it was going to burst through the zipper. He bumped against her body, and the heat of her flesh combined with the tang of her arousal, teased the desire rising up inside him.

Oh fuck, how he wanted her...

Without preamble, he grabbed Katy and drew her close. He slid his hands along her back, splaying his fingers wide as he pinned her to his body. She gasped when she felt his cock press hard against her stomach. He brought his mouth close to hers and tasted the sweetness on her breath.

She struggled against him. Surprised by her response and

wondering if he'd read her wrong, he inched back. He wanted her but he certainly wasn't going to act on those urges if the feelings weren't mutual. "What is it, Katy?"

"I'm all tied up," she murmured in a low seductive voice that had his body moistening. He looked over her shoulder and noticed the tangled belt.

He arched a brow. "And?"

"And I...I want to touch you." The need in her eyes did something to him, and the fact that she wanted this as much as he did touched him on a level that made breathing damn near impossible.

Trent took a moment to gather himself, then shook his head from side to side as wild and wicked ideas pelted him like warm summer rain. Instead of releasing her, he slid his hands down her sides, and in a bold move tightened the belt even more.

Her eyes widened with a mixture of surprise and pleasure. "Trent...?"

He pitched his voice low. "Yeah, Katy?"

Color crept up her neck. "What...what are you doing?" she asked, and he could sense her mounting desire.

"Well, if you must know." He grinned down at her. "I want you at my mercy." With that, Trent drove his knee deep between her legs. "Now widen for me."

She immediately obliged, and he didn't miss the intrigue in her tone when she said, "I've never seen this side of you."

"I'm sure there's a lot you don't know about me anymore."

The lust in her voice nearly pushed him over the edge. "Why don't you show me?" she suggested as the sultry heat in her eyes raised his blood pressure to dangerous proportions.

Trent stood back and looked at her. Jesus, he couldn't believe how much he liked seeing her like this. So needy, so hot, and so goddamn aroused it was going to take every ounce of strength he possessed not to erupt at first contact.

Impatience raced through him. He ached to kiss her, to pull her taut nipples into his mouth, to drag his lips over her flesh and to tongue her sweet, silky cunt the way she liked. Yeah, he knew *what* she liked, and knew how exactly *how* she liked it. Trent knew all her sexy secrets, and God help him, he was about to fulfill them.

"T," she murmured.

His body tightened, and the sound of his nickname on her lips instantly erased the last ten years and brought them to a deeper level of intimacy. Something inside him gave and he felt like he'd been sucker-punched.

"Katy..."

She wet her lips, and the needy look on her face was so potent, everything inside him reached out to her. Desire danced in her eyes, and the way her body beckoned his became his undoing.

Yeah, his plan was to fuck her. Long and hard. Until he got her out of his system. But when she called him T, then parted her lips and welcomed him home, his entire brain shut down, complicating his mission. He cleared his throat, rattled by the emotions she brought out in him.

Her face suffused with color and her breathing changed. God, he loved how she responded to him.

"T, please."

The impatience in her voice and the way she looked at him with such need and desire pushed him over the precipice. His lips crashed down on hers. As he pillaged her mouth, his body screamed *go*, but his last working brain cell screamed *stop,* warning him that sleeping with her was a bad idea. A totally, fucking stupid idea, because once he did his world would never be right again.

Yeah, who the fuck was he kidding? His world hadn't been right for ten years. So what did it matter?

He pulled his mouth from hers and dropped to his knees,

the need to be inside her so powerful he could barely think straight, could barely listen to that inner voice warning that he was headed down a path there'd be no coming back from. Christ, he needed this to stop as much as he needed it to continue.

"Oh God, T," she cried out and arched her back.

He slid his tongue over her quivering body, brushing her nipples and taking his sweet time to draw her pebbled nubs into his mouth. He sucked long and hard until his mouth had had its fill, then his tongue drifted downward. He gripped her legs and spread them even wider.

Christ, he ached to pay homage to her pussy, to feast on her hot, wet clit, and swipe his tongue across her sensitive bundle of nerves. He ached to hear her scream his name during orgasm. Ached to release inside her just one more time.

Just. One. More. Time.

But again something inside him screamed that once would never be enough. Not with her. Not with his Katy.

He was just about to close his mouth over her sex when a noise sounded outside. Someone or something had rattled the door so hard the glass nearly shattered. Heart racing, Trent rocked back on his heels and glanced up at Katy. She was staring down at him, equal mixtures of arousal and unease spreading across her flushed cheeks.

Trent worked to find his voice. "You expecting company, Katy?"

She shook her head quickly. "No."

The noise sounded again, but this time it came from the other side of the beach house. Trent twisted and glanced out the beachside window. "What's going on?" he asked.

"I don't know," Katy said, breathless. "I heard noises outside earlier before you showed up. I brushed it off as the dock."

"That's not the dock."

Trent climbed to his feet and scrubbed his hand over his jaw. He could see how much the banging had scared Katy. Her eyes were wide, blinking rapidly, and her chest was rising and falling erratically, although he could also blame her body's responses on her arousal.

When he noticed the open curtains, he sheltered her exposed body, reached around her and released the bound strap. He draped her house coat over her shoulders to cover her up.

"Thanks." Katy went straight to her window to draw the blinds. Her voice sounded sheepish when she said, "We forgot..."

"I know." Which was so unlike him. He wasn't into exhibitionism and coveted his privacy. Unlike Katy, he could never be a TV personality. He was just a small town boy who liked to remain behind the scenes. But in his quest to be inside her, he'd lost his ability to think straight and it had him forgetting the basics, like drawing the curtains and hiding them from the public's eye.

The front door rattled again, and Trent tensed. He gestured with a nod. "I should go look."

"Yeah. Okay." He could hear the worry in her voice, but underneath he detected disappointment. She wanted this encounter to play out every bit as much as he did. "Do you think it could be an old high-school buddy pulling a prank on you?" she asked.

"I don't know." With the reunion and everyone returning home, the thought had occurred to him. It also occurred to him that no matter how much he wanted to make love to Katy, whoever was out there had stopped him in the nick of time. Before he did something he might regret later.

Trent stepped back and turned as Katy pulled on a pair of jeans and T-shirt. "Wait. I'll come with you."

"No. You stay here."

He left her in the bedroom and walked to the front door. He inched it open and peered outside. When he met with silence, he stepped out into the night and glanced around. He spotted movement at the end of the long sandy lane and bolted from the house.

When he reached the street and heard a whistle, his mind raced. What the hell was going on?

"Harold?"

Harold turned. "Yeah, boy, what is it I can I do for ya?"

Why would Harold be out strolling the streets at night, especially after his recent incident at the hospital?

He tapped an impatient foot. "Well out with it, boy, I ain't got all night, ya know."

"What are you doing out here?"

"Taking a stroll." He tapped his chest and gave a mischievous wink. "Gotta keep the old ticker ticking, boy."

Trent glanced behind him and judged the amount of time it would take to get from the beach house to the street. Harold was old, frail, surely he couldn't have banged on the door then made it to the street in such a short time.

Trent decided to ask anyway, but it sounded crazy, even to himself. "Were you just up at the beach house?"

"No, lad, I wasn't anywhere near the place. Why? What's up?" Curiosity lit his cloudy eyes.

What's up was that someone had banged on the door and broken up an intimate encounter between Katy and himself, and Trent suspected it had been done on purpose, which begged the question was someone trying to get them together, or pull them apart? He considered it a moment longer and then thought about the distance of the lane. Honestly, he had to be crazy to think Harold would—or could —do such a thing. Christ, maybe he'd gotten paranoid over the years.

Just then Katy came rushing down the lane, looking mussed, sexy and breathless.

Harold greeted Katy then turned back to Trent. "So what's up, lad?" he pushed.

Trent didn't dare say anything about anything. Harold along with Byron and Errol, the other two that made up the gruesome threesome—lawless ruffians when younger—were worse than any of the gossiping women at Whispering Salon. Those three would have rumors about Katy and him spread in no time at all.

"Nothing. We heard a noise, is all. Probably the dock coming loose."

"Yeah, prolly," Harold said.

With that Harold turned, resumed his whistling and strolled down the street toward home.

"You don't think..." Katy began.

Trent shook his head. "I don't know." Silence hung heavy as he glanced up and down the road, trying to figure out what the hell was going on.

Looking a little unsure, Katy blinked and pointed her thumb behind her. "Did you want to..."

Trent raked shaky hands through his hair. "I should probably go."

"Oh."

"What?"

"It's just that...I...uh..."

Sexually frustrated and emotionally battered, Trent drove his hands deep into his pockets before he did something stupid, like pull her against him and finish what they started.

"You what?" he asked, unsettled.

"I just thought..."

Flustered, he bit out, "What did you think, Katy? That we could resume our relationship for the summer? Then what?

Then we're right back where we were ten years ago, and I'm pretty sure I can't go through you leaving again."

"Trent, it's not like that. If you just let me..." Suddenly her voice fell off, as if she didn't know what to say, how to explain.

Completely rattled, he asked, "Do you know why I was going to fuck you tonight, Katy?"

She stared up at him with those big blue eyes of hers and whispered, "Because you wanted me?"

"Yes, of course because I wanted you." *Fuck, yeah.* "But also to get you out of my system." When he saw the confusion in her expression, he went on to explain, "Yeah, that's right, Katy. I was going to fuck you tonight, hoping that once and for all it would help me get over you." Jesus, he was being a prick again. "So I guess a lot has changed over the years and there really is a lot you don't know about me anymore."

Her eyes widened with his revelation, then she simply said, "I've never gotten over you either, Trent."

Sweet Mother of God!

Of all the things she could have said, of all the things she could have called him— asshole topping the list—she chose to say that. The one thing that nearly drove him to his knees and had him begging her to stay.

To marry him.

But how could he possibly do that to either of them? He didn't want her to stay only to have her resent him. And he didn't want her to stay because he'd pleaded. He wanted her to stay because she wanted to. Because he was important to her. *This life* was important to her.

Trent pushed past the pain and dug deep, searching for an ounce of control before he followed a path that could very well shatter him. He took a step back. "I should go."

A cool breeze blew her hair off her shoulder as she hugged herself. She shot a nervous glance over her shoulder and Trent felt her anxiety as if it were her own.

Weary despair crossed her face. "I've got some work to do anyway."

Oh fuck, she looked so sweet, so innocent, and so damn vulnerable the gentleman in him didn't want to leave her alone when he knew how much that noise had frightened her.

"Look, I'm heading on over to the Seaside pub for a game of pool. Why don't you come along? You've been working hard since you arrived, and I think a night out and a few beers with old friends might be just what you need."

6

L aughter and music poured out of the window and spilled onto the quiet street as Katy and Trent made their way to the pub. The tang of salt mingled with the aroma of raw seafood and hung heavy in the still air. Trading and selling at the outdoor fisherman's market had ceased hours ago and the vendors had returned to their homes to replenish and rest their voices until first light, when the boats returned with their fresh catches.

Both lost in their own thoughts, neither spoke as they listened to the seagulls squawk out over the water. A few cars passed, and horns sounded, but in the small town most folks simply walked to their destination.

When they reached the pub, Trent tossed her a warm, reassuring smile—one that reminded her of the sweet, caring boy from her childhood—and pulled open the door for her. Before they stepped inside, two black vans passed, vehicles similar to the ones used by the stations. Katy shrugged it off. Maybe the local news had come to town to cover the upcoming reunion.

Katy stepped into the pub, which was alive with activity.

Almost her entire graduating class had overtaken the place. They were bustling about in the darkened room and getting reacquainted. Katy had already spoken to most of them as one by one they made their way to the Seafarer after their arrival, which once again had her wondering why her granddaddy thought business was down.

She redirected her thoughts as Trent slipped his arm around her waist and guided her through the throngs of people to the teak bar overlooking the water. Katy climbed onto a stool and rested her foot on the brass rail as Trent grabbed a drink for each of them.

Trent handed her a cool amber beer and looked past her shoulder. She turned to see him staring at Brody. He leaned in and whispered into her ear. "Wait here for me. I want to talk to Brody about the noises at your cabin."

Katy took a sip of her beer, and swiveled on her stool. She smiled as she perused the room and took in all the familiar faces. She waved to a few girls she hadn't seen in years, and was about to go talk to them when Adam slid onto the stool next to her.

"Hey, Katy," he said, flashing a familiar, charming smile, one that undoubtedly still had the women around town shedding their panties. Dressed in jeans and a long-sleeved T-shirt, with his dark hair a little long and a whole lot wild—like him—Adam still looked as good as he did the day they all graduated. She'd seen him at the Seafarer the other day, but she'd been too busy to stop and chat.

"Adam," she said, and leaned in to give him a big hug. "Sorry I didn't get to speak with you the other day. How are you?"

Always the flirt, he winked and said, "Better now that you're here." He tipped his bottle and Katy clinked her glass with his before taking a drink.

Katy laughed. "So I take it you haven't found anyone and settled down yet."

"Nah, life's too short for that. What about you?"

"Nope, still on the prowl too," she teased.

Something in Adam's expression changed and his eyes turned dark, serious. "So what's going on with you and lover boy?"

"What are you talking about?"

"You two getting…reacquainted?"

She was intelligent enough to know what he meant by reacquainted, but she didn't kiss and tell and Trent was a guy who liked his privacy. Katy respected that. She waved her hand about the room, not about to get into the logistics of her relationship with Trent—partly because it wasn't any of Adam's business, and partly because she didn't understand it herself—and offered Adam a coy smile. "Isn't everyone?"

They both looked up and caught Trent's glance from across the room, and a scowl slid across his face when his gaze went from Katy to Adam. He said something to Brody then started back toward the bar.

"Listen, Katy," Adam said, humor long gone from his expression. "Trent is my best friend. There isn't a thing I wouldn't do for him and I don't want to see him hurt."

"What are you getting at, Adam?"

His eyes locked on hers. "Don't start something you can't finish this time. Okay?"

She nodded, but before she could answer, a strong arm slipped around her waist and lifted her from her seat. In a possessive move, Trent pulled her to him, anchoring her body to his.

His glance locked with Adam's and Adam offered them both a wide grin that could melt the butter cream paint off the walls.

"Come on, Katy. I've got us a table," Trent said, and gestured toward the pool hall in the other room.

Adam gave them a wink. "Want to play three ways?"

"No," Trent burst out, his hand fisting on her back. He turned to Katy. "Stay away from this guy. He's trouble."

The sound of Adam's laughter echoed behind them as Trent led her to the pool table.

As Adam's warning words echoed in her brain, her stomach tightened. The last thing she wanted to do was hurt Trent. In fact, she wanted to love him, and not just in the bedroom. She wanted to put things right between them, wanted to find her way back home to him.

When they reached the table, Trent was mumbling something about Adam under his breath. Katy grabbed a stick. "Adam's a good guy, Trent."

"He's a pain in my ass," Trent responded, but Katy heard the love and respect in his words. Those two were best friends, firefighters, part of a brotherhood, and she loved that Adam worried about Trent. That's how it was in her small town. You grew up together and had each other's back. Katy missed that.

Trent racked the balls and said, "You break."

The rest of the night flew by and Katy couldn't believe how much she was enjoying herself. Trent stayed close to her, his body practically leaning over hers as she took her shots, and for awhile it felt like old times. As they played, the tension between them slipped away and they laughed, joked and teased one another. Before she knew it, she spotted people staring and most likely whispering about them.

"Looks like we're drawing a bit of attention," she said.

Trent glanced up and his jaw clenched. "Want to get out of here?"

"Yeah, it's getting late and I have an early morning anyway."

"Come on. I'll walk you home."

At the thought of going home, and remembering those strange noises, she frowned. Trent, as if knowing exactly what she was thinking, said, "Don't worry. Brody was going to swing by your place and check it out. He said the kids around town have been playing a lot of pranks lately and it's probably nothing to worry about."

"Thanks." Before she realized what she was doing, her hand found his. Their eyes met and she watched his throat work as he swallowed. Keeping their locked hands hidden between their bodies, they walked to the door, but when Trent pushed it open and a camera was thrust into their faces, he stumbled backward.

"What the hell?"

Overhead lights flicked on and blinded them. Katy blinked and shaded her eyes. "What's going on?" she asked.

A microphone was shoved into her face. "So, Kathleen. Is this Trent Parker? The boy from your past? The reason you returned to your childhood home of Whispering Cove?"

"What are you doing here?" Katy demanded.

"A story on you, of course."

"Of course?" Trent asked, his tone accusatory as he stared at Katy. "What does she mean by *of course*? Did you arrange this?"

"No," Katy hurried out, but she saw the seed of doubt before he quickly blinked it away. "I had nothing to do with this."

"Come on." Trent grabbed her hand and hustled her back into the pub, closing the door on the commotion outside. Once inside he called Brody, who'd left the pub shortly after they'd arrived. Katy listened in. A moment later he hung up and informed her that Brody was sending Deputy Peter Veinotte to get things under control but that it might take awhile.

"I guess we'll have to wait it out, since they're blocking the only street leading to my cottage."

When she yawned, the two beers making her tired, Trent said, "I have an idea." He grabbed her hand, made his way to the back of the pub and spoke to Hauk Michaelsen, his old buddy and owner of the establishment.

Hauk ushered them through the kitchen and upstairs to his apartment. Without turning on any lights, he herded them outside and pointed to the long set of wooden stairs leading off his back deck. He tossed Trent a blanket. "Use this to disguise yourselves," he advised in a rich, European dialect, even though he'd grown up in Whispering Cove.

Once outside, they rushed down the back street and Katy followed, not sure where he was guiding her until they reached the foot of Dresden bluff.

He rolled his shoulder. "If we're going to wait it out, I'd rather do it here than in an overcrowded pub."

They climbed the bluff, and when they reached the top, Katy slapped her hand to her chest and drew in air. Waves lapped against the rocks and light glistened on the rolling waves. As old memories came rushing back, Trent stepped up behind her and pressed his chest to her back.

"Is it as beautiful as you remember?" he asked, his voice soft, warm, filled with desire.

His heat reached out to her and she clamped her thighs together as sensations bombarded her body. "More so," she answered honestly.

He positioned his mouth close to her ear and his fingers curled around hers. "I miss coming here with you, Katy."

Her heart twisted and tears threatened. Oh God, she missed it too, so much so that it hurt deep in her core. "If I didn't know better, I'd think you brought me here on purpose."

Trent let loose a long sigh and replied soberly, "Maybe on some level I did."

"I guess Freud would have a field day with you too."

He spun her around to face him. "What?" he asked.

The second she glimpsed the raw need on his rugged face, her heart began pounding and they both knew there'd be no running away for either of them this time. "Nothing. It's nothing," she assured him.

She breathed in his scent, and as the air charged, he lightly brushed her hair from her shoulder. His fingers scorched her flesh and she shivered in response to his touch.

His gaze panned her. "Cold?"

"Not really."

For a long time, quiet fell over them, and when haunted eyes locked with hers, she could see his struggle. Then she saw something in him give and heard the ache of longing in his voice when he said, "Katy, are we really going to do this?"

"Maybe we should, Trent. Maybe it will help get me out of your system," she said, hoping for just the opposite, hoping shared intimacies would help them move beyond the pain of the past and put them back on the path they were meant to travel.

He dropped a soft kiss onto her forehead, and exhaled. "Baby, there is nothing I can do to get you out of my system."

She smiled, his words like a healing balm to her soul. She'd come home to see if Trent could ever forgive her, and as she stared up at him, she felt the shift inside him. Everything in his words and the way he was looking back at her told her they were on the road to recovery, moving on to the future. "Trent."

"Yeah, baby."

"I think you should kiss me."

And kiss her he did.

He dipped his head and pressed his mouth to hers,

parting her lips with his tongue. His kiss was soft, gentle and so achingly familiar and tender that it became her undoing. A tremble moved through her and her entire body shook from head to toe. When he felt her quake, the kiss grew more feverish, more demanding.

Katy moaned and pushed harder against him, savoring every second, every touch. He adjusted his body and a low growl sounded deep in his throat as his cock pushed into her belly. The sudden rush of sexual energy boiled her blood and she too moaned without censure.

Trent broke the kiss, pulled her T-shirt out from her jeans and ran his warm hands over her flesh. She palmed his muscles and ripped at his clothes, desperately needing to see him naked. He peeled off her top and bra, then stepped back to remove his own shirt.

As he exposed his upper body, her glance raced over him, registering every detail of his broad shoulders, hard abdominal muscles and tight, lean waist. "You're beautiful..." she whispered, taking pleasure in the hard man before her.

Trent's mouth curved as he pulled her back to him, and the feel of skin on skin, flesh on flesh, made her hunger for so much more. Desperately needing to touch every inch of him, she released the button on his pants and slid down his zipper. Trent sucked in air when she slipped her hand inside and wrapped her fingers around his cock.

"Oh Jesus," he moaned, and pushed against her.

"Speaking of hoses," she teased as she gave him a light squeeze.

Trent laughed and gripped her ass hard. "What's the matter, Katy? You have another fire you need me to tend to?"

She grinned and stroked him harder. "As a matter of fact..."

"Let me see what I can do about that." His lips crashed down on hers as he backed her up, closer to the edge to use the ocean as a romantic backdrop. He briefly pulled away, grabbed the blanket and laid it out. Then he dropped to his knees and dragged Katy down with him.

"As a professional, my first course of action is to assess the situation." He slipped his hand into her jeans and stroked her cunt.

"Oh God," she murmured.

"Oh yes, I can see how this kind of fire can blaze out of control if I don't give it my full attention right away. Now lie down for me."

Body quivering with need, Katy did just that. She writhed on the ground, aching, needing, as she crooked her finger and gestured him closer. Moonlight spilled over them as Trent slowly pulled her jeans off and tossed them aside.

With a wicked grin on his face, and lust flashing in his eyes, he sat back on his heels, and lightly stroked her pussy. Widen for me, baby."

She spread her legs and impatience thrummed through her. "T," she murmured. "Please." God, if she didn't have him inside her soon she was going to go up in a burst of flames. "I need you inside me."

His eyes darkened and emotion fractured his voice when he said, "There's something I need to do first. Something I've wanted to do for a long time."

With that, Trent bent forward and brushed his tongue over her cunt, the heat of his mouth searing her clit and fueling her need. She tossed her head from side to side then glanced up at the stars as white hot desire claimed her.

Oh Lord, she needed this, needed him in ways he couldn't possibly understand, ways that went well beyond the physical. No matter what Trent thought, she'd never stopped wanting him. Never stopped loving him.

"Please," she begged.

"Is this what you want, baby?"

Trent pressed his lips hungrily into her sex, and their moans of pleasure mingled as he parted her folds and kissed her long and hard. Her flesh began tingling and blood flowed hot and heavy through her veins.

Katy gripped the blanket and arched into him. A whimper escaped her lips. Good God, no one knew how to touch her body quite like he did.

"Jesus, I've missed the taste of you," he murmured from between her legs. She slid her fingers into his hair and held him to her. His hands gripped her hips, his fingers biting into her flesh as the desire in his eyes turned her inside out.

His tongue ignited her blood to near boiling, and she could feel pleasure building in her body. His mouth moved faster, his tongue scraping her clit as he trailed one hand lower and inserted a finger.

He growled low. "You're so wet," he whispered, and she could tell he was fighting for control.

He worked his fingers inside her, brushing the tip over the sensitive bundle of nerves as his other hand slid over her skin. Heat radiated from his hand and he touched her in places so deep she thought she'd died and gone to heaven. His thumb brushed her clit. Pressure began building inside her and her toes curled when he flattened his hand on her stomach and held her down, clearly wanting her at his mercy.

She was close. So close...

"That's my girl," he said. "Come for me, Katy."

She gave a low erotic whimper and pushed against him. "Oh, T," she cried out as her orgasm hit hard. He pinned her with his hand as she clenched and vibrated and rode out the pulsing waves of ecstasy. She reached for him, to pull him to her, but he stayed between her legs and lapped at her hot flow of release until he drank in every last drop.

He tipped his head, and when his eyes met hers, her heart

hammered. She needed him again. Needed him inside her. Needed to join them as one.

He quickly peeled off his pants, slid up her body and settled on top of her. She reveled in the weight of him pressing down on her. His skin glistened with moisture and the intensity in his gaze was as frightening as it was exciting.

Desire twisted her stomach and her pussy ached to feel his hard cock pumping inside her. Warm hands carrying the scent of her sex brushed her damp hair from her forehead, and he shook his head when he said, "Do you have any idea how crazy you make me?"

She smiled, loving that he still cared for her, that he still wanted her in ways she wanted him. Katy widened her legs, trailed her hands over his body until she cupped his firm ass.

"About as crazy as you make me, I believe." She bucked forward and his cock breached her opening.

He clenched down on his jaw hard, and groaned. "What about protection?"

"I'm on the Pill." Despite that, she'd never had sex without a condom before. She never trusted anyone with her body the way she trusted Trent.

As if he'd read her mind, he brushed his thumb over her mouth and whispered, "And I've never ridden bareback with anyone but you, sweetheart."

When his dark eyes fixed on her, a fist squeezed her heart. She recognized that look. It was the same look her father had given her mother—a look that spoke of love and longing. "Trent?"

"Yeah, baby?"

"If you don't do something soon about the flames building inside me, this place is going to go up like an inferno. Then the entire fire department will show up. Including Adam. And if Adam shows…"

"Katy."

She tilted her chin bringing them face to face. "Yeah?"

His mouth curved enticingly and he looked so damn sexy it made her dizzy. Once again her body trembled. Almost violently.

"Shut up and kiss me."

She parted her lips for him and when his mouth closed over hers, he drove his cock all the way up inside her. Katy gasped at the stab of pleasure and widened her legs even more as he sank into her wet heat.

"Katy, Jesus, you feel so good," he whispered into her mouth and stroked a tender caress over her cheek. His hips began moving, his cock sliding in and out, in and out. "I'm not going to last, baby. I can't. It's been too long."

"Same here," she murmured as pressure mounted, gathering in her core and spreading onward and outward until pleasure danced in every nerve.

"It's only ever been this good for me with you," he admitted, and she knew exactly what he was talking about. Sex with him was perfect. Everything with him was perfect.

As basic elemental need took over, they held each other tight. She met each thrust, grinding herself against him and begging for more. Suddenly feeling frantic, crazed, she began burning up inside as he impaled her, harder and deeper, giving her his cock, but also giving her a piece of himself.

As she, in turn, gave herself over to him completely, he drew a labored breath, and slipped a hand between their bodies. He stroked her clit once, twice, and that was it. The world around her disappeared, and no longer could she hear the waves, the ocean or the trees rustling in the breeze. All she could hear was Trent, and the deep, needy moans coming from his throat as he made sweet love to her.

He threw his head back and drove harder, and she sensed he was seeking release, but also sensed, like her, he was seeking something else. She knew this encounter wasn't just about sex, not for her and not for him.

Everything in the way they were touching was more emotional, less physical. Every stroke, every pump was about finding each other again, about regaining what they'd lost and melting away those painful years of longing.

"I want to feel your come inside me, T."

He pinched her clit and that's when she lost it, giving herself over to the sensations pulling at her. Her muscles clenched and tightened, and as her hot cream poured over his shaft, he stilled and let loose a long groan.

His cock pulsed, and he buried his face in her neck as he splashed his seed high inside her. He stayed there for a long time, until they both came back down to earth. A moment later he slid off and snuggled in beside her. Silence ensued as they basked in the afterglow.

Finally Katy tipped her head and smiled at him. "I really needed that."

He grinned, slipped a finger between her legs and stroked her pussy. "Are the flames gone, baby?"

"Yes," she said. "But I suspect it's only temporary. I believe there might still be a few embers smoldering."

Trent laughed. "You're insatiable."

"You make me that way."

"And you make me crazy."

She rolled in to him and gripped his cock, the love she felt for him churning inside her. Trent gave a contented sigh as he drew the blanket around them, but she knew the night was far from over.

They still had ten long years to make up for. Her mouth found his again, and as they exchanged a soft, lingering kiss, her hands roamed over his body. Before long they were making love again, and sometime throughout the night when the camera crews had dispersed, they made their way back to her cottage where they showered and fell into each other's arms again and again. After lovemaking, they cooked together and talked about old times until the wee hours of the morning.

They whispered quietly until both finally fell into a restful sleep, and when Katy woke, she reached for the man beside her. But when her hand came up empty and she found her bed cold and unoccupied, she jolted upright, her heart racing.

$$7$$

Trent hated to walk out on Katy while she slept, but he was needed at the firehouse and didn't have the heart to wake her. She'd finally fallen asleep near dawn and looked so happy and contented he thought it best to leave her and let her get caught up on her rest, especially after all the energy they'd exerted throughout the night.

He'd left her a note on her pillow, in much the same manner he used to years ago when he would slip through her open bedroom window, spend the night cuddled up in bed next to her, then sneak out before her parents surfaced.

Just thinking about those times brought a smile to his face. But thinking about the past also had him wondering about the future. Not once had Katy brought up Chicago, or her job. They'd talked long into the morning and Trent had made numerous attempts to discuss her career, her life in the city, but she'd always redirect the conversation.

Still, he didn't miss the sadness in her eyes, that spoke of longing, loneliness. Katy was a light in the darkness, shining brighter than any lighthouse beacon, but lately, whenever he'd caught her daytime cooking show, he'd noticed that her light had dimmed, the spark gone from her beautiful blue eyes.

He knew her well enough to know that she was unhappy. But last night the spark had returned tenfold. He'd seen it when they were playing pool, and when they were up at Dresden Bluff, which begged the question—was Katy trying to find her way home?

He couldn't say for certain, and he honestly had no idea what she was hoping the next eight weeks would bring, but he was damn well going to give her an incentive to stay. He was never one to be selfish, especially when it came to Katy, but it was about time she realized where she belonged, and he was just the guy to help light the path and show her the way back.

He glanced at the clock as he worked on a new seafood primavera sauce. It was nearing lunch and he was hoping to take a break and catch Katy at the Seafarer. A noise behind him drew his attention, and he spun around to see Katy standing in the doorway, dressed in her sexy, fifties-style uniform from the restaurant. She held a tray with coffee and muffins and her wide smile showcasing perfect white teeth took his breath away.

"I thought you'd run away," she said, her eyes bright, alive and playful when they locked on his.

He shook his head, and without thinking said, "I've never run out on you before."

Katy frowned and he instantly realized it was a poor choice of words.

"Didn't you get my note?" he hurriedly said, not wanting to put a damper on her visit.

The corners of her mouth turned up. "Yeah. Just like old times."

He dropped his spoon and closed the distance between

them. He pitched his voice low and said, "Katy, about last night."

Her smile dissolved and a worried look came over her face. "What about it?"

"I'd like a repeat of it tonight."

She grinned, and looked so damn beautiful it was all he could do not to take her right there. He leaned in and dropped a soft kiss onto her mouth, and took pleasure in the new, easy intimacy blossoming between them.

She kissed him back hungrily, then said, "It'd be my pleasure, but..."

Trent shook his head. "No buts, Katy." When she got quiet for a moment, her blue eyes narrowing with concern, he asked, "Okay, what is it?"

She paused, and seemed to weigh her words carefully before blurting out, "Well, it's just that Granddaddy Errol told me business was down at the Seafarer and he thought I could come up with new menu ideas to attract more tourists. I've been working on a menu and need the kitchen tonight after closing to try them out."

He shook his head, perplexed. "Business is down?"

Katy handed him his coffee and they both sat at the table. "Yeah, I know. I thought the same. But why would he lie about such a thing?"

Trent shrugged, not really sure, and took a slug of the rich brew. "Maybe there are things you don't know."

"I suppose." She opened a napkin and laid out the muffins. She crinkled her nose and added, "Look, he asked me not to say."

Always priding himself on trust and honesty, Trent shook his head and pressed his fingers to her lips. "Hey, did you forget who you were talking to?"

Her smile turned sheepish. "Sorry."

He took a moment to mull over Errol's concerns. As he

considered them, he couldn't help but recall the voice on the other end of his cell, the one that had warned him of the trash-can fire. Something wasn't adding up, but now wasn't the time to be dwelling on such things, not with Katy sitting next to him, smelling like honeyed candy and looking so damn sweet and sexy, she had his cock thickening to the point of pain.

He redirected the conversation. "So if not tonight, tomorrow?"

"I'll be counting down the minutes," she answered, a spark dancing in her eyes as she bit into her muffin. "And besides, aren't you on shift tonight?"

He cocked his head and questioned, "How'd you know that?"

She grinned. "Maybe I really do know more about you than you think."

"Maybe," he said, then frowned. "But soon the world is going to know everything about me too."

Expressive blue eyes met his. "I really don't know what the sudden interest is all about? And I don't know who tipped the media off or even why anyone would do such a thing."

"Did they follow you here?"

"Yeah, but I managed to ditch them before sneaking in the back door."

He leaned into her, and brushed a muffin crumb from her mouth. "You always were very stealthy, Katy."

She arched a manicured brow. "Is that why I was the only girl you let climb the trees with you?"

"Among other reasons." When heat suffused her cheeks, he added, "I'm just glad you were able to ditch them. I hate all the attention."

She chuckled and waved her hand over her bubble-gum-pink uniform. "Yeah, well ditching them with this on was no easy task."

When Trent laughed, she pursed her lips and in a sober voice asked, "Have you been watching television?"

"No." The last thing he wanted to see was himself splashed across the screen.

"Well, the media is making me out to be America's sweetheart, and you, the heroic firefighter, my teenage crush who once again swept me off my feet. Apparently people are eating it up."

"They don't really care anything about us, Katy."

"I know."

"They're not even respecting our privacy."

"I know that too." She let loose a long sigh. "And when the next breaking story hits, we'll be forgotten like yesterday's newspaper."

"Well let's hope that happens sooner rather than later." He slid his hand across the table. "At least it's good to see the townsfolk trying to protect you. They care." Which made him feel secure in the knowledge that no one from Whispering Cove would have alerted the press to her return. Unless, of course, they wanted Katy to realize who she could count on and exactly where she truly belonged.

She gave him a warm smile, then blinked and looked past his shoulder. The pot on the stove and the aromatic scent wafting through the kitchen seemed to draw her attention. She inhaled. "What are you cooking?"

"It's a new seafood primavera."

Katy climbed from her seat and walked to the stove. "Trent, this smells amazing."

"Want to try?"

He grabbed a spoon and gave her a taste. Her eyes widened in delight. "This is delicious. When did you learn to cook?"

"Well, my ex-girlfriend *is* a famous celebrity chef. And because of that, the guys around here expect me to know my way around a kitchen." Trent watched her, gauging her reactions and giving her an opening to correct him on the ex-girlfriend comment. She didn't. Instead she took another bite and looked over the ingredients.

"Will you teach me how to make this?"

Trent straightened. As he stared at her, he jammed his thumb into his chest. "Me? Teach *the* Kathleen Wilson how to cook?"

"I think this would go over great at the restaurant."

He pulled a towel off the counter and tied it around his waist. "Okay," he agreed. "On one condition."

Incredulous, she clutched her chest and feigned surprise. "You have a condition?"

"Sure."

"Okay, what is it?" she conceded.

He gave her a devious wink. "Today we cook in my kitchen, tomorrow night we cook in yours."

"Same old Trent." Katy rolled her eyes and chuckled. "Do you ever give up?"

"No, Katy," he answered honestly, and something warm and intimate moved between them when his glance locked with hers.

A long moment passed as they stared at each other. "I'm glad," she finally murmured in a soft voice that had his heart pounding and his body aching to make love to her on the firehouse floor.

Needing a distraction before he did just that, he handed her the wooden spoon and instructed her to stir the sauce while he took a moment to pull himself together. In no time at all, the two fell into an easy camaraderie, enjoying themselves and the few stolen moments together. Out on the streets, the cameras were still rolling, but here, alone in the firehouse and cloaked in a cocoon of intimacy, they could talk quietly and touch freely.

The next hour flew by as Trent and Katy experimented with new menu ideas, and he couldn't help but think how much it felt like old times. Before he knew it, her lunch break had come to an end and she had to return to the restaurant. Once she was gone, he tidied up and stored the sauce in the fridge. Katy had added a few touches of her own to the sauce. The men working the graveyard shift were in for a real treat tonight. Once he had the kitchen in order, he pulled his cell out of his front pocket and put in a call to Brody.

"Hey, Trent," Brody said when he answered the phone.

"Hey, just checking to see if you had any information on the cottage."

"Yeah, looks like a few of the cedar boards over her door came loose. They were banging in the wind. Nothing serious."

Trent considered it for a moment. Brody's theory was possible, but still he couldn't quite shake the feeling that someone had been outside.

"You'd better get them fixed up before they cause any real damage."

"I'm on it." Trent checked the time and heard Adam outside shooting hoops. He'd come in early, which meant that Trent could get him to cover for the next few hours so he could do the repairs himself. He was about to hang up but then another thought struck. "What's happening with the damn camera crew?"

Jesus, he hated the paparazzi, and the last place he expected to find them was in Whispering Cove. How the hell had they found out about Katy and him? He knew there was a part of her life that was public, but over the last ten years she'd kept her private life...well, private. Why were the media suddenly so interested in her, and her love life *now*?

"We've got them under control," Brody assured him. "We can't keep them off the streets but we can keep them out of the shops and restaurants." He grunted something under his breath and added, "I also can't keep tourists, or anyone else for that matter, from being interviewed. So far it appears the town's protecting her privacy."

Trent clenched his jaw, happy the townsfolk had her back and unhappy about the fact that he couldn't spend time with her without their every movement captured and splashed across the TV.

After hanging up, he talked to Adam then loaded his truck with tools and made his way to the beachside cottage. Waves sounded in the distance and a few blocks away Trent could hear the vendors vying for the tourist dollar as he walked the perimeter and examined the exterior. He stepped onto the cedar deck and shooed away the seagulls that had taken up perch on the railing.

Despite the white paint chips gathering on the rose bushes like dander, and a few broken cedar boards hanging by rusty nails and oxidized from the salty sea water, the place was in pretty good shape. By rights, Alex Sutherland, the owner, should be fixing it up, but something compelled Trent to do it himself. Maybe because he liked doing things for Katy. *Wanted* to do things for her.

He grabbed his ladder and went to work, fixing the loose boards and even doing a few extra repairs on the roof. As he stood back and brushed the moisture from his face, he nodded, pleased with the outcome. Truthfully, he was used to doing such repairs. His own place was old and once belonged to a sea captain.

He could update, buy a newer, more modern home, but he kind of liked the old place, and since he was good with his hands, he could do most of the general repairs himself. As a teen he remembered how much Katy had liked the house with its towering widow's walk and how they'd drive around and point out the houses they'd like to live in.

Disregarding the fact that the house was meant for a big

family and he didn't even have furniture for over half the rooms, he had bought it anyway. Maybe on some unconscious level he'd hoped it would help Katy find her way back to him, and together they could fill it with children.

He'd gotten very little sleep last night and now exhaustion pulled at him. He threw the supplies back into his truck and made his way to the station. He exchanged a few words with Adam then hit the sack. When he woke a few hours later, he spotted a couple of the other guys catching up on their sleep. Quietly climbing out of his cot, he made his way to the kitchen, only to find Adam and Errol playing cards at the table.

Errol? What the hell was Errol doing there?

"Errol," he said, greeting him with a nod and smoothing his mussed hair off his face.

Errol offered him a snarl and pointed his cane. "'Bout time you got your sorry ass out of bed."

"Errol," Trent began, and pinched the bridge of his nose to ward off an impending headache, but Errol cut him off.

"I think there's trouble out on the st*rrr*eets."

Trent made his way to the coffeepot, certain he'd need caffeine before he heard the rest of Errol's story. The guy was not known as an alarmist, but of late Trent was beginning to wonder. He poured himself a mug and when Adam held up his empty cup, Trent refreshed his before replacing the carafe.

He leaned against the sink, took a long drink and asked, "What kind of trouble?"

"A ruckus of sorts. That's why I'm here. I need your help."

Trent pushed off the counter and made his way to the table. "That's Brody's department. Not mine."

Errol gave a dismissive shake of his hand. "You know I don't trust the police."

"Yeah, probably because you were on the wrong side of

the law more than enough when you were a kid," Adam piped in, laughing.

"Never mind that. I'm worried about my Katy."

That stopped Trent in his tracks, and he took in the deep lines on Errol's face. "What about Katy?"

"Them damn paparazzi won't leave her alone. She hasn't even left the restaurant. I think she's still there cuz she don't want to face them."

Trent knew the real reason she was working late. But he'd promised her he wouldn't say anything to anyone so he didn't.

"Why don't ya just do a walk by," Errol said, and Trent didn't miss the glint in his eye. "Make an ole fella feel better."

"I'll cover for you," Adam said. "Just keep your cell on. I'll call if we need you."

Trent couldn't help but think the two were up to something. It all seemed a little fishy, but he also couldn't help thinking how much he'd like to see Katy again, even if only through the restaurant window.

Errol laid out his cards and gathered the loot—which consisted of a handful of old candy bars left over from last year's Halloween—from the center of the table. "Take the back way. Deputy Veinotte blocked the path off and paparazzi have to keep to the main streets."

Trent made a quick trip to the men's room, jumped in the shower and changed his clothes before making his way to the Seafarer. When he stepped outside, the warm, muggy air closed over him. The sound of the camera crew speaking on the street carried in the still night.

Trent slipped around back and cut through the rose bushes lining the walking path. A few minutes later he came upon the back entrance of the Seafarer. He climbed the stairs leading up to the service entrance.

Trent leaned against the rail as the sight of Katy in the window had his pulse leaping. Fully focused and concentrating on her menu, she hadn't noticed him through the pane. He stood on the back deck and watched her, loving everything about her, especially the way she moved with such innocent sensuality. She'd changed out of her work uniform and now wore a light T-shirt and curve-hugging jeans that had his hands itching and his mouth watering.

When she disappeared into the other room, he moved toward the stairs, not about to disturb her when she was so clearly focused on her work, and that's when his cell went off. Shit. He must be needed at the firehouse. He pulled his phone out of his pocket, "Yeah?"

"Fire, Seafarer, hu*rry*..."

The second he slammed his phone shut, the smell of smoke reached his nostrils. He spun in time to see orange flames licking the sky. His feet pounded hard and the sound echoed in the night as he ran down the stairs and took note of the trash-can fire near the recycle bins. He shot a glance around and found the hose beneath the stairs. He turned it on and dashed along the gravel path to the fire. As he doused the flames, he couldn't help but wonder what the hell was going on. It was the second trash fire in as many nights.

A sound at his back had him turning and he spotted Katy rushing toward him. Eyes wide and mouth open in shock, she stared at him. Her glance went from him, to the trash can, back to him again. "Trent," she said. "What's going on? What are you doing here?"

"Just putting out another one of your trash can fires," he informed her.

She frowned and shook her head, perplexed. "Haven't we already done this?"

"Yeah, talk about *déjà vu*."

She gestured toward his hose. "At least this time you didn't soak me."

He arched a brow and lifted it. "It's not too late."

Her soft chuckle teased his nerves and has his cock thickening. He studied her mussed hair, flushed cheeks and big blue eyes. He took a measured step toward her, until his body hovered over hers. "Why do I get the feeling that you're the one starting the fires, Katy?" He tapped the cell in the front pocket of his jeans. "That you're the one making the calls."

She planted her hand on her hip and shot back, "Now why would I do that?"

Trent curled a lock of her dark hair around his finger and watched the desire flicker over her eyes. As their gazes collided, Trent knew she felt the bond between them every bit as much as he did. It was a connection he'd never felt with another, and suspected he never would. "Oh, I don't know. Maybe to get me all alone so you can have your way with me," he teased.

The tip of her finger pressed into his chest and she poked him. "How do I know you're not the one sta*rrr*ting them?" she asked rolling her Rs.

Trent laughed. "Well someone is starting them. If not you, and not me, then who?"

"My guess is either the teens are really antsy this summer or someone is trying to drive us together."

"Either way, we should go inside and call Brody."

When Katy nodded, he slipped his arm around her waist and followed her back along the gravel pathway. He turned off the hose on the way. Inside, the warm scent of melting chocolate hit him hard and just thinking about drizzling that sweet syrup over her naked flesh and licking it off had saliva pooling on his tongue. Lust exploded inside him as he envisioned himself spreading her legs, covering her in chocolate and spending the rest of the night feasting on her.

He cleared his throat, adjusted his pants, and glanced around, trying to take his mind off his erection and doubting it possible. He'd been in the back kitchen before, of course, had done the fire safety inspection himself just a few months back.

Katy gestured toward the stove. "Would you mind giving that a stir for me? I don't want it to burn."

His gaze tracked her as she went for the phone, and his body registered every sexy detail of her curvy backside. As she punched in the numbers, he turned and looked at the sauce warming in the double boiler over the stainless steel range and tried not to think about all the delicious ways he'd like to use it.

Taming his desire, he turned the burner off, gave the sauce a quick stir, then stepped around the long counter positioned in the middle of the room. Bracing his hands on the ledge, he looked out through the service slot and into the restaurant. The lights were off and the place was quiet. The restaurant was locked up for the night which meant they were all alone. While Katy talked to the sheriff's office, he walked back to the counter and examined the ingredients and the recipes spread out over her workstation.

As he looked things over, what he noticed first was the rich, sophisticated menu, one normally found at a fine seafood restaurant. What it wasn't, was something the tourists expected or the Seafarer's regular customers were accustomed to. Since the townsfolk weren't too big on change, he was pretty certain her menu wasn't going to be a hit, but he sure loved how hard she was trying.

He was about to talk to her about it, but when she hung up the phone, drew all the curtains, and moved toward the stove to stir her chocolate, the sight of her tight ass shut down his brain and he decided talking was meant for later. Right then, as she stood with her back to him, her jeans hugging her curves and making her look good enough to eat, he decided to do just that.

"The sheriff said he'd look into it," she tossed over her shoulder, then dipped her finger into the chocolate to test it.

When she removed the chocolate from the heat, Trent stepped up behind her, gripped her hips and pushed his cock against her ass.

She gasped in mock surprise, but then she wiggled. The movement was slight but he noticed it. Katy wanted to play every bit as much as he did and he suspected she'd drawn the curtains and turned her attention to the chocolate sauce for her own naughty reasons.

"I think there is something we should look into too."

"Oh, and what's that?" Katy asked as she went up on her toes to reach the bag of sugar in the cupboard above the stove. Her hot, sexy ass rubbed his cock, so achingly familiar, so achingly erotic, he damn near exploded.

"Jesus, Katy," he murmured, dying to be inside her. Everywhere.

She spun around, her eyes wide, warm chocolate staining her lips. Sexual energy leapt between them and nearly ignited the kitchen. "Trent, are you okay? You sound like you're in pain."

He grinned, licked the chocolate from her mouth, and pushed harder against her. Their eyes locked, the heat between them tremendous. "Yeah, baby, I'm in pain." He stopped to lick his lips. "But wouldn't you just know it, chocolate makes everything better."

He slipped his hands around her ass, and hoisted her onto his hips. As her body molded to his it made him feel wild, crazy, completely out of control. Frenzied with need, he backed her up and pinned her between the wall and his chest.

When she licked the rest of the chocolate off her lips, he whispered, "I need to fuck you, baby." He ran his thumb over her mouth. "I'm going to start here." As she kissed him, he slid his hands along the outer edge of her breasts and squeezed. "Then here."

She moaned and arched into his touch. Trent slid his hand between their bodies and stroked her pussy through her jeans. A growl of longing sounded deep in her throat.

"And here," he said as she thrust her pelvis forward, eager for him to do just that. He circled her waist and cradled her ass in his hands. "And I'm going to finish right here." When her eyes widened in surprise, he said, "Well you can't go around shaking that sweet ass of yours and not expect me to want a piece of it, now can you?"

Lust-saturated eyes met his, and in a low, deeply intimate voice full of sultry invitation, she said, "I suppose not, T."

The promise in her eyes had his body rippling in anticipation and his groin tightening with need. Jesus, he'd missed her, especially her playful, adventurous side.

As his body buzzed to life, he took possession of her mouth and kissed her long and deep. By the time he inched back and let her legs slide to the floor, they were both breathless. A moment later he stepped back to look at her.

Her hair was mussed, her cheeks flushed, and her nipples were so hard they poked out of her T-shirt. His mouth watered for a taste. "I want you naked. Now."

She pointed a finger and wagged it up and down. "You too," she said, her seductive cadence generating warmth and need deep inside him.

He tore his own clothes off as she slowly removed hers, teasing and tormenting his libido with her slow seduction. Trent raked his fingers through his hair, his blood running thick and hot as he watched her. "Christ, girl, you make me crazy."

She offered him a sexy grin, her eyes glimmering with sensuality as she lowered herself into a chair and widened her legs. She gave him a beautiful, unobstructed view of her glistening pussy as she took her breasts into her hands and squeezed.

She moistened her lips. "Come here, Trent. It's my turn to taste you."

His body went weak as he stepped into her and brushed her hair from her face. She inched down in her seat and drew his cock into her hot mouth. "Fuck..." he bit out, and threw his head back as the wet warmth of her mouth enveloped him. Desire thrummed in his veins, and as the tang of her arousal permeated his senses, he had to gulp for his next breath.

The way she drew him into her mouth and kissed his cock with such intimate recognition instantly had him teetering on the edge of ecstasy. His entire body vibrated and Katy, as if sensing his urgency, moaned in delight.

He watched her suck him in deep and use her tongue to lick the precome dripping from his slit. His whole body broke into a sweat as her mouth gripped him hard, and it was all he could do not to give himself over to the sensations. Inching back, he brushed his thumb over her lips and glanced at her heavy breasts.

She smiled at him, knowing exactly what he wanted. She squeezed her breasts together and he stepped back, dipped his finger into the warm chocolate and drizzled it over her mounds. Katy cried out in bliss when he bent his head and drew one rigid nipple into his mouth. His warm tongue brushed over her gently, tasting the sweetness and wetting her hard buds and creamy flesh in preparation. Once she was well lubricated, he stood and met her glance as he slipped his wet cock into the tight channel she'd molded for him.

"Oh baby, you feel so good." He drove upward, and she stuck her tongue out, brushing it over his tip with every hard thrust. His body shook with unabashed hunger and he moved urgently. Sensing he was about to lose control, he quickly withdrew his blood-filled cock before he erupted. Panting and on the brink of losing it, he dropped to the ground and poised his mouth over her pussy as he took a moment to compose himself.

As his blood ran hot, he asked, "Are you wet for me, baby?"

Trent trailed his fingers along her thighs and she widened her legs even more. The sight of her hot, wet pussy practically rendered him senseless.

"Why don't you check," she murmured, and lifted her hips off the chair. His hands spanned her waist and he pushed her back down to anchor her in place.

He slipped a finger inside her and she liquefied under his touch. He groaned deep in his throat. "Baby, you're on fire."

Her pussy muscles gripped him hard and his cock protested, demanding to be the one inside her. Breathing became difficult and it took all his effort to speak. "I need to fuck you now, sweetheart."

Eyes full of want shot to his. "Please, T."

There was a desperation in her voice he'd never heard before, and the tender look of intimacy on her face warmed his darkest corners and knocked him off balance. A surge of love rushed through him and his throat clogged.

When she slid her fingers through his hair, he lifted her from the chair and took her place. "I want you to ride me, baby."

Katy wrapped her legs around him and he gripped her hips and guided her home.

Home. With him. Where she belonged.

She wiggled, wanting to impale herself, but he wanted to draw out the moment and savor it. Trent drew a steadying breath as he slowly drove into her and joined them as one. As they came together, they forged an intimate connection, one that went beyond the physical, one that took two broken pieces and made them whole again. He looked deep into her blue eyes and knew there was nothing he could ever do to sate his need for her. She'd taken up residency in his heart over a decade ago. She was under his skin, inside him, a part of him.

Katy's mouth found his and she began riding him, long hard strokes that pushed him to the edge and tested his control. As he lost himself in her, body, heart and soul, he could feel the pressure building in her body.

Slipping a finger between them, he drew small circles around her clit, and could feel the pleasure resonating through her. Her beautiful breasts bounced with her every movement and color flooded her cheeks. A heartbeat later she took a shuddering breath and he could feel her liquid heat scorch his cock. As she came for him, he held her tight and buried his face in her neck, forcing himself to hold on because he needed to be inside her. Everywhere.

When her body stopped spasming, he lifted her from his cock, slid his hand around her back and stroked a shaky finger over her puckered passage. Her eyes met his and she whispered, "I want it too, T." She pushed against him, trusting him with her pleasure and welcoming him into her body.

Trent glanced around and searched for a place to take her, wanting to make it as comfortable as possible for her.

"Follow me." With a naughty look on her face, she grabbed something from the cupboard, gripped his hand and led him to the small break room off the kitchen. She threw a pillow onto the floor, dropped to her knees in front of the floral sofa and crooked her finger.

He sucked in air. The sight of her bent over that couch and opening her body to him had his cock spasming with pleasure. "Katy, Jesus…"

He dropped down behind her and pushed his hand between her legs. "I don't have any lubricant, sweetheart."

"That's what the almond oil is for," she said as she handed him the bottle.

He groaned, took the bottle from her and poured a generous amount over her back. It dripped over her curves, and he couldn't believe how sexy she looked as it seductively slid over her sweet ass. He spread his palms over her back and massaged the oil in. She moaned in bliss as he moved closer and closer to her back passage, taking his time to prepare her properly. He gently squeezed a finger inside, and when he met with tight walls, he asked, "Katy, sweetheart, is this a first?"

When she nodded, he exhaled slowly, determined to make this good for her, and loving how open and honest they could be with each other.

He put his mouth close to her ear, needing to claim her and put his mark on her in a way he'd never marked another.

"Me too." The truth was he'd only ever wanted to take Katy this way, only ever needed to be one with her like this.

"T." Her voice hitched as his admission seemed to do something to her. She reached around and locked her fingers with his. "Please, T. I want to feel you inside me."

"You're not ready for me yet, baby." Trent wet his dry lips and spent a long time playing with her ass. He worked in one finger, and then two, until her body beckoned his and her passion flared hot. Attuned to her needs, he continued to lubricate her with the oil, to ensure she was completely ready for him.

He positioned his cock at her opening and she wiggled backwards. "Baby, if this hurts, let me know and I'll stop."

Trent took his time, entering her slowly and savoring every inch. When her fingers curled around the cushions and she gave a little yelp, he stopped. He kept still while she got used to the fullness and, wanting to give her pleasure, slipped a finger around her body and lightly brushed her clit until it filled with blood. Soon she was moaning, and when he gave a gentle thrust and pushed past her ringed opening, her body relaxed for him.

"That's my girl," he murmured, and gripped her hips for leverage.

She began moving with him, encouraging him, meeting and welcoming each thrust. Soon the two were rocking in sync, each giving and taking, and coming together in a beautiful new way—a way they'd only ever experienced with each other. That thought turned him inside out, and created a new closeness between them.

Trent slid his hands around her body and hugged her to him. Moisture sealed their flesh together as he rammed home. Her breathing changed, became erratic, and he brushed his finger over her clit to guide her along. As her muscles tightened and she came for him, he drove deep and stilled. Closing his eyes, he released himself inside her as every feeling he had for her pulsed through his body and rose to the surface.

He stayed inside her, lying over her body until his cock grew flaccid. When he finally pulled out, he dropped down beside her and pulled her to him for a long, soul-searching kiss.

A long time later he inched away and she smiled. He ran the back of his hand along her flushed cheek. "I didn't hurt you, did I?"

The emotions in her eyes touched his soul and he could feel himself hardening again when she said, "Maybe a little," she admitted honestly. "But I know you would never purposely hurt me."

As his heart pounded in his chest, and emotions tore through him, Katy yawned. Trent chuckled and gave her a hug. "Am I keeping you up?" he asked.

She laughed and pointed downward. "No, but I think I might be keeping you up."

He kissed her mouth and pitched his voice low. "I can't get enough of you, baby."

"Yeah, but maybe we should get out of here before we lose track of time and the breakfast crew arrives and finds us like this."

Basking in the afterglow of great sex, Trent climbed to his feet and hauled Katy up with him. They made their way into the kitchen and went in search of their clothes.

Katy winked at him as she scooped up her pile. "When you said you wanted to cook in my kitchen, you weren't kidding." She gave a low sigh full of contentment then glanced at the mess. "But now I'm too spent to finish up here."

"Want me to help?"

She pulled on her panties and jeans. "No. Leave it. I think I have my menu figured out anyway."

"Katy about this menu, do you think it's a little too... sophisticated for the townsfolk?"

She shrugged. "It's the kind of food I prepare on the show."

He treaded gingerly, not wanting to offend her, but always wanting to be honest with her. "I know, and as much as I love your show, sometimes I think your menu is a bit too complicated for the average Joe." He rolled one shoulder and added, "Hey, there is something to be said for down-home cooking."

She frowned, and mumbled under her breath, something about her viewership.

"What?" He tipped her chin to bring them eye to eye, and wondered why she suddenly seemed so distressed.

"Nothing," she said. "It's nothing."

"Katy," he pressed, wanting her to share everything with him.

"Come on. I'm anxious to get home, soak in a bubble bath and crawl into bed with my favorite firefighter."

"You'd better be talking about me," he teased.

Katy laughed, stepped away from him and pulled on her shirt while Trent finished getting dressed.

He held his hand out to her. "Come on, I'll walk with you."

"You want to be seen with me?"

"I'm sure as hell not going to let you face the wolves yourself."

She smiled. "Firefighter *and* bodyguard," she teased.

Once they were dressed, they slipped out the back and took the gravel path until it led to the main road. As soon as they surfaced, cameras were directed at them and microphones were shoved in their faces. Jesus, he hated being thrust into the spotlight like this. Deputy Veinotte controlled the reporters as Trent and Katy kept their heads down and hurried along the street. When they reached her cottage, Trent guided her along the lane, stopped at the door and ignored the questions being fired their way from the street.

"Aren't you coming in?" Katy asked.

"Don't want to sully your reputation, lassie."

She angled her head and grinned. "So what, now you're a pirate?"

He gave her a wink. "If you want me to be. I'm sure I can rustle up a costume."

She laughed, went up on her toes and placed a soft kiss on his mouth. "I think I'll stick to my fireman. He's quite good at putting out fires and I don't just mean the ones in my trash can."

When her smile faded, he brushed his thumb along her mouth, knowing what was going through that pretty head of hers. "Don't worry, Katy. You're safe here. Brody said the noise was from loose shingles. I fixed them this afternoon."

Her eyes widened, emotions passed over her face. "You did? Why?"

"Do you really need to ask?"

With that he bent and kissed her with all the love inside him. When she kissed him back, the press taking pictures from the end of her lane, he knew in his heart his Katy had found her way home.

Feeling alive for the first time in a long time, Trent couldn't wipe the smile from his face. He turned to leave, knowing it was time to take their relationship to the next level. A plan began to formulate, and as he warmed to the idea, excitement rushed through his veins. From here on out, when he wasn't working, he was going to spend every moment with Katy, making love to her and proving over and over again just how good they were together before he moved forward with the rest of his agenda.

As he made his way back to the fire station, the paparazzi tight on his heels, he tried to ignore them. Except when someone hinted that Katy was back in town simply to create a buzz, and had found the perfect hero to help her become America's sweetheart, he stopped in his tracks.

"What the hell are you talking about?" Trent demanded.

"Come on, Trent," the reporter said. "Who doesn't love a firefighter? A down-home boy respected by men and wanted by women. You're exactly what Katy needs to draw interest and get her ratings back up."

Trent fisted his hands and worked to keep his anger in check. He resisted the urge to hit the guy only because he didn't want it to look bad on Katy. "Take a hike, pal." Trent turned and reminded himself the guy was nothing more than the damned paparazzi trying to get a rise out of him.

"Yeah, well when the story breaks, we'll see who's going to be taking the hike and who's going to be the one left behind."

Trent's stomach tightened as old, painful memories resurfaced. As he mulled over that worry, a seed of doubt blossomed inside him and his pulse kicked up a notch.

They had to be wrong. They just had to be. Katy said she had nothing to do with the media's sudden appearance and he believed her. She was honest and caring and would never throw her small town into the spotlight for her own selfish reasons.

But as he walked back to the station, something began niggling in the back of his brain, something Katy had said that he couldn't quite put his finger on...

⓼

Katy woke to the sound of seagulls squawking outside her window. She smiled as she recalled the last three days. She and Trent had hung out like old times, relaxing, chatting, cooking. They'd spent every spare moment they could together, sneaking around town, hiding from the paparazzi and making love every chance they could. Katy had never been happier in her life, not just because she and Trent had found each other again, but because of something Trent had said three nights ago when they'd made love at the restaurant, she'd finally figured out what she wanted to do about her contract.

After a restless night of thinking, tossing and turning, and planning for her future, Katy climbed from bed, dressed in her work wear and hurried to the restaurant. She'd scrapped her idea of introducing sophisticated gourmet food to the menu, thanks to Trent's insight, and used the last few days to play with local recipes. As she glanced over the day's menu, good old down-home cooking with a twist, she knew it was time to contact her station and put her plans into motion.

As excitement began building inside her, she jotted down

a quick, bullet-point presentation, determined to prove to the network that she had what it took to increase ratings. It was time to put in a call and get the contract back on the table. Then, once it was signed, she needed to talk to Trent about what their futures held.

After her quick, succinct presentation, the network agreed to her idea, and immediately faxed the contract for her signature. Katy spent the rest of the day desperately trying to focus on her work. The day flew by far too slowly for her liking and she counted down the minutes until she could see Trent, to tell him about her newly signed contract and her exciting new ideas.

Katy couldn't help but think things couldn't have worked out better for her. She and Trent had found each other again, had put the past behind them, and she now knew where her career was headed. All day she'd been bursting to tell someone, but she wanted Trent to be the first to hear it.

After the dinner rush hour, she slipped out the back entrance and cut along the gravel path to avoid the cameras. She came upon Trent's big old Victorian house and her heart tightened as she stood back to look at it. He'd painted it red, changing it back to its original color, a color once used to help the fishermen find their way home in the fog. Had he done that on purpose? To help her find her way back to him? Katy swallowed the lump in her throat and choked back the tears as love rushed to her heart.

As she climbed the stairs, she thought about all the times they'd driven by this particular place when they were young, idealistic teens. Katy loved the old home, had dreamed about buying it with Trent and filling it with kids. They used to talk long into the night about it, excited by the prospect of a future together. But then she'd grown up, and decided she needed to experience more.

When she reached the landing, she knocked on the front

door. When no response came, she checked her watch. Trent wasn't supposed to be on duty tonight. Thinking he might have been called in for an extra shift, Katy hurried to the firehouse and met with Adam. She found him out back shooting hoops by himself.

Still dressed in her work clothes, Katy brushed the moisture from her forehead, and leaned against the brick wall. "Hey, Adam, have you seen Trent?"

Shirtless, Adam took a shot, pushed his hair from his face and met her gaze straight on. "What do you want him for?"

Katy stepped back, surprised by the hardness in his tone. "I need to tell him something."

The ball came bouncing back and Adam picked it up and braced it under his arm. He angled his head and glared at her. "Haven't you done enough already, Kathleen?"

Katy swallowed, a nervous sensation moving through her. "What are you talking about, Adam?"

Adam shook his head and grunted. "I thought you said you weren't going to start something you couldn't finish."

"I didn't."

"Oh no?"

"No. I love him, Adam," she admitted, ready to tell the world how she felt.

He studied her for a moment, then his face softened slightly when he said, "Well you sure have a funny way of showing it."

"Where is he?" she demanded, her knees feeling a little rubbery beneath her.

He gave a long sigh. "I don't know. He seemed out of sorts and tore out of town earlier. I haven't been able to get ahold of him."

As Katy thought through the events of the last few days, she couldn't deny that there were moments where Trent had seemed a bit distracted. She chalked up his distraction to his concerns over the town's new arsonist, but now she was beginning to wonder if it had something to do with her.

Feeling numb and confused, Katy turned from Adam and made her way back to her cottage, only to find Granddaddy Errol standing on her front porch. He looked guilty about something and more than a little concerned. That was when she noticed the reporters on the street. She'd been so lost in her thoughts she hadn't noticed how antsy and excited they'd become. Deputy Veinotte had to employ the help of a few more men to keep them in line.

"What?" she asked when her gaze locked on Errol's.

"You'd better come inside, lassie."

Her grandfather led her to the sofa and told her to have a seat while he flicked on the news. Katy felt the color drain from her face as she listened to the perky blonde reporter state that Kathleen Wilson's return to Whispering Cove was simply a marketing ploy.

After all, who didn't love a juicy story about young love, especially when the male lead was a heroic firefighter? She then went on to report that with Kathleen's ratings dropping, speculation was that she and her publicist had planned the whole event, and now with the public's interest piqued, every network wanted a piece of Kathleen Wilson. The reporter then announced that Kathleen had, in fact, renewed her contract.

"Oh no," she put her hand over her mouth, thinking how quickly the word had spread, and before she could talk to Trent. "Trent must have seen this."

"Everyone's seen it. But Trent heard about it the other day. Apparently some reporter tipped him off. Told him you were using him. I overheard the whole thing."

Katy's jaw dropped. "He never said anything."

But that must have been why he'd been so distracted. Her stomach knotted and she couldn't help but wonder if, now that an official statement had been made, he'd torn out of town so he could leave her before she had a chance to leave him. Again.

"I didn't mean for it to go down like this, Katy."

She turned her head to see Errol. "What are you talking about?"

"I tipped off the reporters."

Katy jumped to her feet. "You did what?"

"Thought it might help you see who really cared about you." He looked so sad and remorseful, Katy's heart went out to him. He gave her a sheepish look. "I'm old, Katy. Sometimes my ideas aren't so well thought out."

"Business wasn't really down at the Seafarer either, was it?"

He shook his head. "Nah, just wanted to get you home, lassie. Just wanted to show you where you belong."

Honestly, she couldn't fault her granddaddy for that. He loved her, cared about her and wanted only what was best for her.

Like Trent.

"The fires?" she asked

"Yup," he admitted. "I was responsible for them too."

Katy shook her head in dismay. "Don't you understand the danger involved? You could have..."

Her granddaddy cut her off. "You were never in any danger, Katy. Not with Trent looking out for you. Besides, Adam was in on it with me."

"Adam?"

"Yeah, he wanted you two together as much as me. Hell, the whole town knows you two belong together." He gave a long, heavy sigh. "Dammit, girl, you're the only one who doesn't know where you belong."

Emotions swelled inside her. "I know where I belong," she said softly.

Just then her door flung open and she turned to see Trent standing there, his eyes were dark and stormy, his mouth tight, set in a fine line. The torment on his face tore at her heart. He looked so lost, so vulnerable, so much like he had ten years ago when she told him she was leaving town.

"And where might that be, Katy?" he asked.

When Katy didn't answer, Trent stepped through the door. "Well, where might that be?" he asked again.

"Trent, I'm sorry." Pained blue eyes met his as she took a tentative step toward him.

His mind raced, hardly able to believe what he was hearing. "Sorry? What are you sorry for?"

Her mouth turned down in a frown. "I didn't want you to find out like this."

The room around him began to spin and a sick feeling welled up in the pit of his stomach as she apologized to him. "So what they said is true?" he managed to get out around the lump in his throat as he shook his head, still unable to believe it.

"No, of course not. Well, not all of it."

He narrowed his gaze, hope rushing through him. "Which part is true?"

"The contract part."

Trent raked his hand through is hair. Chaos erupted inside him and his mind raced. "You really signed it?"

She nodded quickly.

"Katy," he began, perplexed.

"But the terms have changed," she hurried out.

"The terms? I don't understand."

"It was something you said."

"Jesus, Katy. What the hell is going on?"

"You told me there was something to be said for down-home cooking. And you were right." She waved her hand around. "The network loved my idea of setting up a kitchen here in Whispering Cove and preparing some of the Seafarer's famous East coast meals."

An invisible band tightened around Trent's heart as reality dawned. He smiled. "So you're telling me..."

"Yes, Trent, I'm telling you that I'm staying. This is where I belong. It's where I've always belonged." She pressed her palm to the side of his face. "Thank you for giving me the freedom to discover that. Thank you for never giving up on me. And thank you for helping me find my way back home, to you."

Tension eased from his shoulders. "Katy, really, do you mean it?" he asked, needing to hear her say it again.

"Yeah, I mean it. I'm home to stay. I wanted to talk to you. To tell you in person. But Adam said you tore out of town and—" She stopped talking, lowered her head, and whispered under her breath, "I thought the worst."

"I had to go into Colton County."

"Colton County? Why?"

"That's where my savings and trust account is."

Confusion came over her face. "Why did you have to go there?"

"I had an errand to run."

Katy visibly relaxed. "And here I thought..."

"You thought I'd run out on you?" When she gave a remorseful nod, he pulled her in tight and said, "I told you, I'd never run out on you, Katy, and I meant it."

"But after the news..."

"What about it?"

"I thought you believed them, that I'd been using you, and that I was leaving."

He smiled. "Not for a second. Okay, maybe for a second when you started to apologize."

"Granddaddy told me they tipped you off days ago. He said he'd overheard them."

Trent's heart pounded in his chest as he brushed the moisture away from her eyes. "It's true, Katy. The other night some guy told me you were using me to increase viewership, then I remembered what you said at the restaurant, something about your viewership slipping."

"You never said anything."

"Why would I?"

"Didn't you think...?"

"No, I didn't think."

She shook her head. "God, you have so much faith in me."

"That's because I believe in you, Katy. I believe in the strength of our love and know you'd never use me or do anything to purposely hurt me."

Her throat worked as she swallowed. "When I left before—"

"You had to do what you had to do, Katy. I of all people know that. All that matters now is that you've finally found your way home." When she got quiet, he went on to say, "I was sorry to hear about the decreasing viewership. I can just imagine how horrible that made you feel. Is that why you didn't want to talk about it?"

She nodded.

"I want us to share everything, okay? The good and the bad."

"I want that too."

He let loose a slow breath. "Even though ratings were down, you and I both know you weren't happy in Chicago."

Her eyes widened, like something just occurred to her. "Is that why you've been so distracted? Because I didn't want to talk about it?"

"No. I didn't want to press and knew you'd talk about it when you were ready."

"Then why?"

Before she could probe, his mouth took possession of hers and as he kissed her long and hard. In that instant it occurred to him that he'd never felt closer to her in his entire life.

"God, girl, you make me crazy," he murmured, easing the tension around them. "But I can't tell you how happy I am that you get to do what you love, and you get to do it here."

"There is one little problem though," she whispered into his mouth when he inched back.

His heart stilled, his glance taking in her nervous expression. "What?"

"The network agreed to my contract changes only if you'll do guest spots. Lots of them. The public loves you, and I know you like privacy, but I'm still trying to find a way to work around it."

Trent laughed with relief. "I don't care, Katy. As long as you're here, I'll put up with the damn cameras."

"You'd...you'd do that for me?" she choked out.

He dipped his head, his lips hovering over hers. "Yeah, baby, I'd do that for you. I like doing things for you, so get used to it."

Emotions moved over her face and she smiled. "I'm glad to hear that because I'm also hoping you can help me with menu ideas. You're pretty darn good in the kitchen." She winked and he understood the double meaning.

"I'll help you on one condition."

She gifted him with an amused look. "Oh, so now you have a condition?"

"Of course." He stepped back and dropped to one knee. "This is why I took off to Colton County and why I've been distracted, Katy." He held an engagement ring out. "Because this has been waiting to go on your finger for ten years and I wanted to do it right."

Tears welled up in Katy's eyes. "Oh, Trent."

"I want you to be mine. Forever. I want you to move into the house I bought for us. I've been waiting for you to find your way home for a long, long time, sweetheart."

Tears filled her eyes, and when she nodded, Trent jumped to his feet and gathered her into his arms. "I love you, Katy," he murmured as he soaked in her warmth and love.

"I love you too." She rose up on her toes to meet his lips.

Errol cleared his throat and they both turned. Honestly, Trent had completely forgotten he was still in the room, and by the surprised yet embarrassed look on Katy's face, so had she.

"I'm going to go get rid of the reporters," Errol said. "You two need your privacy." If Trent wasn't mistaken, the old man had a tear or two in his eyes as well.

"Don't bother," Trent said, and gathered Katy into his arms.

She squealed. "What are you up to?"

"If they want a show, I'll give them a show."

Trent carried her down the lane, depositing her in front of the cameras. As soon as all the attention was on him, he announced to the world that he loved her and was going to marry her. Then he drew Katy into his arms and kissed her with all the love inside him.

He didn't care if it was broadcast all over the world. All that mattered was that Katy had found her way home to him and they were going to spend the rest of their lives together cooking—inside the kitchen and out.

EPILOGUE

Drinks and laughter and dancing and boisterous music swelled within the pub walls and overflowed onto the deck. Men wore suits and ties, though many had discarded their jackets. Women fluttered like butterflies in their best dresses and flashiest jewels.

"It's good seeing everyone back together and all fancied up." Taryn, Hauk's special-occasion hostess, smiled as she gathered the dirty plates from the table.

"Aye. The reunion is as good a reason as any for a fancy party." Harold poured more rum into his and Errol's glasses and sat back in his chair.

Bryon nodded and tapped his right foot against the table leg. "Weddings are better."

"Aye."

"You have a wedding date yet?" the green-and-red lamp over the table cast a multihued haze over Errol as he petting the backs of his cards.

"Braydon's holding out on a date. It's as if he's on to us."

"Think he'll tell the others?" Harold asked.

"Yeah." Bryon raised his glass in a silent salute to Braydon across the room. Braydon shook his head with a humored grin splitting his face, turned his attention back to his bride-to-be, and led her to join Brody ad Trent. "If he knows. And they'll scheme to keep any one of us from winning our bets."

"So we tied on this one."

"There's the next one still," Harold insisted.

"Yep." Bryon watched Braydon pull Danica close for an intimate dance. While the bragging rights of winning would've been fun, he was perfectly happy to see the young couples in love. Not that he'd admit as much to his buddies. "Like who's the first to get us great-grandbabies."

He happened to know Braydon and Danica were already planning their family. Once his boy had settled down, he and the doc had dived right in to their future plans. Except the setting –the-date-part.

"I'll take that bet." Errol took a swig of his rum. "Ain't no way my Katy will let me down."

"Barnacle plucking ole goats." Harold slapped the table. "My Andie and Brody will waste no time getting back to their old intentions."

"Then we're agreed." Bryon raised his glass in a toast. "Winner names the prize."

Harold and Errol clinked their glasses with his and spoke in unison. "Agreed."

"In the meantime..." Bryon watched Sophie Michaelsen chatting with Victoria Hayes. "I know of some other young ones who need to get on with the business of families"

Just then, Adam Collins escorted a young woman who didn't match his temperament onto the dance floor. Errol nodded. "Yes. Yes. We have our work cut out for us if we're going to ensure the right matches."

"Today's young need all the help they can get."

"Thank the se goddess they 'ave us."

BRAZEN

In Whispering Cove

A barnacle-suckin' hand with a king and a six.

Byron Mitchell placed his second card face-down atop the first and reached for his tumbler of rum. It was a shoddy beginning, but he had bluffed his way out of worse. Then again, so had his weekly poker buddies Harold Adair and Errol Wilson.

Distraction. He could win with the right distraction, and these days the same distraction never failed. 'How are those great-grandbabies growin'?"

"Fast." Harold's mouth curled into a smile as he laid his second card facedown. "Andie's big enough to be having twins, but she won't tell me if there's more than one. Says wondering is what I get for meddling."

Shaking his head, Errol placed his second card facedown with his first. "Place your bets."

They tossed chips into the small pile. Errol dealt round three.

"It's not meddlin'." Harold mumbled.

"Women see it different," Bryon mused. At least according to his wife Ruth and Dani, his new granddaughter by marriage. Braydon's life plan to sail in solitude. "Dani and Braydon are supposed to be paintin' the nursery this week. They won't tell me what they're havin'." Bryon pursed his lips and swirled the rum in his tumbler. "They keep sayin' I'd have too many thoughts on names."

"Women are—"

"The reason we have babies," Errol cut Harold off. "My Katy gave me that same line when she told me to stop coddling her." The left corner of Errol's mouth twitched. The tell made Byron want to smile. His pal had a nice hand, but he was thinking more about his granddaughter and when she might bring him news of a baby. The distraction was working. "Not that she's fessing up to carrying my grandbaby," Errol finished.

"They think they're invincible." Bryon swirled the liquor in his tumbler again. "Maybe we should let 'em think we're leaving them alone."

"How do you mean?" Errol dealt the last round and they all placed their bets.

Whatever Errol had dealt himself wasn't a great hand. He wasn't revealing any of his tells like Harold. Their tells got bigger the better their hand.

"I think it's time to get some other youngsters paired off," said Byron. "Hauk is living in fear of reliving his past. And little Sophie deserves a momma. It's time he figured out he can have it all."

Harold nodded. "Reece has been running from Tabatha long enough."

"And Adam is blind to Josie. Sees her only as his best friend's sister. Doesn't know how good they could be together." Errol's smile broadened. "With the Fall Festival coming, there's a lot to plan."

"They won't be as easy to manoeuvre as the others. They'll be on the lookout."

"And the festival will be a great distraction." Errol chuckled as he shuffled the cards he'd dealt himself. "We'll give the jobs and watch those sparks fly."

"Those boys won't know what hit 'em."

"Neither will the girls."

Bryon nodded, liking the idea more and more. It was always fun to see the young'ns get twisted up over finding love. "The bet?"

"The fastest match with the least interventions?" Harold offered.

"The most creative setup," Bryon countered.

"No. These kids know each other, so they only have to let go their fool notions about each other to see what they'll have."

Errol poured more run into his tumbler. "The match must be made before the end of the Fall Festival."

The all nodded as their budding schemes swam in their eyes.

"Losers eat barnacles," Errol tossed out.

"Losers buys the rum for a month," Harold added.

Byron took a drink and watched the plan unfurl in his mind as clearly as the stars awakening in the fall sky. One thing he'd learned over the years was how to read the town's youngsters. Hauk Michaelsen with his charcoal-touch heart, which was more fragile than he thought, was so used to what was in front of him, so blind to the woman who loved him he would never see Victoria Hayes coming. "Good thing you two have a taste for 'em."

"Chase 'em down with a little run and they won't be so bad," Errol laughed.

9

Adam Collins leaned against old man Henningar's fifteen-hundred-pound, prize-winning pumpkin and plucked a piece of straw from the bales of hay surrounding the freakishly large gourd. He plopped the dry strand of grass into his mouth and glanced around the bustling fair grounds, noting that there seemed to be a new energy and excitement in the air this year. Perhaps it was because all his friends were either hooking up, getting married or having babies. Or perhaps it was because the small town had an influx of people since Katy Wilson's, or rather, Katy Parker's cooking show put their quaint fishing village on the map.

Either way, as he thought more about Katy and her recent marriage to his best friend and fellow firefighter Trent Parker, a delicious medley of tastes—everything from sugary cotton candy, rich, buttery popcorn to greasy, hand-cut French fries —settled on the back of his tongue and had him realizing just how alone he felt in the crowd.

There was no denying that he loved this time of year. Loved when people from the neighboring communities ventured into his beloved town of Whispering Cove to celebrate the land's rich harvest and the ocean's lush bounty. Loved when friends, old and new, all came together in the downtown core to partake in the annual fall festival.

But when the giggles of small children and the laughter of their parents cut through the noise of the fair's activities and wrapped around his heart like a tight vise, it was simply a reminder of what he wanted. And what he could never have.

Fortunately, before he had time to dwell on that disheartening truth, Errol Wilson came hobbling up to him and poked him with his cane, dragging his dark thoughts back to the present.

"Get off your keister there, boy, and try to rustle us up some victims...err, I mean, customers for that dang psychic booth. How do you think we're gonna raise money for the new community center if we ain't drawing in paying folk?"

"Errol," Adam greeted as he removed the butt of the cane from his gut and placed it on the yellowing, sunburnt grass at his feet. "I see your leg is bothering you again."

Errol snarled. "Dang thing's been stiffening up on me. Must be the cooler weather..."

Before Errol could finish his sentence, his thoughts drifted off and his gaze shifted to a distant spot behind Adam's shoulder. If Adam didn't know better he'd think the old guy was losing his mind. But he did know better.

Despite his age, Errol Wilson—bright, energetic and wily —was the spark in every fire, the crest in every wave and was to never, ever be underestimated. Adam twisted to follow Errol's gaze, wondering exactly what it was that caught the old guy's attention and managed to distract him from his constant pestering.

When he spotted Trent, Errol's new son-in-law, hugging his wife Katy, who looked to be putting on a fair bit of weight —right around the midsection—Adam couldn't help but smile. He was happy for his friends, happy to see them moving forward at a breakneck speed in an attempt to make up for the ten long years they'd spent apart.

Adam knew the two had a secret but it certainly wasn't his place to let the cat out of the bag. Hell, as a local fire fighter at station 415, the only cat he planned on freeing was the one trapped in a tree. Those two would tell Errol, one of Whispering Cove's biggest gossips—the other two being Harold Adair and Byron Mitchell, Errol's partners in crime—when they were damn well ready.

Errol narrowed those inquisitive eyes of his, now dark and cloudy from old age, but Adam didn't miss the seed of hope blossoming in their murky depths when he asked, "You think she's got my great-grandbaby in there?"

Adam pushed himself off the pumpkin and stretched out his arms, feeling a bit stiff himself after last night's softball game. "I don't know, Errol. You'll have to ask Katy and Trent that yourself."

"I have. They ain't spilling." He paused to offer Adam a mischievous smirk and gave a slight nod when he said, "But no worries, lad. I know just how to find out."

Fallen maple leaves, crisp and colorful from the changing season, crunched beneath Adam's sneakers as he began walking toward the psychic booth. He cast Errol a warning glance and arched a brow as the older man rushed to keep pace. "I thought your days of meddling were supposed to be over."

Although as of late, after watching Hauk and Vic, as well as Reece and Tabby find love during the fall festival, Adam had begun to suspect the gruesome threesome were up to their old matchmaking ways. Of course the whole town knew those two couples belonged together, and while the meddlesome grandfathers all swore they had nothing to do with it, Adam still had his suspicions.

"Ain't nothing wrong with a little digging, boy."

"Errol," he cautioned.

That brought a grimace to Errol's weathered face. "You youngins are always telling us old folk how to run our business when y'all know nothing about nothing."

Ignoring Errol's rant, Adam stopped a few feet away from the psychic booth, although he could hardly classify it as a booth, not with the long draping curtains Tabby had breathed new life into and sewed together to form exterior walls. With its flowing entrance, soft, welcoming pillows and numerous, multicolored scarves shimmering in the slight breeze, the elegance of the sultan's tent hadn't gone unnoticed by him. Perhaps the classiness was to hide the fact that Madame M, the so-called clairvoyant inside, was as phony as Errol's convictions that he'd stopped interfering in other people's lives.

Adam jammed his hands into his pockets and scoffed as he rocked on the balls of his feet. "Whose idea was it to put up a psychic stand this year anyway?"

"Mine. Why? You got something against psychics?" When Adam gave Errol a dubious look, Errol probed, "What? You don't believe in them?"

"That's right." But before he could elaborate and tell the old man that he believed in psychics about as much as he believed he was the marrying kind, sweet Josie Wells walked by.

Josie Wells.

As his heart picked up tempo, he fisted his hands inside his pockets and tried to appear unaffected, a difficult task considering the prettiest girl he'd ever known had just passed in front of him. A girl he wanted in the worst fucking way.

Wearing a pretty dress that hugged her soft, feminine curves in all the right places, Adam couldn't help but watch the easy, casual way she moved, couldn't help but take pleasure in her innocent sensuality as she sauntered by, or the way that innocent sensuality seeped under his skin and settled deep in his groin.

Her hips swayed seductively and a beautiful smile lit up her blue eyes as she moved past them, but Adam was too damn preoccupied thinking about how that sensuous body of hers would feel beneath his, how that long, silken blonde hair of hers would feel running along his naked flesh to formulate any sort of a response.

As a kindergarten teacher at the local elementary school, not only was Josie compassionate, caring, soft spoken and patient—basically she was the antithesis of the wild and wicked women he was accustomed to—she had flawless skin made for touching, full, sensuous lips made for kissing and a lush body made for making love. Simply put, Josie was real, natural and sensual. With a girl like her, a girl with no hidden agendas, what you saw was what you got. And what he saw made his dick hard. So goddamn hard it was all he could do not to excuse himself and head straight to his bedroom so he could take the edge off.

Before he could stop himself, he made a choking sound, a half growl, half gurgle.

Fully pathetic.

Errol patted him on the back. "You okay, boy? You need a glass of water or something?"

"I'm fine," he answered. Except he wasn't fine. Oh no, he wasn't fine at all. Not where Josie Wells was concerned.

Okay, so Adam was wrong when he once told his best friend Trent Parker that fucking solved everything. Because with a girl like Josie, a girl who not only wanted, but deserved, a loving husband and a big house with a widow's peak overlooking the majestic Atlantic Ocean, things Adam could never give her, fucking would simply complicate matters more than they already were and result in pain and loss.

After all, he knew his fate. And he'd be damned if he dragged a sweet thing like Josie Wells into his troubled life.

Errol made a tsking sound. "There's only one way to scratch that kind of itch, lad."

Adam gave Errol an odd look and shifted uncomfortably under the man's scrutinizing gaze. Surely to God the old man wasn't suggesting...

"What are you talking about?" Adam asked cautiously, hoping he wasn't about to start lecturing him on his sex life.

It was only when Errol put his cane over his shoulder and dragged it along the middle of his back that Adam realized he was running his own fingers over his neck. Except his rubbing had more to do with sexual frustration than any kind of itch.

"So what do you say, boy? You gonna get a reading from Madame M or what?"

Adam gave a quick shake of his head, then stepped back a bit to avoid a direct hit from a rambunctious kid who appeared to be hyped up on sugar and covered in sticky cotton candy. "Not a chance."

"If folks see you going in they might follow."

"Why don't you go then?"

"Cause I'm an old man and I don't need any psychic telling me how my bum leg is about to give out on me. I already know that, lad."

Just then Adam spotted his younger brother Jacob. In typical Jacob fashion, he had a woman on each arm, both vying for his attention while a few giggling girls followed close behind. The sight of his playboy brother immediately reminded Adam of who he was and where he'd come from.

Errol continued to prod him. "Besides, the ladies seem to like you and that will drum up business. When they catch sight of you entering they might be inclined to follow. Ain't no one gonna follow an old man like me in there."

Adam's stomach tightened. Errol might not want any psychic telling him about his bad leg, but Adam certainly didn't want to hear about how much the Collins boys were like their old man, either. Hell, they already knew that. Adam was a firefighter, his brother a veterinarian, and while both found professional success, neither would ever achieve success in a loving, long-term relationship.

They both understood the hand fate had dealt them.

Adam opened his mouth to protest, but Errol poked him with his cane and said, "Come on, Adam. It's for charity. Think of the kids, the community center."

Christ, when he put it that way there was no way he could refuse, despite the fact that everything in his gut told him to run the other way. Cursing under his breath, he blurted out, "Fine," and snatched Errol's cane from him. He pointed it at the man and warned, "But if she delivers bad news, I'll be gunning for you for making me go in there in the first place."

"Don't see what the problem is, boy," Errol said matter-of-factly. "You know, seeing as you just finished telling me you didn't believe in psychics and all."

Humor lit Errol's eyes, and when he offered Adam a wily grin, Adam just shook his head and wondered what the meddling old man was up to this time.

⚫ 10

S hading the late afternoon sun from her eyes, Josie surveyed the packed fairgrounds and searched for her two best friends. When she spotted Vic and Tabby sitting just inside the food and drink tent, she pushed through the throngs of people, taking care to avoid a run-in with a crowd of over-stimulated kids, many of whom were in her kindergarten class, as they ran from one children's activity to another.

As she approached her friends and took in their big, toothy grins, along with the new pink hues brightening their cheeks—a flush that spoke of wild, wicked nights—a small pang of jealousy rose up inside her. Josie was happy for her friends, she really was, but she couldn't deny that after watching them both find love in the arms of two wonderful men, she felt a little envious, and a little tired of waiting for her own Mr. Right to come along.

"Be patient," Madame M had told her a few months back, "and the man of your dreams will come along, a one-woman kind of man with the initials J.A.D."

But honestly, a girl only had so much patience. Not to

mention needs. At twenty-six years old Josie was primed for love, marriage and children—along with great sex—and was getting a little tired of waiting for J.A.D. to profess his undying love to her, whoever the hell J.A.D. was.

"Josie," Vic called out and waved her over when she met her glance. "We saved you a seat."

Josie slipped into the plastic chair that Tabby had pushed out from the table, and took a big sip of the ice-cold soda they had waiting for her.

Tabby grinned. "After that pie-eating contest we thought you might need this."

"Thanks, I do," Josie responded, taking note of the way the two were staring at her as she wiped her mouth and searched the tent for any new faces, or anyone who could possibly have the initials of the man she was supposed to marry. When her glance came up empty, she tried not to look too disappointed, but it was hard to hide anything from her perceptive friends.

Knowing they were about to press about her love life, and hoping to redirect the conversation before they had a chance, Josie pulled a face and rubbed her aching stomach as she glared at them both. "The next time you two want to sign me up for something, do you think it can involve coins or darts, instead of a pound of lard?" Since Josie had been too busy at a school meeting to sign up for any of the activities, her friends had taken the liberty of adding her name to a few of the events.

The two laughed. "We only signed you up for one more thing tonight," Tabby added.

Josie groaned and said, "Please tell me you didn't put my name down for the hot-dog-eating competition, too."

Tabby gave a quick shake of her head. "No, but you need to find your way to Town Square after dark."

Josie racked her brain, trying to figure out what activities were going on after the sun set, when the kids' events shut down and the adult activities took over. She cast an accusing glare her friend's way. "What have you gotten me into this time?"

"Never mind that," Vic said, ignoring her question and asking one of her own. "What I want to know is if you've met the mysterious J.A.D. yet."

Josie frowned and took another hopeful look around the tent, but all she saw was a medley of familiar faces, none of whom sported the initials J.A.D. Well, except for ninety-year-old Judd Daltry, and she was pretty sure he wasn't her soul mate. His wife might have something to say about that.

"Nope, and I'm beginning to believe he doesn't exist."

Tabby toyed with her straw and pulled a face. "Maybe Madame M was wrong and you should just get on with dating."

Just then Lila Sheppard, a young chef who was volunteering in the kitchen, stepped up to them and deposited a huge basket of French fries in the middle of their table. Lila was fairly new in town, hired as Katy's cooking assistant for her daytime show, *Cooking with Katy*.

"Thanks, Lila," they all said, but instead of responding, a dreamy look came over the girl's pretty face as she gazed longingly out into the crowd.

Twisting to see what had caught her attention, Josie followed Lila's gaze until her glance once again fell on Adam Collins. Okay, so clearly the guy was super hot, and clearly Lila wanted a piece of him. Not that she could blame her.

Lila gave a mock shiver. "Jeez, that guy sets my body ablaze with just a simple look." She grinned and arched a playful brow. "Do you think he does house calls for that kind of fire?"

"No, and you should stay away from him." Vic's stern voice caught Josie off guard and had her wondering what it was about Adam Collins that riled her friend so much. Adam might be a playboy, but she also knew he was a nice guy, even though he hadn't spoken to her since she'd returned home from college earlier that year and started teaching at the local elementary school.

"Oh, why's that?" Lila asked.

"Because you're a nice girl and he's hell-bent on staying single," Vic added.

"Who says I'm looking for anything more?" Lila shot them all a wicked grin and continued, "I mean, come on. Sometimes nice girls just have to have really good, down-and-dirty sex too, you know."

Josie laughed and shook her head, unable to deny that. Not that she'd ever experienced really good, down-and-dirty sex before, considering she'd only slept with one guy in her entire twenty-six years. He'd been a gentle lover, considerate enough, she supposed. The fact that he'd never once brought her to orgasm in the three years they dated back in college, however, did have her thinking she might be flawed in some way.

Lack of orgasms aside, Josie also knew that the fire was missing from their relationship. Plus, he'd never once attempted to tap into or satisfy any of her secret fetishes. Not that she'd ever had the nerve to tell him what they were, or anyone else for that matter. Heck, she doubted she'd even tell J.A.D. about all the scintillating things she'd love to experience. After all, she didn't want anyone to think she was some sort of sexual deviant. But she couldn't help it that she found the idea of having sex outdoors with the chance of getting caught, or having her lover spank her, utterly exciting. Just considering it now had blood rushing through her veins and her body hungering for so much more. She clamped her thighs together as her mind drifted in an erotic direction.

Okay, so she might not be a one-night kind of girl, but if

Mr. Right didn't soon appear and help soothe her aching libido, she just might have to rethink her lifestyle choices, because the truth was, she'd gone without sex far too long and was in desperate need of a man's intimate touch—whether he could bring her to orgasm or not.

After Lila turned her attention to the table beside them, Tabby and Vic leaned forward, and from the conspiratorial looks on their pretty faces, Josie braced herself for an inquisition.

Tabby lowered her voice. "So," she said, "since there are no signs of any man with the initials J.A.D., do you think you should forget about what Madame M said and start dating the local men from Whispering Cove?"

Josie grabbed a French fry and dipped it into the ketchup. "The only problem with that idea, Tabby, is that you gals just snagged the last two decent men in town."

With that they both smiled, then Vic said, "Okay, so who says you have to date a decent man?"

Josie jabbed her thumb into her chest. "Uh, I do."

"Why?"

"Why?" Josie asked, dumfounded by the question. Her friends knew her well enough to know that she wasn't about to settle for anyone less than her perfect mate. "Because I want a nice respectable guy and don't want to end up married to an *indecent* man."

"Who says you have to end up with him?" Tabby asked.

A mischievous look came over Vic's face. "Indecent men do have benefits too, you know."

"Oh really, Vic, and how, pray tell, do you know this?"

Vic pointed a finger and redirected the conversation. "This is about you, remember."

"Okay, fine, so what are you getting at?" Josie asked, deciding to humor her friends.

"Well, while you're waiting for Mr. Decent to come along, why not have some fun with Mr. Indecent?"

Josie's eyes opened wide. "What exactly are you suggesting?"

"I'm suggesting that you need to get out and have an orgasm or two. Look at you. You're all tense and stressed out about finding this guy with the initials J.A.D. While you're waiting for him to come along, why not have some fun? Like Lila said, sometimes nice girls just have to have really good, down-and-dirty sex, too."

Shocked at her friend's scandalous suggestion, but unable to deny that her body was aching for the erotic touch of a man, she asked, "And exactly who do you think I should have this fun with?"

"How about with someone who is always up for a good time? Someone who isn't going to go all serious on you and want more than you can give him?"

"Okay, I'm listening."

Victoria pointed a finger and Josie followed the direction. "How about someone like him?"

"Adam Collins!" Josie blurted out.

"Yeah, why not?"

"Ah, didn't you just warn Lila to stay away from him?"

"That's because they're all wrong for each other."

Josie's head jerked back. "Oh, and you think we're right for each other."

"I didn't exactly say that."

"Then what exactly are you saying?"

"That he's the perfect guy to help you pass the time until Mr. Right comes along."

Josie let her glance wander to Adam as he made his way across the fairgrounds. Oh yeah, he was perfect all right. From his thick hair, his sun-kissed skin, his lean, fit body and size-twelve shoe, the man had perfect written all over him. Perfect trouble, that was.

She swallowed and asked, "What makes you think Adam Collins is the perfect guy for the job?"

"Because you're sweet, Josie. The kind of nice girl that respectable guys want to marry and bring home to their mothers."

Josie rolled her eyes. "And where might I find these respectable guys?"

"With Adam you can have a little fun and not risk him falling for you or making things awkward while you wait for Mr. Right."

Josie took another long pull from her straw, trying to wrap her brain around the idea of her and Adam Collins—together in bed. But when she realized it wasn't all that difficult to imagine, she swallowed hard and said, "Vic, I don't know how you come up with this stuff."

Vic's eyes widened. "So you think it's a good idea then?"

"No, I don't. Besides, Adam has never even given me a second glance. At least not since I've returned from college."

Tabby arched a perfectly manicured brow and questioned, "Oh, so you've noticed him not noticing you then, have you?"

She took a moment to think about Adam, about how his rich, earthy smell reached her nostrils and brought on a shiver when she'd walked past him earlier. Thought about how athletic and sexy he looked standing there outside the sultan's tent, hands jammed deep in his pockets and pulling his jeans low to expose tight, oblique muscles—muscles Josie would love to run her hands along, as well as her tongue.

As heat moved into her stomach, she gulped air and wondered what the hell she was doing. She shouldn't be fantasizing about Adam. She should be concentrating on finding her Mr. Right, because everything about the hot, sexy man who undoubtedly knew his way around a woman's body screamed wrong, with a capital W.

When she realized her friends were waiting for an answer, she blew out a breath and said, "Come on, Tabby. He's a little impossible not to notice, don't you think?"

Tabby sat back in her chair. "So then why don't you go for it?"

"Because whenever he sees me coming, he goes the other way. Clearly I'm not his type. I'm a kindergarten teacher looking for everlasting love. He's a playboy looking for lust, and the kind of girls he goes out with are brazen women, women who are only in it for the sex."

"And that's the only reason you'd be in it too, Josie."

As Josie's body quivered in sensual delight, she bit her lip as thoughts of sex with Adam pinged around inside her brain. Her skin flushed, her sex ached and everything inside her urged her to go for it, to have a little fun with the town's playboy until her future husband came along. As a tremor raced through her blood, her pussy fluttered in anticipation and she took a moment to think about what it would take to gain his attention, to get him to finally notice her.

Dear God, she couldn't believe she was actually thinking about it, thinking about having a scandalous affair with Adam Collins.

"So you're going to go for it then?" Vic asked.

"No. Never. And this conversation is over," Josie announced, slamming her palms on the table. But the truth was, now that the two had planted that outrageous idea in her head, it was all she could do to keep her salacious gaze from straying to Adam, Whispering Cove's most eligible bachelor —a man who, according to his reputation, knew how to light a fire in a woman, and, more importantly, knew how to tamp said fire out.

Maybe he really was the guy who could get the job done.

Good Lord, what was she doing? She really, really shouldn't be thinking about Adam like this, thinking about how perfect his hard body was, how his raw sexuality reached out to her and stimulated her body like a lover's caress, or how that sensuous mouth of his would feel on her flesh, between her legs.

Then again, she was growing tired of waiting for J.A.D. to come along and maybe, just maybe, a little afternoon delight with a hot guy like Adam, a man who was anything but a one-woman kind of guy, was exactly what she needed to help her pass the time, soothe her raging libido and get her through the lonely, cold nights ahead.

$$11$$

By the time Adam settled himself into the kissing booth, the sun had set and a multitude of brightly colored lights lit up the downtown core, providing enough illumination for the townsfolk to easily stroll along the sidewalks and partake in the nighttime activities.

The children's festivities had shut down hours ago, and the closed-off streets were now filled with adults, many of whom were hanging out at the beer tent, or getting the life scared out of them over at Hauk's haunted bar down on the waterfront.

Since Adam was always up for a good scare, he thought he might venture on over there later, after his firefighter demonstration in Town Square. He glanced up to see the line of women forming on the street, all eager to trade a dollar for a kiss. Adam grinned, thinking the kissing booth trumped the psychic booth any day, but then a darker, more serious thought wiped the smile from his face.

As his best bud Trent, who was in charge of crowd control, went to work on getting the ladies to form a straight line before he opened the booth for business, Adam took a quick moment to consider what Madame M had told him. That he'd fall in love with a woman with the initials J.C.W., and find true happiness.

True happiness, his ass!

Clearly the woman knew nothing about his fate, or the undeniable fact that he had his father's blood running through his veins. Adam's father—like his father before him, and his father before him—had never been faithful a day in his life, even when he was married. Eventually he'd up and left his wife and two sons, skipping town with a young waitress from the Seafarer. Adam heard rumors that he'd stayed with her for a little over a year before he moved on to something shinier. Sadly enough, there hadn't been a Collins man yet to break the pattern.

With the Collins curse handed down from one generation to the next, no one in the small town of Whispering Cove expected Adam or Jacob to be any different—including their own mother—and so far both he and his brother had lived up to those expectations.

As far as Adam was concerned, Madame M had simply pulled the initial J.C.W. out of thin air, because he clearly had the inability to fall in love or commit for any length of time, which in his books meant true happiness.

Despite knowing that, he wasn't sure why that so-called psychic's prediction had bothered him so much. Like he'd told Errol, he didn't believe the woman had any spiritual abilities anyway. Then again, perhaps it was simply because it hit too close to home, and she was suggesting he could have the one thing he knew he couldn't.

Honestly, he just needed to put her ridiculous prediction behind him and remind himself that she had no idea what she was talking about. Although he couldn't deny that she did seem to know the nickname his father used to call him before he'd skipped town some fifteen years ago. But Adam had always been athletic—joining every sport going. Everyone knew that about him, and a lot of fathers called their sons "sport", right?

"Hey, Adam." The sound of Cheri's voice pulled his focus, and when he glanced at her and noted the pair of dark, sultry eyes looking him over with genuine interest, it helped lighten his mood and bring his attention back around to the task at hand.

"Cheri," he greeted, as she sat down in the chair on the other side of the small booth.

She slid her dollar across the table, and from the way she was looking at him, Adam could tell she was interested in a lot more than a simple kiss.

Puckering her lips, she purred like a kitten and said, "This is just to whet your appetite, baby." She leaned forward, her mouth only inches from his. "Then later, when you're done here, we can really get down to business because I have a pussy in need of a fireman's attention." With that she planted her perfectly painted lips on his.

Adam had kissed Cheri before, and while he thought she was a great kisser, very hot and passionate, this time he felt nothing as her soft lips pressed against his, nor did her sexy little game of firefighter rescuing the kitty excite him either. There was no doubt that she was putting her best efforts forward, but Adam just couldn't muster up the enthusiasm to give her anything more than a small peck.

Madame M and her asinine prediction clearly rattled him more than he cared to admit.

He began to inch away, but before he could break contact, Cheri gripped his T-shirt to prevent him from moving, and tried to slip her tongue into his mouth. That's when Trent broke things up.

"Next," he called out, grinning at Adam as he tapped Cheri on the shoulder.

Adam sat back and wiped his mouth with the back of his hand. Jesus, that woman was so bold. So brazen. So like the girls he always went for. Which begged the question, why was he suddenly so disinterested?

She gave him a wink and said, "Later, Adam," before she disappeared.

"Something bothering you?" Trent asked as he leaned against the booth and crossed his legs at the ankles.

"Nope."

"Cheri looked like she wanted to eat you alive and you seemed a little...distracted."

"Everything is fine," he assured Trent, but the dubious look on his friend's face made it perfectly clear that he wasn't convincing.

Before he had a chance to press, Adam said, "If we want to make our firefighter demonstration, we'd better get this show on the road."

Shaking his head, Trent gestured for another woman to have a seat. Then before Adam knew it, the night had slipped by, and over the course of the last few hours he'd kissed so many women he'd lost track of the count.

But no matter how many pretty ladies had planted their mouths on his, and no matter how many had openly invited him back to their place, he still couldn't get enthused. Finally, after giving his last kiss of the night, he dipped his head to see the stack of money in the box at his feet, pleased to see how much he'd raised for the community center.

He was just about to shout to Trent, who was chatting quietly with Katy, to tell him to close up so he could do a count, when another woman dropped down into the seat across from him. Adam lifted his head to see who it was, and opened his mouth to inform her that his shift was over, but when he caught sight of the beautiful girl sitting across from him, the world around him tilted on its axis and his stomach punched into his throat.

"Adam," Josie greeted, those big blue eyes of hers staring at him as her mouth turned up in a warm, inviting smile—the same breath-robbing smile she'd given him earlier that day.

"What...what are you doing?" he finally managed to ask once he regained control of his voice.

She casually rolled one shoulder, and slid her dollar across the counter. "Like you, I'm just doing my part to raise money for the new community center."

"Oh," he said, and wet his lips. "I guess I just didn't expect..."

She gave him an easy, playful grin, and everything in the way she looked at him had his body reacting with heated need. His glance raced over her face, taking in her big eyes, full, lush mouth and long blonde hair. Christ, she looked so gorgeous and sensual that it had his cock tightening to the point of pain. He shifted, uncomfortable, as his body reacted to her closeness, not to mention what that sweet jasmine scent of hers was doing to him. As his blood went from simmer to inferno, he cleared his throat and tried to relax.

"Didn't expect what?" she asked with bright-eyed innocence, except beneath that innocence he thought he spotted something else. Something that looked like desire. White-hot desire, that was. For him.

Oh fuck!

"I don't know." Flustered, he raked his hair off his forehead. "Never mind."

Her mouth curved. "Shall we get on with it then?" Josie asked, her voice playful, teasing, as she leaned forward to poise her mouth open. With the top two buttons on her dress undone, her actions gave him a perfect, unobstructed view of her cleavage. Adam tried not to stare. He really did. But he was a guy, for Christ's sake!

And a pathetic one at that.

When she toyed with the third button on her dress, Adam nearly swallowed his tongue. With his mouth salivating worse than his brother's Saint Bernard on a hot summer day, he briefly pinched his eyes shut and worked to get his thoughts focused. But how the hell was he supposed to keep a calm demeanor when Josie, the sweet girl who'd invaded his fantasies for as long as he could remember—a girl who suddenly seemed to be coming on strong—was waiting for him to kiss her?

Adam drew a deep, rejuvenating breath and reminded himself this was all for charity. Just thinking of the kids helped him gain a modicum of composure. Okay, he could do this. He could give her a small peck and then once the night was over he'd go find Cheri, or one of the other women who'd openly invited him home for a late-night rendezvous, and fuck her long and hard and well into the morning until he got Josie out of his system once and for all.

"Adam," she whispered, "I'm ready."

When their glances met, sexual energy arced between them and nearly knocked him backward. His dick jumped, his blood pumped faster, and a barrage of emotions tore through him and had his thoughts scattering in a million different directions.

He took a deep breath, but before he could get his head on straight, her warm hands touched his cheeks, igniting a fire deep inside him. That first sweet touch of her lips to his damn near shut down his brain. As tension coiled inside him, she made a small sexy noise, one that had him conjuring up erotic images of their naked bodies coming together, over and over again, and it was all he could do not to climb over that booth and drag her home with him.

Her kiss was warm, full of passion, excitement and something else, something he'd never felt before and couldn't quite put a name to. Before he realized what he was doing, he widened her lips with his tongue and slipped inside for a deeper, more thorough exploration. At first the kiss was slow, sultry, but when he deepened it, needing in the most unfathomable ways to taste every inch of her, her mouth moved urgently under his, seeking, searching, demanding more than just his tongue.

As her mouth pressed hungrily, pressure began brewing inside him, and his body pulsed with raw need. Oh God, how he wanted. His fingers began trembling, and then, as though moving of their own accord, his hands circled her head and he fisted her hair, pulling her impossibly closer. His muscles bunched, his cock ached and a deep growl of longing caught in his throat. In the span of a second, this beautiful, sensual woman caught him off guard and completely turned his world inside out.

Then it suddenly occurred to him that his disinterest in those other women tonight had more to do with Josie than any damn prediction. The truth was, after crossing paths with her earlier that day, and after she'd tossed him that sweet yet sexy smile of hers, he'd been completely preoccupied with her, unable to get her out of his head, either one of them.

Then another thought struck.

Josie Wells!

A shiver raced up his spine, and he slowly inched away. "Josie?" he asked in a strangled voice.

Breathless, she looked at him, and the warm flush coloring her cheeks told him he wasn't the only one rattled by that kiss. "Yeah?" she murmured.

"Uh, what's your middle name?"

She gave him an odd look and said, "Caitlyn, why?"

J.C.W. Josie Caitlyn Wells.

Jesus Christ!

He pushed back in his chair and tried to wrap his brain around this information. "No reason," he choked out.

Her brow furrowed. "Really? Because it seems like such an odd question."

As his thoughts raced a million miles an hour, Trent and Katy approached. Katy shifted her attention to Josie, and the two began talking. As they turned their focus to Katy's growing stomach, Josie climbed from her seat and the two sauntered off.

"Meet you in Town Square," Katy called out to Trent.

"What the hell was that?" Trent asked when Katy and Josie were out of earshot.

"What the hell was what?"

"Oh, come on, Adam," Trent said, grinning like the crazy son of a bitch he really was. "I thought I was going to have to hose you two down."

When the festival's chairman came up from behind, Adam grabbed the box of money and handed it to him, apologizing that he didn't have a dollar count. Then he snatched his windbreaker off the back of his chair, tossed it over his shoulder and started making his way toward Town Square.

Knowing he was unable to keep anything from Trent, he cast him a sideways glance and said, "She really was coming on kind of strong, wasn't she? What do you make of that?"

Trent rolled his eyes. "Geez, I wonder."

Adam took a minute to chew on Trent's response. Was it possible that sweet little Josie wanted him as much as he wanted her? She knew his reputation as a playboy, so why was a nice respectable girl like her, a girl who'd openly admitted to wanting love, marriage and children, suddenly paying him so much attention? What the hell had gotten into her?

They rounded the corner and spotted a crowd surrounding the fire truck parked in the center of Town Square. "So what are you going to do about it?"

"Nothing."

"Nothing? Come on, Adam, you both clearly want each other. What's stopping you?"

"You know what's stopping me." Wanting to change the subject, Adam nodded toward the truck and asked, "What exactly is it we're supposed to be doing anyway?"

"Adam..." Trent began, refusing to let the matter drop.

But Adam just shook his head and said, "You know I can't, Trent. Not with her. Not with Josie."

Before Trent could respond, their captain Doug Simms called out to them and waved them over.

"Get yourselves suited up," he said when they approached, and that's when Adam noticed his colleagues. All three were shirtless and wearing only their pants and suspenders. Confused, Adam wasn't quite sure what the demonstration entailed or why they were doing it after dark. Most fire-fighting displays were done for the children and there wasn't a child in sight at this late hour.

After removing his own shirt and pulling on his pants, the captain lined them up. Adam looked into the crowd, and noted the excitement in the air. As his captain read off names, and five women came forward, one of them being Josie, he turned to Trent. "What the hell is going on?"

Trent grinned and let his glance race over his wife Katy as she stepped up to him. "I guess we'll find out soon enough."

As Doug began to pair them up, and he found himself face-to-face with Josie, he had a sinking feeling in the pit of his stomach that nothing good could come from this. He glanced to his left and spotted Josie's friend's Vic and Tabby cheering her on.

He gestured with a nod as understanding hit. "I take it they put you up to this?"

"Yeah," she said, looking innocent and sheepish once

again, and he also wondered if they were also the ones who put her up to the kissing booth.

"Okay, when I sound the fire alarm, you begin to undress," Doug continued. "With the help of your partners, of course. The first one to get out of their gear wins dinner for two at the Seafarer."

Okay, that seemed simple enough. Perhaps this wouldn't be too bad after all.

"But there's a catch," Doug went on to explain. "Neither one of you can use your hands." When he added, "Bodies only," cheers erupted from the crowd.

Sweet mother of God!

Adam had no idea what he'd done to deserve this kind of torture. He did a quick tally of the day's events—first Madame M said he was going to fall in love with Josie, then the two shared a smoking-hot kiss that had him wanting to forget his vow to stay away from her, and now she was about to use that sexy body of hers and nothing else to help him undress. Adam had a sneaking suspicion that the fate gods were conspiring against him, trying to complicate his mission to keep his distance from the one woman who got to him in a way no other woman ever had. As he envisioned her wiggling that tight little ass of hers against him, his cock thickened and he groaned out loud.

Adam swallowed hard as Josie looked at the competition. She had a mischievous grin on her face when she turned back to him and said, "I think we can beat them." Her tone was light, playful, but he didn't miss the desire smoldering in the depth of her pretty baby blues when they met his. Nor did he miss the tremble that moved through her body as the crowd gathered in for a better look. Tonight he was seeing another side to sweet Josie Wells, and if Adam had to guess, he'd say this public display of intimacy was a turn-on for her.

The second the alarm sounded, Josie stepped up to him,

and the closeness of her body nearly had him shooting off in his pants, with the whole goddamn town watching. Fuck. Adam rolled his shoulder and tried to loosen the strap on his suspenders, but his efforts proved futile. When Josie twisted her head to glance at their competition, Adam followed her gaze in time to see Katy using her mouth to remove Trent's suspenders.

Josie turned her attention back to him and said, "Maybe I should try that."

Before he could respond, she put her mouth close to his neck. Her breath felt so fucking erotic on his flesh as she gripped the strap with her teeth and began to slip it over his shoulder, that he damn near dropped to the ground and dragged her along with him.

She wiggled against him and suddenly Adam couldn't move, couldn't breathe, couldn't think with any clarity, because the way she was undressing him with her mouth had to be the sexiest thing he'd ever seen. With his own mouth agape, he stood there staring at her as she went to work on removing the next strap. Once complete, she stood back and her sensuous lips puckered as she gave consideration to his pants.

He quickly moved his hips in an attempt to shimmy them down his legs before she got too close again, but in a brazen move she pressed against him, stomach to stomach, hip to hip, pussy to cock.

Holy fuck!

"Let me help you." The crowd went wild, and when they started screaming encouragement out to Josie, cheering her on, Adam didn't miss the heat in her eyes, the way her flesh suffused with color or the way her nipples hardened and pressed against his bare chest.

Slowly, methodically, they began to move in sync, working their bodies together and creating friction as they dragged his pants to his ankles. When her eyes met his, her baby blues darkened and he could sense her mounting desire. Christ, seeing her this aroused became his undoing, and when she made a sexy little bedroom noise, it took every ounce of strength he had to remain vertical. Okay, he stood corrected. This was the sexiest thing he'd ever seen.

Everything in the way she moved, the way the audience seemed to turn her on, evoked a myriad of sinful thoughts and there wasn't a damn thing he could do to purify them. In no time at all impatience thrummed through him. Impatience to taste her, to touch her, to spread her long, silky legs and fuck her until she cried out in orgasmic bliss.

When his waistband hit his ankles, he kicked his pants off and the crowd began to clap and whistle. As he stood there in nothing but his jeans and boots, his heart crashing hard against his chest, Josie's hot glance skated over his body, then in the softest, sexiest voice she whispered, "See what we can do when we put our minds to it?"

Except in this case, it wasn't her mind she put to it, it was her body. A smoking-hot body that had him so hard he was certain he was going to do permanent damage. Since a reply was beyond him, he just nodded and continued to think about all the ways he wanted to undress her, all the things he wanted to do to her naked body.

Once the applause settled down, the other guys disappeared around back to hang up their gear, and Adam worked to tame his raging hard-on before the entire town took note of it. Thank God it was nighttime and Town Square wasn't lit up like a Christmas tree, the way the closed-off side streets were.

When Josie went to get their dinner certificate from Doug, Adam stepped back into the shadows of the truck to use that time to get his head on straight. Needing a distraction, he gathered his gear, and by the time he walked around to the back of the truck to put it away, the crowd had dispersed, save for the few stragglers who continued to hang out near the monument honoring all the fishermen lost at sea.

Knowing he needed to get the hell out of there before he did something he might regret, he grabbed his shirt and windbreaker, but before he could dress, and find someone to help him take the edge off, Josie's sweet scent reached his nostrils. He spun around and gulped when he found her watching him with heated interest.

"Josie..." he managed to get out.

In a bold move she stepped close, too close. Her hot breath whispered over his skin and her voice was full of invitation when she said, "I wonder what else we can do if we put our minds to it?"

Dropping his shirt and jacket, he raked shaky fingers through his hair. "Jesus Christ, you can't say something like that to me."

She leaned against the truck, looking casual and innocent, even though everything in his gut told him she was anything but. Her laugh was edgy, churning with passion when she asked, "Oh, why not?"

"Because it makes me want to fuck you, that's why. Right here. Up against the truck."

The second the words left his mouth, a fire lit her eyes, and a strange noise sounded deep in her throat.

With his dick throbbing and his body urging him to lift that flimsy dress of hers, and drive his erection all the way up inside her, he drew a heavy breath, put his hands on either side of her head and pressed against her, pinning her body between his and the truck.

She tilted her head back, her eyes full of urgent need. "Adam."

He heard the impatience in her voice and everything in

the way she breathed his name into his mouth spoke of raw, unbridled want. With his own body beckoning her touch, he pushed his cock hard against her pussy, letting her know in no uncertain terms what she was doing to him.

Pressure brewed deep in his groin, and some small coherent part of his brain reminded him that this was a bad idea. But the other part of him, that part of him that wanted her so fucking badly, told him to give her what she wanted, to take her beyond her wildest fantasies, and deal with the consequences tomorrow.

Her nipples pressed against his chest, her body calling out to him in ways that made him frantic with the need to fuck her. As he waged an internal war, he knew he needed this to end almost as much as he needed it to continue. Digging deep to gain a modicum of composure, he sucked in a fortifying breath, placed his hands on her shoulders and began to inch away, not wanting to do anything to hurt her, but when she wet her lips, her sultry glance dropping to his mouth, he knew he was done for.

So totally fucking done for...

As she slid her hands over his back, he gave himself a quick consultation. The truth was, everyone in town knew his reputation, and women only came to him for one reason and one reason only. Sex. And from the brazen way she was coming on to him, she clearly wanted him to fuck her. He might not be able to give her the other things she wanted, like love and commitment—not that she was asking him for it—but he sure as hell could give her the ride of her life.

He was about to grab her by the hand and haul her back to his place, but when a noise sounded in the distance, she bit her bottom lip and a tremor raced through her. Adam grinned, reading her reactions and understanding exactly what they meant.

Sweet Josie Wells got off on an audience.

He couldn't deny that he liked this adventurous, daring side of her, a side she clearly hid from the world. For a brief moment he wondered if any other guys had tapped into her secret fetishes, or if he was the first. Damned if he didn't want to be the last.

Moving with purpose, he slid his palms to her sides and gripped a handful of her dress. Gauging her reaction as he inched it higher and higher on her hips, he pressed them deeper into the shadows. When her tongue snaked out to brush over her bottom lip and she thrust her hips forward in a sexy, intimate move that nearly drove him mad, Adam knew everything he needed to know. Josie wanted him to fuck her right there against his truck, in the middle of Town Square where anyone could stumble upon them.

Sexual energy leapt between them as he slid his hand between her legs, and when he felt her damp panties, he was pretty damn certain he'd died and gone to heaven. Her heady scent curled around him and he inhaled, pulling it into his lungs so he could savor it in its entirety later that night when they were done playing and he was alone in his bed, reliving every minute of this night.

When she moved against his hand, he slipped a finger inside the satin material and scraped it over her aching clit. He exhaled slowly when he felt her silky softness and it took all his effort to speak.

"Is this what you want, Josie? Is it what you need?"

Before she could answer, he grabbed the scrap of material covering her pussy and ripped it from her hips. She gasped in surprise, but he pressed his lips to hers and swallowed the noise, not wanting anyone to overhear them. While he might be all about fulfilling her sexual fantasies, he really didn't want the two of them to get caught. It might be fun and exciting for her tonight, but she had to think about tomorrow. Word spread fast in their small town, and he wouldn't want to do anything to hurt her reputation.

When he put his hand back between her legs and inched a finger into her hot opening and felt a small tremor, his blood began pulsing. "Jesus, girl, you're already halfway there." He pulled his hand away, purposely dragging his thumb over her clit before he gripped her slim hips.

"Adam, please..." she begged.

"Don't worry, baby," he whispered into her mouth before he moved his lips to the long column of her neck, fully intending to kiss his way to her pussy. "I'm going to give you what you want, but when you come for me, it's going to be when my mouth is on you. I don't want to miss a drop of your sweetness."

His words seemed to trigger a reaction in her. He felt something in her stiffen. He inched back, his heart pounding as his gaze searched her pretty face. Her blue eyes looked troubled and her lips pinched tightly together, a telltale sign something was wrong.

His stomach plummeted as he inched back again, not about to do anything she was uncomfortable with. "Second thoughts?" he asked and brushed a strand of hair off her face to better see her.

"No. It's just. It's nothing..." Her words fell off and she gave a quick shake of her head. "Never mind."

He felt a rush of tenderness as he put his finger under her chin, tilting it up to bring them eye to eye. "Hey, you can tell me. What is it?"

"It's just...well. I...uh...I might be flawed."

Everything inside him told him that she was sharing something very private, and the fact that she felt comfortable enough with him to share warmed him all over. Then he frowned when he digested her words, because he knew she was the most perfect creature he'd ever had the pleasure of touching.

"Flawed?"

She gave a forced, uncomfortable laugh. "Yeah, you know, in the orgasm department."

He got quiet for a moment, taking a second to absorb what she was telling him. Then it hit him. "You've never had an orgasm before?"

"Well, not with a guy," she said, her honesty taking them to a comfort level he'd never before experienced.

"And that makes you think you're flawed somehow?"

She nodded.

Adam gave a shake of his head. "Did you ever once stop to think it wasn't you? That perhaps the guys you were with weren't taking the time to understand what you needed?"

"There was only one," she admitted, lowering her head like it was something to be ashamed of.

Adam swallowed hard as his chest tightened. "Only one?" he asked, and there was nothing he could do to keep the emotion from his voice.

She gave a slight shrug and he could sense her embarrassment when she said, "Yeah, I've only ever been with one guy before."

Her openness had his heart clenching, and the fact that he was only the second guy she'd ever gifted with her body made him weak in the knees. A wave of possessiveness tore through him as his glance panned her face, and suddenly he wondered if she was telling him this because she wanted to warn him not to expect too much, or was it because she really wanted him to change it?

Either way, it made him question what he was doing. Josie was sweet and innocent and he was just so wrong for her. He needed to get away from her and he needed to do it now.

Except, when he tried to extricate himself, she wrapped

her arms around him to pull him to her. As her warm hands scalded his flesh, his body went weak, his resolve puddling at his feet. And when her heat wrapped around his heart, he knew he was doomed, because everything inside him wanted to be the man to bring her to orgasm, to show her just how perfect she was and just how good he could make this for her.

"Josie..." he murmured into her mouth, his eyes connecting with hers.

"Yeah?"

"I can make you come."

"Adam," she whimpered, eagerness lacing her voice as her entire body quaked with pent-up need.

With that, Adam pushed against her, taking full possession of her pleasure. He pressed his mouth to hers, giving her a soft, sensuous kiss before beginning a leisurely exploration down her body. The warmth in her kisses burned him from the inside out, and as she became pliable in his arms, he cupped her breasts and gave a light massage.

She moaned and arched against him, and that's when he pulled her dress open to lick her hard nipples through the thin lace. She gripped the cups of her bra and pulled her gorgeous breasts free. As his blood pressure soared, he swiped his tongue over her sensitized nipples, then drew one marbled bud into his mouth for a hard suck.

"So good," she cried out, and wrapped her hands around his head to hold him to her breasts, but Adam had other ideas, ideas that involved taking her beyond her wildest fantasies.

Inching away, he kissed a path down her body, pulling her sun dress up so he could run his tongue over her stomach, her belly button, going lower and lower until he reached the spot that needed his attention the most. Her aroused scent teased him, had fire licking over his thighs, and Adam feared if they weren't hosed down soon, they'd both go up in a burst of flames.

Needing a moment of reprieve before he did just that, he inched back on his heels and took a long moment to stare at her sweet pussy. When he glanced up at her and saw the heat and desire swimming in her blue eyes, he grinned, loving that he could do this to her.

He stroked her damp sex. "So pretty," he whispered, lightly running his finger over her soft curls before inching her lips open for a better look. The sight of her gorgeous pink pussy, all wet and ready for him, had his muscles bunching and his cock throbbing, aching to be inside her.

He pressed his tongue to her wet lips and widened them, and when that first sweet taste of her hot cream settled on the tip of his tongue, lust exploded inside him, and his throat dried.

"Jesus," he murmured from between her thighs, wondering how he was going to slow himself down and bring her to orgasm when all he wanted to do was drive deep inside and go at her like a wild animal in heat.

She gyrated her hips and his mouth connected with her swollen clit. She cried out and pushed harder against his face, and he could tell she was desperate, frantic for an orgasm. But that urgency also spoke of stress. Everything in his gut told him she was worried it wasn't going to happen, that there was something wrong with her.

"Slow down, baby," he murmured. "I'm going to take care of you. I promise."

His confident words seemed to do something to her. A strangled cry sounded in her throat and she gripped his hair tighter, moving her pussy against his face.

Slowing himself down so he could learn what she liked, what her body craved and exactly what it was going to take to push her over the precipice, he pressed his mouth over her pussy to gauge her responses. As he brushed the soft blade of his tongue over her engorged clit, a shiver moved through her, and from her body's reactions, he began to understand just what it was going to take to bring her to orgasm.

He pressed his tongue deeper and took a moment to savor the sweet taste of her before circling her clit with firm, deft strokes. Teasing her senses, and drawing out her pleasure, he probed her opening, but when her hips jutted forward, demanding more, he knew it was time to end the torment.

Loving the way she reacted to him, and knowing how desperate she was to climax, Adam slipped a finger inside her. When her walls wrapped around his index finger, a fit so snug he wondered how he'd ever fit inside her, he sucked in a tight breath.

He pushed deeper and her walls closed in on him. She was tight, so fucking tight, and it instantly reminded him that she was virtually inexperienced. A melee of emotions ripped through him as he inched his finger in higher, until he found the hot bundle of nerves he was searching for. Wanting to please her more than he'd ever wanted anything in his entire life, he touched her lightly, testing the sensitivity of her G-spot as he acquainted himself with her body.

"Adam," she cried out. "Please. I need you inside me." Adam didn't miss the raw ache of lust in her voice or the way it sent shockwaves rocketing through him.

He tipped his head to look at her, and when she began shaking, her pleasure escalating as her body came alive, he growled deep and struggled to maintain his composure.

"I know, baby. I know." He breathed the words over her sex, letting the warmth of his mouth stimulate her pussy. There'd be time for fucking later, he'd make sure of it, but he desperately wanted to make her come using his mouth first.

As raw need streaked through him, demanding he drive into her, he turned his attention back to her sex, deciding it was well past time to give her what she craved. He pinned his mouth to her inflamed clit, and laved her with his tongue, alternating between soft licks and hard nibbles. Meanwhile, deep inside her pussy he sinuously circled her G-spot, each furtive brush taking her higher and higher. Her chest began to heave, her breathing grew rapid and in no time at all she began trembling from head to toe. When a noise sounded in the near distance, a reminder that they could get caught at any moment, he could feel small quakes pulling at her core. Jesus, he loved this naughty side of hers.

He pushed another finger inside, and when her body opened for him he knew she was close. So fucking close.

Heart racing, pleasure forked through him as he continued to feast on her, and when he felt that first sweet clench, her quaking body sucking his fingers in deeper and deeper, he knew his life was about to get a hell of a lot more complicated.

She gripped his shoulders, her nails cutting his flesh. "Oh. My. God." She cried out, tossing her head from side to side as he paid homage to both her clit and her G-spot, the dual assault making her delirious, crazed.

"Adam," she whimpered, her flesh tightening with the impending approach of an orgasm.

"Just relax, sweetheart," he encouraged, "and let it happen." He continued to knead her sensitive areas until her body pulsed and throbbed in sensual bliss. He licked harder and pushed deeper, and when her mouth opened but no sound came, he knew she'd finally found the sensual ecstasy she'd been so desperate for.

"Come hard for me, baby," he murmured as her liquid heat singed him. His chest puffed up with pride and he buried his face in her pussy to drink in her sweet release. Wanting to prolong and nurture the pleasure for as long as possible, he continued to move his fingers in and out of her.

After the tremors finally subsided, he shot her another glance.

"Oh. My. God," she whimpered again, and the surprise in her voice brought a smile to his face. "You're...you're..."

Adam climbed to his feet and smothered her words with a kiss. Desperate to feel her tight walls wrapped around his cock, he unzipped his pants and inserted his knee between her legs to widen them. "What I am, Josie, is not nearly finished with you," he murmured between kisses. "I need to be inside you. I need to fuck you, hard and fast, okay?" He wasn't sure whether he was asking or telling, all he knew was that he was mad with want and if he didn't soon get inside her he was going to explode into a million tiny pieces.

"I need that too," she rushed out, and he loved how rattled she looked, loved that he could do that to her. Then she bit her bottom lip, her expressive eyes questioning as they searched his.

"Yes, sweetheart," he assured her, answering her unasked question as he grabbed a condom from his back pocket and quickly sheathed himself. "I'm going to make you come again." His cock slipped between her silky legs, and brushed over her hot opening. He gripped her ass and lifted her clear off the ground. "Wrap your legs around me."

When she did as he requested, he gave her an inch, then stilled to let her get used to the fullness, but the pleasure was excruciating, so goddamn excruciating, he had no idea how he'd last.

"More," she said, bucking against him. "Harder."

Fuck, yes!

He inched out, then drove all the way inside her, ramming his thick shaft so deep and so hard, she gasped out loud and scratched her nails over his back. As he pushed open her walls and her cunt clenched hard around him, pleasure like he'd never before experienced swamped him and it took every ounce of strength he possessed not to lose it.

He took a quick fortifying breath, then began moving, rocking his hips and creating a rhythm. As their bodies joined as one, her mouth pressed hungrily against his, and her hard nipples scraped over his chest.

"Oh fuck," he whispered, his body tensing as his cock screamed for release. He drove harder, because he simply couldn't get enough of her, and when her body began pressing against him, seeking release, he knew she was teetering on the brink. He slipped a hand between them to brush her clit and a moment later she cried out in orgasmic bliss. Her hot juice taunted his cock as she climaxed, and Adam threw his head back and gave himself over to the intense pleasure pulling at him. Her sex gripped him hard as he came on a growl, completely letting himself go. They stayed like that for a long time, until he softened and they both came back down to earth.

Adam slipped out of her and she lowered her legs to the ground. Grinning sheepishly, he disposed of his condom and helped her adjust her dress, taking note of the pair of torn panties on the ground. He looked her over and brushed her hair from her face. At least one of them should have some semblance of order. As he thought about the way she'd come for him, and the surprised but excited look on her face, he whispered, "You're so fucking beautiful when you come."

Her hand found his face and she closed her palm over his cheek. "Honestly, Adam, I can't believe I came."

His glance moved over her face, taking in the flush on her cheeks, and in a low tone he whispered, "I told you I could make you come, Josie."

Her grin was slow, sexy. "I wasn't so sure, but then not only did you do it once, you did it twice." With that, Adam laughed and she added, "Maybe I'm not so flawed after all."

Everything in the way she touched him made him weak. "What do you mean, maybe?" he asked, and grabbed her hand and pressed it to his mouth for a kiss, then he gave her a warm smile. "Listen, if you're still not convinced I'd be willing to go another round. You know, just to prove it to you once and for all."

The gleam in her eyes turned wicked. "Well, when you put it that way…"

Her words trailed off as his mouth found hers for a slow, simmering kiss. Deep in the shadows of the truck, with the two of them cloaked in contentment, he continued to hold her and share intimacies with her until footsteps heralded someone's approach.

"Hey, Adam, is that you?"

Adam quickly zipped his pants, turned around and tucked Josie behind his back. He cleared his throat and worked to sound casual, but from his disheveled state, to the scent of their lovemaking still lingering in the air, he knew it was going to be hard to pull off normal.

"Jacob," he returned. "What's up?"

"I guess I should be asking you that," his brother said with a knowing grin. He tried to look past Adam's shoulder. "Then again, I think it's safe to say nothing is up anymore."

Adam cursed under his breath. "Beat it, little brother."

Jacob held his hands up and laughed. "Whoa, easy there, big bro. What's gotten into you?"

"Jacob," he growled. "So help me, if you know what's good for you—"

"Okay, okay. I'm leaving," Jacob rushed out, humor in his tone. "Christ, when did the big bad wolf suddenly turn into the protective woodsman?"

Despite the precarious situation, Adam found himself smiling at the reference to Little Red Riding Hood, recalling his younger brother's favorite bedtime story, one Adam had to read to him over and over again, when he had no choice but to take over the role as father.

Still chuckling, Jacob turned to leave and Adam breathed a sigh of relief. A few minutes later Josie squirmed behind him and he turned to see her. When a smile lit up her face and she said, "I never knew you were such a gentleman," his heart clenched.

Okay, so Jacob was right and he knew he was acting out of character, but this was sweet Josie they were talking about, and while she found fucking outside titillating, the last thing he wanted to do was soil her reputation.

Then Adam took a moment to think about his own regrets. There was no denying that their lovemaking created a new intimacy between them, a warmth he'd never felt with anyone, and the truth was, he had no idea how to deal with those kinds of emotions.

As he thought about the way she affected him, unease hit him like a sucker punch and he cursed under his breath. Fuck, he never should have gone so far with her, and the fact that he was the first man to bring her to orgasm, the only man to ever tap into her fantasies—as well as fulfill them—did something to him, something, he feared, there was no coming back from.

Warm morning light filtered in through Josie's open window as she stretched out on her bed. Even though two days had passed since her Saturday night rendezvous with Adam, memories of the way he touched her, attended to her every need and brought her to orgasm, still danced around inside her head and had her grinning like the village idiot. Just thinking about it now, thinking about the careful way he caressed her body, the way he put her needs first and the way he protected her when his brother came along had her pussy moistening and her heart swelling.

Honestly, she knew Adam was a nice guy, but he'd surprised her with his protectiveness and by not making her feel foolish when he'd discovered her exhibitionism tendencies. It made her secret desires feel natural and brought Adam and her to a deeper level of intimacy, not only physically but emotionally. The fact that he took the time to tap into her fantasies, as well as fulfill them, gave her a new confidence in herself, and it was that confidence that had her embracing her fetishes and eager to explore the naughty side blossoming inside her.

Thinking about Adam, a very astute man who understood her wants and desires without her ever having to voice them, had her reaching between her legs to stroke herself. She widened her lips and lightly brushed her finger over her clit, imagining it was Adam's hands on her body.

Everyone knew she was a nice girl, the marrying kind, but there was just something so erotic, so forbidden about stepping out of character and getting naughty in public with the town's bad boy, that had her craving his touch, again and again.

She brushed her fingers over her clit faster, mimicking the way Adam stroked her. Her body began burning up, and as her breathing grew ragged, her mouth dried. Swallowing hard, she pushed one finger inside herself, and when her walls clenched, she shivered with delight, knowing her orgasm was only a few strokes away. Desire moved through her as she imagined Adam's mouth on her, his tongue circling her swollen clit, his fingers pumping deep. Her body tensed, moisture broke out on her flesh, and there was nothing she could do to keep herself from crying out in ecstasy.

Immersed in pleasure, she rode out the waves of her climax, not ever wanting to move, even though it was Monday morning and she had to get ready for work. Then she remembered the activities she had planned for her students today. A class trip to the fire station. Doug Simms usually gave the tours and she wondered if Adam would be there. How would he act around her?

She understood he was into casual affairs, which had her wondering if he would simply go about his business and ignore her, or would he be interested in a repeat performance of Saturday night? It was that thought that had her climbing from her bed, anxious to see the man who'd taken her beyond her wildest fantasies.

Less than two hours later, Josie hustled twenty kindergartners into the firehouse, and as the scent of fresh coffee and cinnamon reached her nose—Trent must have been whipping up something delicious in the kitchen—she eagerly looked around for Adam.

She spotted Errol chatting with Doug, and they both waved to her when she entered. Just then Adam stepped out of the back room, looking like sex incarnate dressed in a T-shirt and pair of jeans. When she saw the ruffled, wet state of his hair, she guessed he'd just gotten out of the shower. Their glances locked and her entire body reacted with heated need. Knowing this was neither the time nor place to let her emotions get the better of her, she squared her shoulders and put on her best professional face.

"Adam," Doug said, calling him over as Errol disappeared into the kitchen.

She watched Adam saunter over to his captain, and the two spoke quietly before Adam turned to face her, and the captain followed Errol into the other room.

The kids fidgeted restlessly as he walked up to her. "Ms. Wells," he greeted with a slight smile, making him look so sexy. "Looks like I'll be in charge of the tour today."

"Mr. Collins," she returned, surprised by this turn of events, but not able to consider it longer because everything in the way he looked at her elicited a response from deep within. As she took a moment to consider the way he affected her without even trying, alarm bells began jangling in her mind, warning that maybe she was getting in over her head with Adam. She wasn't supposed to have feelings for him. But after the way he took such painstaking care of her needs, and treated her with genuine respect, how could she not? Oh boy, this wasn't good. This wasn't good at all.

Schooling herself, she turned her attention to her class and worked to put him out of her mind. "Can everyone say hello to Mr. Collins?"

"Hello, Mr. Collins," the kids shouted out.

Adam gave them a warm, welcoming smile, and seeing the way his eyes lit up when he focused in on the kids, tugged at her emotions and had her wondering more about him. Did Adam like kids? Did he want any of his own? Then she considered his brother Jacob. When they were younger she remembered the way he took care of him. He obviously had a nurturing side. And it was that nurturing side that would make him a great father. The direction of her thoughts unnerved her and had her mind coming to a screeching halt.

Cripes, hadn't she just lectured herself on putting him out of her mind?

Adam clapped his hands together. "So what do you say, gang? Who wants to see the fire trucks?"

As collective cheers rang out, Adam hustled them through the fire house and into the garage where the trucks were parked. Josie followed along behind, but when she entered the garage, and spotted the truck that she and Adam made love against, her body warmed in all the wrong places.

She gave her head a good hard shake to clear it, then stood back to watch Adam as he gave the kids an external tour of the truck, explaining what all the dials were for, and how the equipment was used. She was especially happy when he talked about safety, and the dangers of fire. For a man with no kids of his own, it was amazing how good he was with her class of youngsters, amazing how he could talk to the children on their level and hold their attention—likely a result of having to be the father in the family after his own ran out, she supposed.

As the kids watched on in mute fascination, it occurred to her that Adam was full of surprises, and she soon found herself smiling and enjoying herself as he entertained her class. Every now and again he'd toss her a secret grin, and it never failed to rattle her. Adam might be a bad boy, but he really was a sweet guy. It was no wonder every woman in town was crazy about him.

At that thought nervousness stole over her, and once again alarm bells jangled in the back of her mind, reminding her that he wasn't the settling-down type and she was spending far too much time thinking about him. She blew a long, slow breath, trying to figure out what she could do to fight this growing attraction she felt for him. When she couldn't see any way around it, her stomach clenched.

Okay, so maybe she was getting in over her head here. Everything from the way he looked at her to the way he joked and laughed with the kids did the strangest things to her insides. He was just supposed to be a guy to have some fun with until Mr. Right came along, yet here she was, completely smitten with the town's bad boy, a guy who wasn't interested in long term. And even if he was, what about Madame M's prediction? She took another moment to mull over that worry. Josie was supposed to fall in love with a man with the initials J.A.D., not A.C. She wasn't sure what his middle name was, but supposed it didn't matter anyway. What mattered was that she liked him—too much—and it was time to distance herself before this brief affair ended in heartache.

Just then Trent stepped into the garage. "Who wants to sound the alarm?" he asked, taking over for Adam.

"I do. I do," the kids all chirped in unison.

"Okay, form a straight line here and you can each take a turn in the front seat."

With that Adam stepped back, and she tensed as he

approached her, because from the look on his face she could tell he had something on his mind.

His dark eyes searched her face, and she wondered what he was looking for as he assessed her. "Hey," he said.

"Hey yourself," she managed to get out as her throat began to close over.

He gestured with a nod. "Great bunch of kids."

Okay, so they were at his workplace and he was keeping it casual. She could do this. She could play along and act like nothing happened between them. "They seemed to really like you too."

His eyes darkened, and he pitched his voice low. "So what are you doing tonight?"

Cripes, what the heck happened to casual? Folding her arms, Josie swallowed, and from the heat in his eyes she knew exactly what he was getting at. Putting on her best professional face when Jason Fraser came running up to her, she bent down, spoke quietly to the child, then turned her attention to Adam when the child moved out of earshot. "I promised Tabby I'd help her at the dunk tank." Then, out of politeness she asked, "How about you?"

"Softball game. It should be over fairly early. Want to head to Hauk's with me afterward?"

She shook her head and waved her hand toward the kids, knowing she had to put a stop to this thing between them—whatever this was—now, and get out before she got in any deeper. "I can't. I have an early morning."

Something passed over Adam's face, and he stepped close, his expression dark, tortured. "Josie—" he began, but was cut off when two children started a shoving match, both wanting to be the first to sit in the truck.

"I have to go," she said, cutting him off.

He closed his mouth, but when his glance fastened on hers, she could tell he wanted to say something else, but she wasn't so sure she wanted to hear what it was. Because as she slipped past him, her heart pounding erratically, she understood she was in serious trouble here. Right from the beginning she knew she wasn't a love 'em and leave 'em sort of girl, and she never, ever should have seduced Adam, despite how amazing they were together.

Adam was the town's bad boy, a guy who went from woman to woman, and she wasn't the kind of girl who could love casually, which meant he wasn't the guy for her.

J.A.D. was.

S tanding in the dugout with Trent while they waited for the rest of the softball team to arrive, Adam blurted out, "Okay, that's it. I want her."

Trent balanced his baseball bat on his toes and angled his head to see him, a knowing grin spreading across his face. "Yeah, pal. I could have told you that."

"I mean it, Trent. I really want her," he admitted.

Trent paused for a moment, as though considering his next words carefully, then all humor left his face when he questioned, "I thought you said you wouldn't go for it with her because of your ridiculous belief that you're no better than your old man."

"I know, but she makes me want to try," Adam confessed as he tore off his T-shirt to pull on his jersey. It wasn't a decision he'd made lightly, and he'd spent the last two days doing some serious soul searching before coming to the conclusion that maybe, just maybe, Madame M's prediction was fate's way of telling him he could—with Josie at his side—change his ways. "She really, really makes me want to try to break the pattern."

"It's all in your head, you know," Trent scoffed. "There is no pattern. I've been telling you that for years."

"Yeah, yeah, I know, and you've also been telling me that when the right girl comes along I'll know it, and I won't even want to look at another woman."

Trent offered him a smug smile. "Feel free to tell me I was right all along then."

"Would a *fuck off* suffice?" Adam plunked himself onto the bench and ran his hands through his hair.

Trent laughed. "Jesus, Adam. I've never seen you like this before. What the hell happened between Saturday and tonight?"

Adam took a moment to think about Josie, sweet, sexy, naughty Josie. Earlier that morning, when he was out for a jog, he'd run past her place, but when he heard a low moan coming from her open window, it stopped him in his tracks. At first he thought she was in there with some other guy, and the jealousy he felt rose sure and swift. It was that jealousy that spoke volumes and had him realizing just how much she meant to him. Then, when he realized she was alone and it became clear that she was masturbating, he damn near knocked down her front door to join her. Instead he bolted down a side street, and spent the next few hours thinking things over as he jogged long and hard, until he was late for work. He'd only just made it to the fire station and showered when she showed up with her class.

"So...what the hell happened between Saturday night and now?" Trent asked again, pulling his thoughts back.

"A lot."

"Want to elaborate?"

"No."

"Well if you want her so bad, then what the hell are you doing hanging out here with me? Go get her."

"That's just it. We had a great time Saturday night, but

then today at the station and tonight at the fair she's all but ignored me."

"Well, well, isn't that a twist of fate?" Trent took a practice swing of his bat. "The one time you really want a girl and she doesn't want you back."

The mention of fate had Adam thinking of Madame M's prediction. Maybe the woman really was on to something. Maybe he really was meant to be with Josie and maybe he really could be a one-woman kind of guy. Because in the span of a couple of days, Josie had turned his world upside down and sure as hell made him want to try.

"You're not helping me, pal."

Trent gave him a sly grin. "Okay, so everyone knows your reputation with the ladies, right?"

"What are you getting at?"

"Maybe you just need to show Josie that you've changed your ways. Maybe then she'll see you as something more than a good time at the back of the fire truck."

Taken aback, Adam cringed and asked, "So you know then?"

"Well, that was just an educated guess," he said, grinning. "How could I not have come to that conclusion? You two both disappeared after our demonstration, and you haven't stopped smiling for two days."

"And she's been ignoring me for just as long." Well that wasn't entirely true. He'd spent Sunday at the station, while she was with her friends at the fair, which meant he hadn't been able to hook up with her. But Monday morning during the school tour, he'd felt her pull away from him.

Trent shrugged, and whacked his bat against his runners, knocking the dirt from the spikes. "So do something about it."

Just then Reece McGrath joined them in the dugout. "Do something about what?" he asked.

"Our man here's got it bad," Trent said.

"Oh yeah, and who might he have it bad for?"

"Sweet little Josie Wells," Trent announced.

"Oh really?" Reece paused and said, "I guess I can see that. She really is a nice girl." Rolling one shoulder, he added, "Hard to believe that she's still single."

"Uh, I'm right here, guys."

Trent looked at Adam. "What's hard to believe is that this dumb-ass took so long to realize what I've always known."

Reece said, "Well, from what Tabby told me, a few months back the psychic gave Josie the initials of the guy she is going to marry, and I hate to break it to you, pal, but they weren't yours." He glanced at Trent. "I guess that's probably why she's still single. She's waiting for her Mr. Right to come along."

"Do you really believe in that psychic shit?" Trent asked as the two began a debate on the merits of Madame M.

At the mention of Madame M and her prediction for Josie, an uneasy feeling moved into Adam's stomach. Okay, so maybe the crazy woman didn't know what she was talking about after all, because he'd be damned if he'd give up on Josie now. Not since he'd spent the last two days agonizing over her, and had come to the conclusion that so long as she was at his side, he could and would break the Collins curse.

Not only did he want to do it for Josie, he wanted to do it for Jacob. It was about time someone in the Collins family took responsibility for their actions. Jacob deserved to have a better role model, and up until now Adam had been doing a piss-poor job of that.

Before he could consider it further, the team showed up and Adam put his concerns away for the time being. He joined the team on the field and blinked under the bright lights, wondering if Josie was in the stands. Unable to see past the glare, he stepped up to bat.

Three hours later, after winning the softball game against the neighboring town, Adam showered and made his way back to the fairgrounds. It was late, and since it was a work night, things were shutting down early. As the temperature dropped, he jammed his hands into his jeans and walked around in search of Josie, but she was nowhere to be found. No doubt she was at home preparing her agenda for her class tomorrow.

The thoughts of living such a normal life, of crawling into bed early with someone you loved, someone who loved you back, had his heart clenching. Adam never thought he could have those things, but goddammit, it sure didn't mean he hadn't spent years wanting them.

Deciding to make his way to Hauk's haunted bar, he cut down a side street and walked along the water, but when he heard a loud noise up on Dresden's Bluff, and saw a spark in the air, he cursed under his breath.

How many times had he warned those teens about the dangers of fireworks?

Passing by the bar, he made his way to the bluff to read the riot act to the irresponsible youth who should have been at home asleep and not out causing trouble. After all, it was a school night.

He hurried up the bluff, but when he found Errol at the top, jumping around because he'd singed his fingertips, Adam cursed and looked at the pack of firecrackers on the ground. "Errol, what the hell do you think you're doing?"

Like a school kid caught with his fingers in the cookie jar, Errol glared at him in surprise. "What are you doing here?" he asked.

"What do you think I'm doing here?" Adam grabbed the old man's hand to examine it and blew a relieved breath to find it was nothing more than a light surface burn. Next time, however, he might not be so lucky. "You're going to get your self killed one of these days." He reached into his pocket. "I'm calling Trent."

"No, don't do that, lad. Was just out having me some fun. No harm. No foul."

Adam shook his head. "I think you need to find another hobby."

"Well, y'all put a stop to my meddling, so I have to find something fun to do."

When Adam saw real sadness come over Errol's face, it reminded him that after the man's wife, Margaret, passed away, Errol was alone in that big old house of his. Then it had him thinking of his own grandma. Errol and Delilah had been friends for years and maybe it was time someone opened their eyes to the fact that they'd be great companions for one another. Maybe it was time someone used Errol's meddling tricks on him.

"Errol..." he began.

"Okay, I'm leaving, I'm leaving. Don't get your panties in a twist, boy."

Adam laughed and drew the night air into his lungs, thinking he might just hang out on the bluff a little longer. It would do him good to get his head on straight and think about his best approach with Josie. But when he noticed Errol favoring one leg, he said, "You want me to walk you home?"

"Come on, boy, I ain't no invalid. I can make my own way home. And I might just pick up some rum on the way. I suppose ya got something to say about that too?" Before Adam could respond, he added, "You just stay put and make sure all those sparks are out. Make yourself useful for a change."

Twirling his cane, Errol began whistling as he made his way down the hill and Adam looked skyward, wondering what the hell he was going to do with the cranky old guy. After a few minutes Errol's whistling grew faint, and once he disappeared into the dark, Adam stood on the bluff and looked out over the town. But when his gaze zeroed in on Josie's bungalow, and he spotted her unlocking her front door and entering her foyer, his heart began to race, thinking about what he'd heard her doing in her bedroom earlier that morning.

He watched the lights flick on inside her small house, and when he watched her grab something out of her closet and disappear into another room, he suddenly felt like it wasn't such a coincidence that he was standing on the bluff, at the exact same time she was arriving home.

Speaking of meddling...

Was Errol up to his old tricks again? Had he led Adam there on purpose, knowing he would spot Josie arriving home? Still not convinced that the three granddads weren't involved in pairing Reece and Tabby as well as Vic and Hauk, Adam considered this turn of events longer. But as he tossed it around in his mind, the more convinced he was that Errol couldn't have known the precise time Josie would arrive home. Christ, maybe all these new emotions were just making him paranoid.

He was about to gather the firecrackers and head back to Hauk's when a movement inside her bedroom gained his attention. Peering into the dark, he could see her moving around, and from the way her hair hung down her back he'd hazarded a guess that she'd just showered. Through the gap in her curtain, he watched her climb into bed and grab a book, but in no time at all she'd abandoned the book and sank lower into her sheets.

She writhed around, and when her lamp flicked off, Adam swallowed. Because if she was doing what he thought she was doing, he was going to lose it and lose it hard.

His body vibrated and his thickening cock urged him to join her before he went up in a burst of flames. Barely able to think straight, he hurried down the bluff and headed straight for her walkway. Working to regulate his breathing, he rapped on her door. He waited a long time for her to answer, and when she finally pulled her door open, and he caught sight of the gorgeous woman before him, he knew his world would never be the same again. His throat tightened as expressive blue eyes looked up at him, and the pink flush on her cheek—a flush that spoke volumes—combined with the soft white robe draped over her naked body, told him she had been doing precisely what he suspected.

With his mouth salivating, his fingers itching and his body quivering with raw need, he decided to go for broke. Hey, nothing ventured, nothing gained.

Adam cleared his throat and asked, "Need a hand?"

$$14$$

Josie was shocked to find Adam standing outside her door, and she was even more rattled, not to mention turned on, to discover that he seemed to know what she was doing before he'd arrived. She wasn't sure how. All she knew was that he was offering a hand.

And oh, what amazing hands he had!

A girl would have to be crazy to turn down such a scintillating offer. Then again, hadn't she just lectured herself on staying away from him? Wasn't turning down his offer the logical thing to do?

But as he stood there awaiting a response, his expression tender and hot, it wasn't logic calling the shots. Oh no. It was the furthest thing from logic urging her to drop her robe and invite him in.

It was obvious that she wanted him. There was no denying that. And she was pretty damn certain there was nothing she could do to fight her traitorous libido, especially after seeing him on the ball field tonight. God, he looked so hard and sexy when he swung the bat and ran the bases, that it had just about done her in, and it certainly had her thinking about him while she touched herself tonight. And now, seeing him there, an intent look on his handsome face as his glance moved over her curves, had her resolve melting and body beckoning his touch. Suddenly every reason she had for staying away from him seemed so insignificant.

"Adam," she managed to get out as she reached for him, her acceptance of his offer clear in her actions. When he stepped into her, closing the door behind him, sexual energy like she'd never before felt zinged between them and nearly took her breath away.

Everything in the way he looked at her was deeply intimate and she hungered for him in ways that scared her. Okay, so he might not be the man of her future, but from the heat in his eyes when they locked on hers, to the way her body trembled with anticipation, she knew he was the man of her present. She'd have to figure out a way to deal with her emotions later, because right now she needed him like she'd never needed another.

"Josie," he said, the raw ache of lust in his voice teasing all her senses as he pushed her up against the wall. "You're so beautiful."

He grabbed her hands and braced them above her head, and Josie's heart hammered, her excitement mounting as he took control of their play. His knee slipped between her legs to widen them and the scent of her arousal reached her nostrils.

"Tell me," he questioned in a soft voice, "were you thinking of me?"

"Yes," she admitted, knowing full well what he was talking about. Her admission seemed to do something to him, trigger a reaction from somewhere deep.

His lips crashed down on hers, and a low growl caught in his throat. His hands gripped her belt, and when he untangled it from her waist, her robe slid open to expose her naked body. Adam stepped back, taking his time to look at her partially bared flesh, her uncovered cleavage, the warm spot between her legs. He reached out and stroked her neck, then ran his hand the length of her body until he reached her pussy. As she watched him, she shivered under his touch and an erotic whimper escaped her lips.

"Show me," he said.

She began to widen her robe, but he shook his head to stop her. When she gave him a confused look, his mouth curved enticingly. "Show me how you touch yourself."

"Oh God," she cried out, remembering how he seemed to know about her secret fetishes.

"Do it now, Josie." The pleasure she heard in his voice excited her, and something in the way he encouraged her to embrace her naughty side warmed her from the inside out.

Their glances locked and her heart clenched, loving him for allowing her to play out her fantasies like this, loving that he cared about her needs. Wanting to make this as good for him as it was for her, she cupped her breasts, and noted the darkening of his eyes. She played with her nipples, then slowly dragged her hands down her contours, taking her time to tease him, wanting him as wild with desire as she was.

When she reached her pussy, she dipped into her liquid heat. She stroked her curls, which were damp with passion, then eased one finger inside herself.

"Fuck," Adam murmured. He dragged his fingers through his hair, mussing it as his nostrils flared to pull in the scent of her arousal.

Longing moved through her, and she knew it had everything to do with the heated way he was watching her, not to mention the sexy, disheveled state he was in. Feeling bold and brazen, she arched her back and ran her fingers over her clit, and she could tell Adam's composure was about to slip. A hard shudder raced through her as she toyed with her clit, taking herself higher and higher as he watched, hardly able to believe she was actually masturbating in front of this audience of one—albeit a sexy, captivated audience of one. In no time at all she could feel an orgasm pulling at her, and her breathing grew labored, erratic.

She began moving, pressing against her hand, seeking what her body needed, but before she could finish, Adam stepped up to her and pulled her hand away. When she opened her mouth to protest, he silenced her with a kiss and slipped her robe over her shoulders.

Standing there naked in front of the man who did the strangest things to her insides, her body hungered for him with an intensity that made her shake. He kissed her long and deep, and when he inched back, his voice was edgy, rough when he ordered, "Bedroom. Now."

She pushed off the wall, but before she could make her way down the hall, he stepped up behind her. He kissed her bare shoulders, and the intimacy in the way he tenderly brushed his lips over her flesh had her heart tightening, but when he gave her a light slap on the ass, she gasped, her entire body going up in a burst of flames.

He pulled her tighter against his chest, his hands on her hips as he whispered into her ear, "You really are a very naughty girl, aren't you?"

With that he tapped her ass again, and set her into motion. She hurried down the hall, Adam tight on her heels. When she entered the dimly lit room, Adam said, "Get on the bed and spread your legs for me."

As her blood ignited, she climbed onto her mattress. When Adam walked in front of her window and she spotted the gap in the drapes, she knew in an instant he'd been watching her. That realization raised her passion to new heights and had her body quivering.

"Now show me your pussy," Adam said as he tugged off his

T-shirt. She slipped her hand between her legs and stroked herself as he removed his clothes, stopping to grab a condom out of his pocket before reaching for his zipper. He tossed it onto her nightstand and then unfastened his pants. When he released his hard-on, she pulled her bottom lip between her teeth. She took her time to look at his magnificent cock, hard and ready to plunge inside her, and as she took in his impressive girth, not to mention the precome pearling on the swollen tip, her mouth watered for a taste.

"Nice," she murmured, and wet her bottom lip.

He began to move toward her, mischief dancing in his eyes. He slid onto the bed beside her and pressed his mouth to hers. His lips travelled lower, skimming down her body, and before she realized what he was doing, he flipped her over.

"Such a beautiful, beautiful ass," he said, rubbing his hands over her backside. He pressed his lips to her shoulder and then, catching her off guard, he gave her ass a good hard whack.

Blindsided by emotion as Adam tapped into her fetishes, she gasped and writhed against the mattress.

He pressed his mouth against her ear and whispered, "I love this side of you, Josie, and I love discovering all your wants and desires."

When she heard raw passion in his voice, she knew she was in way over her head because she in turn wanted to discover everything about the man who was so sensitive to her needs, a man she was falling for. Hard and fast.

After another slap, he flipped her back over and settled himself over her body. "Let's see what else you like," he murmured, moving his mouth to the soft hollow of her neck.

As he trailed his lips over her body, his hands touching every inch of her naked flesh, she felt like she was drowning in emotion. Her breath caught in her throat when his mouth reached her pussy, and when he pulled her lips open and gave a long, slow lick, she knew she was well past the point of no return with Adam.

She couldn't chalk her feelings up to love at first sight, considering she'd known Adam since she was a child. But it was only the last few days that she'd really gotten to know him on a deeper level, and what she saw in him had her wanting him to be a bigger part of her life—a part of her future.

He spent a long time between her legs, licking her and pushing deep with his fingers. Good God, the man knew just how to touch, when to apply pressure and when not to as he brought her closer and closer to the edge. Blood began flowing hot and heavy in her veins as his fingers glided over her pussy. Her toes curled as pressure began building, coming to a peak.

"Adam..." she cried out.

"I know, baby." He settled his mouth on her pussy, and when his tongue pressed against her clit, she closed her eyes and gave herself over to the sensation. As his tongue did the most mind-shattering things to her body, she let go and instantly tumbled into orgasm.

Adam growled as she came in his mouth, and she reached down to touch him, to feel his flesh beneath her fingers as her body screamed to have him inside her.

Once her tremors subsided, he climbed up her body. Dark, intense eyes met hers and everything inside her reached out to him.

"Adam," she said, her throat drying as she saw a bevy of emotions pass over his eyes.

"I want you to ride me, baby." Josie didn't miss the ache of longing in his voice or the need in his eyes when he added, "I want to watch you when you come for me."

With that he flipped her over until she was on top of him.

As she straddled him, he slipped on his condom, then gripped her hips and lifted her higher, until his shaft was poised at her opening. Their eyes met and powerful emotions passed between them as she lowered herself, taking him into her body to join them as one.

"Holy Jesus," he cried out, and she watched the muscles along his jaw ripple as he clenched down. "You are so hot and tight."

Never having felt so full, Josie whimpered with pleasure and began moving against him. He touched her so deep it sent ripples of pleasure straight to her core. As desire prowled inside her, she could feel color bloom high on her cheeks, her body breaking out in moisture. Her lids slipped shut as she concentrated on the pleasure.

"Look at me, sweetheart."

She did as he requested, and as his eyes visually caressed her, she could feel another orgasm pulling at her. She moved harder, faster, riding him with wild abandon as she ground her clit on his pelvis. Feeling out of control, she bit back a breathy moan, her thoughts fragmenting as the world around her spun out of control.

"Jesus, Josie. Slow down or I'm going to lose it." He gave her a small smack on the ass and her body trembled almost uncontrollably.

"I want you to lose it, Adam. Lose it with me."

With that Adam groaned and powered his hips upward and her pulse raced, wanting them to come in unison.

"I'm...there," she cried out, drawing a shaky breath, and she could hear the urgency and emotion in her voice.

He drove into her harder, and as he stabbed deep, he pressed a finger over her clit and before she knew it, before she could even scream his name, her body went up in a burst of flames and another powerful orgasm ripped through her.

"Oh God," Adam roared as her juices ran over him. A

second later he gripped her hips to still her as he released inside her. She squeezed her muscles tight, milking every last drop out of him before she leaned forward. After dropping a soft kiss on his hot mouth, she collapsed on his chest and stayed like that for a long time, until Adam pulled her down beside him.

When she looked at him, his warm smile was full of tenderness. He smoothed her hair from her face as she snuggled in next to him.

"That was amazing," she whispered as he pulled her in tight and brushed his lips over her forehead. "You're amazing."

"Yes, yes I am," he teased. Then he rolled into her and tipped her chin until they were eye to eye. All humor was gone from his eyes when he said, "What's amazing is the two of us together, Josie."

A riot of emotions tore through her, because he was right. They *were* amazing together. And she couldn't deny how good it felt to be with him, how right it felt to be there in his arms, snuggling together after a beautiful night of lovemaking. The truth was, she'd never felt such fulfillment before—physical or emotional.

As she considered that longer, she thought about Madame M's prediction. The psychic had to be wrong. She had to be. Because deep in her heart she believed Adam just might be the man for her. Everything in the way he touched her and pleasured her created a powerful bond between them, moving them well past casual acquaintances or bed partners.

She thought more about his playboy nature. From what she'd heard he'd spent Sunday night alone and tonight, well tonight he could have been with any woman he wanted, but instead he'd come looking for her. She'd seen the emotions in his eyes when she'd first opened the door, and when he made love to her with his mouth, his hands and his cock, she could feel him reaching out to her on another level.

There really was a lot more to this man than met the eye, and despite the fact that he played the field, and most towns-folk believed he was inflicted with the Collins curse, she'd seen the wanting in his eyes tonight. It was that wanting that told her he craved so much more.

As his glance moved over her face, her heart missed a beat and she knew it was well past time to get to know Adam better, to discover if this connection between them was the lasting kind—the kind that the two of them could build a future on.

15

Over the last week Adam had spent every moment he could with Josie, taking in the fair every night after work, or just hanging out as they got to know each other better, and Adam couldn't deny that she was the most amazing woman he'd ever been with, inside the bedroom and out.

The truth was, he loved everything about Josie, from her sweet, sexy nature, to her wild and adventurous side. She was fun and playful, honest and real, and everything about her had him wanting to be a better man. Trent was right about one thing—he had no interest in looking at another woman and hadn't since the first night he and Josie had made love outdoors. Josie fulfilled him, completed him in ways that baffled him, and had him walking around with a permanent smile on his face. He'd soon have to try to get himself under control, considering the guys at the station were razzing the hell out of him. But right now he didn't want to pull himself together. He just wanted to bask in Josie and ride the waves of emotions as she took him on a journey of happiness.

Honestly, who knew Madame M was the real thing,

because everything she'd told him had come true. Here he was, crazy in love with Josie, and to him that equated to true happiness. And he couldn't forget that Madame M had known his father's nickname for him either. He'd tried to pass that off as a lucky guess, but now, deep in his gut, he really suspected the woman was on to something.

A high-pitched scream broke into his thoughts and he glanced up to see Josie swinging her legs in the dunk tank. Adam laughed as the ball came too close for comfort, missing the target by inches. Josie was yelling, trying to distract Hauk who was laughing and gunning for her as she taunted him, boasting that no one had been able to dunk her yet, and in one hour when the festival was over, she'd be this year's winner. Adam grinned, knowing Hauk was simply playing with her. He was their softball team's ace pitcher and could take her out anytime.

Just then Lila came up to him and he turned to see her. "Hi, Adam," she said around a bright smile.

"Hey, Lila. How are things going?" he asked, then remembered this was her first fall fair. "So how was your first Whispering Cove festival?"

She crinkled her nose. "I spent most of it inside a kitchen and didn't get to see much. Next year remind me to volunteer less."

Adam glanced at his watch. "Hauk's haunted bar will be open until late. He's having too much fun watching people get scared. You could still make that."

"Want to join me?"

He didn't miss the invitation in her voice, and before last week, before he found true happiness with Josie, he would have gone for it. "Josie and I went last night."

"Oh," she said, genuine surprise on her face as her gaze waved back and forth between him and the dunk tank. "Are you two still...?" She paused and added absently, "I guess her Mr. Decent hasn't arrived yet."

"Her what?" he asked, taken aback, his voice coming out harsher than he meant.

Looking embarrassed and upset, she began to backtrack. "Oh, nothing really. It's nothing. I just thought you knew."

"Knew what?" he pressed.

She bit her bottom lip nervously and wrung her fingers together. "It's just...well..."

"What is it, Lila?"

"I heard her and her friends talking at the food tent last week, and from what I understand they talked her into playing with Mr. Indecent—you—until her Mr. Decent came along. I thought you knew. I'm sorry."

After Lila explained what she overheard, a knot tightened his stomach. Adam instantly thought back to what Reece had said and realized how much it fit in to Lila's theory. Josie was waiting for her Mr. Right to come along. He knew Josie's friends had put her up to the firefighting demonstration, and had wondered about the kissing booth as well. Was Lila right? Was he simply a distraction until her Mr. Right came along?

Just then he caught a glimpse of Errol sneaking out of the sultan's tent, and his world went a little fuzzy around the edges, his gut warning that something wasn't quite right. Suddenly, the hairs on his nape began to tingle, and for some odd reason his thoughts raced back to Dresden's Bluff, to when he had the sneaking suspicion that the old man had been trying to lure him there. As his mind raced, trying to puzzle things out, he excused himself from Lila—who looked completely distraught—and went in search of Errol, determined to find out what he was up to.

A short while later he found him inside the beer tent, a sly grin on his face as he shared a beer with his buddies, Byron and Harold. When he approached, the three glanced up, and from the mischief in their eyes, Adam knew they were in cahoots about something, and he was smart enough to know it had everything to do with Josie and him.

"Errol," he said, eyeing him suspiciously. "You've got some explaining to do."

With that Harold and Byron quickly finished off their beers and excused themselves, leaving Errol to fend for himself.

Errol poked Adam with his cane. "Have a seat, lad."

Adam folded his arms and widened his legs. "I think I'll stand."

"Suit yourself."

"You want to tell me what's going on?"

"Ain't nothing going on," Errol hedged.

Adam blew a heavy sigh and pressed. "Come on, Errol. I saw you sneaking out of the psychic's tent. What are you up to?"

Clucking his tongue, Errol said, "Suppose it don't matter now." He glanced at his watch and added, "Festival's over in one hour and it looks like I won't have to buy the rum for the next month." He winked and added, "You had me worried for a bit there, boy."

"What are you going on about?"

"You and Josie."

Adam braced himself. "What about us?"

"You're a couple, ain't ya? A hot item, as the teens around these parts say."

Adam angled his head, wondering exactly what he was getting at. "And..."

"And well, now I ain't stuck buying the rum."

"Can you tell me what the hell that has to do with Josie and me?"

That question earned him a scowl. "For a smart guy, you're kinda dense," Errol said, shaking his head.

Thinking about Hauk and Vic's recent union, not to mention Reece and Tabby's love affair, and having always felt the old men had something to do with bringing those couples together, he questioned, "What have you done, Errol? Why were you in the psychic's booth?"

"Cause sometimes you youngins need a hand."

"Errol," he warned.

"It's no big deal. I just told Madame M to tweak her reading."

He waited for Errol to continue, but when he turned his attention to his beer as if the conversation was over, Adam pressed, "Keep going."

Errol rolled his eyes. "She told you that you'd fall for a girl with the initials J.C.W., right?"

"Yeah."

"Well that was the tweak, lad."

Perplexed and trying to sort things through, he thought about what Reece had told him, that Madame M had given Josie the initials of the man she'd marry and they weren't Adam's. "What I don't get is, why did Madame M give Josie initials that weren't mine?"

Looking thoroughly confused, Errol's glossy eyes widened. "I don't know, lad. I didn't have anything to do with Josie's reading. Was only messing with yours. Someone had to open your eyes. How else could I get you to go for it with Josie? You avoided her like she was a damn storm at sea when I knew all along how right ya both were for each other."

While Errol continued to drone on, Adam faltered backward, feeling physically ill. His mind shifted, sorting through all the events of the past week, not to mention what Lila had just told him.

When the pieces of the puzzle began to fall into place, he dropped down into a chair, his knees giving out on him.

"You okay, boy?" Errol asked.

Adam shook his head, pretty certain he'd never be okay again because the psychic had been right about him falling for Josie and finding happiness. Those things had happened. But what if she was right about Josie too? What if she was supposed to fall in love, marry and find happily ever after with a man who didn't have his initials? And what if she was simply biding her time with him until her Mr. Right came along? Jesus. Adam never would have gone for it with her if the psychic hadn't planted the idea in his mind in the first place. Christ, here he thought it was fate that had brought them together, when in fact it was Errol and his meddling.

Old insecurities and fears rushed to the surface. Maybe it really was impossible to change his ways. Maybe the Collins boys would always be a product of their father, unable to change their lives, their fate. If that was the case, would he only end up hurting Josie in the long run?

The only thing he'd ever wanted was for Josie to be happy and he never, ever wanted to hurt her, which was the reason he'd always avoided her in the first place.

Josie deserved to be with the man meant for her. Yes, he wanted her, and hadn't looked at a woman since he'd been with her, but for how long would that last? It was possible he'd revert back to his old ways because he had his father's blood in him. From the way Josie looked at him, he knew she had feelings for him, even if this affair started out as a distraction until her Mr. Right came along. So maybe he could convince her he was the man for her. But if they weren't really meant to be together for the long haul, was he going to risk her true happiness for his own selfish purposes?

16

Josie climbed out of the dunk tank, soaking wet and cold as the last of the afternoon sun went behind a cloud. Laughing as Hauk cheered in victory, she glanced around, looking for Adam, but when her gaze came up empty and she saw Errol standing there watching her, a forlorn look on his face, her heart sank into her stomach.

She grabbed her towel, wiped her face and made her way toward him. But as she approached, a movement behind him drew her focus. Craning her neck, she looked past his shoulders, and what she saw soured her stomach and had her blood pounding.

Oh God. No.

Errol caught hold of her hand as she watched Adam turn his back on her, two pretty girls flanking him as he sauntered away, moving in the direction of his house.

Confused and not understanding what was happening—after all, things had been going so good between them and Adam hadn't glanced at another woman since they'd been together—she looked at Errol, her damp eyes questioning.

"Josie, I…I…" he said, his voice broken.

Barely able to comprehend what was going on, she shook her head. "What…?"

Errol squeezed her hand tighter and she saw real sadness on his face. "Dangit, girl. The lad don't know what he's doing."

"What happened?" she rushed out.

"All I wanted to do was show him how good you two could be together."

The bile in her stomach pushed into her throat. "What did you do?"

Josie stood there, her towel pressed against her damp body as Errol confessed everything, explaining how he and his buddies had meddled once again, and now, after finding out what they'd done, Adam believed Josie and he weren't really meant to be together.

Once he was done confessing, Josie drew a deep breath, and while she knew she should've been enraged that Adam had just walked off with two women, she was actually touched. Because in her heart she knew who Adam was, and knew who he wasn't. He was a wonderful, amazing and caring man—a man nothing like his father—and he'd only turned his back on her because he was afraid of hurting her.

How could she not love and fight for a man like that?

"I have to go," she said to Errol, and with that she wrapped the towel around her shivering body and made her way to Adam's house.

Less than ten minutes later she stood on his front porch, banging on his door, refusing to give up on him.

When he opened it, looking lost and lonely, her heart ached for him. She looked past his shoulders. "Do you have company?"

"Josie, listen—" he began, but stopped when he noticed her wet clothes. A flood of emotions passed over his eyes as he pulled her inside and slammed the door shut, his gaze tortured as his glance moved over her shivering body. "You're freezing. You need to get out of these clothes."

Her heart tightened with the love she felt for him, and his concern for her well-being touched her deeply. She drew a breath to clear her thoughts and asked again, "Do you have company?"

He gave a hard shake of his head. "No. But you don't understand."

Her heart soared because this only proved that the girls were for show only, to get her to turn her back on him. She poked Adam in the chest. "No. You don't understand."

His gaze moved over her face, assessing her. "I know your friends put you up to sleeping with me."

Taken aback, she blew a long breath and rushed on to explain. "I'll admit things started out that way, but I fell in love with you. You must know that."

He raked shaky hands through his mussed hair, and despite her confession of love, she could feel him trying to distance himself emotionally.

"Josie, you know my reputation, you know about the Collins curse."

"What I know is that you're an amazing man, Adam. I believe in you, so why can't you believe in yourself?"

Sadness passed over his eyes and he pitched his voice low when he said, "I don't want to hurt you."

Warmth moved through her and she stepped close to him. "I know. And that's why I love you."

She watched him soak in her words, watched the way need flashed in his eyes. "But the psychic, she's been right about everything so far, what if she's right about the man you're supposed to be with? The man with the initials that aren't mine."

She drew a shaky breath. "So you know about that too?"

"Yeah."

"I don't care what she says." She wrapped her arms around Adam. "I love you, Adam, and that's all that matters."

Looking confused and vulnerable, he crushed his hands into her hair. "Oh God, Josie. I love you so much it scares me."

With that, Adam kissed her, a deep, passionate kiss that spoke of want and longing and had her needing more.

"Let's go to your bedroom," she whispered.

He slipped his arm under her and carried her down the hall. When they reached his bedroom, he set her down beside his bed, and the silence that hung over them as they both undressed was profound, and not the least bit uncomfortable.

She looked at his gorgeous body as he shed his clothes, and when he climbed between the sheets and pulled back the blankets for her, she slipped in beside him.

With a gentle touch, Adam pushed her hair off her face, then ran his hands over her body to warm her. "Baby, I don't ever want to hurt you," he admitted, his voice shaky.

"You won't," she assured him, her lips finding his. "I believe in you, Adam." Her hands slid over his naked body, touching, exploring, unable to get enough of him. "I honestly don't care what that psychic said. Everything about us feels right," she said, emotion thickening her voice. "I want to be with you and I don't care if your initials aren't J.A.D."

She felt him stiffen beneath her hands, and his voice sounded strangled when he said, "No. You're wrong, Josie. The psychic was right."

When she inched back and caught the incredulous look on his face, Josie's heart missed a beat, wondering what she'd said. Fearing he was about to pull away from her again, she slipped her arm around his shoulder and held him to her.

"Adam, wait—"

A smile split his face. "Josie, don't you see? *I'm* J.A.D."

Confused, she shook her head. "What?"

"I was named after my father. Jack Adam Dempsey."

Josie's eyes widened. She was hardly able to believe what she was hearing. "Oh. My. God."

"After my father skipped town, my mother started calling me by my middle name, and she changed our last name back to her maiden name of Collins."

Josie searched her mind, but it had happened so long ago, when they were only kids, that she'd forgotten that. "The psychic couldn't have known that. She must have been right after all." When his lips found hers again, her heart filled with joy. "So it really was fate that brought us together," she said between kisses.

Adam pulled back and grinned. "Actually, I think it was Errol and his meddling that brought us together."

Josie laughed. "I think you might be right."

Adam groaned and raked his hands through his hair. "And now he feels bad because he thinks he's ruined everything, doesn't he?"

"Do you think we should go find him and put him out of his misery?"

Adam furrowed his brow. "Actually, I think we should let him suffer a few more hours. After all, he's not supposed to be meddling." Climbing on top of her, Adam pushed his cock against her leg. "Besides, I have other more urgent matters pressing right now."

Josie opened her legs for him, welcoming him into her body, heart and soul. "Yes, I believe you do."

Adam quickly sheathed himself, then in one quick thrust entered her, pushing open her tight walls and making her feel so gloriously full and happy.

She held on tight as she murmured, "I love you, J.A.D."

"And I love you, J.C.D."

"J.C.D.?" she asked, angling her head, confused. "My last name begins with a W, not a D."

"Only until you marry me."

Her eyes widened in joy. "Adam," she choked out.

As Adam looked at her, she could feel his love reach out to her. He swallowed, and said, "That is, if you'll have me."

She pulled his mouth to hers, happier than she'd ever been in her life. "How could I say no to a man who makes me burn the way you do?"

"So that's the only reason you want me then, for my body," he teased, breaking the kiss as he pulled out an inch.

Josie laughed and tightened her legs around his ass, driving him back inside her. "Well, for one part in particular," she returned, moaning as he impaled her.

He brushed his lips over hers and murmured, "You really are a bad girl, Josie."

"And you're my bad boy, Adam. Today. Tomorrow. Forever," she said, and when he realized it meant she was accepting his proposal, he gave her a hot, soul-searing kiss, one that branded her brazen heart and told her she'd finally found her Mr. Right. And as luck would have it, her Mr. Indecent was a very decent man.

And she wouldn't want it any other way.

"Here's to another round of successful meddlin'," Byron said, holding his tumbler of rum out for a three-man salute.

Harold grinned, and the old deck boards creaked under his weight as he shifted in his rocker to clink glasses with Byron. "And here's to not getting in trouble for it."

Feeling a little warm under the collar, despite the cool fall breeze that would soon drive the three poker-playing buddies inside until next year's Spring Fling, Errol adjusted his shirt and watched the last of the autumn leaves fall to the ground.

"I wouldn't go so far as to say that," he said, thinking how he'd nearly gotten into trouble with Adam. Lord, the boy had looked like he was about to throttle him when he found out he'd tweaked the dang psychic reading.

Byron and Harold both laughed out loud and tossed a handful of chips into the center of the table, but Errol threw his cards down, leaned back in his rocking chair and folded his arms across his chest.

Harold furrowed his brow and studied him with cloudy

eyes. "You just lost your hand, Errol, so why the hell are you sitting there grinnin' like the village idiot?"

"Cause Katy and Trent were by earlier," he announced, bursting at the seams to share the good news with his best friends.

"And?" Byron asked, as he swirled the last of his rum in his tumbler.

"And she's having my great-grandbaby." Errol threw back the last of his rum and reached for the bottle to refill their tumblers.

Harold harrumphed. "'Bout time those two spilled the news."

Byron clicked his tongue and smiled. "We did good with that match."

"We did good with them all," Harold added.

"So what do y'all think?" Errol asked. "Any more youngins around these parts in need of our help?"

As the other two men lowered their heads in consideration, Errol thought about the three couples who'd found love at the fall festival thanks to their guidance. A moment later his thoughts drifted to his great nephew, Jon. He couldn't help but think it was time the good doctor left that damn clinic in Miami and found himself a nice young girl in Whispering Cove. And with all the new babies on their way, there was no denying that Dani could use a bit of help down at the hospital.

Just then a car drove by and the young lady inside gave them all a wave. Errol smiled, his mind racing with ideas, and suddenly he knew exactly who'd give Jon-boy a run for his money and have him rethinking his big city lifestyle.

After refilling their tumblers, Errol slammed the bottle back down on the table.

"So what do ya say? Y'all up for a little more meddlin'?" he asked.

"Depends. What are we putting on the table this time?"

"Maybe we'd better put up for a month's worth of rum again, seein' as our bottle is empty," Errol said.

"Did someone mention an empty bottle?"

At the sound of a female voice, the three men sat up a bit straighter. Errol angled his head and narrowed his eyes to take in the attractive lady climbing his steps. A bottle of rum was under one arm and a tin, which, from the decadent smell, could only be his neighbor's famous ginger cookies.

"Delilah," Errol said, jumping to his feet. "What brings you by?"

Blue eyes blinked up at him and he couldn't help but notice the quickening of his pulse.

"Adam asked me to bring these things by." She paused to glance at the two men still seated. "But if you're busy—"

Son of a bitch!

Errol grinned, and realized that for the first time the player was finally getting played. Damn youngins and their meddlin'.

"No worries, Delilah, these two were just leavin'," he said.

SILK

In Whispering Cove

.

"Damn that officer, closing up the bar and sending us home 'cause there's a storm blowing through. Pffttt..." Errol Wilson closed the door against the cool winter wind and placed his battered cane on his coat rack. He shook the snow from his wool overcoat and scowled. "It's winter. All we get are storms. Ain't the first one we've weathered."

Harold Adair harrumphed and grabbed his usual seat at the long oaken table the three men had been sitting around for the last fifty years. He began dealing the cards and said, "You got that right. We've been weathering storms long before that lad was a gleam in his father's eyes."

"Well if we can't drink at Hauk's, we'll drink here," Errol announced, pulling a bottle from the stash he had hidden way behind the boxes of bran flakes his granddaughter, Katy, kept buying him and he kept refusing to eat. He might as well head up to Dresden's Bluff and gnaw on a hardwood tree. Roughage his ass. He didn't need no damn roughage. All he needed to keep him regular was his trusty bottle of rum. "What the hell is wrong with the young'ns today anyway?"

"They don't know nothin' about nothin'," Harold declared.

Byron stretched out rheumatoid swollen fingers and grabbed three shot glasses to line them up. After Errol poured the rum, Byron took a swig and said, "You know my Dani's got me eating dried apricots." His face turned sour. "Do you have any idea how much I hate apricots?"

Errol set the bottle of rum aside and picked up his cards to study them before tossing a few chips to the center of the table. "Those kids need something to do other then watch over us."

"And they accuse us of meddlin'." Byron refilled his glass, swallowed it in one gulp, and then poured himself another.

"Yeah, and I think our bar-closin' Officer Leo Caan needs something to occupy his mind other than the law."

Harold's bushy brows show upward as he laid his cards down. "Something or some*one?*"

Errol perked up. "Oh yeah? You got someone in mind?"

Before Harold could answer, the phone rang. Errol climbed to his feet and checked the display. "Damn. That Lila's a persistent one. Always after me to sell her the B&B."

"You can't," Byron said flatly.

Harold gave a slow shake of his head. "Ain't right."

Ignoring the ringing, Errol sat back down and thought of his great-nephew, Jon, the rightful owner of the old B&B. It had been left to him after his folks died and he needed to be the one to decide to sell it or keep it. Errol missed that dang boy, and it was about time he left Miami and came back to where he belonged. He'd argue that he couldn't leave his practice, but Dani could use his help. They could all win.

Errol rubbed his balding head, his mind racing, scheming —even though half the town had warned the three to stay out of everyone else's business. "So, what's this you're saying about getting Officer Caan out of our hair?"

Wind whispered outside and Byron's weathered yet shrewd eyes glistened as they shot to Harold. "Yeah. What are you thinking?"

Harold tossed two cards down, his cloudy blue eyes lighting with excitement. "I think I smell a bet."

Errol nodded toward his cupboard. "If the bar gets shut down more than just tonight, my stash will be gone in no time. It'll be real nice to get a month's worth when you two bloated puffer fish lose."

He took a drink, knowing just how he'd get his couple together in time to win a bet. His mind raced with an idea on how to catch two fish with one lure. Get his great-nephew home for good and get Lila Sheppard off his dang back.

Harold swirled his glass on the table and jabbed his thumb into his chest. "We'll see who the bloated puffer fish are when it's my stash you two will be refilling."

They both turned to Byron.

"You in?" Errol asked.

"Damn straight," Byron said. He shook his head. "'Cause it ain't right that sweet Aimee is raising that little angel all alone. That girl needs some support."

"You mean meddlin'," Harold corrected.

Errol took in the twinkle in Byron's gaze and knew the old goat was scheming. And scheming good. "You been thinkin' about this?"

Byron shrugged. "A Christmas concert, with a surprise guest."

As Errol and Harold nodded their heads, knowing exactly what Byron was up to, the smile fell from Byron's face. "But you two barnacle-suckin' old blowfish got to keep the name of the surprise guest a secret."

"I'm real good at keeping secrets," Errol said with a nod toward Harold. "Unlike some people."

Harold looked offended. "Why you no good, creatin'..."

Byron held his hand up to cut him off. "I'll bet my own bottle neither of you can."

"You're on." Errol grinned and tossed his cards down. "First one to make a match without being caught wins." Harold held his glass up for a three-man salute and they all clinked glasses.

"Here's to getting the young'ns out of our hair," Errol said.

"If we had any," Byron said, his mouth twitching.

17

Jon Carver wasn't sure what he disliked more, Christmas or homecomings.

That thought had him wondering why he'd left Miami and was currently weaving his rental vehicle through the snow-powdered streets of his childhood home. The coastal fishing town might be small in both size and population, but the decorated store fronts, the garland wreaths hanging from the lampposts and the twinkling lights in every window of every house reminded him that the tight-knit community of Whispering Cove, Maine, celebrated Christmas in a big way.

As snowflakes fell on his windshield warm childhood memories ambushed him. He flicked on his wipers and, despite his aversion to the holidays, couldn't help but take pleasure in the festive sights. The bulbs and ribbons took him back in time, specifically to the Christmas when he was twelve and his mother and father had bought his first mini bike.

But thinking of his folks had a chaotic lump crawling into his too-tight throat. He drew in a sharp breath and desperately tried to swallow the pain, locking it behind the wall he'd built some seven years ago, right after the accident that had changed the face of his future.

Looking for a distraction, anything to get his mind off that horrific night, he recklessly negotiated a twisting turn and cut down a side road. But there was no escaping the holiday jubilation in this festive town. Every image on every street spoke of family and fun, love and laughter, and made him remember what he'd lost. He tightened his grip on the steering wheel, his fingers itching to spin the vehicle around and drive straight back to the airport. At least in Miami he could get lost in the anonymity of his life. No one on the streets knew his name or his history.

His heart beat quicker in his constricted chest and he worked to desensitize, to bring back the numbness, because there was no denying that deep down he wanted to be a part of the celebrations, wanted to laugh and share eggnog with friends, trim the tree and hang stockings with family.

Except he didn't deserve the ideal life that seemed to go on without him.

Moments before he was about to give the wheel a good hard yank and pull a one-eighty right there in the middle of the street, he spotted his great-uncle Errol's house overlooking the ocean. As he recalled their phone conversation just last week, and remembered how urgent and out of sorts Errol had sounded, Jon knew he couldn't turn his back on the man who'd always been there for him. Errol had been vague on the phone and Jon had no idea what was wrong, he only knew something wasn't right.

Night fell over the town as he pulled into Errol's driveway. He lightly tapped the brakes, and when the vehicle came to a complete stop, the porch light flicked on and his uncle hobbled out with a cane. Jon frowned as he killed the ignition and hurried out of the driver's seat. During his brief visit some three years ago, when he'd come back to check on his estate, an old Victorian house Errol was renting for him, and trying to sell, Errol had been robust, healthy and bustling around town without any kind of assistance. What had happened since Jon had been gone? A knot twisted in his stomach as concern for his uncle's well-being washed over him like a cold Atlantic wave, and it made him worry about the real reason Errol had insisted he come home this holiday season.

Jon climbed the three stairs and Errol jabbed him in the ribs with his cane when he reached the landing.

"'Bout time you got here, boy."

"Nice to see you too, Errol," Jon said. He buttoned his wool coat against the bite in the air, a reminder that he was a far cry away from the sunshine state he now called home.

A moment of awkward silence hit as they stood there staring at each other. As Jon looked into Errol's cloudy blue eyes an eerily familiar feeling invaded his gut. Almost seven years ago to the day, when tragedy hit like a hard punch to the stomach, the two had stood on this exact same porch, both staring at one another in much the same manner.

Jon sucked in a breath and blinked against the flood of sadness and loss. He fisted his hands at his sides and valiantly struggled to get himself together. He'd known this home-coming wasn't going to be easy, but there was no way he could tuck tail and run. If Errol needed him, then he was damn well going to be there for him, despite the demons.

Errol finally cut the tension by saying, "Well get on over here and give an old man a hug, will ya?"

Jon bent forward and put his arms around the aging man. As Errol hugged back, Jon once again considered the man's health and couldn't help but worry about the medical care he was receiving at the clinic. It was becoming more and more difficult to get doctors to practice in small towns. Most wanted to be in the big city. Jon was no exception. Well, that wasn't entirely true. When he'd first left for college some twelve years ago, his plan had been to come back and hang his shingle in Whispering Cove, but... Sometimes things change.

After the hug Jon inched back and gave his uncle a good, hard look. Concern washed over him and guilt that he hadn't been overseeing the aging man's health settled in the pit of his stomach like a lump of cold oatmeal. "What happened to your leg, Errol?"

Errol glanced at the sky and snarled as snowflakes fell over the town. "Damned bum leg. Always acts up in the damp weather."

Instantly going into professional mode, Jon asked, "You want me to take a look at it?"

Looking indignant, Errol blurted out, "You wanna look at a leg, look at your own damn leg."

That brought a grin to Jon's face. Despite whatever was going on with Errol, it gave Jon a measure of comfort to see that his great-uncle had remained his spirited, ornery self.

"When was the last time you had blood work done?"

"Blood work?" Errol tapped the inside crook of his elbow. "Only thing running through these veins is rum, my boy. Don't need no doctor poking me with a needle to know that."

When Errol gave him a look that suggested it was time to switch topics, Jon gave a resigned sigh, knowing he wasn't going to get anywhere tonight. Perhaps after they'd both had a good night's sleep he could investigate a little deeper. Maybe even a trip to the clinic tomorrow to look over Errol's health records was in order.

He gestured toward the vehicle. "Let me grab my bag."

Errol poked him with the cane again. "You best not be talking about no medical bag."

With his hands up and palms out Jon said, "Just going for my duffle bag, Errol. Scout's honor."

Errol's bark of laughter carried in the quiet night. "You never were much of a Scout. Always lighting fires and getting into trouble."

Jon laughed in response. "Yeah, well you're one to talk. You and Dad taught me everything I know."

At the mention of his father, silence once again hung heavy. Fighting back a wave of pain, Jon turned from his uncle. "I'll...uh...I'll get my bag."

"Jon."

Errol's somber voice stilled Jon. When Jon angled his head to see his uncle and spotted worry moving into his cloudy eyes, it stopped his breath.

Even though his gut was in turmoil, Jon kept his voice level when he asked, "What is it?"

"Got me some bad news, boy."

Jon stiffened, his pulse leaping in his throat. He didn't visit his uncle often enough, but that didn't mean he didn't care about the man. He did. He cared enough to clear his schedule as fast as he could and head straight to the airport from the hospital first chance he had.

He cleared his throat and wrapped his hands around the paint-chipped rail beside him, gripping it until his knuckles turned white. "What is it, Uncle Errol? Are you ill?"

"I'm fine, boy. Never been better." He paused and gave a mischievous wink. "The rum keeps me young and healthy."

Jon loosened his hold on the rail as his mind raced for answers. Okay, so if Errol was fine—and the jury was still out on that one—and hadn't called him back home for medical reasons, why then had he sounded so anxious on the phone? Why had he been so insistent that Jon drop everything and return to Whispering Cove without delay?

Jon scrubbed his hand over his chin, his mind trying to sort things through. "What's the bad news, Errol?"

"You can't stay with me."

Jon looked past Errol to see into the house. "What are you talking about? I stayed with you three years ago when I visited."

"You call that a visit? You holed up in the bedroom and I barely saw you," Errol scolded and Jon didn't miss the way his uncle had shifted his stance to block Jon's view.

"What's going on?"

"Termites."

"Termites?" Jon shook his head, incredulous. "So let me get this straight, you call me and insist I come home for no apparent reason, and then tell me I have no place to stay?"

"Don't need no reason. Besides, it ain't like I knew I had termites when I called." Jon looked past Errol's shoulders a second time, but Errol straightened to his full height and asked, "You got something to say, boy?"

Jon pinched the bridge of his nose, trying to figure out what the hell was going on, and more importantly where he going to stay for the next few days. He could crash with his cousin, Katy, and her husband, Trent, but with the new baby, he didn't want to interfere. Then there were Katy's parents, Aunt Annette and Uncle Pete, who were in that big old Victorian house all by themselves. They went all out at Christmas, decorating every inch of their place, inside and out. Since his dad and Pete were first cousins, the families had spent a lot of time together when Jon was young. While he loved his relatives dearly, staying at their place over the holidays would simply bring back too many memories.

"Termites?" he asked again. "This time of year?"

"Can't control when them critters are gonna chew their way inside, boy. Those pests have a mind of their own."

Jon exhaled slowly and instead of dwelling on the problem he turned his attention to a solution. "Okay, so where are you staying then?"

Errol offered him another mischievous wink. "Delilah Kean's putting me up."

"Oh." Jon looked two doors down to Mrs. Kean's house, and when he remembered that she was all alone in that big place of hers, her husband having passed away a few years back, his eyes widened. "Oh," he said again, as understanding dawned. Well, good for the old man.

When he glimpsed a twinkle in his great-uncle's eyes, Jon smiled, happy to see that Errol had found love again. Jon, on the other hand, had pretty much buried himself in his work, and while he had the occasional bedmate, most of the women from his social circle were either high maintenance or trying to climb the social ladder—certainly not the kind of girl he'd want to settle down with. Not that he was looking to find love or get married. He wasn't. But if he were, he'd want an easy-going, low-maintenance kind of girl who knew how to let her hair down. Perhaps it was because deep down he was just a small-town boy who liked the simple things in life.

"I was thinking," Errol said, pulling his thoughts back. "Why don't you go stay at Sleepy Cove?"

Jon stiffened and gave a quick shake of his head. "I don't think—"

"That's your problem, boy. You do too much thinking."

"Errol."

"Here are your choices. You come stay with me and Delilah, but them walls are pretty thin and if you value your sleep—"

Jon cringed and held his hands up to cut his uncle off. "Errol, I get it. No need to explain any further."

"So you'll go to Sleepy Cove then?"

As his mind drifted to the Victorian house his folks had bought with the intention of turning into a B&B, an invisible fist squeezed his heart. Thanks to him, they'd never lived to see their dreams to fruition. After the accident, Jon had put the homestead in Errol's hands and asked him to sell it, but Errol swore there were no buyers and instead rented it to Vivian and Doug Osmond, old family friends who eventually went on to fulfill his late parents' dreams of turning it into a B&B.

He hadn't seen the Osmonds in years, and the thought of facing them again and seeing the blame in their eyes, albeit justified blame, was more than he could take.

As if knowing exactly what he was thinking, Errol said, "Vivian and Doug retired. They're spending their winters down south now. Lila Sheppard's renting the place from me now." Errol folded his arms across his chest and balanced on his good leg. "She refurbished the entire inn. Doesn't even look like the same old house anymore."

Jon's head came up with a start. "Who's Lila Sheppard?"

"Just a young'n who came here from Chicago to help Katy with her cooking show. Now she's fulfilling her dream of being a chef in her own bed and breakfast."

"She's renting it?"

"Yeah."

Jon arched a brow. "She's not interested in buying it?"

"Nope."

Jon thought about that for a moment. "So she completely redid the whole place?"

"Yeah, you wouldn't even recognize it now."

Jon glanced over his shoulder and in the far distance he glimpsed the B&B. His gaze went to the widow's peak overlooking the ocean and he noted that the light was still on. He swallowed hard, because he could almost picture his mother in that room. It was a place she'd retreat to and stare out over the ocean as she waited for Jon's father to return from one of his many fishing trips.

Jon turned back to Errol. "Maybe I should just check in with Aunt Annette and Uncle Pete."

"Can't."

"Why not?"

Errol frowned, and poked Jon in the ribs with his cane. "Well, I ain't supposed to say nothing, and you know I'm real good at keeping secrets, but those two have been having some marital troubles. Need time alone to work things out."

Taken aback, Jon stared at his uncle. "Really? I had no idea."

"'Course not. But don't say nothing to no one. I was sworn to secrecy."

Jon nodded. "I understand. I just...I'm just surprised. They always seemed so happy. Is there anything I can do?"

"No, they just need quiet time. I'm sure they'll work it out."

Jon looked out over the snow-covered streets and considered his next course of action. Here it was late at night and he was smack dab in the middle of his childhood town with nowhere to stay. Once again his gaze strayed to Sleepy Cove. If Lila Sheppard had completely refurbished the place, then perhaps it wouldn't be so bad. Maybe it wouldn't evoke childhood memories and remind him of what he'd loved and lost.

"You'd best get your keister on over to Sleepy Cove. It's late and Lila's probably fixin' to lock up." He clucked his tongue. "Besides, Delilah's waitin' and you don't want to keep a catch like her—"

"Okay, Errol." Jon spun on the balls of his feet. He shook his head and grinned. "I really don't need to hear the details." When he reached the SUV he turned. "I'll see you in the morning then?"

Errol winked. "Not too early now."

Grinning at his feisty great-uncle and hoping to get away before he divulged any more details of his relationship with Delilah, Jon hopped back in his vehicle. As the engine turned over, he wondered more about Errol's termite infestation, as well as Pete and Annette's marital troubles. It was true that he hadn't been around in three years, but he'd kept tabs on his friends and family and knew Errol well enough to know that he'd been acting kind of strange. First he'd pleaded with him to come home, only to turn him around and insist he stay at Sleepy Cove, which had Jon wondering... What the hell was his uncle really up to?

$$18$$

Lila Sheppard took one look at the gorgeous man standing on her front porch and wondered if Santa had delivered her Christmas present early. And if so, when could she start unwrapping him?

"You must be Lila," Mr. Gorgeous said, flashing perfect white teeth as his piercing blue eyes met hers.

Lila nodded and instead of politely shaking his hand, she continued to stare at him, her manners completely forgotten. As she took pleasure in his thick, dark hair, fine, chiseled face and well-dressed body, she didn't miss the way his deep, sexy voice played down her spine or the sexual awareness prowling restlessly through her bloodstream.

Fully aware that she was gazing at the hottest guy she'd ever set eyes on, a guy who made her think of sex—wild, steamy, up against the wall kind of sex—Lila continued to gawk at him in frank appreciation.

As her libido kicked into high gear, Mr. Gorgeous stood there watching her in return, like he was waiting for something, but for what she had no idea, considering her brain was preoccupied with other things at the moment.

Looking a bit restless, he shifted on his feet and high overhead the snow fell harder, matting his hair to his head. He brushed it back, but that didn't distract from his good looks one tiny bit. In fact, watching the fat flakes melt on his warm skin and drip down his chiseled face made him look sexy—downright delicious—and had a bevy of fantasies rushing through her salacious mind.

But when he looked past her shoulders and asked, "Do you have any rooms for rent?" she realized just how hard she'd been staring, drooling, hoping her wish to Santa had come true.

"I'm Jon Carver. Errol Wilson sent me. He said you'd have a room."

Ah, so that's what he was waiting for—a room. Disappointment settled in her stomach. Since Errol was no Saint Nick, it meant this man wasn't an early present for her personal enjoyment. Too bad, really, because this stranger was hot enough to melt the ice sculptures in the town square.

Working to tamp down the desire zinging through her veins, and realizing just how long it'd been since she'd crawled between the sheets with a man—clearly the lack of orgasms was playing havoc with her mind—she remembered her manners. Offering him a warm greeting, she widened her door to welcome him into her beloved B&B.

"You bet I do," she said, as she marshaled her libido and gave herself a hard mental shake to get her head on straight. "The place is pretty quiet this time of year."

Jon stopped to rub his wet boots on her doormat, and that small, thoughtful gesture surprised Lila. Not only was he gorgeous, he also had manners, a unique combination indeed. The city boys she knew never concerned themselves with such trivial things—which was one of the reasons she'd left that life behind—and she had to admit, she kind of liked that he cared.

She studied him for another second and that's when she felt a brief moment of recognition. Had she seen him around town before? His name didn't ring a bell, but that didn't mean he wasn't a local. Then again, everything from his expensive leather boots to his wool coat and designer scarf gave the impression that he was a polished city boy. And if he were a local, wouldn't he be staying with family or friends?

Wondering who he was and where he'd come from, she hurried behind the counter to sign him in. But when she looked up and caught the storm brewing in his translucent blue eyes as he perused her front lobby, she thought more about the stranger who studied his surroundings like he was trying to orient himself.

"So what brings you to Whispering Cove?" she asked, more than curious about the gorgeous man who'd landed on her doorstep six days before Christmas.

"Just some things to take care of," he mumbled under his breath, but she didn't miss the melancholy in his voice, nor did she miss the way he quickly blinked the emotion from his bedroom blues.

"I'll be checking out on the twenty-fourth."

"You're not staying for Christmas?" Lila stole a quick glance at his ring finger, only to find it empty. "I guess you must have a family to get back to?" she probed, even though it was none of her business. But Lila never was one to skirt around an issue, and the truth was, this man intrigued her in so many ways.

At the mention of family his entire body stiffened and he swallowed hard before saying a second time, "I just have some things to take care of."

Lila knew some people struggled with the holidays and from his reactions, she could tell he was one of them. But getting to know the people who stayed at her B&B and making them feel warm and welcome, especially this time of year, was important to her. Since he was going to be here for five long days that gave her plenty of time to make him feel special and figure out who he was and what made him tick. He might be a tough nut to crack, but she was up for the challenge. Besides, it wasn't like she had anything else to do. The place had been empty until he arrived, and her folks, two sisters and three brothers weren't flying in until Christmas Eve, which meant she had lots of free time on her hands.

"I'll put you in the Captain's room right at the top of the first landing. It has a great view of the ocean." She paused, wrapped her arms around herself and gave a mock shiver. "Plus it's cool tonight and that room has—"

"A fireplace," he said, finishing her sentence. "I know."

Lila's head came back with a start. "So you've stayed here before?"

"Something like that," he answered.

Angling her head in thought, Lila gave him a once over. "Do I know you?"

"I don't think so."

Lila nibbled on her bottom lip and watched the way his gaze dropped to her mouth. Something passed over his eyes, something that sent a little rush through her blood. Her hand went to her hair, which undoubtedly looked like it had been combed with a blender. As she smoothed the wild curls that had a mind of their own in this damp weather, she glanced at her bedraggled state. Honestly, with an icing-covered apron tied over comfy old yoga pants and a sweatshirt with a flashy Christmas tree on it she undoubtedly looked like a sorry sight to him. A hot guy like Jon, one who was put together very nicely, was probably used to well-dressed, sophisticated women who doused themselves in perfume and makeup.

Getting her thoughts back onto the conversation at hand she said, "I'm sure I've seen you before."

"Have you ever been to Miami?"

Ah, so he wasn't from around these parts after all. Such a shame really, because he was all kinds of yummy. But Lila had sworn off fast-talking city boys with even faster hands. She wanted a small-town guy, one who enjoyed slow-cooked meals and lazy Sunday afternoons. Except, thanks to Errol, Byron and Harold and their matchmaking antics, the single guys were getting snatched up quicker than the catch of the day at the Seafarer restaurant.

"Nope, never been to Miami." She narrowed her eyes. "Have you ever been to Palmer's Hotel in Chicago? I was the sous chef in their restaurant before coming here."

"Can't say as I have."

When he bent to pick up his small duffel bag, Lila handed him his key, and that's when she noticed how cold and tired he looked. "We can do the paperwork in the morning. Breakfast is served between seven and nine. Do you have any allergies that I should know about?"

When he stood back up and his eyes met hers, Lila sucked in a breath. There was something so mesmerizing and hungry in his gaze as it moved over her face that it had her heart racing and her pulse jumping in her throat.

She watched the way his Adam's apple bobbed as he lifted one hand toward her face. Then, as if reconsidering his actions, he quickly pulled it back again. "You...uh...you have...." His voice fell off and he rubbed his hand on his cheek. That's when Lila's palm went to her own.

The second she felt dried icing on her face, she gave a breezy laugh. Okay, so maybe he wasn't looking at her like he wanted to eat her alive. The man was hungry, but it wasn't for *her*, it was for the gingerbread men she'd been baking for tomorrow's Whispering Wonderland skating festivities at the outdoor rink.

"I was baking."

"Is the kitchen still open?"

She hesitated for a second and glanced at the clock. "Yes," she lied. The truth was the kitchen had been closed for hours, but not only did this man look cold, tired *and* famished, Lila loved cooking for others and loved when people appreciated her homemade meals. Plus, with no guests, she'd been a bit lonely lately, and with Christmas just around the corner she was beginning to feel a little homesick.

His brow furrowed as he followed her glance to the clock. "It's late," he said. "I can order in."

Lila laughed at that. "You're in Whispering Cove, not Miami. No one is doing delivery this late."

"Right," he said. "My mistake." When his mouth curved up in a sheepish yet sexy grin, Lila swallowed a breathy moan and didn't miss the way her body trembled with need.

By God, he was good looking.

"I'll make you something."

He raked his fingers through his wet hair, and there was something so boyish, and so vulnerable in his look when he said, "I don't want to put you through any trouble," that it had her thinking about all the trouble she'd like him to put her through.

Okay, she really needed to get herself together. Either that or finally find herself a man to settle down with so she could get her mind off her libido—and off every handsome guest who walked through her door—and on to running her inn.

"It's no trouble at all. Go get yourself settled. I have some leftovers in the fridge. I'll heat them up for you."

Grateful eyes moved over her face and his warm, genuine smile did the strangest things to her. "Thanks. I'll be right back down."

He turned toward the winding staircase. As she watched him go she thought more about the stranger who stirred her restless libido and reminded her she was a woman, a woman who hadn't been with a man in a very long time. But she wasn't just looking for sex, although a little roll between her silk sheets would be nice. No, she wanted long term, because when it came right down to it, she was tired of going to bed alone and, more importantly, waking up alone.

Once he reached the top of the stairwell, Lila pushed those depressing thoughts out of her mind and hurried to the kitchen. She glanced at the countertop full of gingerbread men in need of icing. Stifling a yawn, and knowing she still had hours of work ahead, she pulled the pot of chowder from the fridge, placed it on the stove and returned her attention to her cookies.

The warm gingerbread scent and the recipe that had been handed down from generation to generation had her thinking of her late grandma. Lila missed her dearly, missed the summers she spent in the small Iowa town both her grandma and grandpa had grown up in. Lila's father had moved to Chicago for work when he was young, but his heart always belonged in Iowa.

Lila smiled, remembering how her grandmother swore that small-town boys made the best husbands. Cleary she was on to something, considering she'd been married to the same man for forty years while the divorce rate in Chicago was climbing at an alarming speed. It wasn't easy for Lila to leave her family behind when she'd made the snap decision to move, but she belonged in a small town and wanted to raise a family in a community where everyone cared about each other.

When she'd heard Katy was looking for an assistant for her daytime show, *Cooking with Katy*, she'd packed her bags and headed straight to Whispering Cove. As soon as the previous renters turned the B&B back over to their landlord, Errol, and she saw the chance to run her own kitchen, she made another snap decision and jumped on the opportunity. She had no plans to ever leave the place, and because she was hoping Errol would eventually let her buy, she invested heavily into making it her own.

Lila did a quick count of the cookies and hoped the twelve batches she'd baked would be enough for the party tomorrow. Too bad she hadn't brought her skates to Whispering Cove. She did, however, recall seeing a box full of hockey gear in the shed out back, likely left behind from the previous owners. So what if they were boys' skates. As long as they fit her, she was good to go. Heck, maybe she could find a pair to fit Jon. She had no idea what he was doing in town, or how he knew ornery old Errol, but she'd spotted the tension in his posture earlier. Perhaps an afternoon at the rink would help him unwind and forget about whatever it was that had him so tense this holiday season.

When a Bing Crosby Christmas song came over the radio, Lila punched up the volume and began humming along. She continued to decorate cookies until the delicious scent of savory chowder filled her kitchen. She put down the icing and grabbed a ladle to give it a stir and when she scooped up a big chunk of lobster, it gave her a moment of pause.

Jon never did tell her if he had allergies, which led her to believe he didn't. In her experience people with food sensitivities usually jumped all over that question when she asked, but she still didn't want to take a chance. Honestly, the last thing she wanted to do was serve him shellfish and have him blow up like a balloon. As the only doctor in town, Danica Kent, or rather Danica Mitchell now that she'd taken on her new husband's last name, was always on call, but with the sniffling season here, she was completely run off her feet.

Lila took a look at the clock again and wondered what was taking Jon so long. Deciding to check in on him, and to make sure everything was okay, and confirm he had no allergies before she served him chowder, she turned off the gas, wiped her sticky hands on her apron and hurried up the winding staircase.

She listened outside his door, and her ears met with silence. Could he have fallen asleep? She knocked quietly. "Jon, is everything okay?"

A split second later the door swung open, and when she caught sight of Jon standing before her in nothing but a fluffy towel tied at the waist it was all she could do to drag in a breath.

"I'm okay," he answered.

Oh, he was right about that. Except he was more than *okay*. He was downright perfect.

Desire twisted her insides as her glance moved over him, taking in a long, lean body that instantly filled her libidinous mind with rich, sensual fantasies. As she visualized herself beneath his hardness, her nipples tightened and a shudder moved through her. She sucked in air, a quick breath that filled her nostrils with the heady scent of his freshly showered skin. His rich aroma raced through her bloodstream and had her thighs tingling in a way they'd never tingled before.

"I went to the airport straight from the office and wanted to get out of my work clothes," he added. When she didn't respond he said, "Lila?"

Okay, so she'd never been stunned speechless in her whole life, and while she'd seen naked before, she'd never seen this kind of naked. Heat moved through her as she soaked in the sight of him, and it took all her effort not to throw herself into his arms, to beg him to take her right then and there. From behind his left shoulder she spotted the bed. As she thought about rolling around on the white sheets she'd personally put on his mattress, his towel slipped an inch. But dammit, he managed to grab it seconds before it fell from his hips.

She watched his sculpted muscles ripple and her pulse

beat quicker. Need curled through her and her womb tightened with want as her glance traveled back to his face. The air charged, sexual awareness leaping between them.

Feeling breathless and unable to form a coherent thought, she stared, fully aware of the saliva pooling in her mouth. His skin was dark, sun kissed from the Miami rays, and there was nothing she could do to stop her flesh from moistening.

Jon cleared his throat and broke the quiet, "I didn't mean to keep you waiting."

There was that vulnerable look again, the one that was sweet and sensitive and did the weirdest things to her insides. As her entire body trembled with want, it made it that much more difficult to find her voice.

With her thoughts derailed, she struggled to keep from sounding as shaky as she felt. "Actually, I, uh, I just needed to know if you have any shellfish allergies."

He dipped his head and his voice came out husky, deeper than before, when he said, "Nope. No allergies at all."

"Oh, okay," she mumbled as sparks shot through her body, sizzling all the way to the warm juncture between her legs.

As he leaned against the doorjamb looking like sex incarnate, the heat in his gaze licked over her body. She turned her attention to the water dripping down his well-carved chest, only to get absorbed by the fluffy towel hiding the hard ridge of what looked to be a very well-endowed body part.

Damned if she didn't want to find out.

"Give me a sec. I'll just pull on my jeans and come back down with you."

He turned from her, and when her gaze dropped to his backside, a shiver of anticipation raced across her flesh, because as her glance followed his gorgeous towel-draped ass across the room, Lila instantly decided another snap decision was in order.

Jon Carver might be a fast-food, fast-hands kind of guy,

the kind of guy who likely reached out and touched more women than Hallmark, but her body was telling her to go for it with the sexy city boy who was only going to be around until Christmas Eve. After all, like she once told her friends, sometimes even nice girls need a little down and dirty sex too. Since the holidays were all about overindulging, why shouldn't she indulge a little?

She'd always been told that the way to a man's heart was through his stomach. Did that old saying also apply to getting him naked?

"Hurry up," she said. "We don't want the chowder to get cold."

19

The noises coming from outside his window, combined with the smell of bacon from the kitchen below, pulled Jon from his deep slumber. His joints groaned in protest as he stretched his arms over his head, and when he blinked his eyes open it took a moment to orient himself and figure out where the hell he was. The shrill shriek of laughter cut through the quiet of his room. He pushed off his blankets and quietly padded to his window.

He pulled back the heavy curtains. When he caught the familiar sight of kids sliding down Dresden Bluff at the back of his old homestead, he couldn't help but smile, remembering all the times he and his friends had raced down the icy slope on the wooden sleds Errol and his pals had handed down to them.

He missed the friends he hadn't seen in years. Missed them horribly. But he'd distanced himself on purpose, pretty damn sure they wouldn't want anything more to do with him after the accident.

Burying those painful thoughts, he turned to peruse the room, taking in the soft blue color on the walls, the embers still smoldering in the fireplace and the decorations that made him feel like he was on board a fishing vessel. When Lila had said she was putting him in the Captain's room, she wasn't kidding. Everything about the space captured the true essence of Whispering Cove and the industry that had supported the townsfolk for decades.

Jon was impressed with Lila's creativity, and the touches that made the B&B her own. Errol was right, the place looked completely different from when he was a kid. Then again, he'd never spent much time in this particular room when he was little. Never gave it any thought really. His folks had bought the place when he was ten and since they hadn't planned to turn it into a B&B until after his father had retired from the sea, most of the rooms had been left empty.

The beeping of his cell phone gained his attention and he was thankful for the distraction. He really didn't want to think about being back in his childhood home or how it felt both disturbing and consoling at the same time.

He grabbed the phone off his nightstand and was shocked to find the message was from Great-Uncle Errol. Okay, so when had Errol stepped into the twenty-first century and learned to text? Jon gave a slow shake of his head, realizing that a lot of things had changed since he'd been home three years ago. But when the shrieks outside once again filled his room, it gave him a measure of comfort to know that some things hadn't.

Worried that Errol might need him for medical reasons, Jon opened the message and read it. He frowned, and after reading it a second time, he couldn't help but feel his uncle was avoiding him. It was just last week that Errol had called and urged him to come home. While Jon had hoped to spend the day with his great-uncle, to find out what was really going on with him, Errol clearly had other plans, ones that didn't involve him.

Wanting to get to the bottom of matters, Jon grabbed a pair of jeans from his bag and tugged them on. When he opened his door, he was accosted with Christmas music and savory smells. Lila was down there making him breakfast, but she'd fed him so much chowder, rolls and gingerbread cookies last night that his stomach felt like it was swollen to three times its normal size.

It was easy to see that Lila was at home in the kitchen and took pleasure in feeding others. After surviving on take out for the last decade, Jon planned to take advantage of her culinary skills and enjoy everything she had to offer. Although if he continued to gorge on her scrumptious homemade food, he'd be able to fill out Santa's suit at the Christmas Eve children's parade without the use of added padding. Not that he planned to go to the parade, or still be in Whispering Cove on the twenty-fourth. He didn't deserve to celebrate with friends and family on the night he'd lost those closest to him, considering he was the one responsible for their deaths.

Another laugh outside his window prompted him into action, and he stole a quick glance at his bedside clock. Surprised to find that he'd slept in so late, he shoved the phone into his front pocket and tugged on a T-shirt. When he reached the winding staircase, he considered sliding down it for old time's sake but quickly changed his mind.

The lamps had been dimmed last night, but the morning sunshine streaming in through the big bay window gave sufficient light for him to see that Lila had decorated every square inch of the main living space. There were no stockings hung on the mantle, and he could only assume she was waiting until Christmas Eve when her family came—something he learned while chatting with her over his late-night meal—but no one could ever accuse Lila of lacking in holiday spirit.

The smell of pine from the huge tree filled his nostrils. He pulled it in and turned his attention to the pictures decorating her walls. His heart squeezed as he looked at all her photos. Clearly family was important to her, which made him wonder why Lila had moved so far away from them.

He made his way to the kitchen and opened his mouth to greet her, but when he noticed her singing and swaying that gorgeous body of hers to an upbeat Christmas song, his words died an abrupt death. Okay, so there was no denying that he'd *noticed* her last night. Noticed how she made yoga pants and a sweatshirt look damn good, how she smelled like sugar and spice and all things nice, and how that pink frosting on her face had made her look so adorable that it was all he could do not to draw her into his arms and lick it off. Talk about the proverbial icing on the cake.

What he noticed this morning, however, was that she looked warm, mussed and so incredibly sexy as she stood over the stove singing off-key, that it had his body reacting in a primal way. He drove his hands into his pockets to adjust his jeans, which suddenly felt too tight around the zipper area.

He leaned against the doorjamb. Even though the holidays brought nothing but bad memories for him, there was little he could do to wipe the stupid grin off his face.

Dark curls fell down her back in a tousled mess as she bobbed her head to the beat, and she didn't need to look his way for him to know that her honey brown eyes would be filled with life and laughter. This morning she was dressed in a pair of snug jeans that accentuated her perfect heart-shaped ass, and a pink blouse that highlighted her slim waist and looked soft and sensual beneath her curls. It occurred to him that it didn't matter what she wore. She could make a potato sack look sexy.

Even though he hadn't spent much time with her, he could tell she was honest and open, completely lacking in artifice, so unlike the women he knew. In fact, the women he knew wouldn't be caught dead in the kitchen, let alone an apron. He also got the sense that she was completely oblivious to her sensuality and to how she affected him on a primitive level. Not that he was going to show her or act on his impulses. He was here to tend to his great-uncle. That was his one and only priority. Once he was sure the old man was getting the medical attention he needed, he planned to get the hell out of Dodge.

She angled her head and her big brown eyes lit up like a Christmas tree when she spotted him, and oddly enough it gave his heart a little jolt. Then she puckered her lips and planted her hands on her slim waist.

"You're late," she admonished.

Jon pushed off the doorframe and took a step toward her. "I'm sorry. I never sleep that late."

Lila crinkled her cute little nose and nodded like she completely understood. "It's the fresh ocean air here. Knocks you right out. Plus you looked pretty worn out last night." Balancing a plate full of bacon, eggs, hash browns and toast in her palm, she turned toward him and everything from her easygoing nature to her warm, inviting, laid back look, had his breath catching and a riot of foreign emotions racing through him. "But I'll forgive you this time."

Even though he still had no appetite, his stomach took that moment to grumble, although he was beginning to wonder if the hunger prowling through him was for her food or because he wanted to feast on something else entirely.

Christ, hadn't he just lectured himself on staying away from her?

Jon examined the pots and pans on the stove. "You didn't have to go through all this trouble. Not for me."

"No trouble at all," she announced, then turned toward the room just off the kitchen. That's when he noticed the dining room table—his mother's old table—beautifully set for one. It touched him that Lila liked the table enough to keep it when she'd redone so much of the place. In fact, as he looked around now, taking in the gingham curtains, the antique pottery in her china cabinet and the rugs covering the hard wood floors, it occurred to him that she'd kept quite a few of his mother's belongings.

He grabbed one of the two stools tucked under the island and asked, "Is it okay if I just sit here again?"

"Oh, sure." She pushed his plate toward him, filled his coffee cup and grabbed another set of utensils from the drawer. After she handed them to him, she went back to humming and started packing cookies into a big plastic container.

Jon looked at the plate then back at Lila. Catching him by surprise, a sharp pang of loneliness cut through his heart like a serrated knife. Before he could think better of it, he asked, "Aren't you going to join me?"

She gave him an odd look. "I already had my breakfast."

"Oh."

"What?"

"Nothing," he said, feeling a bit foolish. Cloaking his disappointment, his glance moved over the woman before him. Even though he'd just met her, she had the uncanny ability to make him feel all peculiar inside. Oddly enough, watching her prepare his food had him thinking about all the meals he'd eaten alone over the years. Dining solo had never bothered him before, never made him think about how alone he really felt in Miami, so why then, was he suddenly so aware of it now?

Heck, maybe he was just feeling sentimental because he was back in his childhood hometown, or perhaps the peculiar feeling in his gut was a matter of indigestion from overindulging last evening.

Needing to get his mind on something else, he took a slug

from his coffee cup and asked, "What are you doing with all those cookies?"

A smile lit up her pretty face. "It's the Whispering Wonderland skating party today. Everyone is going to be there. You should come."

Jon frowned. "I don't think so." He actually preferred to keep a low profile when in town. Errol was right, when he came home three years ago, he'd pretty much holed up in Errol's back bedroom.

"Why not? You have something else to do?"

Jon arched a brow. "Are you always this forward?"

"Yes," she answered. Refusing to let him off easy she asked again. "So, do you have something else to do?"

"As a matter of fact I do," he answered, thinking how he'd planned to spend the day with Errol, only to get a text saying he wasn't going to be around because he'd be too busy helping out at the skating party. But if Errol was occupied, then it would make getting to the clinic to read over his records that much easier.

"Is Danica running the clinic?" he asked before tossing a piece of bacon into his mouth.

Lila gave him a concerned look. She bent forward to put her palm on his forehead, then ran her hands along his cheeks. While the position afforded him a view of her cleavage, he tried not to look, but more importantly, he tried not to choke on his bacon.

"No fever. Are you sick?"

As her silky soft fingers caressed his face, the warmth of her touch went right through him. "No," he answered, as every muscle in his body tightened. "I was just wondering."

She pulled her hand away and her face relaxed. "Actually, she's the *only* one running the clinic." She looked at Jon's plate. "Need more bacon?"

Jon swallowed and shook his head no. "You're kidding me? She's the only doctor in town?"

Lila nodded. "Yup, and she's pretty much run off her feet these days."

Could that be why Errol had asked him to come home, to help out at the clinic?

"So you know Dani?" she asked.

Jon nodded, his mind going to all the friends he'd grown up with. Most of them were married with kids now. In fact there seemed to be a baby boom going on in Whispering Cove.

Jon swallowed the last of his coffee and stood to get another cup, but Lila took it from him. "I'll get that for you."

"You don't have to wait on me."

"It's no trouble. Besides, I need a favor."

"Ah, so that's it," he teased. "Tit for tat."

The second the words left his mouth, he tried to snatch them back, because as they hovered over them like a loaded weapon he realized just how sexual they sounded. "Wait," he rushed out. "I mean, you scratch my back I'll scratch yours." He groaned inwardly. "No...I mean..." Shit.

Lila grinned at him, a soft, seductive smile that turned him inside out. Her fingers went to the top button on her blouse, and as Jon watched the sexy movement his cock thickened in his unforgiving jeans. As she toyed with the little white button, popping it in and out of the hole in a manner that had his thoughts careening in an erotic direction, her look was warm, playful, drawing him into a place he swore he wasn't going to go. Lila was a nice girl, and he was the last person she needed to get mixed up with.

But then, in a sensual voice that had him thinking about naked bodies, and hot, uninhibited sex, she asked, "Do you have an itch you need scratched, Jon?"

"I mean..." Less than five minutes ago he'd said he was going to enjoy everything Lila had to offer, but now he was suddenly wondering exactly what it was she was offering. Not that it mattered. He was in town to take care of Errol, not flirt with or take advantage of Lila, no matter how much he'd like to get her naked and have his way with her. Besides, even with the way she gawked at his near nakedness last night—yes, he'd noticed *and* he'd felt the pull every bit as much as she did—he didn't take Lila for the kind of woman who indulged in brief affairs.

The woman was settled down and running her own B&B, which meant she was most likely a forever kind of girl. Right now a brief roll between the sheets was all he could offer. And he wasn't even sure about that. On some level he knew that a night with a sweet girl like her just might have him wanting things he didn't deserve.

"I mean," he tried again, but when she grabbed the carafe and refilled his cup, her sexy body crowding his, he shoved another slice of bacon into his mouth before he said something else he just might regret.

As sexual energy arced between them, Jon scarfed down the rest of his food. Averting his gaze, he finally broke the silence by asking, "What did you need, Lila?"

"Well," she began, her voice like a rough caress over his flesh. "There is a box full of skates in the shed. They're up high with lots of other boxes packed around them. I was hoping you could lend me a hand to get them down."

Jon jumped up, dumped his scraps into the garbage disposal, then put his plate in the dishwasher. "How about I just get them for you?"

"You don't know where they are."

"I'll find them." Before she could voice an argument, he left the kitchen, needing a moment of reprieve from the sexy woman with a body made for sin. After grabbing his coat and boots, he made his way out to the backyard but not even the brisk winter air could help cool down his overheated body.

He trudged through the deep snow and as soon as he pulled open the double doors to the woodshed, his heart lodged in his throat and a bevy of memories shook him to the core. A cold morning breeze rushed around him and the sound of the kids on the hill in the distance faded to a distant buzz as his glance went to the long abandoned mini bike propped up in the corner, like it was waiting for a new owner, a new kid to play with. He swallowed and looked at all the boxes. Had his parents kept *every* single toy from his childhood?

Steeling himself against the flood of emotions, his glance went to the carvings on the inside wall and when he saw JC+TT he couldn't help but smile. Good God, he'd had such a huge crush on Tabby Taylor when he was fourteen that he'd carved their initials into the wood. But he never did ask her out. Her older brother, Devon, was enough to scare any kid straight. As a barrage of old, happy memories swamped him, he ran his finger along the carving. He'd heard Tabby and Reece McGrath had hooked up. He grinned, wondering how that had played out, seeing as how Devon and Reece were best friends and all.

Snow crunched behind him and pulled his attention. He spun around to see Lila tromping toward him.

"I didn't expect you to do this alone," she said, her coat swinging wide open as she glanced at the carved letters he'd been mulling over.

Jon watched her approach and when she stopped just outside the door, he saw the pink flush on her cheeks and took note of the way her teeth were chattering.

He grabbed her by the shoulders and hauled her inside. "You're going to catch your death of cold out here, Lila. And like you said, Dani is busy enough as it is." He fastened her zipper, then pulled it all the way to her chin.

Lila angled her head and gave him an odd look.

"What?" he asked.

"You sound like Errol. I've heard him use those exact words on the kids around town."

Jon's thoughts traveled to his great-aunt Margaret, Errol's late wife. It was originally her turn of phrase, but Jon kept that information to himself.

"And besides," Lila added, tilting her chin in stubborn determination. "You can't get sick from the cold weather. It's an old wives' tale."

"Oh, and who are these old wives you've been talking to?"

"It's just something folks tell kids to get them to bundle up."

"Well," Jon began, when he suddenly noticed how close he was standing to Lila, how her fragrant scent was seeping under his skin and making him wonder if she'd taste as good as she smelled. While he somehow knew she would, that didn't stop his body from urging him to take a nibble, to lick a path down her body until he found the spot that tasted the sweetest. Jon gave a hard shake of his head and struggled to keep his thoughts focused, a difficult task considering they way Lila continued to crowd him, her lush body practically crushed against his. "It just so happens that those old wives know a thing or two."

She tipped her head to look into his eyes. "Really? Do tell."

Jon fished his leather gloves out of his pocket and put them over her small hands. As skin brushed skin, sexual longing pulled at him. Okay, so he swore he was going to keep his distance, but everything about her urged him to throw caution to the wind, to indulge in the beautiful woman and sate his sexual needs before he left town.

"You see, when you get cold, it can affect your immune system and when you're in a weakened state you're less able to fight off the viruses that cause colds."

She lifted her chin higher, and as Jon studied the small but fiercely independent woman before him, he suspected she was completely unaware of her allure, even when her lips were turning blue. "And you know this how?" she challenged.

He smiled at her. "I just do."

She planted her hands on her hips then suddenly those pretty amber eyes widened like she just had an epiphany. "So that's how you know Dani. You're a doctor."

Even though it was a statement, not a question, he answered with, "Something like that."

Lila shook her head, her wild curls flaring around her face. "You really don't like talking about yourself do you?" But before he could answer she said, "Wait! Are you here to help out at the clinic? Because you know this town can really use the help." She clapped her gloved hands together. "The townsfolk will be so thrilled to find out we're getting another doctor."

"I'm leaving on the twenty-fourth," he reminded her.

Lila puckered her lips and cast her eyes downward. "Oh, I just thought—"

Feeling like he'd been sucker punched, and instantly hating himself for disappointing her, he said, "Well, I supposed I can check in with her. Maybe I can help lighten her load while I'm here."

Her brow furrowed. "If you're not our new doctor, then what brought you to Whispering Cove this time of year?"

Jon should have expected the question. After all, she wasn't the kind of girl who held her punches. Whispering Cove was a small town and it wouldn't be long before she found out that nearly seven years ago to the day he was the young resident doctor at Miami General, the one who'd been too busy, too caught up in his career and big-city life to come home to family and friends. He'd forgotten what matter mattered to him—family, friends, helping others—and because of it his parents had died on Christmas Eve during a surprise visit. Their deaths reminded him of who he was, what was important, and what he truly held close, but by then it was too late. They were gone. Because of him. Once Lila found out that his actions had ultimately resulted in their deaths, she'd likely join those who rightfully looked at him with blame.

"I just have some things to take care of," he said, giving her his usual answer.

She shrugged like it was nothing, but he didn't miss the hurt in her eyes. "It's fine. You don't have to tell me. It's none of my business, anyway." She gazed past his shoulder, her glance once again passing over the initials carved into the wood. He could almost hear the wheels spinning, her curious mind trying to put together the pieces and figure out exactly who he was and what he was doing in town.

Even though he was glad she hadn't pressed, he still felt like a world-class prick for brushing off her question. "Lila, wait. It's not like that. I just don't want to get into it."

"It's okay, Jon, really." She stole a glance at her watch. "I'd better get those skates and get going. I told Errol I'd help with the set-up and if I don't deliver those cookies on time, I'll have a horde of hungry kids on my hands." She perused the shelf and redirected the conversation. "Now, where did I put those skates?"

Jon spun around and looked at the boxes lining the shelves. When he spotted one marked skates, he pointed and tried to lighten her mood by saying, "My guess is in that box."

Lila grinned. "Good call." With that she pushed past him and when her sweet scent flared around him, he pulled it into his lungs. Grabbing a ladder, she balanced it against the shelf and climbed up two steps. She reached up and tried to shimmy the box free.

A rush of tenderness moved through him as he watched her struggle. There was something about her independence that brought out the protector in him and had him yearning to do things for her.

Maybe it was the doctor in him wanting to help others, or maybe it was the man in him who simply wanted her. Either way, she threw him off his game and had him feeling things —*wanting things*—he didn't deserve to have.

He stepped up behind her and pressed his chest to her back. His voice came out a little rough, a little raspy when he said, "I can get that, Lila."

Her body stiffened against his, and a wave of lust curled around him as he helped her free the box from the shelf. Jon took the bulk of the weight as he placed it on the floor at the foot of the ladder.

Lila stepped down and sounded a little breathless when she dropped to one knee and said, "You sure you don't want to come?" She held up a pair of his old skates and said, "These look like they would fit you."

As Jon saw the bright-eyed enthusiasm in her gaze and noted the flare of desire as she looked up at him, he suddenly wasn't sure what he wanted anymore. He twisted around and as his breath turned to fog he recalled the days when he wouldn't have dreamed of missing the Whispering Wonderland skating festival. He could almost taste the creamy marshmallow hot chocolate, hear the music and laughter, and see the smiles on everyone's faces as they gathered around the ice and shared outrageous stories from their fishing season.

But he didn't belong there. Not anymore.

"I don't think it's a good idea," he said, his eyes going to Lila's snow-covered car, to her bald tires specifically. He spun to face her, his heart pounding a little harder in his chest.

"Lila, you're not planning on driving to the skating oval are you?"

"Yeah, why?"

"You can't go anywhere on those tires."

She crinkled her nose. "I know. They're a little bald. Winter tires just weren't in the budget this year."

"A little bald? Errol is a little bald, Lila. Those tires are a death trap."

She gave an apologetic shrug. "I usually walk everywhere."

"Well, you can't walk today. It's freezing out and the roads are icy."

She exhaled slowly, like she was mulling his concerns over. Then she blinked up at him and said, "I'll drive slow."

Jon gave a hard shake of his head. "No, you won't."

She waved her hands in the air, and one of his gloves went flying. "I just made one hundred and forty-four cookies, so if you think I'm—"

"I'll drive you."

Her head came back with a start, and there was something so warm and honest in her eyes that it had his heart racing. "You will?"

"Yeah, that car isn't going anywhere until you get a set of winter tires."

"That might not be until spring. I've been saving for other things."

"They won't do you any good in the spring." He grabbed a pair of skates from the box. "Come on. I'll take you."

He stepped out of the shed and when he realized she hadn't followed he turned to see her. That's when he noticed the smile on her face and the way her inquisitive eyes were studying him darkly.

Uncomfortable under her scrutiny, he angled his head and asked, "Why are you looking at me like that?"

Her grin was slow, sexy, heating his blood from simmer to inferno. "Because you don't strike me as a big city doctor."

"Well, I hate to disappoint—"

"I never said I was disappointed."

As Jon looked at the gorgeous, laid back woman staring up at him, he took in the pretty pink flush on her face, the seductive way her amber eyes moved over him and the way she made a bulky winter coat look hotter than skimpy lingerie. He took a moment to think about all the things he said he wasn't going to do while he was home, mainly getting her naked and having his way with her. Yet here he was realigning his priorities and going to a skating party he hadn't planned on attending, partly because of her bald tires and partly because she asked him to.

Which begged the question, what else would he do if she asked?

20

Lila knew there was a lot more to this man then met the eye. He might live in Miami, but she didn't get a city vibe from him at all. She stole a sideways glance at him as he drove his vehicle through town. It occurred to her that he knew his way around without her guidance, which once again had her wondering who he was and why he seemed so familiar. He might not be willing to divulge information about himself, but that didn't mean she couldn't do a little snooping of her own.

When they reached the skating oval, Jon slammed the SUV into park. She didn't miss the tension in his posture as he watched the townsfolk all come together on the manmade rink smack dab in the center of town square.

Emotions passed over his eyes as he perused the dozen or so ice sculptures near the monument honoring all the fishermen lost at sea. "Who won the sculpting contest?"

"Mr. Henningar." She pulled a face and looked at the kids running around in the gazebo that Hauk built for last year's fall festival. "That man wins everything."

Jon grinned. "I take it he's still growing the biggest pumpkins?"

Okay, so he clearly knew a lot about the place, which meant he either visited often or he really was from around these parts. But if he was from around here, why wasn't he staying with family or friends? "Yeah, I think he has them on steroids."

They shared a laugh. When two kids ran in front of his vehicle, racing toward the rink at breakneck speed, Jon pulled the keys from the ignition and went eerily quiet.

"Hey, you okay?" Lila asked.

He smiled but she could tell it was forced. "Yeah, I'm fine." He cracked open his door. "We'd better deliver those cookies. Obviously the kids aren't hyped up enough as it is."

She gave him a playful whack. "Hey, it's Christmas. In my book that means we get to indulge guilt-free." When he cast a glance her way and she spotted heat in his eyes, the air around them charged. She wet her dry lips and his scorching glance dropped to her mouth. "Don't you agree, Jon?"

Before he could answer, Errol was at her door tapping his cane on her window. "What's taking so long, lassie?"

She rolled her eyes, cursing Errol for his bad timing, because she really, really wanted to hear Jon's answer. "Someone ought to take that cane away from him. I don't think he needs it, anyway. He just likes the power it gives him."

With the intimacy between them severed, Jon asked, "How well do you know Errol?"

"He's my landlord," she supplied. "And the most cantankerous old man in town." She paused, then added, "But underneath all the crustiness he's a pretty good guy." She grinned. "I like him a lot. Of course, I'd like him more without the cane." Seeing an opportunity to learn more about Jon, she asked, "How do you know Errol?"

Instead of answering, he asked. "What makes you think he doesn't need the cane?"

"Rumor has it that he took to using it a few years ago when he was trying to convince Katy—" Before she could finish, Errol gave another hard tap on the window.

"What's the hold up? Got a bunch of screaming kids on my hands. Get your damn keisters out here and start handing out them gingerbread cookies." Even though his words were harsh, he still had that same old twinkle in his eyes.

"See what I mean," she said, laughing. "Cantankerous."

Exasperated, Lila climbed from the vehicle, tossed her skates over her shoulder and grabbed the plastic container full of cookies from the back seat. "Okay, okay, Errol. Don't get your cane in a knot." With that, she carried them toward the table, then turned to say something to Jon only to realize he wasn't behind her.

He was speaking with Errol, and she had no idea what he was saying, but whatever it was it seemed to brighten the twinkle in the old man's eyes. It still didn't stop him from poking Jon in the ribs with his splintering cane. Lila laughed at them but when Byron and Harold moved in beside Errol and blocked her view she turned her attention to her surroundings, soaking in the festive sights of the beloved town she now called home.

As the familiar sounds and smells of the winter carnival curled around her, happiness welled up inside her and had her looking forward to hanging stockings and reuniting with her family on Christmas Eve. But memories of family had her thinking more about Jon. Where did he have to rush off to on Christmas Eve?

She set her container down next to the huge, five-gallon thermos dispenser. If Jon thought the kids were hyped up now, wait until after they'd polished off all the marshmallows and hot chocolate sloshing around inside that jug.

Tabby stepped up to her. Eyes full of curiosity, her friend rubbed her small baby bump and asked, "Is that who I think it is?"

"First you'll have to tell me who you think it is?" Lila teased.

"Jon Carver."

"You guessed it. He's staying at the inn."

Tabby's jaw dropped. "You're kidding me."

At Tabby's strange reaction, Lila arched an inquisitive brow and probed, "Why would I be kidding you?"

"I just... I never..."

They both turned and when Jon spotted her talking to Tabby, something moved over his face, an emotion she couldn't quite identify. Swallowing the uneasy feeling closing in on her, she looked back at Tabby.

"How do you know him?" As soon as the question left her mouth, she could feel Jon's tension reaching out to her, confusing her feelings in the most bizarre way. While it was in her nature to be open and honest, it suddenly felt so wrong to be prying into his personal life. He valued his privacy, that much she knew, and everything in her gut told her she should respect that.

Tabby went quiet for a moment, then said, "We, uh. We knew each other growing up."

So he *was* from Whispering Cove. "Are you going to say hello?"

When Lila spotted Katy's husband, Trent Parker, and his best friend, Adam Collins, both firefighters at the local station, step up to Jon and the others, Tabby inched away. "I'm not sure he'd want me to." She frowned. "He blames... thinks we blame... I mean...after the... Well, he kind of distanced himself a few years ago."

As Lila wondered about the secrets Jon held close, a few kids came skating up to the table and before long she was lost in the chaos known as the Whispering Wonderland festival, handing out cookies to animated kids and parents alike.

Even though she was busy, chatting easily to all those who made their way to her, she was still fully aware of Jon, fully aware of the way he stood back from the crowd, his eyes mainly on her. Despite his distance it didn't stop the towns-folk from greeting him with open arms. Every now and then she'd glance his way, only to find him looking at her in return. The strange way he watched her made her feel edgy, restless, hyper aware of her body and the way it was reacting to the guy who, for some unknown reason removed himself from those who obviously cared about him, and by the looks of things, still did.

The local veterinarian, Jacob Collins, Adam's brother, came skating up to her table and poured himself a hot choco-late. "Hey, Lila," he said as she handed him a cookie. He took a bite and moaned in frank appreciation. "You know, it's been said that the way to a man's heart is through his stomach, and if you keep feeding me the way you do, I just might fall in love with you."

Lila laughed out loud and Jacob gave her one of his infa-mous grins, the same grin that had the girls around town shedding their panties. Jacob was her neighbor and often came over for breakfast at her B&B, which made him feel more like a brother to her than anything else. She really liked him, loved the way he cared for animals, which in her book proved he was a great guy. But even though he was a great guy, he wasn't the settling down type. He had a bevy of women following him around, and love was the last thing he wanted to fall in to.

"I'm not too worried about that," she said. When he pulled a twig of mistletoe out of his back pocket and held it over her head, she leaned forward to give him a peck on the cheek. Except Jacob had other plans. He turned his head and planted a hot kiss on her mouth.

Lila wiped cookie crumbs from her lips and rolled her eyes at his mischievousness. Even though there was no sexual chemistry between them it never stopped Jacob from flirting. Lila pulled a disgruntled face. "I guess I should have seen that coming."

"What, you didn't like it?"

Teasing, she said, "No, I loved it, Jacob. No one gives cookie kisses quite like you do."

"I can do better," he whispered, his voice holding all kinds of promises.

"Not with me you can't."

"Oh you know you love me."

"Of course I do." Lila angled her head and a wave of heat moved over her when she spotted Jon watching the exchange.

"So I see you have a guest for the holidays," Jacob said, the teasing gone from his voice.

She turned back to Jacob. "Yeah, do you know Jon?"

He nodded. "Not well. When we were kids he was friends with Adam. He left for college years ago and never came back." He lowered his voice and almost to himself he murmured, "He's too hard on himself." He shook his head. "Thinks we blame him," he added, and Lila guessed he assumed she knew what he was talking about.

Lila instantly thought about how Tabby had also mentioned something about blame, but before she could probe, Jacob redirected the conversation and asked, "So, are you going to take a break and come skating with me?"

She looked at the small stack of cookies still left in the container, then spotted Errol coming her way. She gave another eye roll. "If I leave my post now, Errol—"

Errol narrowed his eyes. "Errol will what?" he asked, his voice rough and crusty.

As if expecting a poke in the ribs, Jacob drove his hands into his coat pockets and skated backward a few feet. "I was just asking Lila if she wanted to go skating but she said she has to man her post."

Errol pointed his cane at Lila and waved her away. "Go on, go skate, lassie. I'll give out the rest of the cookies."

She grinned and gave Errol a kiss on the cheek. "Thanks, Errol."

Errol grumbled something under his breath as she bent down to grab her skates but when she stood up, electricity zinged through her body and she didn't have to turn around to know Jon was standing behind her.

He put his mouth close to her ear and his warm breath elicited a shiver from deep within. "I have to go," he whispered

Swallowing, and without turning to face him she said, "But you didn't even get a chance to skate." She really was hoping some time on the rink would help relax him.

"Maybe later," he said. "Right now I have to check in with Dani at the clinic."

Lila turned to face him and found him close. "Oh, okay. I'll see you back at the inn later then."

He shook his head. "No, I'll be back to get you."

Jacob came skating back up to her table. "I can drive her home. She lives right beside me."

Lila didn't miss the flare in Jon's nostrils as he lifted his head. "Jacob," he greeted. "It's nice to see you again. How are you?"

"I'm good. It's nice to see you too, Jon." If Lila wasn't mistaken she was certain she spotted real sadness in Jacob's eyes as he greeted Jon, but she also saw real concern. What the heck was going on with Jon and the people in this town? Why had he distanced himself?

Jon looked back at her. "Wait for me, okay?"

When she agreed, Jon nodded to both Jacob and Errol, then cut across the town square to make his way back to his vehicle. But it wasn't a quick trip to the SUV. Every few seconds he was stopped by folks wanting to talk, to hug even. Once he finally reached his vehicle, Lila tugged on her skates and joined the others on the rink.

She soon lost herself in the fun and before she knew it the afternoon hours had passed. Over the course of the day, she'd spoken to many people who all seemed surprised to hear Jon was staying at the inn. But the conversation never went any further than that. No one wanted to talk about Jon, which was odd, considering gossip spread quicker than the sniffles in Whispering Cove. But it occurred to her that they considered him one of their own, and in this small coastal village, the townsfolk went to great lengths to protect and care for their own, which was one of the things she loved most about the place.

As the crowd parted and the sun set, everyone began making their way home for dinner. Lila packed up her container and wondered what was taking Jon so long. Deciding to walk to the clinic to meet him, she tossed her skates over her shoulders. With night approaching, the air had turned chilly, but the clinic was only a few blocks away.

Hurrying her steps through the snowplowed sidewalks, she rushed to the clinic and saw three vehicles parked outside. When she realized one was Katy's she frowned, hoping Katy's daughter, Katherine, wasn't sick. Lila pulled open the door and crinkled her nose against the scent of antiseptic.

"Hello," she called out quietly. "Anyone here?"

Her call was met with silence, so she wandered into the waiting area. When she heard voices coming from the back of the clinic and saw a light on in the examination room, she tiptoed quietly down the hall in search of Jon.

She stopped outside the open door and when she looked in and spotted Jon with little Katherine in his arms, air rushed from her lungs in a whoosh. There was something so lost, so sad and so damn vulnerable in his eyes as he cuddled the baby girl that it had her heart squeezing to the point of pain. It also had her thinking about how much she wanted a family of her own—a baby and husband to help fill that big old house with love and laughter.

But as she looked at Jon, it wasn't only her body that was growing needy, aching for something far more intimate from him. Lila swallowed and wondered if she should re-evaluate her snap decision to seduce him, because it never occurred to her that she could actually fall for him. And even though he really was from around these parts falling for him would be a colossal mistake. He was only here for a few days, and while there was no denying that there was an attraction between them, he seemed less than interested in acting on it.

As if sensing her presence Jon looked up. When his glance met hers, it took the wind right out of her. "Lila," he said, his voice soft, the emotions in his eyes so incredibly raw as they met hers it had both her legs and her heart wobbling. She locked knees to keep herself standing, but there was nothing she could do to stabilize her heart.

Rattled she began to back up. "I'm sorry. I didn't mean... I was just... I thought..."

"Lila, come in," Katy said, jumping from the chair facing Jon. Lila had been so caught up in watching Jon interact with Katherine that she hadn't even noticed Katy sitting there.

When Katherine coughed, Lila looked at her. "Is Katherine okay?"

"She's going to be just fine," Jon said, his professional demeanor back in place. "A little bronchial infection that we're going to take care of right away. She'll be as good as new on Christmas Day." He handed a wiggling Katherine back to Katy and turned his attention to writing out a prescription.

Just then, Dani came out of her office and moved down the hall toward them. "Lila," she greeted. "I was just about to call you and see if we're still on for the craft bazaar tomorrow?"

Lila nodded eagerly. "I'd love to, but I know how busy you are so I wasn't sure you could get away."

She gave Jon a wide grin. "Jon said he'd be happy to help me out while he was here and I really appreciate the break so I can spend more time with Braydon and Ashton." As Lila thought about baby Ashton and how fast he was growing, Dani turned to Jon and folded her arms in thought. "Now if there was only some way I could convince him to stay for good."

Jon stood and moved in beside Lila. Instead of responding to Dani's not so subtle hint about keeping him in Whispering Cove, he dipped his head. "Sorry about taking so long."

"I don't mind at all. I'm glad you could help out here."

"There is one more thing I need to do, then I'll drive you home, okay?"

After Lila nodded, he looked at Dani and said, "Can I speak to you for a moment?"

Before the two of them disappeared into Dani's office, leaving her with her good friend, Katy, Dani called out, "I'll swing by and pick you up around two tomorrow."

"See you then." Lila turned her attention to Katy. "Here, let me help you." She reached out and helped Katy bundle Katherine in a pretty pink snowsuit. "Are you going to be able to join us tomorrow?"

She nodded. "I'm hoping to get some more blown glass items from Tempest Sky. Her work is beautiful."

"I'd like to grab a few things for the B&B too."

As they retraced their steps back to the lobby, Katy

looked at her hesitantly and said, "Jon mentioned that he'd be leaving on Christmas Eve."

"Yeah, he's in a big rush to get back to Miami," she answered, wanting to ask what her friend knew about Jon, but feeling a bit torn about prying.

"That's too bad. I hate to see him spend Christmas Day alone."

"He's really going back to Miami to be alone?" Katy nodded, and Lila touched her friend's shoulder to stop her. When Katy turned to face her, she couldn't help but ask, "What is he running away from, Katy?"

"Something that happened a long time ago," Katy supplied, but before she could elaborate, they heard Jon's footsteps in the hall. Katy leaned in and whispered, "I sure wish he'd stay. Maybe if he had a reason to..." Leaving that statement lingering in the air, Katy pushed open the front door, and said, "See you tomorrow."

As Lila thought more about the man who was kind and sensitive, a man who looked so lost and wounded that it made her heart ache, she wondered exactly what it would take to get him to stay in Whispering Cove, a place where he obviously belonged.

21

Jon drove his truck through town and stole a sideways glance at the woman beside him, noting that she was unusually quiet as he drove her home. Considering she was the chattiest girl he knew—a quality he'd never found endearing until her—he could only assume she had something on her mind.

"You okay?" he asked.

When she offered him a smile, the same playful grin she'd given Jacob, he felt a weird tightening inside him. What was it about this woman that had him feeling things he didn't want to feel?

She stifled a yawn. "I think all the fresh air made me tired."

Jon flicked on his signal and carefully negotiated the slick street as he turned toward the B&B. "I'm sorry about keeping you waiting for so long."

"It was no trouble at all."

He smiled.

"What?"

"Nothing ever gives you trouble, does it?"

"I guess I'm just an easygoing kind of girl." She gave a breezy laugh and added, "Either that or I'm very simple."

"You're far from simple, Lila."

She went quiet for a moment then said, "When I left Chicago I decided to leave all my stresses with it." She waved her hand around. "Things are much less complicated here."

"What was complicated in Chicago?" he asked.

"Besides dating?" she asked with a grin.

"Ah, I see."

"The truth is, I worked most nights at the restaurant and didn't have a whole lot of time for dating, or for anything really. When I did date it always seemed to end in disaster."

"How so?"

"I either attracted fast-food/fast-hands kind of guys, or the city was just full of them. And at the restaurant I got tired of cooking for people who rushed through their meals the same way they rushed through life. I was simply going through the motions and for a while there I lost my love of cooking, and pretty much everything else. I hated all the hurrying and watching my life fly by faster than a Chicago cab." A small smile touched her mouth as she glanced at the huge snow banks. "When Katy had an opening on her show, I immediately applied."

"Did you find it hard to move so far from your family?"

"I miss them." She put her hand over her heart. "But they'll always be here with me."

"You're just a small town girl at heart aren't you?"

Lila smiled. "My dad came from a small town and I spent my summers with my grandma and grandpa in Iowa. I just think small town life is in me."

Jon nodded, understanding it was in him too.

"There is just something special about Whispering Cove. The pace is slower, the people are nicer and I know this is a place where I can settle down with my own family, cook big

Sunday dinners and eat and play at a relaxed pace. Besides," she added with a wink, "my grandma always said small town guys make the best husbands."

Jon's chest tightened as she poured her heart out to him. While it should have surprised him that she was telling a virtual stranger something so personal, he wasn't shocked at all. Lila wore her emotions on her sleeve, and when it came to her, what you saw was what you got. She had no hidden agenda and the only ladder she was looking to climb was the one in her shed. Damned if he didn't like that about her.

She laughed out loud and he couldn't deny that there was a strange new intimacy between them. Sure, he just met her, but she was so easy to be around, so comfortable and honest that it felt, inexplicably, as if he'd known her for a lifetime.

"I guess I sound pretty jaded for a girl my age, huh?"

Jon smiled, loving the way she laughed. In fact, there were a lot of things he loved about her. And he wasn't the only one. Earlier today he could feel the town's affection for her. She might not have been born and raised in Whispering Cove, but the townsfolk had taken her under their wings and treated her like she was one of their own. Then again, she put everyone around her at ease, which made it so easy to like her.

"Not jaded, Lila. You just know what you want, and that's a lot more than I can say for most people."

"What do you want, Jon?"

Jon didn't miss the hitch in her voice, the soft invitation lingering beneath her words. The air changed, sexual energy arcing between them. Jon gripped the steering wheel tighter as he pulled into her driveway. When her heat reached out to him, he instantly reaffirmed his vow to stay away from her. Two seconds ago she'd pretty much just told him she wanted the white picket fence and a family to fill her house, which meant he wasn't the guy for her.

He swallowed the lump in his throat and said, "Well, right now I'd like to gather some wood and get a fire going, because it's damn cold out here."

"Right," she said, disarming him with a seductive smile that has his cock thickening. "A fire is a great idea." She rubbed her stomach. "Why don't you get that started while I prepare dinner for two." She wet her lips and added, "You are staying for dinner, right?"

"I didn't realize the B&B came with dinner too."

"It's good to learn something new every day," she teased, tossing her long hair over her shoulder. "And hurry up with the wood. I'm starving."

Jesus, everything in the way she was looking at him spoke of a different kind of hunger, and if he knew what was good for him, and for her, he'd back his vehicle right out of her driveway and get out while he still could.

"Meet me in the kitchen when you're done."

Despite his best interests, he nodded, and with that Lila fished her key out of her pocket and made her way inside. As soon as she disappeared from his line of sight, he grabbed his cell from his pocket and called Errol, fearing if he stayed in the house one more night he might do something he could only regret later. After three rings his great-uncle picked up.

"What's up, boy?" Errol answered.

"Has your place been fumigated yet?"

"Not yet. It's the holidays. Hard to get anyone to come by over the holidays."

Jon gave a frustrated sigh and took note of the time. It was well past work hours, but he made a mental note to call the exterminator himself first thing tomorrow.

"Are you free to meet up tonight?" Jon asked.

"Can't. Helping get things ready for the craft bazaar tomorrow." Before Jon could ask when his uncle would be free, Errol said. "Nice thing you're doing for Dani. That girl needs a break." Jon was just about to ask if that was why he'd wanted him to come home, but Errol said, "Gotta go. Delilah's got dinner on the table and you don't want to—"

"I know I know. Don't want to keep a catch like her waiting," Jon said, finishing his uncle's sentence. "Listen, I'll be at the clinic tomorrow. Stop by to see me, okay?"

Errol got quiet for a moment then asked, "You're not going to try to poke me with a needle, are ya?"

Jon exhaled a frustrated sigh. "No, Errol. I came home because you asked me to, and I really want to spend some time with you."

"You will, boy. You will." With that, Errol hung up and Jon shook his head as he shoved his phone back into his pocket. What the hell was going on with that man? After talking with Dani today he knew it wasn't health related. So what was really behind the need for Errol to have him home for the holidays only to end up too busy to spend time with him?

Jon climbed from the SUV and made his way over to the tarp covering the pile of wood. He gathered a few logs and hurried inside the house. He turned his attention to the fireplace in the main living room and spent the next fifteen minutes getting a small blaze going. Once he was done, he noticed the delicious smells coming from the kitchen. He followed his nose and found Lila humming to a Christmas tune as she tossed spices into the dish she was preparing.

"Smells good. What is it?"

"Nothing fancy," she answered. "Just something I had in the freezer."

He walked over to her and when he noticed the dining room table beautifully set for two his heart thumped.

"Are you eating dinner with me?"

"Of course."

"Do you always eat with your guests?"

She turned and instead of answering she just smiled at

him. When he looked over her shoulder and saw a pot filled with stew, the rich, hearty kind he could never find in Miami, his stomach grumbled.

"That looks good."

She shrugged. "It's just stew," she said, except it wasn't just stew to him. It represented everything she was. The warmth and comfort of home and hearth.

Christ, did she realize she was seducing her way into his heart with her home-cooked meals?

He cleared his throat but his voice still came out sounding gritty, like he'd swallowed a handful of dirt. "I'll get the bowls."

Once the bowls were filled they made their way into the dining room and Jon dug into his food with enthusiasm.

He glanced up to see Lila smiling at him.

"What?" he asked, and wiped his mouth with a napkin.

"Can I get you more?"

When he noticed that her bowl was still full and his was almost gone he gave a sheepish grin. "It's just so good."

Lila laughed. "I take it you don't cook at all."

He shook his head and held up his hands. "Nope. These hands were made for surgery, not cooking."

"Then you need to find someone to cook for you," she said matter-of-factly as she reached for his bowl. When she stood, he noticed she was eating with her apron on, the same way his mother used to. His body tightened against the flood of emotions. Everything about Lila screamed of family and fun.

"You don't have to serve me, Lila."

She grinned. "It's no trouble at all."

"Of course not," Jon said as she left the room. "But if you keep this up, I might never leave."

As soon as the words left his mouth, he realized what he'd said, and how happy she made his childhood home.

Lila came back with another bowl of stew and when she sat, he redirected the conversation, keeping it on her. Twenty minutes later they rose from the table and he tried not to think about how much he wanted to eat with her on a regular basis. How much he wanted her. How much he didn't deserve either.

Fighting off the wave of emotion, he gathered the two bowls and carried them into the kitchen. After helping Lila straighten up, he feigned exhaustion. "I guess I should call it a night. I'm covering for Dani at the clinic tomorrow and have to get up early." Without looking at Lila, he made his way out of the kitchen.

"Will you be having breakfast here before you go to work?"

"I'll be leaving early so I'll just grab something at the coffee shop." His feet slapped the wood floors as he hurried up the stairs to his room, needing time to pull himself together.

Turning his attention to building a fire, he tossed some kindling onto the grate and tried not to think about Lila and how she was crawling past his defenses without even trying. There was no denying the attraction between them, one they both clearly wanted to act on. But no way, no how, was he going to act on his feelings. Lila deserved someone who could give her what she really wanted.

After lighting the fire he jumped in the shower and turned the water to cold, striving to get his erection under control. He stayed in there for a good long time, until his room was blistering hot.

Jon stepped from the shower stall, wrapped a towel around his waist and padded to his window. He was just about to draw the curtains when a movement down below caught his attention. He narrowed his eyes, looking closer, and when he spotted Lila facedown in a snow pile, dressed in nothing but a cotton robe and slippers, his pulse leapt in his throat.

"Jesus," he cursed and quickly tugged on his jeans, pulling his T-shirt over his head as he rushed down the staircase. At the door he tugged on his boots and hurried outside.

When he found Lila struggling to her feet, a load of wood still in her arms, he hauled her up and looked her over. He brushed snow from her face. "Lila, are you okay?"

"I slipped," she sputtered through a mouthful of snow.

"Give me that." Jon grabbed the pile of wood from her arms. "What are you doing out here in your robe? You're going to catch your death of cold."

He hurried her inside and after he locked the door behind her, he shook his head. "Jesus, Lila. You could have asked me to do that."

Her teeth chattered as she said, "Running the B&B is my responsibility."

"Well at least let me help while I'm here," he mumbled as a part of him realized how much he wanted to help her, and not just until Christmas Eve.

Fuck.

He dropped the wet wood at the door and guided her into the living room. He threw a few pieces of dry kindling onto the dying fire, but when he turned to see her shivering he knew she needed heat now.

"Come on," he said, catching her hand. As he passed her liquor cabinet, he tucked a bottle of brandy under his arm and grabbed two glasses.

"Where are you taking me?" she asked.

"To my room."

"Your room?" Despite the cold, heat moved over her eyes. The way her robe inched open enough to expose her lush cleavage hadn't gone unnoticed by him.

"Yeah, it's the only room with a good fire going, and I

need to get you warmed up." Using his shoulder, he pushed open his bedroom door and guided Lila to the foot of the bed, a few feet from the fireplace.

He took off her slippers and gathered her ice-cold feet in his hands. "You probably shouldn't be in the snow in your bunny slippers."

She forced a quick laugh. "I was in a hurry."

After warming her feet, he poured a generous amount of brandy into her glass and pressed it into her hand. "Drink this." As she took it from him, skin touched skin, eliciting a shiver from deep within. Jon poured a glass for himself, took a huge swig then put the bottle and glass aside. He ran his hand up her calf to create friction.

"Does anything hurt?"

"Only my pride," she answered, crinkling her nose.

Jon shook his head and couldn't help but smile. "No need to be embarrassed in front of me." When his hand reached her thigh, he said, "We need to get you out of this robe. You're still freezing."

A strange, garbled noise sounded in Lila's throat. He glanced up to see her, and that's when he noticed two things. Her eyes were flaring hot and his hand had traveled far too high on her thigh. He was about to pull it away, but Lila closed her hand over his, holding it in place. As her touch turned him inside out, lust bombarded him and his cock began tightening.

She wet her full, plump lips and her voice dropped an octave. "I agree about the robe, but don't agree that I'm still freezing."

"No?" he choked out.

She drained the rest of her brandy before setting her glass beside his. "No," she said. "In fact, I'm feeling a little...hot."

Her robe slipped open another inch and he made the mistake of sliding a look over her bare skin. His imagination kicked into high gear, and his body reacted, unable to ignore her blatant femininity.

As he ached to lose himself in her, a growl of sexual frustration climbed from his throat and there wasn't a damn thing he could do to stifle it.

Working to marshal his lust, he said, "It's the fire. It's blazing hot in here."

"Nope. Don't think that's it."

With one hand still trapped under hers, Jon grabbed his tumbler with the other and took another swig. She began moving his hand, running it along her thigh, creating heat and friction on her leg as well as in his pants. As sexual tension built inside him, he noted the way her honey-flecked eyes glimmered with sensuality, the way her body vibrated with want, the rich scent of her skin flooding the room and making her so damn impossible to resist.

"Jon."

"Yeah."

"I was thinking."

"About what?"

"About the holidays."

He exhaled slowly and went back on his heels, wondering where she was going with this.

"What about them, Lila?" he asked his voice sounding deeper, more intimate, even to himself.

"Well, I was thinking that holidays are about overindulging."

Jon finished the brandy in his glass and set his tumbler aside. "Yeah."

She nestled against him. "And well, since you're here alone, and I'm here alone, maybe we could...you know...indulge."

"Indulge?"

"Yeah, in each other."

His jaw clenched and as her proposition rattled around inside his brain like a runaway pinball, she rushed out, "You know, just for the holidays."

Even though he'd sworn he was going to stay away from her, because he was here for Errol and Errol alone, everything in the sexy way she looked at him had him rethinking his priorities.

"Lila—" he began, knowing he couldn't give her what she really wanted.

"It's just a simple holiday fling, Jon. Nothing more," she assured him.

As she grabbed the belt on her robe and started loosening it, Jon began warming to the idea of tossing her onto his sheets and having his way with her. Just for the holidays. Honestly, it was a perfectly sensible proposition, one he'd be a fool to pass up. But he didn't want to sleep with her until she knew the truth about him. Knew he was a selfish bastard who chose to stay in Miami and work instead of coming home for the holidays, only to end up losing his parents because of it, the two people in the world who loved him the most. If she chose to look at him with blame instead of desire, chose to walk out of his room, then so be it.

"Lila, we need to talk."

She removed her belt, widening the opening of her robe. "No, Jon. We need to get out of our clothes."

The sight of her gorgeous, naked body, save for the silk panties, nearly rendered him senseless. He swallowed. Hard. "I need to tell you something."

Her warm seductive chuckle curled around him. "Oh, so now the man of few words wants to talk. Well guess what? I'm not in the mood for talking."

"I thought you were always in the mood for talking," he managed to get out and struggled to remember what it was he needed to tell her.

She rolled her shoulder and let her robe fall down one arm, shutting down his ability to think with any sort of clarity.

"Not always," she assured him. "Sometimes I'm in the mood for moaning," she said, teasing him in a playful manner that drew him deeper and deeper into her seduction.

"Lila—" He tried again, and struggled to remember what it was he needed to tell her as equal amounts of lust for this woman and fear for what she made him feel raced through him.

"Jon," she said, sliding her fingers through her damp hair. "Whatever it is, it can wait until breakfast tomorrow."

When he heard the raw ache of lust in her voice and saw the sexy pink flush on her cheeks, all he could think about was laying her out on his bed, spreading her legs and nibbling on her like she was his personal holiday feast.

"Tonight, however—"

Jon pressed his fingers to her lips to hush her. "Lila."

"Yeah," she asked.

"It's time to stop talking."

"It is?"

"Yeah." He positioned his lips over hers, creating an instant intimacy, and murmured into her mouth, "Because it's time for indulging."

22

The second Jon's lips came down on hers, Lila knew Santa had indeed answered her holiday wish. He deepened the kiss, but there was nothing hurried in his touch. His palms slid inside her half-draped robe, and her body came alive as his fingers roamed leisurely over her skin. With excruciating slowness, he trailed his palms over her curves, taking his time to acquaint himself with her body.

Reaching out, Lila explored his chest in return, eager to get him naked, to feel his body pressing down on hers. When she gripped the hem of his shirt and gave it a little tug, Jon groaned out loud, inched back and peeled it from his body.

As she took in his gorgeous chest and rock hard abs, Lila leaned back on the bed, shrugging her other shoulder out of the robe in a silent invitation. Jon stared down at her nakedness, like he was savoring the moment, savoring the sight of her. He took his sweet time to peruse her contours, his glance lingering over her breasts then sliding downward to take in her panties. She bent one knee, and when Jon's nostrils flared, the intensity in his gaze frightened her as much as it excited her.

He kicked off his boots. "You are so damn sexy," he murmured, then made quick work of the rest of his clothes, abandoning them on the bedroom floor.

When Lila got a glimpse of his impressive cock, big, hard and ready to play, her body flushed hotly.

"You're not so bad yourself," she murmured seductively.

Aching to feel his mouth on hers, his hands on her body and his cock inside her, she shimmied backward until she reached the pillow. As her nipples tightened with arousal, she crooked her finger, urging him close.

Jon climbed onto the foot of the bed, then caged her legs between his. He crawled upward until his mouth found hers again. She parted her lips for him, welcoming him to her body, and that's when his tongue slipped inside to tangle with hers. He slid deft fingers through her hair and spent a long time kissing her, tasting every inch of her mouth before his lips danced over her skin. He buried his face in the crook of her neck, and she whimpered, taking pleasure in the warm and wicked sensations he aroused in her.

Sexual heat flooded her and she moaned without censor as he ran his tongue over her sensitive flesh and widened her legs with his knee. He settled his weight on top of her and she wrapped her arms around his back to hold him tight.

With her trapped beneath him, he slowly kissed a path down her body, his mouth claiming one hard nipple. He licked and sucked until she felt small spasms in her core. God, no man had ever made her come from nipple stimulations before, but she was close, so damn close to losing it with him.

She let loose a long moan, and he lifted his head until their eyes met. His smile was slow, sexy, as he cupped her breasts and brushed his thumbs over her nipples.

She arched into him and trailed her hands over his hard muscles. "I love how you touch me," she murmured, her body becoming pliable in his arms. The man didn't just have hands made for surgery, he had hands made for the bedroom. He was so skilled, so familiar with the erogenous areas of the female body.

"That's good, because I think it's pretty clear just how much I'm enjoying it too," he murmured in response.

As heat radiated from his palms, emotions and sensations streaked through her and she felt herself grow slicker, her body preparing itself for his impressive girth. But Jon was busy familiarizing himself with her body and didn't seem to be in any hurry to slip between her legs and join them as one.

Inching away from her aching breasts, he licked downward, stopping to tease her bellybutton before he reached the band on her lace panties.

"Very sexy," he murmured. Then he licked her through the material and the wet heat of his tongue had her hips coming off the bed. He splayed his big hand over her belly and pushed her back down, and there was something so primal and sexy in his take-charge attitude that it had her pussy clenching, eager to be filled.

Feeling edgy and needy, she writhed beneath his expert touch. "Jon, please," she begged, her body beckoning so much more from him, needing him in a way she'd never needed another, a way that actually scared her.

"Please what?" he asked, his soft whispering covering her like a blanket of warmth. "What is it you want, Lila?"

"I want to feel you inside me," she murmured.

"Soon," he answered. "But right now there are many, many things I need to do to you first." He hooked his thumbs under the lacy band of her panties and ever so slowly slid them down her legs, purposely swiping his thumb over her swollen clit.

She gasped, and as the heat in his eyes licked over her body, she moistened all over. Tension grew between her thighs, and Jon tossed her panties aside, gripped her legs and spread them wide.

"So pretty," he murmured and wet his bottom lip. He lightly petted her sex, touching her with such soft, gentle hands as he brushed his thumb up and down her pussy, widening her engorged lips.

He leaned into her and she exhaled a shallow breath. Shivers of warm need rushed through her bloodstream as he pressed a soft kiss over her sex, his erotic but gentle touch flashing through her blood.

He licked her with the soft blade of his tongue, and the satiny warmth of his mouth had her crying out his name. "Jon. Oh, yes. So good."

Her body grew hot. Too hot. Her skin was on fire everywhere he touched. A low growl came from his throat and drowned out her low whimper. Lila propped herself up on her elbows to see him, and as she watched him lick her, it occurred to her that it was the most erotic thing she'd ever seen.

He lifted his head and she saw the raw ache of lust on his face when he said, "You are the sweetest thing I've ever tasted." Lila reached out and ran her palm over his face and she didn't miss the way he leaned into her touch. Or the way he looked at her with such need and desire.

Turning his focus back to her pleasure, he pushed one finger inside her and cursed under his breath. "You're so wet. So hot for me, baby."

His warm scent curled around her and her heart missed a beat as she looked at him. Everything in the way he tended to her needs, indulging her with sheer pleasure, touched her on a deeper level and warned that she just might be getting in deep.

When he pushed another finger inside all rational thought fled and she quivered beneath the gentle assault, the sweet stab of bliss filling her with a new kind of passion. He took full possession of her pussy, licking, sucking, stroking deeper and deeper until her body went up in a burst of flames. A cry escaped her lips as he drove her to the edge of ecstasy and took her beyond her wildest fantasies.

But he wasn't in any hurry to let her tumble over. Oh no, he didn't appear to be finished with his slow seduction. Instead, he delicately brushed her G-spot, and the light furtive touch had air ripping from her lungs. He eased his finger out only to sink it back inside again. His touch was slow, deeply intimate, making her feel things she'd never felt before. As she slipped deeper and deeper into a place she said she wouldn't go, she raked her fingers through his hair, needing him to end the sweet torment before she shattered into a million pieces. She began trembling and panting, her body exploding from the inside out as tingling sensations overtook her.

Slowly, methodically, his thumb circled her swollen clit, and, giving her no reprieve from the sheer delight burning through her blood, he continued to feast on her like a man starved for so much more than just sex.

Honestly, he knew just how to touch, just how much pressure to apply to bring her to the edge and keep her hovering there. No man had ever been so in tune with her body before, so thorough, so unselfish.

Jon continued to stroke her with expertise, his tongue searing her clit as every nerve in her body screamed for release. Small tremors pulled at her core, and her breath came in jagged bursts.

As if knowing she was close he burrowed a finger inside her and she could feel the pressure building, coming to a peak. Her body began thrumming, entirely lost in the moment. Entirely lost in Jon.

"That's it, sweetheart. Come for me now."

Warmth pooled between her thighs and the pleasure was so intense, she gripped his shoulders to hang on. She grew slicker with each stroke and her breath caught in her throat as white-hot desire claimed her. She threw herself back on the bed and concentrated on the heat in her body as her pussy pulsed and throbbed with the hot flow of release.

Jon stayed between her legs for a long time, licking her gently until her muscles finally stopped spasming. Then he filled his lungs with her scent before he lifted his head and offered her a smile, one that was so full of warmth and tenderness it made her worry about what she'd gotten herself into. She suddenly wasn't so sure she could actually do casual sex with him.

"Jon," she said as her body and heart hummed for so much more from this man. That's when she remembered she hadn't bought condoms in a long time. Her heart leapt in her chest, and she met his glance.

"Yeah?" he asked, as he pressed himself over her body, caging her between the mattress and his hard chest.

"Tell me you have a condom."

He frowned. "I don't. I never thought…"

"I'm not on the pill," she rushed out.

Jon smoothed her hair from her face. "It's okay, Lila. We'll pick some up tomorrow."

"Tomorrow? But I want you now."

His soft laugh trickled through her veins and her toes curled when he tucked her hair behind her ears. "Believe me, I want you too, sweetheart."

He slipped off her body and when she felt his hard cock, she knew there were ways to please him. "What about you… we didn't…"

"Lila, you don't have to—"

He didn't get the chance to finish his sentence because

the second she wrapped both hands around him and stroked his length he sank back into the sheets.

"Jesus," he murmured and when she felt his cock thicken with blood she knew how close he was. She dipped into the juice pearling on his crown and used it to lubricate him. With her hands sliding over his impressive girth, she shifted on the mattress and climbed between his legs. His eyes met hers when she wet her lips in preparation.

She cupped his balls and stroked quicker but when she leaned forward, Jon cupped her face and stopped her from wrapping her mouth around his cock. He held her back, which was too bad really, because her mouth was watering for a taste of him. His hips came off the bed, and when he powered upward, once, twice, she could feel the blood pumping through his veins.

Knowing the pressure was mounting, she ran her hands over his crown. "Come for me, Jon," she murmured, and that's when he let go.

He pulsed in her hands, and she loved that she could do this for him, loved that she could make him feel this good.

Once his tremors subsided, he pulled her to him. She was about to ask him why he'd stopped her from going down on him, but he pressed his mouth to hers. His kiss was so soft and gentle it caught her by surprise and stole her words. Then he murmured into her mouth, "At least one good thing came from having no condoms." His lips curved into a crooked smile.

Rattled by the things this man made her feel, Lila crinkled her nose and tried to keep her voice light. "Really? And what is that?"

"We get to do this again tomorrow."

Jon pulled her in tight and when he kissed her again, a slow, lazy kiss meant to carry them through until morning, she realized just how nice it felt to be held by him. She looked into his gorgeous eyes, and her heart stuttered at the tenderness on his face.

She swallowed hard, because Jon was everything she was looking for in a guy. Not only was he utterly skilled in the bedroom, he was the least-selfish man she knew. Tonight he'd taken the time to pleasure her, asking for nothing in return. Honestly, she was beginning to give up hope that men like Jon actually existed.

Lila instantly knew that rolling in the sheets with a guy like Jon was scarier than riding the winter roads with bald tires. Because there was no denying that she was falling for him. Not a wise move on her part, considering he was only going to be around for the holidays.

Unless someone gave him a reason to stay...

23

The piercing sound from the fire alarm had Jon turning off the gas burner and opening the back door to let in a gust of cold, morning air. He coughed on the smoke clouding the kitchen, and when he heard the sound of footsteps rushing down the stairs, he spun around. The second he set eyes on Lila's sleepy, mussed state, warm intimacy curled around him and he tossed her a sheepish smile.

"I was trying to make you breakfast in bed." He held up the pan and showed her four strips of bacon, or what used to be bacon before he got his hands on them. Right now they were charred and crispy and looked like he was preparing some sort of sacrificial offering. "But I'm not very good at this."

Lila tightened the belt on her robe and as she hugged herself against the chill in the air she gave a lighthearted laugh that went right through him. Her mood was playful when she said, "Why don't you just stick to doing things in bed that you are good at."

Jon shut the door and moved toward her. "But you've

been doing so much for me that I wanted to do something for you."

Lila tossed the pan in the sink and grabbed another. "But I like doing this for you, remember." She nodded toward the upstairs. "And besides, it's not like you haven't done anything for me."

Jon couldn't help but grin at her sexual innuendo. In fact, he could feel himself getting warm all over again. "I liked doing that for you, Lila."

"Good, because we still have a few days before you leave and since you like it so much, I plan to let you do a lot of it."

His grin widened. "That's awfully kind of you."

Her chuckle was breathy, intimate, and his body tightened, anxious to crawl between her legs again.

Lila shuffled around in her fluffy bunny slippers and grabbed some eggs from the fridge.

Jon felt a little pinch in his heart. "You don't have to go through all this trouble."

She gave him a sassy wink and turned the kitchen thermostat up a notch. "Maybe I think you're worth the trouble."

As he looked at her he realized just how much he liked her, just how much he'd lost himself in her last night, which was one of the reasons he'd stopped her from going down on him. In his book that act was more intimate than intercourse. If a girl like her, one who was the epitome of home and hearth, ever wrapped her mouth around his cock, then the wall he'd built around his heart just might come crumbling down.

There was no denying that Lila made him forget, made him feel things other than guilt and sadness. And even though he swore he was going to stay away from her, the second she opened herself to him, he knew he was done for, knew he couldn't stop even if he wanted to.

Christ, he really was a selfish bastard.

He stepped up to her and ran his hands up and down her arms to warm her. When he noticed the sexy pink flush on her cheeks, all he could think about was once again losing himself in her sweetness.

With a bemused expression on her face, she said, "Why don't you have a seat and let me finish this."

Before he could respond, the back door flung open and they both turned to see Jacob Collins darkening the doorway, a huge Saint Bernard dog by his side.

Jon broke the embrace and stepped back as Jacob's gaze went from Lila to Jon back to Lila again. "Is everything okay? I was out walking Charlie when I heard your smoke detector."

Lila smiled at him and Jon had an instant pang of jealously. He cursed under his breath, because this thing between them was just supposed to be about sex, a little holiday indulgence. He was not supposed to be feeling more for her.

"Everything is fine. Just some charred bacon."

Jacob rubbed his dog's head. "Ah, Charlie's favorite."

Lila crinkled that cute little nose of hers. "I think this might be a little overdone even for Charlie." She patted her leg. "Here, boy."

As Charlie raced across the room, barreling into Lila, she waved her hand toward the stools. "Grab a seat, Jacob. Have breakfast with us."

Jacob hesitated and looked at Jon. "Are you sure? If you're busy..."

Lila laughed and Jon could feel the affection and comfort between the two. "Give me a break, Jacob. You and I both know it wasn't the smoke alarm that had you running over here, it was the smell of bacon." She pointed a spatula at the stool. "Now sit."

Jacob shot Jon a glance as he plunked himself down. "She knows me too well." Then he looked at the ingredients she was pulling out of the fridge. "Are you making those yummy blueberry pancakes too?"

Lila rolled her eyes, but Jon didn't miss the gleam, one that told him how much she loved cooking for others. "For you Jacob, anything."

"Well, only if you're making them," he said, rubbing his stomach as she poured him a big mug of coffee. He turned to Jon. "I told her if she keeps feeding me like this, I'm going to fall in love with her." He gave Jon a wink. "Careful there, pal, or the same thing will happen to you too."

As an uneasy feeling closed in on him, Jon glanced at the clock and said, "I should get going."

Lila turned to him. "But you didn't eat and I thought we were going to talk after breakfast."

"We'll talk later, and no worries, I'll just grab something at the coffee shop. Besides, I want to get in early and get some paperwork done that I brought with me." He was just about to leave when he remembered Lila's bald tires. "Do you have to go anywhere today?"

"Dani is picking me up at two."

"I just don't want you driving on those tires."

"I can drive her anywhere she needs to go," Jacob piped in as he took a swig of coffee.

"Fine," Jon said, pushing down an ugly wave of jealousy as Jacob continued to sit at the counter looking so at home with Lila that it made Jon want to punch him in the face.

Christ, he had no claims on her. They both agreed that what was between them was sex and he'd be wise to remember that.

Jon snatched his coat off the rack and made his way to his vehicle. After grabbing a bagel and coffee he drove to the clinic to begin his day. In no time at all the waiting room filled up and patient after patient came to see him. And as he greeted old friends, no one brought up the accident and for that he was grateful. If he didn't know better, he'd think they were genuinely happy to see him, most even asking if he was home for good, because not only did they appear to miss him, each one voiced that the town really needed another doctor.

Before Jon knew it, noon was upon him, and he was grateful for the break, needing time to sort through his feelings about the town and the way the people in it were reacting toward him. He pushed back in his chair just as Kira Doherty, Dani's receptionist, poked her head in.

"Your morning appointments are finished which means you're free until one thirty." She pointed at her watch and her straight white teeth flashed in a smile. Jon returned her smile, thinking back to when Kira wore braces and climbed the trees with him and her brother, Sam. Kira had certainly changed since those days, and the last he'd heard, Sam Doherty had become a ghost hunter in New Mexico. Jon had never thought he'd see the day when Sam believed in the paranormal. Then again, when they were kids, camping out in the backyard and getting ready for sleep after pouring over superman comics, Sam always left his flashlight on. Perhaps he really could see things that Jon couldn't.

Kira tucked a blonde curl behind her ear. "I'm heading to the Seafarer for lunch. Would you like to join me?"

He considered joining her and his stomach grumbled, a reminder that the bagel he'd scarfed down after ruining breakfast hadn't been enough to carry him through the morning. But thinking of his failed attempt to make Lila breakfast in bed had his thoughts lingering on the incredible night they'd had and he suddenly found himself smiling.

"Everything okay?"

"Fine," he answered, "Just remembering something." As warmth moved through him, he knew he was treading on dangerous territory when it came to Lila, but he couldn't seem to resist her or her offer for a little holiday indulgence.

"So you'll join me then? Everyone will be there, and Errol, Byron and Harold will be at their usual table, meddling, and scheming up their next bet."

At the mention of Errol, he glanced at the phone. He'd yet to call the exterminator. Since he really didn't want to hang out at the Seafarer, a place where good friends all came together for a meal—a place he no longer belonged—it was the perfect excuse to turn down her offer. Plus, he had to put a call into his old friend, Jonah, the town's top mechanic. Then something else Kira said caught his attention, which had him thinking about what Lila had said the other day, something about Errol not really needing the cane. "Wait, what did you say? What about Errol meddling and scheming?"

She opened her mouth to answer, but a noise at the door in the waiting room drew their attention. Kira spun around, and he caught disappointment on her face when she turned back to him and said, "Never mind. Looks like lunch came to you."

Jon glanced past Kira's shoulders as she moved down the hall toward the receptionist's counter and that's when he saw Lila walking toward him. After noting that she was dressed in a parka and a sexy skirt, he looked at the huge lunch basket in her arms.

The second he set eyes on her he felt a rush of sexual energy. She greeted him, but this time her smile was more sexy than sweet when she said, "I figured you might be hungry."

Jon stood, worry pulling at him. "You didn't drive here did you?"

"No need to worry. Jacob drove me." She laughed and added, "That guy will do anything for food."

Jon looked down the hall. "Where is he now?"

"He had to run some errands and then he'll be back to

pick me up later." She closed and locked the door behind her, then plunked the basket on his desk. She pulled out a stack of sandwiches, followed by fruit, drinks and cheese.

He looked at all the food. "If you keep feeding me like this—"

"What, you'll fall in love with me?"

He swallowed hard, because he was beginning to believe that could very well be the case. "I was going to say, I'll be able to fill out Santa's suit without the stuffing."

She poked him in the stomach. "I saw you naked, Jon, and believe me, you won't be filling that out anytime soon. Besides," she added, her mouth turning up in a devious smile, "it's not your heart I'm after."

She was right, this was about sex, and that was exactly what he wanted. So why, then, did it bother him to hear her say it? And why did it have him feeling like he'd been punched in the gut. Christ, what the hell was going on with him? He really needed to get it together.

Feeling edgy and a little out of control, he turned his focus to the food. "You didn't have to go through all the—"

She poked him in the chest and cut him off again. "Oh, did you somehow think this little afternoon rendezvous was all about you?"

Confused, he raised a brow. "What do you mean?"

"You see, Jon." She shrugged out of her parka, then reached back into the basket. "It might be lunchtime, but I'm not hungry for food." She pulled out a box of condoms and pressed her body against his. "It's you I want. Right here. Right now."

Jon darted a nervous glance around the examination room. "Lila, what are you doing?"

"Finishing what we started." The air instantly charged, sexual energy arching between them.

Jon pinched his eyes shut, understanding what she had in

mind probably wasn't a good idea, for numerous reasons, but when she released the button on his pants and pulled them wide open, his body turned traitorous. The little vixen was seducing her way into his pants and his heart and there wasn't a damn thing he could do about it. He wanted to say something to stop this, but when she sank to her knees and drew his hard cock between her lips before he even realized what she was doing, the only thing that came out of his mouth was a loud growl of pleasure.

"Jesus, Lila." He groaned and closed his eyes against the flood of heat.

She ran her tongue over his swollen tip, then drew him deeper, but it wasn't just what she was doing to him that had him all tangled up inside. It was the soft, sexy moans of pleasure in her throat, moans that told him how much she enjoyed doing this for him.

He gripped her head, but couldn't stop her. She was hell bent on pleasuring him orally, and despite how intimate he found the act, how her soft purrs of delight were crumbling the walls around his heart, his traitorous body began rocking against her, his composure blown to bits.

His hands followed the movement of her head as her hot mouth scorched him. He began trembling, his body coming up to speed in record time. Hunger for her consumed him, and tension began building in his body.

"Lila," he managed to get out, his tongue so thick it was a wonder he could talk. "I want to be inside you." Even though it could very well shred his last measure of control, he needed to feel her body wrapped around his cock more than he needed air.

Climbing to her feet, Lila gave him a little shove and he fell backward into his chair. Taking control of the situation, she a grabbed a condom from the box and ripped open the package. Jon sat there in mute fascination as she proceeded to sheathe him. Christ, no woman had ever put a condom on him before, and he had to admit that he found the whole process rather exciting.

He looked at the examination table, ready to scoop her up and spread her out, but she shook her head no.

"No?" he asked.

"No," she said, and threw her legs over his to straddle his lap. That's when he realized she had no panties on and the skirt had been worn on purpose. She really did have every intention of seducing him out of his pants this afternoon.

"Christ, Lila." She shimmied into position, but before she could impale herself, he slipped a hand between her legs, but when he found her sex sopping wet and so damn ready for him, all he could do was hang on for the ride.

As she lowered herself, he opened her blouse and tugged her bra down to expose her breasts. His mouth watered as her pert nipples hovered inches from his lips, and as she sank onto him, his cock burrowing deeper and deeper into her tight wet channel, he buried his face between her breasts and drew in the sweet smell of her skin.

She writhed against him, and pleasure like he'd never before experienced swamped him. His mouth found one nipple and he drew it inside. Lila threw her head back and his blood pressure soared as she gyrated, increasing the tension inside his groin.

"You fill me so nicely," she murmured.

Her arms snaked around his neck and she held him close, crushing her body to his as they joined as one. Jon held her tight, and as he savored the sensations, it was almost as if time had suddenly stood still for the two of them, like a lifetime had passed, creating a deeper, more meaningful intimacy between them.

When she began rocking her hips and sliding his cock in and out of her tight pussy, it prompted him into action. He slid his fingers through her hair and shifted in his seat for deeper thrusts. He drove higher and higher into her, and when her muscles clenched around him she cried out in sensual bliss.

Seeing her this aroused had passion and possession racing trough him. He loved that he could do this to her. Loved the way she reacted to his touch. He slipped a hand between their bodies again and swirled his finger over her slick clit and the look of ecstasy that came over her face had to be the sweetest thing he'd ever seen.

Her honeyed scent saturated the room as she continued to ride him. He gripped her hips, and eased her up and down, up and down, being sure to scrape her clit over his pelvis with every glorious thrust. Together they established a rhythm, each moving, giving and taking, except he quickly realized it wasn't just a physical release his body was seeking.

As pressure brewed deep in his groin, his thoughts whirled a million miles an hour. His muscles bunched, his cock tightened, and he feared he was going to lose more than just orgasmic control with her.

"Lila," he murmured through clenched teeth as he struggled to hang on. "You've got me right there, baby."

"Me too," she cried out as she tilted her head back to meet his glance. Eyes full of urgent need moved over his face and he knew just what to do to take them both over the edge.

He took possession of her mouth, and gripped her shoulders to pull her down harder, burying every last inch of him inside her. When her clit smashed against his body, her muscles gripped his cock hard, and the second he felt her hot cream drip over his balls, air ripped from his lungs and he let himself go, joining her in orgasm.

They held onto each other for a long time, clinging to one another like their lives depended on it. Lila finally broke the quiet, cupped his face with her small hands and whispered into his mouth, "That. Was. Incredible."

Jon rested his forehead against hers, and worked to get his breathing under control. "Jesus, Lila."

She inched back to see him, and her lips twitched in amusement. "What?"

"You're amazing is what."

The look in her eyes touched something deep inside him, something he feared there was no coming back from. With contentment written all over her, she continued to cup his face. Then she placed a soft kiss onto his mouth. Jon didn't miss the fact that her touch felt more emotional than physical and had him wondering if this afternoon rendezvous was simply about sex, simply two people indulging in one another for the holidays.

But then he remembered what Lila had said. She wasn't after his heart.

Which was a good thing, right?

Rattled by the emotions she brought out in him, he shook his head. He'd been prepared for a lot when he first came back to Whispering Cove, but nothing could have ever prepared him for Lila and the things she made him feel. With each passing second she was pulling him into a place he didn't deserve to go.

It was his own damn fault really, because he knew he could never just have sex and keep his emotions out of it. Not with a girl like her. Of course, that still didn't change the fact that in two short days he'd gotten himself in completely over his head and had no idea what the hell he was going to do about it.

24

There was nothing Lila could do to wipe the ridiculous grin off her face when Dani stopped by her place to pick her up. Lila jumped into her friend's car and did her best to keep the conversation casual, but from the sideways glances Dani kept giving her, she knew the astute doctor had picked up on the changes in her.

"Is Katy meeting us there?" Lila asked as Dani drove through town.

Instead of answering, Dani asked, "Uh, Lila is there anything you want to talk about?"

"Nope." Lila smiled and while she was rather frank and honest about pretty much everything in her life, she wasn't quite ready to talk about what was going on with her and Jon. No, she wanted to keep the memories all to herself and close to her heart, a place where she could protect, nurture and savor them in their entirety.

Her mind took that moment to revisit her rendezvous with Jon. Honestly, when he talked about her feeding him and she'd used the word love, he stood there staring at her like a deer caught in the headlights, which was the reason she'd told him she was only after his body. After all, he was already spooked enough about something and she didn't want to scare him any more than he already was.

Deep in her heart she knew he felt the connection every bit as much as she did, he just wasn't ready to come to terms with it. But Lila wasn't one to give up so easily.

Even though she was torn about prying into his personal life, she said, "Actually, I'd like to know what Jon blames himself for."

Dani frowned and stared straight ahead for a long moment before saying, "He lost his folks a few years back. He blames himself. Thinks we all blame him too."

"Oh," she said, as something niggled in the back of her mind, something that was just out of reach.

Before Dani could say more, they reached the new community center and spotted Katy waiting at the doors for them. Deciding to press Dani for more information after the bazaar, they caught up with Katy and made their way inside to examine all the wonderful crafts and local fares. After picking up a few new glass pieces made by the talented Tempest Sky, Lila spotted Errol chatting with Jacob, who had a booth set up to raise money for rescue dogs.

The two looked like they were in deep conversation. In fact, they looked like they were conspiring about something. When Errol drove his cane into Jacob's rib, Lila cut her way through the crowd and walked over. It was the perfect time to work on Errol and talk him into selling her the B&B instead of renting it to her.

"Errol, Jacob," she greeted and patted Charlie on the head before she dropped a few bills into the fundraising jar.

Jacob smiled at her and looked a bit relieved when Errol turned his attention to her.

"Errol, can I talk to you for a minute?"

"Sure, lassie. What's on your mind?"

They moved away from Jacob to find a quiet corner at the back of the community center. Lila drew a breath and prepared herself for an argument. It wasn't like this was the first time she'd talked to Errol about selling her the house.

"I think you know."

"Nope, not a mind reader," he said, and twirled his cracked cane in his hands.

"I want to talk to you about the B&B."

"Ah, I see."

"Have you thought anymore about selling it to me?"

"Can't."

"Why not?"

"Ain't mine to sell. Told you that already, lassie."

Frustrated with all his cryptic answers, Lila rooted her feet. "How can it not be yours to sell? I pay you the rent money so you must own it. And if you don't, can you tell me who does so I can contact them?"

Errol puckered his lips and his cloudy blue eyes moved over her face, assessing her. For a minute she felt like he could see right into her soul, see that she'd been having the best sex of her life. But thinking of Jon had her feeling all warm and wonderful inside, and there was nothing she could do to stop herself from smiling, despite how frustrated Errol made her.

"What's goin' on with you? You seem...different."

"I'm fine."

"My great-nephew isn't giving you trouble now is he?"

Lila's head came back with a start. "Your great-nephew?"

Errol glanced past her shoulders and he had a distant look in his eyes when he said, "It's nice to have him home and it's good to see him helping out at the clinic. I just know his folks are looking down at him with pride in their eyes."

As his words sank in, Lila felt her blood run cold, because suddenly the puzzle known as Jon Carver began to fall into place.

"I...I have to go," she said, then pulled her phone out to text both Katy and Dani, who were still browsing the craft tables, to tell them something came up and she had to leave. She rushed outside and ran the five blocks to her B&B. Once there, she dropped her purchases onto her kitchen table and darted up the stairs. At the top landing, she pulled on the rope and the hatch leading to the attic lowered.

She hurried up the stairs and glanced around at the old dusty boxes, ones she'd peeked through last year during renovations. Pulling open the one labeled "Photos", she sank to her knees and poured through the pictures.

Her heart raced faster in her too-tight chest as she spent hours looking at Jon through the years. This was why he'd seemed so familiar to her. She'd seen his pictures before. When Jon had first entered the B&B and glanced around the front foyer like he was trying to orient himself, it was because he *was* trying to orient himself. She shook her head, everything now making sense.

Errol wasn't lying when he said this wasn't his house to sell. Because this house didn't belong to him. It belonged to Jon. It was his childhood home.

She swallowed the lump pushing into her throat when she found the old newspaper article amongst the pictures. She didn't need to read it to know what it said, because she knew the people who once owned this home were related to Errol and had been in an automobile accident years ago when they were going to visit their son on Christmas Eve.

Feeling like the air had been sucked from her lungs, Lila shimmied along the floor until her back was pressed against the wall. Her mind raced, sorting through things.

After a long moment, Lila dropped everything and made her way down the stairs and out to the back shed. She traced her fingers over the carving JC+TT.

"Ohmigod," she whispered, as Jon, his life—his past and

his present—all fell into place. Thinking about what Dani had said about Jon blaming himself, believing others blamed him, she looked at the mini bike, the skates and all the things from Jon's childhood.

He had no idea just how much everyone cared.

She gave a slow shake of her head, her heart aching for the man who was so incredibly lost. When a shiver moved through her, Lila hugged herself and made her way back inside. Now that she knew exactly who he was and why he'd run away from Whispering Cove, it gave her a new purpose. Getting lost in his arms last night and this afternoon was an experience she wanted to relive, night after night, and deep down, she knew Jon belonged here. Jon needed to find his way back home. And she was just the girl who was going to show him the path.

A noise at the front door had her spinning and when she spotted Jon walking through the threshold her pulse leaped in her throat. As she stood there staring at him, her heart aching for him, but also longing for him in ways it had never longed for another.

"Lila? Is everything okay?" he asked, his brow knitting into a frown.

She hated how he blamed himself, how he thought others blamed him, and while she wanted to blurt out that he was wrong, he wouldn't believe her, and it could very well send him packing. She'd have to find a way to show him, one that would help him understand.

"Everything is fine," she said, biding her time until she could put a plan together. "How was your day?"

"Lunch was pretty damn good," he said grinning. "But the afternoon was a bit rough."

"Oh?" she asked. "And why was that?"

"I...uh...I had a bit of a hard time concentrating."

Lila feigned innocence. "What on earth had you so distracted?"

He tugged on his collar, and looked at the smoldering embers in the fire. "Gee, I wonder," he said, his grin crooked as he grabbed two logs to toss into the pit.

Lila followed him into the room, and as night fell around them she bent to plug in her Christmas lights. When she stood she felt Jon close behind her and her entire body came alive.

She spun to face him and his eyes met hers. Lila wasn't sure who moved first, but the next thing she knew she was in his arms, kissing him with everything she had inside her. They dropped to the floor and spent the next few hours making love in front of the fire. Over the course of the night, they somehow made their way to his bedroom where they fell asleep in each other's arms.

Warm morning light streamed in through the open curtains, and Lila smiled when she heard kids sliding down Dresden Bluff. Her heart tightened as she listened to the laughter, and she ran her hand over her stomach, imagining the day when her house was full of children. She turned and when she caught Jon staring at her, a crooked grin on his face, her heart beat a little faster.

"What?" she asked.

"You snore."

"I do not snore," she bit out, indignant, and hit him with the pillow.

Jon took the pillow from her and slid her under his body. The next thing she knew they were making love again, burning through the box of condoms in record time. A long time later, Jon rolled off her and pulled her close. A comfortable silence fell around them as they both became lost in their own thoughts.

"What time are you going into the clinic today?" she asked, breaking the quiet.

"Dani is covering this morning. I'm in for the afternoon."

His fingers curled in her hair as she ran her hands up and down his hard chest. When his stomach grumbled, she laughed. "How about breakfast in bed?"

"How about I come help you?"

"Just stay away from the bacon," she warned, as she shoved the blankets off. They both showered, then tugged on their clothes and made their way to the kitchen. As Jon made coffee, she noticed he was suddenly quiet.

"So," she began, wanting to draw him in to conversation. "The other night you wanted to tell me something, but we never did get the chance to talk."

"No, something always seems to come *up*."

Lila laughed and took her coffee from Jon, and that's when she noticed he was looking at his cell phone, his expression serious.

"You okay?"

"I just got a text from Errol saying he couldn't see me today."

"What's going on?"

"That's what I want to know." He ran a hand through his hair. "I asked him to come by the clinic yesterday and he never showed up, and every time I try to see him, he has other plans. And just now I got a text saying he was going to be busy tonight at the tree lighting festival and won't be able to see me." He shrugged. "I don't get it. He asked me to come back for the holidays, then tells me I can't stay with him because he has termites."

Lila crinkled her nose. "Termites?"

"Yeah, and I called the exterminator myself yesterday afternoon and they said they hadn't received a call from him." Jon took a slug of coffee. "I'm not sure what is going on with him." He peered at her over the rim of his mug. "You even said something about him using a cane that he didn't need, and at the clinic yesterday Kira mentioned something about him meddling. What is going on with him? Do you think he's okay?"

"I think he's fine," she assured him. "He's just always butting into everyone else's business."

"So you don't think he's losing it then?"

Lila shook her head, knowing Errol wasn't losing it at all. He, along with the other two men who made up the gruesome threesome, were the wiliest old men she knew. They were always interfering in everyone's lives and making bets on who they could hook up first. As she mulled that over for a moment longer, and thought about how Jon had landed on her doorstep six days before Christmas—Errol having sent him—understanding hit like a hard snowball. Oh. My. God.

Her heart leapt in her chest and her blood rushed a little faster, because as she considered all the events over the last few days one thing became glaringly apparent to her.

Cantankerous old Errol Wilson really was her Santa Claus.

$$25$$

After a late day at the clinic, and still having no luck in catching up with Errol, Jon returned home to find Lila sitting in front of the Christmas tree, stitching names onto stockings.

A smile lit her face and she jumped to her feet the second he entered the house. "I was getting worried about you."

Jon struggled to sound casual, but the hitch in his voice belied his emotions. "The clinic ran late."

She glanced at her watch. "No worries, we still have time to make it."

Jon angled his head. "Where?"

Lila grabbed her coat off the hook. "To the tree lighting ceremony. Then to Hauk's bar for drinks and food."

"I wasn't really planning—"

"Oh," she said. "I thought you might like to come. Errol will be there and it might be a good time to talk to him." She paused and looked at the snow falling outside. "I guess I'll walk over there myself—"

"I'll drive you."

"You don't have to drive me. It's less than five minutes away."

"It's cold and slippery," he said. As he took in the soft blush on her cheeks, the warmth in her eyes as she looked at him, he knew the cold and slippery streets were just an excuse. Even though he no longer belonged here, and didn't deserve to be a part of the festivities, he hated the thoughts of her going alone. But it was more than that. He wanted to be with her, wanted to enjoy every moment of her while he was still in Whispering Cove.

Less than five minutes later, Lila was bundled up in the car, sitting beside him, and she had a grin on her face. One that said she seemed rather pleased with herself.

He should tell her who he really was, but the truth was, he just wanted to enjoy this thing between them for a little longer, until he went back to Miami. Then he'd bury himself in his work and try to forget about the girl who'd turned his life upside down in a few short days. But thinking of his life in Miami had him thinking of Lila's hometown.

He turned to her. "Do you plan to settle in Whispering Cove for good?"

"Yes, why?"

"Are you planning to run the B&B forever?"

"I hope so."

"I know this isn't any of my business, but don't you think it would be a better investment to buy the place instead of renting it?"

"I can't. Errol won't sell it to me."

Okay, that took Jon by surprise, considering Errol had said he could never find a buyer for the home. Perplexed, Jon probed, "So you do want to buy it, then?"

Probing eyes met his and when she said, "Errol told me it wasn't his to sell," he got the distinct impression that she was waiting for him to elaborate on the subject.

Confusion welled up inside him, and needing to get this perfectly straight in his head he asked, "You'd buy it if you could?"

"In a heartbeat."

"And Errol knows this?"

"He should. I keep asking him to sell it to me instead of renting it."

Jon swallowed the lump pushing into his throat. Errol had blatantly lied to him. He had no idea what was going on with his uncle, but he needed to talk to him and he needed to do it now.

After squeezing his rental vehicle between two cars, Jon and Lila climbed from the SUV and made their way to the town square. As they approached, the familiar sights, smells and music bombarded him with old memories and had him feeling emotional inside. He peered into the crowd and when he spotted Aunt Annette and Uncle Pete hugging one another, an uneasy feeling moved through him, because everything in the way they looked at each other spoke of love and happiness, not marital troubles.

Lila slipped her hand into his, and gave him a comforting squeeze. He looked at her and had the oddest sense that she knew far more about him than he ever wanted her to know.

"You okay?"

He nodded. "I need to find Errol."

"Can it wait for a minute? They're just about to light the tree."

Jon nodded and when Trent, Katy, Dani, Braydon, Josie, Adam, Tabby and Reece all greeted him with open arms, the lights flicked on and lit up the whole town square. Everyone clapped, the sound mostly muffled by gloved hands, and when the carolers started singing, Lila went up on her toes and kissed him on the cheek.

"What was that for?" he asked.

She laughed and instead of answering, she said, "Come on. Let's go to Hauk's for drinks."

"Lila," he said feeling uneasy inside. "I need to find Errol."

"He's probably at Hauk's by now." She grinned and added, "The eggnog Hauk serves is spiked with rum, and believe me, Errol wouldn't miss that."

Together they walked the few blocks to Hauk's bar and as soon as they entered through the heavy front door, a glass of eggnog was pushed into his hands. Trent walked up to him, and his wife, Katy, waved Lila over to the crowd of women gathered around a long oaken table.

"Lila, get on over here for a Pina Cock-a-lada and a Screaming Orgasm," Josie said. Jon gave Lila a strange look, and she laughed. "Hauk's waitress, Aimee, renamed all the drinks." She gave him a wink and said, "You should try Sex at My House." She went up on her tiptoes and whispered, "Oh wait, we already did that."

Trent pressed a pool cue into Jon's free hand. "Come on. We're playing doubles and I need a partner."

He turned to Lila to gauge her reaction. "I'll catch up with you soon," she said, and disappeared into the crowd.

Since Errol was nowhere to be found, Jon joined the guys at the pool table, and before he knew it, he and Trent were whipping Adam and Braydon at a game of eight ball. The guys all laughed and taunted one other about their pool abilities, and feeling like he was back with his old gang, Jon joined in the teasing. As the hours slipped by, Jon fell into an easy camaraderie with his childhood friends and not once did anyone mention anything about his parents. If he wasn't mistaken, no one looked at him with blame in their eyes. Instead, they all made him feel warm and welcomed, like he was back where he truly belonged.

From across the room, he caught Lila's glance and his heart turned over in his chest. Christ, he was in so much trouble. As the night flew by and the crowd dwindled, not to mention the rum, Jon excused himself from the guys and went in search of Lila.

He wasn't sure what compelled him to do it, perhaps it was the rum, or perhaps it was because he just really wanted to, but, discretion aside, the second he reached her, he planted a warm kiss on her mouth.

She grinned. "What was that for?"

Instead of answering, he gestured with a nod. "Want to get out of here?"

When she gave him a sexy, knowing grin, Jon looked up and thought he spotted Errol by the door. He blinked and just like that the man was gone. For an old guy who relied on a cane, he was pretty damn swift on his feet. "Was that Errol?" he asked Lila.

She spun around. "I'm not sure."

Jon shook his head. "I think he's avoiding me."

She shimmied close, put two fingers on his chin and turned his face until he was looking at her. "I'm not." Jon felt his cock thicken when she added, "What was that you said about getting out of here?"

"Can you drive?" he asked.

"Nope. I had too many Screaming Orgasms."

Grinning, Jon asked, "So you're not up for one more?"

She returned his grin. "I'm always up for one more, maybe even two."

"Then let's hurry." Jon zipped her coat to her neck and she pressed against him. His cock ached, wanting to take her right then and there. "Jesus, it's a good thing my place is close." As soon as the words left his mouth, Jon realized what he'd said, realized how at home he felt in the old homestead. "I mean..."

"Want to race?" Lila said, and before he could answer, she was running out the door.

Jon darted after her, but she was damn fast. As he chased after her, she scooped up snow and tossed it at him.

"Oh, so that's how it's going to be is it?" he asked, catching up to her. He captured her in his arms and swung her around, threatening to throw her in the snow bank.

Lila was laughing so hard she could barely talk. "Okay... okay," she managed to get out through giggles. "Truce?"

His lips twitched in amusement. When was the last time he'd had such fun? Jon set her down, and when a cool ocean breeze rushed over them, they hurried past Dresden Bluff. Lila's eyes were bright with laughter and he fought the compulsion to make sweet love to her right there at the foot of the hill. The truth was, she made him forget, and while he didn't deserve to ever forget the tragedy that changed the lives of so many, it felt so damn good to experience something, anything, other than guilt and pain.

Once inside the house, they both kicked off their boots and tossed their winter wear aside. Before long, they were in front of the fire making love. They stayed there until the fire died down, then he took her to his bed.

There was a new intimacy between them, one that had him thinking about something more permanent. He was getting in too deep, falling into something he had no right to be a part of.

Despite that knowledge, their entire next day consisted of making love on her silk sheets, cooking, showering and making love again. Earlier that evening they could hear music coming from the town square, but they chose to stay in each other's arms, missing the concert. As the moon peered into the window, Jon knew he needed to climb from her bed and contact his uncle so he could get to the bottom of matters before he left town. But slipping from the bed and leaving Lila's arms had his heart squeezing and his stomach punching into his throat. Tomorrow was Christmas Eve, which meant he'd be flying back to Miami, and right now he just wanted to soak in her warmth while he still could.

"Lila?"

She stretched her arms out. "Yeah?"

"I really do need to find Errol."

A look he couldn't quite identify came over her face. "I know," she said her voice barely audible. She turned to see the clock. "But will he still be up?"

Jon followed her glance, and was shocked to find that it was after midnight. He shook his head. "Where did the day go?"

Lila laughed and as soon as she said, "Merry Christmas Eve, Jon," his heart sank into his stomach.

Christmas Eve...

With his mood sobering, he climbed from the bed. He sat on the edge for a moment and worked to get his emotions under control.

"I have to go."

"I know," she said softly, and once again he got the sense that she could see right through him, that she knew more about him than he ever wanted her to.

Jon pulled on his clothes and made his way outside. He walked past Lila's car and glanced at her new tires. Jonah must have come by and replaced them sometime throughout the day when he and Lila were locked inside the bedroom. It was clear to Jon that she'd been saving her money to put a down payment on the B&B. He understood that, but he wasn't about to let her drive around town on bald tires. What if something happened to her? What if a car accident stole someone else he loved?

Loved.

Oh Jesus, he really was in trouble here.

It was well after one in the morning when Jon walked to the town square to get his vehicle, which had been sitting there since the night at Hauk's bar. After climbing into the driver's seat, he drove around town and stopped at Errol's house, then Delilah's. But when his search came up empty, he made his way to Hauk's bar. Since the lights were still on, he parked his SUV and hurried inside to find Errol, Byron and Harold drinking rum over a game of poker. All three were laughing and talking about who had to buy next month's rum.

"Errol," Jon said, stepping up to them. "We need to talk."

Errol folded his cards. "What's up, boy?"

"That's what I want to know."

Harold finished his rum and slammed his glass onto the table. "Guess that's our cue to leave," he said to Bryon.

As soon as the two older gentlemen disappeared, Jon pulled out a chair and met his uncle's cloudy eyes. Getting right to the point, he asked, "Why did you ask me to come home?"

"'Cause I missed ya."

"Missed me? You call me back for no apparent reason then continue to avoid me."

"It wasn't for no apparent reason," Errol said, his eyes twinkling mischievously.

"Then let me guess. It was so you could meddle in my life."

"Who told you I've been meddling?" he asked, accusingly. "I bet it was Jacob." He cursed under his breath. "That boy's got a big mouth."

Jon had no idea what Errol was going on about, but redirected the conversation. "You lied to me about Lila. You said she wasn't interested in buying the house."

"That's 'cause you aren't ready to sell it," he said, his cloudy eyes suddenly clear, full of wisdom.

"Did you lie about the termites and Aunt Annette and Uncle Pete too?"

Errol didn't need to answer because his sheepish expression told Jon what he needed to know. He exhaled slowly, anger rushing through him as he planted his elbows on the table.

Errol touched his arm. "Don't be mad. I just wanted you home."

"Why? So you could turn me away at your door?" As soon as the words left his mouth, Jon realized what his great-uncle had done, realized that he hadn't just been meddling where his property was concerned, he'd been meddling in his personal affairs, and in Lila's livelihood. "Jesus," he whispered under his breath. "I get that you wanted to interfere in my life because we're related, but you didn't have to drag Lila into this too."

"I saw you with Lila the other night and from the glow on her face I'd say she's pretty happy with my meddling."

"Errol—"

"Jon," he said cutting him off, "your parents were good people who wanted what was best for you, and Miami isn't it. You need to be home, surrounded by those who love you. And you need to stop blaming yourself, because no one else does."

With emotions getting the better of him, Jon jumped up and his chair scraped across the wooden floor as he said, "Sell her the house, Errol."

Flying past Byron and Harold, Jon made his way outside. He hopped into his vehicle and hurried back to the B&B. When he opened the door and found Lila fully dressed, with a worried look on her face, his gut tightened.

"Are you okay?" he questioned.

She nodded, and he spotted genuine concern in her eyes when she asked, "Are you?"

"We need to talk."

"I know."

"I spoke with Errol."

"And?"

"And he's going to sell you this place."

Air left her lungs, and he didn't miss the wounded look on her face. "I don't want it, Jon."

Perplexed by her reaction, he said, "But you—"

"I changed my mind."

He ran a shaky hand through his hair. "What's going on around here anyway?"

She reached for his other hand. "I want you to come with me."

He gave a hard shake of his head and glanced at the clock. "No. I have to go."

"Why?"

"Because it's Christmas Eve and your family will be here soon."

"That's no reason to run away."

"I don't belong here, Lila. I shouldn't be at a family gathering that I don't deserve to be a part of."

"Jon—"

"No, you don't understand. There are things you don't know about me. I tried to tell you that first night we made love, but you stopped me and then...well, then I never told you because I didn't want to ruin what we had."

"And what do we have, Jon?"

"It's just...I don't..."

"Well, I do know. And if you think I'm going to let you run away from this thing between us, like you've run away from this town and the people in it, then you've got another thought coming."

His head jerked back. "What are you talking about?"

"Come with me."

Going against his better judgment, because he was getting far more involved with her than he ever should have allowed, he followed her up the stairs and into the attic.

Swallowing the knot in his throat, he glanced around at all the boxes. "Why did you bring me up here?"

"Because it's Christmas Eve, Jon."

"I don't understand."

"Sit down."

He sank to the floor and she shuffled in beside him. Then she reached into a box and pulled out a stack of pictures. With a soft smile on her face, she said, "Tell me about this Christmas."

Jon's heart turned over his chest when he saw a picture of himself standing next to his mini bike. "I loved that bike," he said, his voice cracking slightly.

"I guess that's why your parents kept it, so you could pass it on to your own child." She grabbed another picture, one of his mom and dad. "Tell me about them."

Jon scrubbed his chin. "Lila, what are you doing?"

She cupped his face. "Helping you heal. It's time you learned to celebrate the lives of your parents, not spend all your time mourning them and feeling guilty."

He blew out a slow breath and stared at the picture of his mom and dad. "So you knew, then? You knew all along who I was and you still wanted to be with me?"

"I realized who you were after talking to Errol at the craft bazaar, and it never changed how I felt about you."

"Why didn't you say something?"

"I figured you'd tell me when you were ready."

He felt his throat close over. "It was my fault, Lila. If I hadn't been so selfish..."

She pressed her finger to his lips. "You are the least selfish man I know and the only one blaming you, is you. The people in this town care about you and what you're seeing on their faces isn't blame, Jon, it's sadness. They want to reach out to you and help you but you won't let them. You're the one running away, and it's time to stop."

Jon took deep breaths as he thought more about the way the townsfolk greeted him and he couldn't deny that he felt their warmth, their genuine happiness to see him. He considered things longer, and as her words rattled around inside his brain he wondered if he'd been mistaken all these years. Was it possible that they didn't blame him? That both Lila and Errol were right?

"It's time to create new, happy memories on Christmas Eve, Jon."

"I miss them."

"I know," she said, and pressed her hand over his heart. "But they're still with you. In here."

He looked at the picture of his folks and before he knew it, he was opening up to Lila, telling her all about his childhood, his parents, his friends and his life in Whispering Cove. When they finished going through one box, Lila opened another, pulling out his baby clothes, pictures and toys.

As dawn approached, Jon felt his shoulders relax, because maybe, just maybe, Lila was right, and maybe he really was the only one blaming himself. He would never forget what happened to his folks, but maybe it was time to let go of the pain. Like Errol had said, it's what his parents would have wanted.

Jon gathered Lila into his arms. A hug turned to a kiss, which led to something far more intimate. Soon, after they each took a turn to slide down the old banister, they found themselves on the main level, kissing passionately in front of the Christmas tree. Lila tossed a heap of blankets on the floor and after another round of lovemaking they both fell asleep in front of the fire.

The sound of kids playing on the hill outside pulled Jon awake and he glanced at the beautiful woman snuggled up beside him. He pulled the blankets around her and his heart beat quicker as he looked at the sparkling lights on the tree she'd decorated. His thoughts drifted to Errol and all his meddling, and when he looked at Lila, a wonderful, caring, independent woman who lit the darkness inside him and allowed him to come to peace with the loss of his parents, anger at Errol's meddling dissolved. How could he be upset with his uncle when he only ever wanted what was best for Jon?

Lila's lids fluttered open and she smiled up at him.

"Hey," she said.

"Hey, yourself."

Her glance moved over his face and she frowned. "What's on your mind?"

He brushed her hair back and laughed. "Am I that transparent?"

She chuckled and marched her fingers over his chest. "Maybe to me."

"I was thinking of Errol."

"Ah, meddling Errol."

"Did you know what he was up to with us?"

"Not at first, but I figured that out the other night."

"Why didn't you say something?"

A mischievous grin curled her lips. "Because I wanted to see how things played out."

The rest of the walls surrounding his heart came tumbling down, because everything in the way she looked at him, with heat and desire, trust and respect—never blame and pity—spoke of a deeper, more meaningful emotion.

He felt a little jolt inside him, and asked, "Does this mean you want more than just sex from me?"

Lila laughed. "Pretty much from the minute you walked into this place."

He went quiet for a moment as he considered everything that had happened over the last few days. "I changed my mind about selling you this place, Lila."

He felt her body stiffen. "You did. Why?"

"I don't want to sell it anymore."

He spotted a mixture of hope and worry in her eyes. "You don't?"

"No, because I want to stay here and share it with you. If you'll have me, that is."

The smile that came over her face pushed away the last traces of coldness inside him. Answering his question without words, she threw her arms around him and gave him a kiss so full of love and passion he wondered what he'd ever done to deserve her.

He inched back and looked deep into her smiling eyes. "How is it possible that someone like you has come into my life?"

Before she could answer, the sound of a car pulling into the driveway gained their attention. Lila squealed and jumped up to peer out the window. When she looked back at him, her mouth was agape, her eyes wide, tears pooling inside them.

Unease moved through Jon as he climbed to his feet. "Lila, what is it?" he asked, pulling her into his arms.

"My car."

"What about it?"

"It has new snow tires on it."

He wiped her face. "Don't cry. I just wanted to get you something for Christmas."

Before she could say anything, the doorbell rang. They both hurried into their clothes and picked their bedding up from the floor. Then Lila opened the door to let her family inside.

Jon stood back and took in the chaos. Seeing Lila so happy as her family all hugged and kissed one another had his heart swelling, and when he thought about what Lila had done for him last night, how she helped him create happy memories, he knew he was the luckiest guy in the world.

He also knew he wanted this, all of this, and he wanted it with her, a woman who opened his eyes and made him feel so deserving. First chance, he planned to clear out his life in Miami and place his shingle beside Dani's, where it had always belonged, where his parents would have wanted it to hang.

Once the flurry of activity inside his childhood home slowed down, Lila captured Jon's hand. She introduced him to her family, who all greeted him with open arms. Even her sister's dog, Molly, who gave him a big lick across the mouth, seemed happy to meet him.

As her parents and siblings all went off to put their suitcases in their bedrooms, Lila dragged him back into the main room. He stood in front of the tree as she reached into a box, and when she pulled out a stocking with his name on it, his heart tightened painfully.

He took it from her, and traced his fingers over the stitching. Everything inside him reached out to her, and he swallowed the lump in his throat. "Lila," he choked out, "you didn't have to go through—"

She pressed her lips to his and whispered, "How many times do I have to tell you that you're worth the trouble?" When she inched back, she searched his face. "Will you hang it with me tonight?"

As he looked at her and realized how many good memories they were going to create, he said, "I wouldn't miss it for the world." Then he gave a slow shake of his head. "How is it possible that someone like you has come into my life?" he asked again.

"Errol," she said laughing. "Or should I say Saint Nick, because he sure answered my Christmas wish."

As Jon laughed along with her, his phone beeped. He

pulled it from his pocket and opened the text. "Speaking of Errol."

"What is it?"

"Looks like he's still at it." Jon couldn't help but grin at the old man's antics. "He said he was supposed to play Santa in the parade this afternoon, but he's feeling under the weather and needs me to do it."

Lila wrapped her arms around his waist and hugged him. "I guess he thinks you still plan on leaving today."

"And this is his way of keeping me here."

"Well, since you're staying..." She poked him in the stomach. "We'd better get you into the kitchen and get some food into you if you're going to play Santa." She gave him a playful wink and added, "Besides, isn't the way to a man's heart through his stomach?"

Jon cupped her face and as his heart soared with love and laughter, home and hearth, he planted a warm kiss on her mouth. "You've already got my heart, Lila." He grinned and added, "It comes with the house."

"Oh does it now?"

"Yes, it also comes with lazy Sunday afternoons, a house full of kids and slow-cooked meals."

She kissed him and he felt her love reach out to him when she whispered, "I'm so happy I finally found someone to cook for."

Jon pulled her in tighter and they both laughed when he said, "That's good, because you and I both know I really, really need someone to cook for me."

"Another round of couples mated." Byron raised his tumbler for a toast. "Couldn't ask for better Christmas presents."

"Especially the one of us with a month's supply of rum comin'." Errol laughed.

"That wouldn't be you, you old codger." Harold rearranged his cards and then moved them back to their original arrangement. He'd convinced himself long ago that playing with his cards would keep Byron and Errol off guard. It never did.

"You can't think you won," Bryon exclaimed. "Your plan was an afterthought."

Errol rolled the bottom edge of his tumbler on the table and nodded thoughtfully. "An afterthought he couldn't pull off without us to help."

"That desperation made you easy to read." Like too many of their bets there was no clear winner, but Byron had decided that somebody was paying up this time. "The kids saw right through you."

"You think they didn't see through you pulling Josh Byran in?"

"You may as well have been waving a flag declaring yer plans."

"But I was never doubted." Bryon smiled. "See, it's not a hard sale that Josh loved the town enough to come here a second time."

"And Jon would've had to deal with his house whether Lila had been there or not." Harold huffed in apparent triumph.

"Ye claimin' victory by the simplicity of your plans?"

Bryon shrugged. Never knew you to be such a sore loser."

"Fine." Errol groused. "You think I lost. Tell me who won."

"Bryon and Harold looked at each other, neither of them able to say one had beaten the other. It dawned on Byron that maybe they got so wrapped up in getting couples together they failed to get specific in their terms.

"You can't do it," Errol laughed. "You can't say it cuz it ain't true."

"You're right," Harold drawled. "But if neither of us won, then we tied."

"Which would mean Errol owes us both a supply of rum."

"That was not part of the bet," Errol argued. "But it's Christmas so I'll be the better man and give ye each half a supply."

"No way," Bryon shook his head and rested his swollen fingers over his cards. "We don't want your pity rum, but I have a new proposition."

Harold and Errol both straightened in their chairs.

"We lay low until spring, planning our next couples." Bryon smiled as the idea grew firmer. "We each have the same start and end date. Our couples must declare their love publicly. The most unique declaration, determined by the complexity of their vow, wins the bet.

Harold and Errol each grinned. Nodded slowly. "And the two losers owe a month's supply of rum."

Bryon raised his tumbler and waited for his poker pals to raise theirs "Doe we have a deal?"

They clinked glasses and began debating the rules of their next wager. They would be specific.

FLIRTY

In Whispering Cove

A salty breeze blew off the ocean, whispering through Harold Adair's hair as he sat in his lounge chair and pushed his toes beneath the warm sand. His heavy eyelids began to droop, but the chill against his palm reminded him he held a half-full glass of his favorite rum propped on his barreled chest. He raised the tumbler to his lips and took a swig, allowing the amber liquid to quench his parched throat.

"Ahhh." Life couldn't be any better.

His granddaughter, Andrea Adair—now McGrath—was home where she belonged. Married to her high school sweetheart, Andie had two healthy boys with her husband Brody. Said boys were playing beneath their watchful parents' eyes.

Harold smiled.

Donal followed a sand crab moving sideways to avoid the stick the naughty boy used to poke at it. His twin brother, Daniel, chased a receding wave. When the wave made an about-face, the boy squealed. He spun around, his chubby little legs going a mile a minute as he tried to outrun the water licking at his ankles.

Daniel's giggles warmed Harold's heart, until the crab Donal harassed got wedged between two rocks and the child turned his attentions to his brother. With a shove, Daniel ended up facedown in the sand and water. Before the ocean could engulf the child, his father ran to his side, jerking him into the safety of his arms.

The scream Daniel released as he spat sand out of his mouth made Brody, the local sheriff, frown. "If your momma wasn't here I'd tan your hide, Donal."

The twenty-month-old puckered his lips. His big blue eyes took on a sad puppy-dog look that always did Harold in.

As Andie approached, she shook her head and narrowed her sights on her husband. "Who are you trying to kid? You've never raised a hand to either of these boys." She dropped to her knees before Donal. "You know what you did was wrong. I think you need a time out."

"Momma—"

"No, Donal." She pushed to her feet, her hands propped against her slender hips. She glared down at the child, who inhaled a ragged breath, clearly on the verge of tears. "You don't treat your brother like that. Now get to the blanket and sit beneath the umbrella until I say you can get up and play."

"Andie?"

"Brody, I don't want to hear 'boys will be boys'." She extended her arms toward Daniel and he crawled into them. Brushing away the sand caking his face, she held him close and kissed his forehead.

Daniel was the quieter of the two—a gentle soul. His brother? Well, that was another story. But they were both angels in Harold's eyes.

"Let's clean you up. Brody, he's yours to watch while I'm gone." She glanced to where Donal sat. Silent tears streamed down his dirty cheeks. "I want to see him sitting right there when I return." She leveled a firm eye on her husband, who had the good sense to simply nod, before she pivoted and walked away.

Errol Wilson chuckled. "She's a good mother." A stiff breeze blew the thin piece of gray hair that was usually combed over his bald head to the side. After he patted the stringy stuff back in place, he reached for the half-empty bottle of rum propped in the sand by the leg of his lounge chair.

"Aye. She be the best." There was no better in Harold's eyes.

Errol filled his glass and frowned at the remaining contents of the bottle. "Looks like it's time for another bet."

Byron Mitchell swirled the amber liquor in his glass, making the ice cubes clink against the sides. "My cupboards are bare too."

The arthritic man made up the final member of their threesome. Together they had finagled their wayward grandchildren to return home. With a little more conniving, they had even gotten them hitched and settled down. Now and then they tried their hand at matchmaking and had become quite successful.

The way Harold saw it, they were doing this town a service. "I agree." It was time they put their matchmaking skills to work again.

"I've been thinking," Errol said.

Laughter burst from Byron's mouth. "Did it hurt much?"

"Real funny, you ol' blowfish." Yet Errol chuckled at his friend's teasing. "What do you say we make this bet a little more interesting?"

Byron leaned forward in his chair. "What do you have in mind?"

"Let's change it up a little. How 'bout a public declaration by either the man or woman."

Byron's brows shot upward. "In front of a crowd?"

Harold liked the idea. "The most creative expression of love."

"Anywhere? Any size group?" When Harold and Errol nodded, Byron continued. "Since today is June first, the deadline should by the Fourth of July Parade."

The gleam in his eyes had Harold a little concerned. His friend of many years was up to something. "Who should we be focusing on this year?"

Byron looked over Harold's shoulder. "Here comes my man now."

Harold's gaze followed both of his friends'. "Ryan Alden? The boy recently returned to town."

"Two months ago. After twelve years in the Marines, it's time he settled down."

It dawned on Harold exactly what Byron had been up to. "Why you scalawag. You've been sneaking around and preparing for our next bet."

Harold shot a look of disbelief toward Errol. When he expected his friend to join in berating Byron and he didn't, it became clear he'd been the only one waiting for the next bet to be announced. But to confirm it, he asked, "You too?" When Errol shrugged, Harold grumbled, "Well, you liver-lily pond-suckers. Who have you chosen?"

"Sam Doherty." Errol grinned ear to ear as he glanced over to Sam, who was playing catch with young Jake Caan on the other end of the beach.

"He be old man Doherty's grandson, right? The ghost hunter?" Harold shook his head. Whoever heard of a grown man who believed in ghosts?

"This wouldn't have anything to do with the young woman who purchased Ol' Lady Landry's old Victorian house?" Byron asked.

A sheepish expression spread across Errol's weathered

face as he looked at the big house overlooking the ocean at the far end of the beach.

Byron took a sip of his drink. "What have you been up to?"

"Just a little funny business. You know I have a key to Ol' Lady Landry's place."

"You be scaring the poor lassie out of her wits." Harold thought of the big, creaky house. It was perfect for a little mischief. He glanced toward Byron. "Suppose you have someone in mind to match Alden up with?"

Byron nodded toward Carmen Smith as she walked from the water in her fifties-style swimsuit. "It's about time that young chickadee settled down."

Her older sister, Aimee, had captured Byron's attention at Christmas time. Two months ago she had married her daughter's baby daddy, as it should be.

Byron raised his glass and Errol clinked his against it. "Best you get to fishing or cut bait." He rose from his chair and glanced to the large Victorian house down the beach. "I have a little tomfoolery in mind."

Harold harrumphed. Of all the rotten things for his two best friends to have done, he was now behind the eight ball.

He gazed around the growing crowd, stopping when he caught sight of Lauren Savage, Brody's secretary from the police station, playing volleyball. Now *she* showed possibility. The attractive blonde had been in town for almost two years and hadn't reeled in any particular man.

A very pregnant Tabby and her brother Devon Taylor walked up to Brody, reminding Harold one of their sisters had come of age. If Harold remembered correctly, Katrina, or Kat as she was known around these parts, had recently returned from college this year.

"Yes!" Lauren's squeal of delight as the volleyball she served struck the sand inside the boundaries on the other side of the net grabbed Harold's attention, before he glanced at Devon once more.

Hmmm. Lauren? Devon?

After the sworn bachelor helped his sister sit down next to Donal, he pinned his sights on the game of volleyball before him. But he didn't have eyes for Lauren, who again served the ball over the net. Instead his gaze was locked on a shapely redhead in a teeny-tiny bikini, playing on the opposite team.

Now there held some potential.

Instead of focusing on the bet between his friends, he'd choose a couple who would give him a run for his money. Devon was a laid-back construction worker. He lived life one day at a time and to its fullest. With his dark, shoulder-length hair and that bandanna, he wore the bad-boy persona well, but he wasn't fooling Harold. The young man had a heart of gold. No one messed with his sisters or mother and he was always there for someone in need.

The statuesque redhead was Leo Caan's sister, who had come to town early to help her brother and soon to be sister-in-law with their wedding arrangements, another couple Harold was responsible for hooking up. Sahara Caan was a Supreme Court Justice's daughter and a real estate developer. She was everything Devon wasn't. Different as black and white.

When she flashed Devon a drop-dead smile, Harold eased back in his lounge chair. From where he sat it didn't appear getting them together would be difficult at all.

But keeping them together... There lay the challenge.

$$26$$

Alexis Miller, aka Lex, shook her head in dismay and wondered what the heck she'd gone and gotten herself into. Here she was, stuck in the Podunk town known as Whispering Cove for thirty days now...*thirty whole days*, and had yet to accomplish a damn thing.

Her steel-toed work boots echoed in the silence of the attic as she spread her arms for balance. She picked her way along a dusty beam, doing a final count of the last few boxes and remaining pieces of antique furniture that had been collecting cobwebs for years.

When she'd purchased the century-old Victorian home in the coastal town of Maine a few months back, it had been with the intention of bringing in the crew she'd hired in Portland, flipping it within sixty days and having it sold by the first of July. Little did she know the old homestead had been deemed a heritage property. Which meant she had to have her plans approved by a restoration committee—one that moved at a snail's pace—before she could so much as screw in a new light bulb.

Damn. Damn. Damn.

So much for patting herself on the back for being such a smart and savvy business woman, saving enough money and securing loans to convert the old house into a gorgeous, state of the art, twenty-first-century modern home before any one of her four, overbearing brothers found out. She could only imagine the looks on their faces if they ever discovered the mess she'd gone and gotten herself into. Instead of finally proving she could be a competent, contributing member who could flip houses with the best of them—in their "boys only" construction company—she'd end up being the laughing stock of the Miller clan. Cripes, as if it wasn't hard enough being the youngest and only girl in a male-dominated family.

A low groan crawled out of her throat and when she lowered her head to shake it, she walked straight into a spider's web. She slipped off the beam, let loose a little yelp, and brushed dirt and dead insects off her clothes as she stumbled backward, her long ponytail slapping against her heat-flushed cheeks. Good Lord, it had to be at least a gazillion degrees in the attic.

She turned direction, flipped open the octagon vent and sneezed as she disturbed a decade's worth of dust. At least while she waited for the proper permits to come in, and the town's only restoration company to get back to her, she was able to keep herself busy by clearing out most of the attic and part of the basement. She'd already unloaded numerous pieces of furniture that looked to be about as old as the crazy old fella who'd been snooping around the place for weeks now.

She'd donated a few items to charity and had taken a few antique pieces to the local pawn shop. What wasn't salvageable she dumped, all with the help of Jake Caan, a teenager who was more than happy to do odd jobs for cash.

Jake, nephew of Officer Leo Caan, was a nice kid, here for his uncle's upcoming wedding to Skylar Wellington. He'd come in early with his Aunt Sahara, and his parents would be following later for the wedding. As far as Lex could tell, Jake was the only one in the tight-knit community who didn't give her the big stink eye when she talked about making changes to the house. Probably because he wasn't a local.

Cripes, the more she thought about it, the more she realized how caught up she'd gotten in the lives of everyone in town. Learning far more about the folks, their families, their kids and jobs than she ever intended, seeing as she was just passing through.

But the truth was, while most of the people were helpful and nice, they had also urged her to embrace and preserve the heritage in the old homestead instead of refurbishing from the ground up. Apparently the folk in Whispering Cove didn't like change. Since the Miller construction business focused on modernization and installing the latest and greatest technology, she had no choice but to bring the house up to today's standards. How else would she prove to her brothers, and maybe to herself, that she was good enough for their all-boys club?

She had a meeting with Devon Taylor tomorrow. Apparently the company he ran with Reece McGrath was the only one in town licensed to handle preservation work. She hoped that once she got the proper permits his company would be able to do the work, otherwise she had no idea where she'd turn. But she'd cross that bridge when she came to it, because the first thing she needed to do was secure the necessary permits.

"Uh oh, now you've gone and done it."

The sound of a gravelly voice behind her had Lex spinning around. Speaking of the crazy old coot.

"Gone and done what?" she asked, as Errol Wilson, one of the locals who liked to pop by unannounced, waved his glass cane in her direction.

His cloudy eyes narrowed and he pinched his thin lips into a straight line as he held one hand out, palm toward her. "Can't you feel it?"

She eyed him suspiciously. "Feel what?"

"That cold spot?"

Cold spot?

Lex wiped the moisture from her brow. "It's stifling up here, Errol."

He gave a slow shake of his head, his gray brows furrowing as he made a *tsking* sound. "I'm afraid I knew this would happen."

Deciding to humor him—after all, he really was a nice old man and she needed something to keep herself occupied with while she waited for the restoration company to call—she asked, "Okay, what happened, what have I gone and done?"

He waved his cane toward the boxes, then walked over to the small door leading to the rooftop and ladder outside—an access point to the lower deck that made roof maintenance much easier. He fussed with the lock, then jimmied the small door open and closed it before saying, "You went and disturbed Ol' Lady Landry is what you've done, lassie."

"Ol' Lady Landry?"

"Meanest teacher in town." He looked past her shoulders like he was remembering something. "If I had a nickel for every time she took her ruler to my knuckles." He chuckled and added, "I probably deserved it, though. Especially when I put that rubber snake in her desk." He laughed a little harder. "That woman did not like snakes."

"Why are we talking about Ol' Lady Landry?"

"Because this used to be her place and you've disturbed her rest with all the messing around ya been doing."

Disturbed her rest?

"Ah, are you suggesting I have a ghost?" She eyed him carefully and considered putting a call in to Doc Jon Wilson

—who she'd come to learn was Errol's great-nephew—to find out if Errol had come off his meds. Or perhaps he'd been dipping into the rum a little too early on this beautiful June afternoon. Oh yeah, she'd heard all about the drinking habits of the gruesome threesome.

"Ain't suggesting nothin'. Telling you straight up ya got yourself a ghost." He gave a mock shiver and hugged himself. "A dang mean one too." He took a step forward and felt the air. "Oh yeah, she's here and she's madder than a flounder caught in a trawler's net with all this nonsense of modernizing the place." He glanced at her. "You can't tell me you don't feel that?"

The only thing she was feeling was the beginning of a headache. "Errol..." she began, thinking that the cold spot in the room was between Errol's ears.

He waved his cane, the beautiful colors catching in the stream of light shining through the attic's open vent. "Don't 'Errol' me, lassie." He went quiet for a moment, like he was mulling something over, then his eyes lit with childlike excitement, making her think he wasn't quite as crazy as she had originally thought. "What you need is someone to cleanse the place. Let Ol' Lady Landry know you ain't gonna mess with her homestead. That'll get her settled back down." He pursed his lips and nodded his head, looking rather pleased with himself. "And as luck would have it, I know just the guy to help."

Real concern gnawed at Lex's gut. Not wanting to insult him, but genuinely worried that something upstairs might not be firing correctly, she asked in a soft voice, "Errol, have you talked to Jon lately?"

He gave her an odd look. "Jon? What's my great-nephew got to do with this? No, I'm talking about Sam Doherty, Jon's best friend. He's a ghost hunter, you know."

"A ghost hunter. Errol I don't believe—"

"Yup, down in New Mexico. And wouldn't you know it, he's home visiting for the month." He frowned and added under his breath, "Damn time that boy grew up and came back for good too." He pounded his cane into the old plank floor. Dust rained from the ceiling and the sound echoed around them as he leaned forward to put his weight on it. "I can send him your way."

"I'm sure I don't—"

A squeal outside caught her attention and her words fell off. She took a tiny step backward and glanced out the vent to see the waves of the beautiful Atlantic Ocean splash against the sandy shore. On the wide stretch of beach below, the townsfolk gathered in groups. With their arms filled with kids, and food and blow-up floaty toys, the women all huddled together in a circle, smiling and chatting loudly. Lex felt a little hitch in her heart as she watched them congregate, everyone filing from their houses and coming together on the massive expanse of shoreline like one big family.

Errol smiled. "That sounds like my little Katherine. She loves to play in the water, that one." He crinkled his nose. "Don't matter how dang cold it is, either."

Lex noted the way his eyes lit when he talked about his great-granddaughter. It was easy to tell how much he liked being surrounded by his family. It had her thinking of her own family, and how much of an outcast she felt amongst them. She loved her brothers and father dearly, but when her mother ran out on them all, shortly after her fifth child was born, Lex always carried a sense of loss and responsibility. Even after her mother had finally gotten the baby girl she'd always wanted, it still wasn't enough to keep her around.

She wasn't enough to keep her around.

Lex swallowed against the tightness in her throat. She'd had plenty of girlfriends over the years, of course—rarely a boyfriend for long since her brothers always scared them off —but she'd never had a real sense of belonging, of sisterhood.

Of being good enough.

"I best be going." Errol turned to leave, then tossed his next words over his shoulder. "Ain't ya coming?"

"Coming?"

"To the beach party." He moved toward the steep staircase. "It's tradition, lassie. The whole town gathers at the beach to kick off the summer."

Lex was about to ask if he needed help negotiating the steps, but bit her tongue. It was easy to tell Errol was a prideful man and she didn't want to insult him by taking his arm. Instead she slipped ahead of him. If he fell, he'd land on her. She might be small-framed, but at least she'd help beak his fall.

When Errol reached the bottom step, she closed the attic hatch behind them. He poked his nose into her bedroom. "I see you're sleeping in the back room. Nice view of the ocean. Makes ya feel right at home, don't it?"

Even though she never really had a true sense of home or belonging, she nodded in agreement. Not wanting to talk about home and hearth anymore, she led him to the next set of stairs going down to the main level. Once they reached the hallway, she walked Errol to the door and opened it. As the cool breeze rushed up from the ocean it felt refreshing against her overheated body.

"Well, you comin' or what?"

She looked at her oversized navy-blue coveralls. While they were heavy and uncomfortable, if she wanted to be taken seriously in a male-dominated field, she had to look, act and dress the part. "I don't have a swimsuit."

"You look to be about the same size as my Katy." He paused and crinkled his nose as he perused her baggy clothes. "Although it's hard to tell under all that dang material. But

I'm sure my granddaughter, or any one of her friends, can rustle you up a suit."

"No, it's okay. I still have a lot to do."

Errol tapped his cane on the floor. "Damn young'uns don't know how to have any fun anymore." Before he left, he shot her one last glance. He had an ominous look in his eyes, and his voice turned serious when he said, "Now you heed my warning, lassie. Don't go messin' with Ol' Lady Landry."

"Okay, Errol, I won't," she said, unable to keep the grin from her face.

"If she causes you any trouble, you let me know and I'll get my boy Sam right on it."

After Lex saw him out, keeping an eye on him as he hobbled down the sandy path leading to the water, she walked to the kitchen. Squeals of delight echoed through the big, empty house, and she couldn't help but sneak a peek at the fun taking place on the beach just beyond her back veranda. She opened her back veranda door and walked out. She might have been in Whispering Cove for one whole month, but she was sure she'd never get used to the magnificent views. The place was a far cry from the concrete jungle she glimpsed through her condo window back in Portland.

The smell of food being grilled over coals at the far end of the beach reached her nose and her stomach growled. Flames shot up from a small barbeque and she looked past it to spot a few adults playing volleyball. She scanned the beach, smiling at the kids making a castle in the sand, until her glance landed on two guys tossing a football around on the sand below, merely a few feet from her back veranda.

She narrowed her eyes, and realized it was young Jake tossing a ball to a guy she hadn't seen around town before— and a very fine-looking guy he was.

With swim trunks hanging low on his hips, her gaze zeroed in on his oblique muscles, her favorite part on a man's body. Oddly enough, warmth tingled in her belly, and the fine hairs on her neck stood at attention. Intrigued, she moved to the paint-chipped wooden rail for a better look. Hoping to go unnoticed, she watched him, watched the way his eyes lit up when he laughed, the way his tight muscles bunched and relaxed again as he threw the ball. She took in his dark hair, his sun-kissed skin, and the easy way he carried himself, like he didn't have a worry in the world.

Jacob Collins, one of the town's veterinarians, along with his Saint Bernard, Charlie, strolled up to talk with Mr. Hottie. She spotted a pretty blonde girl walking beside Jacob, her own dog, a big chocolate lab, on a leash. From her peripheral vision she caught Errol walking over to Jake. The teen had been staying at Errol's place while he was in town. Apparently there was way too much girly stuff going on at his uncle Leo's place as Skylar prepared for the wedding. Jake shot a quick glance her way, and she thought she caught a mischievous grin on his young face before he walked away with Errol. She watched the two for a moment, wondering what chore Errol was currently giving Jake and why he wasn't playing with little Katherine.

When they were out of her line of sight, Lex turned her full attention back to the girl in the string bikini, if one could even classify the skimp of material a bikini. The girl moved to Mr. Hottie's side. She touched him in a very flirtatious, very suggestive manner, and naturally he responded like any man would. When he gave her a smile that had "my place or yours" written all over it, Lex instantly pegged him as the playboy type. Having grown up with four brothers, she knew every type, from Mr. Responsible to Mr. Carefree. And that man digging his toes in the surf, looking like some sort of perfectly sculpted sand god, definitely leaned toward the latter.

Since she wasn't into one-night stands, Lex went out of

her way to avoid the love 'em and leave 'em kind of guys. She glanced at her unflattering apparel and backtracked. Okay, maybe it was more like *they* went out of their way to avoid her, and when it came right down to it, she wasn't into any kind of "stands"—one-night or long-term. Still, Mr. Hottie was nice to look at.

So look she did.

Her glance moved over his broad shoulders and his rock-hard abs before going lower, halting just below the belt area. As she checked him out, her blood warmed and desire moved into her stomach. The guy was smokin' hot, and as sunlight spilled over his body, her mind strayed in an erotic direction.

With her nipples tightening, her gaze moved back to his handsome face. When she found him staring back, a wide, knowing grin curling his lips, her stomach bottomed out and her blood burned hot.

Oh, shit.

Mortified that she'd been caught ogling him, she ducked back inside. As she hid behind her door, embarrassment flooding her veins, she vowed never to step foot outside again. But when a loud noise overhead shook the house to its very foundation, followed by a strange cackling sound, she bolted though the house, out the front door, and straight into a waiting Errol's arms.

Sam Doherty stared at the now-empty veranda overlooking the beach and wondered if he was seeing things. One second a beautiful young woman was standing there staring down at him, and the next thing he knew she was gone, appearing and disappearing faster than a ghostly apparition. Maybe Errol was right. Maybe the place was haunted.

At least that's what his best friend's great-uncle, Errol Wilson, had told him over the phone when he called him home from New Mexico. He'd insisted he needed to cleanse the house and send Ol' Lady Landry back to her resting place.

Sam wasn't opposed to coming home, and when he'd heard that his best friend, Jon, had moved back to town, living in his childhood home nonetheless, with a girl who'd turned it into a bed and breakfast, he was excited to hang out with him and catch up on life.

He also loved springtime in his hometown, and since his ghost-hunting team was on a break while his two co-workers ran off to get married, he had nothing better to do with his time then come home and relax with family and friends.

He'd flown in late last night and after sharing a few stories and a few drinks with his folks at Hauk's bar, he crashed and crashed hard. But the sound of the afternoon beach party pulled him from his childhood bed—and a room that his parents hadn't changed since he'd left some ten years ago. Anxious to get out and see all his old friends, he headed straight for the ocean, hoping to eventually catch up with Errol and get the deets on the alleged haunted house.

Excusing himself from the overfriendly girl Jacob had introduced him to, he took a few steps toward the Victorian house, scanning the windows and back veranda. He stood there for a long moment, waiting for the apparition to reappear. But when he heard a loud noise inside, he rushed around to the front door, only to find Errol with his arms around the prettiest girl he'd ever set eyes on. The same one who was staring at him from the deck.

"Oh, I...excuse me," Sam said, giving Errol a playful, atta' boy wink. "I didn't mean to interrupt."

Errol's head came back with a start and when his eyes lit with understanding, he snarled. "Dang, boy. What's the matter with you? Ain't nothing going on here. You're seeing things again."

"Hey, Errol," Sam said, holding his hands up palms out as

he began backing away. "I know what I saw, but you don't owe me any explanation," he said, teasing. "Your business is your business."

"You think I could catch me a fine filly like this?" Errol waved his cane, and Sam caught the small swagger in the elderly gentleman's step as he let go of the girl and inched back. He gave a cocky shake of his head and added, "'Course, in my younger days..."

Sam turned toward the petite woman, who was staring up at him with those almost-too-big blue eyes, and asked, "I heard screaming. Is everything okay?"

She blinked twice, then shrugged, her big old coveralls flapping around her body. "I'm not sure." She jerked her thumb toward the house. "I was inside and, and well... earlier Errol thought he felt cold spots...and then I heard this bang... and I think a scream, and there was a rush of air." She stopped talking, and took a breath. "I'm sorry, I don't usually ramble on and I'm sure there is a logical explanation for all this. I mean, it's not like I believe in ghosts."

Sam held his hand out for a shake and gave her a wide smile. "I'm Sam Doherty. Ghost hunter."

Her eyes widened as they went from Sam to Errol back to Sam again. "Oh, I didn't mean... I didn't realize it was you."

"You know me?" he asked, the richness in his voice seeping under her skin and affecting her in the strangest ways.

"Errol mentioned that he could get you to help me." She slipped her hand into his, and when his fingers curled around hers for a shake, he realized just how small she really was. His glance moved over her again. As he took in her five-sizes-too-big coveralls, he couldn't help but wonder more about the girl who kept her figure hidden and her hair pulled back into a tight ponytail. The tomboy look she was going for didn't really seem to suit her, yet it did prove to intrigue him more.

Since Sam was a man who could see more than most, he took a moment to look beyond the image she presented to the world. He suddenly found himself visualizing what she'd look like in clothes that actually fit her small frame, or better yet, no clothes at all...

"And here Errol never mentioned a thing about you," he said.

His eyes moved over her flushed cheeks, taking a long time to access her. Even without makeup she was gorgeous, in a girl-next-door, wholesome kind of way. And that mouth... wow. With just a little pout to it, that mouth was made for kissing. His lips twitched, and he fought the natural inclination to lean into her, to press his lips to hers to see if they felt as soft as they looked.

Of course, unlike all his friends, who were settling down and having kids, he hadn't come back to Whispering Cove looking for long term. *Been there, done that.* But while he was here, he sure wasn't opposed to getting to know the girl that Errol had seemed to take a liking to. Not that he could blame him. There was just something about this girl, and the sweetness she exuded, that brought out the protector in a guy.

With her hand still in his, he asked, "And you are?"

"I'm Lex Miller."

A wide grin split his mouth.

"What?" She pulled her hand from his, a challenging look on her face as she glared at him, like she was waiting for some smart-assed comment.

Since he didn't want to disappoint her...

"Lex?" he asked, thinking back to all the times he and Jon had camped out in their backyards, spending hours poring over Superman comic books. "As in Lex Luthor, Superman's nemesis?"

"No," she said. And even though the stain on her cheeks was deepening, she angled her head in a defiant manner and held her own against his teasing. Damned if he didn't like that about her. "As in Alexis Miller, old house restoration and modernization specialist."

He stepped closer and when he caught the sweet citrus scent of her skin, he bit back a moan. "Now what a team we make," he said, giving her a playful wink to let her know he was teasing...sort of. "You don't believe in ghosts, and I don't believe in restoring old houses."

At least not anymore.

Before he could say more, he got a glass cane to the gut. Hard. He bent forward and let out an agonized oomph.

Errol poked him again and growled, "What's your dang problem, boy? You leave your manners in New Mexico? Why, if your father..."

As Errol continued with his litany, Alexis mouthed the words, "I think he's off his meds."

Loving her sense of humor, and knowing they were going to get along just fine, Sam let out a laugh. Once he was able to straighten back up, he asked, "So, Alexis, what is it that Errol said I could help you with?"

"He thinks I have a ghost."

As she looked up at him with those bedroom blues, his mind raced, thinking about all the naughty delicious things he'd like to help her with, and not one of them involved cleansing her house of a ghost.

$$27$$

Since the last thing Lex believed in were ghosts, and despite the fact that her traitorous body was urging her to invite this gorgeous man inside to explore her...*house*...she opened her mouth, completely prepared to tell him that she didn't need his help, only to find herself blurting out, "I think the noise came from the upstairs bedroom."

Sam's lips twitched. "Would that be *your* bedroom?"

"Yes, just temporarily, until I can get the place restored and on the market."

He slanted his head, his eyes moving over her face. "So it's odd to hear noises, or even screaming, coming from your room."

When she caught the teasing glint in his dark eyes, her pulse leapt, totally knowing where he was going with this. Feeling a bit flustered as he stepped closer, his mere presence overwhelming her senses, she answered with, "Well yes... I mean no... I mean..."

"Well, what is it, Alexis? Is it or is it not normal to hear screaming coming from your bedroom?"

"No, it's not."

"Now that's a damn shame," he murmured under his breath as he turned his attention to her house.

Before she could respond, Errol poked Sam with his cane again and said, "Why don't you grab your gizmo thingies and check it out. You did bring them with you, didn't you?"

Sam ran his hands through his shoulder-length hair, humor in his voice when he asked, "My gizmos?"

Errol nodded. "Yeah, those gizmo things you use to trap ghosts."

"Ah, you mean my state of the art, electrometric gauge, pulse meter, strobe light and cage?"

"Yeah, boy. That's what I said, your gizmo thingies."

"Yeah, I brought them." He turned to Lex. "But first I need the lady's permission to enter her house."

A fine shiver moved through Lex, and she gave a breathless laugh. "You make it sound like you're a vampire, not a ghost hunter."

A sexy look came over his face and since she'd given him such a great opening, she was certain he was going to come back with another smart-assed comment. But then he looked at Errol and cleared his throat before explaining, "My team and I just don't believe in doing anything or going anywhere where we're not wanted." He met her glance straight on before he added, "I need to know you want me, Alexis."

Oh, God...

The guy was a big flirt, and every word that came out of his mouth was so suggestive, so sexy. Then again, maybe it was just her imagination, and she was simply reading him wrong, because everything about him made her think of sex. Either way, hell yeah she wanted him. But his teasing manner and easygoing nature told her he was a playboy and she wasn't about to get involved with a guy who read comic books and hunted ghosts in New Mexico.

"Yes, you have my permission," she said.

"Good, then I'll go grab my gizmos and be right back." He was about to leave, but turned back, real concern dancing in his dark eyes. "Will you be okay here, or did you want to come with me?"

Looking like the cat that swallowed the canary, Errol said, "Of course she's not going to be okay. You need to keep her close, boy."

Lex shook her head. She'd had enough coddling from brothers and didn't need the men here doing it, too. "No, Errol, I'll be fine."

"You ain't fine. You got yourself a ghost. And you shouldn't be alone in that big old house. Especially at night. I hear ghosts are more active after dark." He poked Sam with the cane. "I'll have a cot sent over and my boy Sam here will stay with you until the house is clean. Won't you, Sam?"

Dark eyes locked on hers, and his mouth turned up at the corner, a half smile that warmed her blood and curled her toes. "If it's what the lady wants."

"Of course that's what the lady wants. And don't worry, lassie. You're in good hands with this one."

She shook her head, knowing that if this handsome, hormone-stirring man was sleeping in the room next door a mean old ghost was the last of her problems.

"No. I'm fine. Sam, you go get your equipment and, Errol, you go and play with that sweet great-granddaughter of yours."

Errol was about to protest, but she pointed toward the shore. He followed the direction and smiled when he spotted Katherine. "Well, if you say so."

He seemed to have a new spring in his step, and a wide smile on his face as he walked toward the path. Lex watched for a second, and was pretty sure she heard him mumble something about a month's worth of rum as he went.

When she looked back at Sam he was grinning. "I think that man's losing it."

Lex gave a slow shake of her head, suddenly not so sure anymore. "I've got a sneaking suspicion he has all his wits about him, and then some. I also think he carries that cane so he can poke people with it."

Sam pulled a face and rubbed his gut. "I think I've got internal damage," he teased, and while she tried to focus on what he was saying, her gaze kept dropping to his bare chest. As heat moved through her body and she swallowed against the dryness in her throat, she hoped like hell that when he came back he had a shirt on.

Were all ghost hunters this buff?

"Are you okay?" Sam asked. "You're getting really flushed."

"I...uh...I was in the attic and it was hot and dusty. I just need to get a glass of water."

He pointed to the house and gave a wink before saying, "Okay, you go get a drink and try to avoid a run-in with Ol' Lady Landry before I get back."

She thought about Errol's ghost for a moment, then her thoughts shifted to the townsfolk and how they really didn't want her messing with the Victorian house. Was it possible that someone was trying to scare her on purpose?

"Sam," she said quietly when he turned to leave.

He twisted back around, and the smile fell from his face when his glance met hers. "Yeah, what is it?"

She shrugged. "You're from this town and know these people better than I do..."

"And?"

"And I was wondering if someone could be trying to scare me on purpose. To drive me out of town. No one seems to like what I'm doing here."

His face softened. "I don't think anyone here would do

that. But let me just get my gear, and see if Errol is on to something first, okay?"

After she nodded, he turned back around. As she watched him go, her gaze following his ass until he disappeared down the street, Lex walked back to the house. She opened the door and peeked inside. "Hello," she whispered. "Is there anyone here?"

When her question was met with silence, she gave a hard shake of her head to get it back on right. Ghosts weren't real! Shaking off her unease, she walked inside and glanced up the wide staircase as she made her way back to the kitchen. Even though she didn't believe in ghosts, she thought it best to wait for Sam to return before she went up to check out her bedroom.

She paced the main hall, and within fifteen minutes, Sam was back. He'd changed out of his swimsuit and now wore a pair of khaki shorts and a T-shirt that had a picture of a spoon and said "Cereal Killer". She held open the door for him and resisted the urge to roll her eyes. Some guys just never grew up.

Sam entered, carrying an armful of equipment. He stood in the foyer for a long moment, taking his time to look around. With his legs wide, and his eyes narrowed in deep concentration, it occurred to her that while he had a carefree nature, he took his job very seriously. He moved to the foot of the staircase and turned on some long wand-like piece of equipment. It made a high-pitched sound before settling into a steady beep.

He looked back at her. "Do you want to wait here?"

She shook her head and tried not to appear nervous. After all she didn't believe in ghosts, right? "I should probably come. To show you which bedroom is mine." Although she suspected a guy like Sam had no problem finding his way to a woman's bedroom, and probably did it on a regular basis. Not that she cared. She didn't.

The first step creaked beneath his weight as he began his ascent, and Lex stayed close behind. When they reached the top landing, she pointed to her bedroom. He gave the door a little push and stepped inside. Embarrassment flooded her when his glance strayed to her unmade cot and the stack of delicates that she'd rinsed by hand and taken off the line earlier.

His gizmo continued to beep steadily as he swept her room, then walked to the empty closet. He waved the wand thingy around inside and glanced up at the small, closed hatch overhead, one of the many access points to the attic.

"Your place is clean, Alexis." He turned to face her but she was standing so close, he bumped her. She faltered a little but he slipped his arm around her waist to hold her.

"It's...it's Lex," she corrected.

He smiled at her and his voice dropped an octave when he said, "Yeah, but I think Alexis suits you better." His hand splayed over the small of her back, the soft stroke of his fingers on her sensitive flesh sending skitters through her body when he added, "It's pretty, like you."

Did he just say I was pretty?

"Nobody calls—"

"Are you saying I'm nobody?" he teased.

"Okay, fine," she murmured and wondered what it was about this guy that had her feeling all silly and girlie inside. Maybe it was because she was standing inside a dimly lit closet with him, his strong arms around her waist as he anchored her body to his. Or maybe it was the way he looked at her, not through her like most guys, and didn't want to call her by a boy's name.

She wiggled to free herself from his arms, and if she

wasn't mistaken she thought she heard a low groan catch in his throat.

"So...uh...no ghosts?"

"No ghosts."

"Maybe Errol really is losing it," she said.

Sam cleared his throat and shifted his stance. Under his breath he grunted, "He's not the only one."

"What?"

"Nothing." She backed out of the closet and he followed her. As he stood over her, crowding her, he said, "I'll talk to the sheriff to see if any of the kids around town have been getting into mischief."

"Thanks, I'd appreciate that. I guess that's it then. I should probably let you get back to the beach party."

With her pulse pounding hard at the base of her neck, she practically ran down the stairs. Sam followed her, and when they reached the landing, she hurried to the door, needing a reprieve from the hot guy who smelled like an ocean breeze on a warm summer day and stirred all her senses.

He opened his mouth to say something, but before he could get any words out, a loud scream sounded from upstairs. Frightened, Lex clutched her chest and nearly jumped out of her skin. Before she realized what was happening, she once again found herself all wrapped up in Sam's arms. He dipped his head, his open lips so close to hers she could almost taste the sweetness of his mouth.

"It's okay. I've got you."

"What...what was that?"

He looked past her shoulder and up the stairs. "I don't know, but why don't you wait here and I'll go check it out again."

With her heart beating impossibly faster, her mind took that moment to revisit all the slasher movies she'd watched as a teen. "Have you never watched a scary movie?" She ran her finger over her neck in a cutting motion. "Whoever goes up the stairs alone is the first to get it."

"Alexis, it's okay," he said, equal measures of warmth and amusement moving into his eyes. "This is what I do for a living, remember?"

"I don't care. I'm still coming with you."

"Fine, but just stay behind me."

He gathered his equipment in one hand, and held her hand in the other.

"Maybe your gizmo isn't working," she whispered.

A strange sound rumbled in his throat before he said, "Oh my gizmo is definitely working."

When she caught the humor in his voice she suddenly wondered if he was talking about his ghost-hunting equipment or something else entirely. But she had no more time to think about it when he positioned her behind him and guided her up the stairs.

She couldn't deny that having him lead the way gave her a measure of comfort, and while she'd spent her whole life feeling suffocated by her overprotective brothers, there was nothing stifling in the way Sam was currently shielding her. In fact it made her feel all warm and safe inside, and she somehow knew that as long as he was with her, no harm would ever come. Errol had said she was in good hands with him, and deep in her gut, she knew he was right.

She kept tight on his heels, her chest practically pressed up against his back as they climbed higher. She breathed in his warm scent, and once again that delightful combination of sand and surf and something that was uniquely Sam stirred her body. When they reached the top landing, her bedroom door slammed shut with a resounding thud.

She gasped, but Sam just held her tight, and as he absorbed her tremors, it gave her a new sense of calm.

"Stay here," he whispered, positioning her against the

wall. His lips brushed her cheek, and every nerve in her body jumped when he put his mouth close to her ear to whisper, "Don't make a sound."

She held her breath as he left her there and moved to her bedroom door. He turned the knob and pushed, but it wouldn't budge. He ran his palm over the door trim, his brow furrowed in concentration.

When he looked at her she mouthed the words, "What is it?"

He walked away from the door and glanced into the other bedrooms before tipping his chin to examine the hallway hatch that she and Errol had come down earlier. "I'm just checking for a draft. Do you have any windows open up here?"

"No, the windows are the original rolled glass and the trim has been painted so many times they're sealed shut."

Just then the bedroom door creaked open and they exchanged a long look before Sam inched his way into the room. She waited in the hall, every nerve on edge, but then he stuck his head out and said, "There must have been a gust coming from the attic." He ran his hands along the edge of the old oak door. "And the wood is so old, it's probably just swollen in this humidity."

"Which is why it would have jammed," she said, following along with his explanation.

"Exactly."

"And I was up in the attic today," she explained. "I was clearing out old boxes. I left the vent open and Errol was doing something to the access door."

"There you go. That explains everything," he said, even though it didn't. Not really. Doors didn't just jam shut, and then creak open on their own. He gestured with a nod. "I can go up and check it out if you like."

"No, you've done enough."

He pressed his hand to the wall beside her head, and a small tremor moved through her.

He must have felt it, because he asked, "Are you sure you're going to be okay?"

"Yes," she said, knowing full well that tremor had little to do with fear and everything to do with this man and how close he was standing.

He got quiet for a moment, then dipped his head. "I could stay the night if you like."

"You...you want to stay the night."

"You know, in case you have any more trouble, or in case Ol' Lady Landry decides to make a visit. You heard Errol, ghosts are more active at night, and it's best not to be alone in this big old house."

"But your gizmo, you said it didn't sense anything. Are you now saying it might not have been working properly?"

"Believe me, Alexis. My gizmo senses everything and it's most definitely working properly."

It was nearing late afternoon by the time Errol had a cot sent over and Sam finished doing a thorough check of Alexis's house, sweeping it from top to bottom. Once he was convinced the place was ghost free and that no one was sneaking around inside, he'd tried to convince Alexis to go to Hauk's bar with him. Even though the beach party was still going on at the far end of the shore, he wanted to go somewhere quiet for dinner and drinks, so he could talk to Jon and get to know his wife Lila better. She'd declined, telling him she had phone calls to make but insisted he go. In fact, she seemed eager for him to go.

While he hated to leave her alone, he wanted to talk to Sheriff Brody McGrath and Officer Leo Caan, who were still kicking back in the sand, to make sure no one in Whispering

Cove was messing with Alexis and trying to scare her out of town. Not that he thought any of the good folks would do that, but still...

What Sam had discovered during his conversation with the sheriff, as well as over a glass of beer and pub food with his best friend Jon, was that the townsfolk really liked Alexis. When he mentioned all the strange noises she was hearing, and how he planned to stay in the old house to keep an eye on things, no one seemed surprised. In fact, Brody simply smirked and nodded. Even though he assured Sam he'd stop by to check on things, Sam had the strangest feeling the sheriff wasn't taking any of his concerns seriously.

After leaving Hauk's he cut through town square and hurried back to the house, a takeout container with a club sandwich and home fries tucked under his arm. He knocked but when no answer came he tried the front door and found it open. He stepped inside.

"Alexis, are you here? I brought you food in case you were hungry."

When his call met with silence, he did a quick check of the main level, putting the food in the fridge, before heading upstairs. Her bedroom door was open and he peeked inside.

"Alexis, you in here?"

With worry gnawing at him, he moved to the end of the hall and climbed the winding set of stairs leading to the widow's peak, the highest room in the house. Thinking perhaps she was in the glass turret overlooking the shore, he hurried up the steps. Other than a small loveseat and a table with an open book on it, the room was empty. Pushing his hands into his pockets, he walked to the window to look out, and what he saw jumpstarted his heart, not to mention his cock.

Sweet mother of God and all that was holy!

As the full moon glistened on the water, it gave him sufficient light to see Alexis's body. Dressed in nothing but a pair of skimpy panties and bra, she waded into the water alone, her end of the beach now empty, the sand castles washed away after a spectacular day of family and fun.

He spent a long time looking at her, unable to wipe the ridiculous smile off his face because he damn well knew it... knew that underneath those too big coveralls existed one hell of a sexy woman. Small framed, yet curvy in all the right places, she had a body made for sin, which made him wonder more about the girl who kept her figure hidden and had come to Whispering Cove with the intention of modernizing the big old Victorian house.

He could help her, of course. Call in a few favors. During his teen years, he'd worked under his father and grandpa, both members of the restoration committee who oversaw every aspect of a renovation to ensure it adhered to the town's code. They both taught Sam so much about the century-old houses, about how one needed to look beyond the surface and see the beauty and art in old world crafts-manship.

Except Alexis specialized in modernization and he knew that meant she wanted to strip the place of all that was weathered and worn, and replace it with the latest and great-est. It was no wonder the restoration committee wouldn't give her the permits or return her calls.

Beneath his feet he looked at the old plank floors that stood the test of time. He thought about all the kids who had played on them, all the scuffs and scratches they made with their toys, all the history and stories the house had to tell. Sure the wood could use a good sanding and polish, but what they didn't need was to be replaced with some fabricated product that had a life span of ten years.

Then again, Alexis wasn't the first girl he knew who couldn't see beyond the nicks and notches. His mind traveled back in time, but then he quickly shook his head hard to clear it. The last thing he wanted to think about was the house he'd secretly and painstakingly restored for his girlfriend some ten years ago, or how she turned down his marriage proposal and ran off with a guy from two towns over because he'd promised her shiny and new. Sam loved that house, loved every minute he'd spent working on it and couldn't be happier that Josie Wells, or rather Josie Collins, now called the place home and shared it with her husband, Adam, and their soon-to-be newborn. Yeah, he'd caught her small baby bump at the beach today.

But the whole situation left a bitter taste in his mouth, and he walked away from the business, swearing he'd never waste another second of his time restoring a house to its original beauty—especially for some woman who wouldn't appreciate it and would only end up leaving.

Turning his attention back to Alexis, he watched her release her hair from the ponytail and let it slide down her back as she ducked under the waves. His nostrils flared, the sweet citrusy scent of her skin still lingering in the air, making him harder than he'd been in a long time. She surfaced a few feet out, only to duck back under. Unable to take his eyes off her as she swam, he continued to watch like a regular old voyeur, keeping to the shadows so she didn't catch him.

As raw lust swamped him, everything inside him urged him to go down there, to slip into the water, and have his wicked way with her. The sexual tension between them was undeniable, he knew she felt it every bit as much as he did. Except Alexis was the kind of girl he could fall for, which meant he'd be wise to keep his distance, because he had no intention of getting in deep—or helping her with the house— only to watch her pack up and leave town when all was said and done. Christ, he'd already fallen for one sweet, girl-next-door type and look where that got him.

But dammit if he didn't want one small taste of her.

One tiny fucking nibble.

After her swim, Alexis stayed to the shadows and walked back to the shore, keeping her distance from the group still partying and sharing drinks over a bonfire at the other end of the beach. She picked up her towel and glanced up at the house as she wrapped it around her body. Sam jerked back from the window, hurried down the winding set of stairs and slipped into his bedroom. He paced as he listened to the front door open and close below. Deciding he needed something to keep his mind occupied before he went down there and dragged her to his bed caveman style, he pulled his cell phone from his pocket and flipped through his game apps.

He listened to her tiptoe up the stairs, the sound of her bare feet on the wood floor stopping outside his door. He practically stopped breathing, because for a second there he wondered if she was going to knock, wondered if she was going to drop her towel and beg him to take her right then and there. The next thing he heard was her shuffling to her bedroom and her door shutting behind her.

Ah, so much for wishful thinking...

Even though he knew staying put was probably for the best, it still didn't stop the disappointment from settling in the pit of his gut, but the ungodly scream he heard next had him dropping his phone and bolting from his bed.

28

hat the hell...

With her heart racing so hard she feared it would pop right out of her chest, Lex locked her knees to keep herself upright and tightened the towel around her shaking body.

She looked around her empty room, her mind racing as she struggled to swallow down her unease and figure out what was going on. With fear forcing her to move her legs, to get her out of her bedroom and out of the house before she disappeared next, she took a tiny step backward. But the sound of her door flinging open and heavy footsteps rushing up behind her had her turning around. When she came face to face with Sam, and he put his big hands on her shoulders in a protective manner, she let out a relieved breath.

Eyes full of concern moved over her face. "Jesus, Alexis, you're as white as a ghost. What is it?"

"My stuff. It's all gone. My suitcase, my clothes. Every-thing. It's gone."

"Shit." Sam stiffened and looked past her shoulder to scan the room. "Christ, all that's left are your bed sheets." He pulled her to him, crushing her wet body against his. "Okay, it's okay, Alexis. Nothing is going to happen to you," he soothed in a reassuring voice as her body quivered in his arms. "I promise I'll get to the bottom of this."

Feeling absurdly safe in his arms, she explained, "I wasn't gone for very long. I just took a quick dip in the ocean and then hurried home." She inched back and met his dark eyes. "I took the key with me and thought I locked up, but I guess I forgot...my mind... I've just been so preoccupied with other things. I must have left the door open by mistake." Then another thought hit and she whispered, "Do you think someone is in the house?"

"I don't know." He scanned the room a second time. "Have you checked your closet to see if your stuff is in there?"

"No."

"I'd better take a look. Maybe you put your belongings in there and forgot."

"I think I would have remembered that." She hugged herself as Sam padded quietly to her closet, and when he glanced back at her she began shivering, her body cold from the ocean water.

"Nothing," he said, his brow furrowed in concern.

She touched the air. Had the temperature in her room dropped? "Why is it so cold in here?" She exhaled, almost certain her breath would turn to fog in the frosty room.

"I don't know, and it's even colder in your closet. But first things first. We need to get you out of those wet clothes." He captured her hand and tugged. "Come on, I'm sure I have something you can wear." But the second he took a step toward the bedroom door—the closed bedroom door—he stopped mid-stride.

"Whoa," he said. "I left the door open when I came in here." He ran a hand through his hair, the look on his face perplexed. "What the fuck?"

"Sam?" she asked, her voice as shaky as her body as she stepped closer to him. His hand slipped around her waist, and he pulled her tight against his warm torso. "What's going on?" she whispered.

"I don't know." He reached out, wrapped his other hand around the knob and gave it a yank. It wouldn't budge, and from the look on his face as he angled his head to see her, his glance moving over her quivering flesh, she knew he suspected it had little to do with drafts or swollen wood. With a tug, he tore off his T-shirt and handed it to her. "Here. Put this on to stay warm until I can figure out what's going on."

He stood there watching her, but when she twirled her finger, he nodded and spun around to give her privacy. She dropped the damp towel and reached for her bra strap, then left it in place, deciding to leave her underthings on, despite how cold they felt against her body. She hurried into his warm T-shirt, which hung to mid-thigh on her, and drew in his scent before she murmured, "Okay, I'm done."

Sam twisted back to face her, and a strange expression came over him. Half-naked and looking like sex incarnate, he stood there looking at her longer than was comfortable. She shifted, suddenly aware of the libidinous way he made her feel, of the sexual energy arcing between them. If he kept staring at her like that she'd be warm in no time.

"Sam?" she asked, her voice coming out a little rougher than usual.

His eyes slid over her, his expression hot when he answered with, "Yeah?"

Lex gulped air. Everything in the distracted way he answered, like he had something else on his mind, brought heat to her most intimate places. "Ah, how are we going to get out of here?"

"I don't know."

"Do you think someone is in the house?" she asked again.

He shook his head. "When I came back earlier, I searched the place looking for you. There was no one here." He ran his hands through his hair, a familiar habit. "And I talked to both Sheriff McGrath and Officer Caan tonight. They don't think anyone is trying to scare you out of town, but they did say they'd stop by and check things out."

"Maybe we should call them right now."

Sam nodded and reached into his pocket. "Shit."

"What?"

"You wouldn't happen to have your cell phone would you?"

"It's in my purse." She held her arms out.

"And your purse is missing, like the rest of your things?"

She shook her head. "I left it in the kitchen downstairs."

Sam walked to the two windows overlooking the ocean and tried to jimmy them. "They're both stuck."

"I know. I wanted to replace them but I can't do a thing without a permit."

He looked almost physically ill when he asked, "You wanted to replace them?"

"Yeah."

He opened his mouth to say something more then seemed to change his mind. Instead he just stood there, his brows furrowed.

"What are we going to do?" she asked.

Sam walked to the closet. "We should try the hatch. At least if we get to the attic, we can get out on to the lower roof and call for help. There's still a bonfire going on down the other end of the beach."

She followed him inside the closet, and frowned when she looked up. "How are we going to reach it?"

"I'll have to lift you."

"Lift me?"

As he dwarfed her small frame he tossed her a skeptical look and said, "Unless you'd rather lift me."

She thought back to all the times she roughhoused with her big brothers when she was younger. "I'm stronger than I look, you know?"

His eyes glistened as he glanced up and down her petite body. "You'd have to be."

"Hey," she shot back, giving him a whack. "I used to wrestle with my older brothers all the time."

His eyes visually caressed her before he asked, "So what are you saying, Alexis, that you'd rather wrestle with me than get out of here?"

As she envisioned herself rolling around on the floor with Sam, their bodies touching, grinding, pushing and pulling, wrestling suddenly took on a whole new meaning.

"I...uh...I don't want to hurt you, or embarrass your pride." She cleared her throat. "So we should probably concentrate on the hatch for now."

The corner of his mouth turned up in a sexy, flirty grin. "Yeah, that's what I was thinking too." Then he gave her a wink and said, "We'll save the wrestling for later." He glanced at the hatch then back at her. "Ready?"

She nodded and he bent to wrap both his arms around her knees. Exerting little effort, he hoisted her up. With his mouth somewhere in the vicinity of her wet panties, Lex worked to concentrate on opening the hatch, a difficult task considering how hot and erotic his breath felt on her thighs. Actually, come to think of it, the chill was gone from her room, and her body.

She pushed at the hatch then made a fist to pound on the corner. "It's stuck," she groaned.

"It probably hasn't been open in years," he said, his voice sounding a bit deeper than usual.

She tried a few more hits, and the next thing she knew

she was sliding down his body, the movement creating heat and friction between them as he lowered her to her feet. He continued to hold her against him, his large hands splayed over the small of her back.

Feeling breathless, she said, "Now what?"

Instead of answering he pulled a confused face and asked, "Is it getting hotter in here?"

For a moment Lex thought it was because of the heat they were generating inside the closet, but then it occurred to her that something else was going on. The temperature in the room had spiked dramatically, making her uncomfortable in her wet underthings, as well as his oversized T-shirt.

She broke from the circle of his arms and inched away to step back into the bedroom. She checked the radiators, to see if they were on, then moved to her window to look out. When she spotted plumes of smoke coming out of the chimney on the lower roof, she whispered, "Oh my God."

"What?" Sam strolled up behind her.

"I think there is a fire in the main level hearth. How can that be? I didn't light a fire."

"Neither did I." Sam pressed against her, his body so hot and hard against hers as he looked past her shoulder. Her skin moistened, and the hungry little spot between her legs quivered with want. "But I think I'm convinced," he said, his breath whispering over her neck.

"Convinced?"

"Someone *is* messing with you."

She turned to face him, and her hard nipples scraped against his bare chest. He must have felt it, because he glanced down, then eyes that seemed too dark, too hungry, locked back on hers.

"What...what should we do?" she asked.

"I don't think anyone is out to harm us, so I don't believe

we're in any danger. Whoever is messing with you just wants to keep you...or us...locked up in this room, for some reason."

"What kind of reason?"

"I don't know. I'm sure Errol will stop by in the morning to check and see if I caught his alleged ghost, and we can ask if he knows what's going on. Why someone would want to lock us in together."

Her breath came shallow as she looked at his near nakedness. She could only think of one reason why someone would lock the two away in a hot room, especially if they felt the sexual tension between them. But surely to God no one would go to such extremes would they?

"And until then?" she asked.

He wiped his brow and shot her a suggestive look, one so full of mischief and playfulness her stomach tightened. "Until then I think it's imperative that we cool down our bodies."

As she acknowledged the flare of desire deep between her thighs, she jerked her thumb over her shoulder. "Should I break the window?"

"No."

"No?"

"It'd be a shame to damage century-old rolled glass when we have other options," he explained, the deepness in his voice coupled with the intent look on his face curling her toes and firing her blood from simmer to inferno.

"Then what do you suggest?"

For a brief second she thought she spotted conflicting emotions moving over his face, then his jaw relaxed as he touched her T-shirt. His voice sounded darkly seductive and highly suggestive when he spoke. "We should probably shed these clothes." He dipped his head and wet his mouth, the promise of something far more intimate in his cadence when he added, "You know, for safety reasons. Heat exhaustion can be very dangerous."

A wheezing sound escaped her lips, and she briefly closed her eyes. "You think we should get naked?"

"I'm certain of it."

As she entertained the idea, her mind raced, sifting through all the things a guy and a girl could do inside a locked bedroom, sans clothes. She took a moment to picture his hard, completely nude body on top of hers, his mouth on her neck, her breasts, between her legs.

Longing moved through her and she pulled in a fortifying breath to help jumpstart her lust-saturated brain. She tried for casual, like she got naked in front of smoking-hot men all the time, but failed miserably. "Don't you...ahh...don't you think that's a bit drastic?" she asked, her voice lacking conviction as she considered taking advantage of the situation they found themselves in, a situation someone or some ghostly *thing* put them in.

"Drastic times call for drastic measures."

As she mulled that over, the sound of his zipper curled through the air, and her thoughts scatted, her passion-rattled brain suddenly wanting one thing and one thing only. To see this gorgeous hunk of a guy naked.

Feeling anxious and nervous, she watched, transfixed, as he released the zipper, popped the button, then kick off his khaki shorts. Lacking any sort of modesty, Sam stood before her in his tight boxer briefs, ones that showcased a hard ridge that her hands itched to explore.

Her body stirred, and as the hungry spot between her legs began calling the shots, she gripped the hem of her T-shirt, marveling at this turn of events. *Do it*...some lusty part of her brain screamed. *Just get naked already*...

Sam's nostrils flared, the muscles along his jaw clenching and unclenching again as he met her gaze unflinchingly. "I think you should take it off, Alexis, otherwise you run the risk of overheating."

She already was overheating.

He thumbed the hem, running the soft pad back and forth, back and forth over the cotton material. As she pictured him touching another part of her body in much the same manner, it prompted her into action and she quickly peeled the shirt from her body.

The possessive, hungry way he looked at her, combined with the growl ripping from his lungs stoked the fire inside her, and she began burning from the inside out. Good God, never had she felt so needy, so wanton before.

Without his eyes ever leaving hers, he removed his boxer briefs, and her gaze dropped, registering every detail of his gorgeous body, taking special note of the impressive erection between his legs. And by impressive, she meant *enormous*.

Sexual tension hung heavy and when she caught the naked want in his eyes—not to mention between his legs—she could feel color bloom high on her cheeks. As his beautiful body overwhelmed her, she ran her fingers along her bra straps, hardly able to believe the way this man wanted her. *Her.*

He gave a lusty groan, its rich baritone sending a barrage of erotic sensations through her, and her body responded with a shudder. With need unleashing inside her, urging her to shed her clothes, as well as her inhibitions, she pulled the straps off her shoulders, then reached around to release the latch. Good God, was she really going to get naked with this sexy, laidback playboy? She dropped her wet bra on the floor, her body nearly delirious with want as Sam stood there taking in her near nakedness.

"And your panties," he said, his intense voice resonating inside her and eliciting a shiver from deep within. "You should definitely remove your panties."

She slipped her finger under the elastic band and drew the panties down her legs. She dropped them into the pile on the floor, then stood back up, baring herself to Sam. When his gaze slid over her, she shifted her body weight from one foot to the other, suddenly feeling a little unsure, a little self-conscious in front of him.

With her nerves getting the better of her she made a move to cover herself but Sam ran his hands down her arms, and stroked the insides of her wrists, his touch burning through her skin. Ripples of sensual pleasure moved through her and she blew a wispy strand of hair from her face. Looking for something to say, anything to break the awkward moment, she found her voice and asked, "Are you feeling cooler?"

"No."

"No? You mean getting naked isn't helping to cool you down?"

"Actually, it's making me hotter."

The heat in his eyes and the way he looked at her with such need filled her with want and reminded her that underneath her boy clothes she was all woman. A woman who hadn't been touched by a man in a very long time, and never one as hot as the guy looking at her like he wanted to eat her alive.

Her body trembled, despite the warm air. "That's not good, Sam. Not good at all."

She bit back a breathy moan and felt a rush of excitement when his glance traveled over her flesh, halting and lingering at the apex of her legs.

"No, it's not. But don't worry. I have an idea on how we can blow off some steam."

It didn't take a genius to know that he wanted to take advantage of the situation they found themselves in every bit as much as she did, but that didn't stop her from playing along and asking, "What would this idea involve?" She blinked up at him, anxious to hear more, despite the fact that getting intimate with a comic book guy who hunted ghosts on the other side of the country wasn't in her best interest, for many reasons. Then again, they were both consenting adults, and there was no denying that she wanted this... needed this in some inexplicable way. The way he looked at her made her forget that she wasn't in to one-night stands— or that she wasn't into stripping in front of a guy either—and there was no disputing the erection between his legs. He wanted this as much as she did. So why couldn't she just have a little fun with Sam tonight, answer the demands of her body and then when he returned to New Mexico and she returned to Portland, she could put it behind her and go back to concentrating on her career.

"Well," he began, and shot her a suggestive look, the message clear in his eyes as he brushed his thumb over her bottom lip. "Have you ever heard of evaporative cooling?"

"Yes, I paid attention in science class, but in order for water to evaporate off our bodies and cool us, we have to be wet first."

"Yeah, that's right."

Her throat constricted. "How will we get wet?"

"I was thinking I could use my mouth. My tongue, specifically." He ran his fingers over her neck, his touch doing delicious things to her body. "I could start here," he began, as he stroked the underside of her breast. His hand dipped lower, caressing her skin, softly, barely touching, his knuckles nudging her clit before his hand came to rest between her legs. "And I could stop here."

The temperature in the room skyrocketed and it had nothing to do with the fire in the hearth below her room. "You think that will help?"

"There's only one way to find out."

She opened her mouth to speak but her words turned into a soft moan when he bent forward to take her nipple into his mouth. "Oh, God," she cried out. Ruled by lust, with her mind abandoning any rational thought, she wrapped her hands around his head to hold him to her. He made a slow, skilled pass with his tongue, making her body a little hotter, and a whole lot wetter—mainly between her legs.

"Sam," she murmured and arched into him, running her fingers through his hair. His mouth moved to her other nipple, and he moaned in delight as he drew it between his teeth for a little nibble.

His hands caressed her waist, and he shaped her contours as he sank to his knees. "You are so beautiful," he murmured as he dragged his tongue over her stomach, stopping to dip into her sensitive bellybutton.

She threw her head back, her legs wobbling beneath her when he slipped his hand between her thighs to widen them. He went back on his heels, his breath hot on her flesh when he said, "Jesus, you have the prettiest pussy."

Heat flitted across his face as he looked at her sex, and pleasure gathered in her core when he reached out and parted her lips. He growled, and lightly stroked her clit. "But it looks like this part of you is already wet." He glanced up at her, his eyes warm and teasing, torturing her in the most delicious ways. "Maybe it doesn't need my tongue after all."

"Sam," she cried out, frantic for him to lick her, to take her pussy into his mouth and run his tongue over her swollen clit.

"Unless, of course, you want me to make you wetter."

"Yes," she cried out. "I want you to make me wetter."

His laugh was edgy, churning with passion as he turned his attention back to her pussy. Positioning himself between her legs, he leaned in and ran his tongue all the way from the bottom to the top, paying special attention to her throbbing clit. A violent quake moved through her, and she nearly collapsed into a quivering heap as he applied the perfect amount of pressure.

"So good," she bit out. "So damn good."

His tongue toyed with her clit, and he drew circles around it, the slow, torturous seduction pushing her to the precipice in record time. He pushed a finger inside her and as he burrowed deep, hunger clawed at her insides, and she began panting. Good God, no man had ever made her pant before.

"Mmm, so goddamn good," he murmured from deep between her legs, the pleasure in his voice pulling soft quakes from her inner core.

She looked at the man acquainting himself with her body and could hardly believe what was happening, could hardly believe that she was getting so intimate, so quickly, with this man who seemed hell bent on giving her the best oral sex of her life.

As he continued to pillage with his tongue, her skin tightened and a moan caught in her throat. He inserted a finger, and she pushed against it, her hips rocking frantically beneath his invading mouth.

"Look at that, you *are* getting wetter," he said, and tossed her a grin before he scraped his teeth over her clit.

Oh, God, the man definitely knew his way around a woman's body.

Another finger joined the first and her hips jerked, her muscles tightening, preparing for the onslaught of pleasure. But she didn't want to come, didn't want this moment to ever end.

"Sam," she cried out, the pleasure so intense, so mind-numbingly glorious she was sure she'd died and gone to heaven, or hell, or wherever. Not that it mattered, because at the moment all she cared about was the man between her legs and what he was doing to her.

"That's a girl," he murmured. "I think if you come it will really help cool down your body."

As soon as the words left his mouth, her skin began to

tingle, every ounce of her being focused on her pussy and the delicious points of pleasure. He applied more pressure to her clit, and her body shuddered in surrender.

"Yes, oh, God, yes. Just like that..." she murmured, as her pussy pulsed and throbbed in erotic delight. Sam kept his mouth on her clit and his fingers high inside. She rode out the pleasure, and knew beyond a shadow of a doubt that she was, indeed, in the right hands.

Her cream dripped over her thighs, tickling her flesh along its downward path, and once her body stopped spasming, Sam slid up her body, crushing her to him. His cock brushed between her legs, and the heat and urgency in his eyes when they met hers sent a shiver skittering through her.

His lips found hers, and when she tasted herself on his mouth, she moaned. Needing to touch him, she stroked his body, running her hands over his sides, trailing the line on his hard oblique muscles, unable to get enough of him.

"You're burning up," she murmured. "Your skin is on fire." She shook her head, and tossed him a concerned look. "I'd better wet you down right away."

"Jesus, Alexis," he murmured when she pressed her mouth to his chest. She licked him, loving the salty taste of him on her tongue as she trailed a path over his chest. "Is this helping?" she asked. "Is my tongue helping...is it doing anything?"

"Oh, it's doing something all right," he murmured, and she couldn't help but smile at the agony she heard in his voice.

She continued to trail her tongue over his body, stroking his washboard stomach and noting the way he was responding to her seduction. When she sank to her knees and took his cock into her hands, his entire body trembled.

"Oh Christ, Alexis," he groaned, his hands fisting her hair.

She looked at the pre-come dripping from his crown, and tossed him an innocent look. "Well now, look at that. It doesn't look like you need my mouth after all."

"Alexis…" he growled and she couldn't help but smile. She truly loved the way he wanted her, the way his body needed her touch.

Deciding not to torture him too much—after all, he'd just given her a mind-blowing orgasm—she flicked her tongue over his head. Their moans mingled when she tasted his sweetness. She leaned in, took as much of him into her mouth as she could, and wrapped her hands around his girth when his hips jutted forward.

She worked her tongue over him and could feel him thicken, his veins filling with blood as he chased an orgasm. Relaxing her throat as much as possible she took him a bit deeper, and he exhaled sharply. As she pleasured him, her body quaked, wanting desperately to climb on top of him and sink down on his cock until he filled her in a way she'd never been filled before. Maybe then she'd be able to sate the hunger building inside her.

"Sweetheart," he murmured. "I'm there." She could feel him trying to pull her away, but she wouldn't let him. She wanted to stay between his legs until he came, and she wanted to drink and savor every last drop of him.

"Oh, Jesus, Alexis," he growled, when he clearly realized what she had planned. "What the hell are you doing to me?"

She cupped his balls and gave a gentle massage. A second later they tightened against his body, and she felt him stiffen. "Alexis," he bit out, taking heavy, serrated breaths as he threw his head back and released deep in her throat.

Staying between his legs until he stopped trembling, Lex rested her head against his pelvis, and when she felt him tug on her, she allowed him to pull her up his body. He drew her tight, and they both just stood there in the middle of the room holding one another, both lost in their own thoughts. She took a moment to think about what they'd just done, the way they'd used the situation to pleasure each other orally.

Even though her body felt gloriously sated, she couldn't help but worry that there might be awkwardness between them when she broke from his arms. Since she never jumped into bed so quickly with a guy before, not that they used the bed or had gone all the way, she had no idea what to do or say next.

Sam broke the quiet. "Hey," he murmured, inching back to see her.

She wasn't sure what to expect when her glance met his, but when she saw the playful smile on his face, it somehow relaxed her, let her feel more comfortable and secure with the intimacies they'd just shared.

It also made her realize how easy it would be to fall for him.

He ran his hands over her body. "Uh, oh..." he said.

"What?"

He began backing her up, leading her toward the cot. "You don't feel cool at all. In fact your body is still way too hot."

When she heard the teasing in his voice, all rational thought fled, and she touched his skin, noting the way his cock was hardening all over again. "Actually, so is yours."

When they reached the mattress he gave her a little push and she fell onto the bed. He stood there looking at her for a moment, his grin mischievous. "I think we might have to try that cooling technique again."

"Drastic times do call for drastic measures."

His eyes darkened, deepened with want. "I think we're going to have to continue wetting our bodies down all night." He glanced at the door, then back at her. "I don't see any other option."

Tension coiled through her, her pussy heating and moistening in anticipation. "It might be the only thing to keep us alive until help arrives."

He climbed over her. "Of course, if my technique doesn't work—"

She pulled his mouth to hers and murmured, "Oh believe me, Sam. Your technique works…it works just fine…"

Bright light streamed in through the curtainless windows as Sam stretched out on the cot—well, as much as he could stretch out considering how small it was. But he had no trouble sharing it with Alexis, or keeping her small body close to his throughout the night. As he looked at the woman asleep beside him, tucked in so nicely next to him, he felt a strange pinch in his heart.

By rights he shouldn't have played such a sexy game with her, no matter how fucking amazing it was to make love to her with his fingers and mouth, because she was way too easy to fall for. But no way, no how was he going to do that. He should have tried a little harder to find a way out of the room. But once he started down the path of seduction, and once she started to play along, basic elemental need took over and there wasn't a damn thing he could do about it.

This morning, however, he needed to talk to her. Even though last night took them to a deeper level of intimacy, one he hadn't felt in a long time, ten years to be exact, he had to let her know this was just about sex and sex only.

She blinked up at him, and when she gifted him with a sweet, girl-next-door smile, his words lodged somewhere in his throat.

"Good morning," she whispered.

Since a response was beyond him, he just pulled her in tighter, but when he felt her stiffen he looked at her. "Hey," he said. "You okay?"

"About last night," she began, the warmth in her eyes

doing the strangest things to his insides. "It was…it was really amazing."

He swallowed. "Yeah, it was."

"But I need you to know that it was just a one-time thing."

She took the words right out of his mouth, so why did it bother him to hear *her* say it? Why did it give him a strange knot in his stomach?

"I think that's for the best."

She nodded. "Good, then it's settled."

"Yeah," he agreed, and even though he should have left it at that he found himself saying, "But I will be here for one more month, and by the looks of things here, you're not going anywhere for a while."

She gave him a perplexed look. "What are you saying?"

He gave a casual shrug. "If we both enjoyed it, maybe we can keep doing it?"

"You want to keep doing *this*?"

"Sure, it doesn't have to be a one-time thing."

"No?"

"Maybe we can keep doing it until we both go back to our respective lives outside Whispering Cove." He winked, gave her shoulder a kiss and said, "And maybe we can do more than just *this*."

"You want to do more?"

"And really, I'd like to finish what I started."

"Oh, I think you finished pretty well."

He rolled on top of her, pinning her down with his weight. His hard cock pressed against her leg and her eyes widened. "I didn't *quite* finish."

She nodded. "Oh, right. There was that other *little* matter…"

He chuckled. "Little?" He was about to say more when her stomach rumbled. "Shit, you must be starving."

"I missed dinner."

"I brought you food back from Hauk's, but then we got locked in here."

Warmth moved into her eyes, and she angled her head like she was perplexed by the gesture. "You brought me food from the bar?"

"Yeah, I..." He gestured toward the door, his thoughts trailing off when he saw that it was ajar. "Holy shit."

Alexis twisted. "What?"

"When did that happen?"

She frowned, and shook her head. "I'll be glad when I can just get my permits, get the work done, and be finished with all this."

Sam nodded, but knew with the demolition she had in mind, the restoration committee would never get back to her. He should probably talk to her, tell her what needed to be done, help her see the beauty in refining the old Victorian house and keeping with the heritage craftsmanship, to respect the significance of it. That way she'd get the job done and get out of here sooner rather than later. But of course, he'd wiped his hands of the business, and wasn't about to roll up his sleeves—again—and work endlessly for a woman who all along only appreciated shiny and new.

"I'll talk to the sheriff again, and I'm going to check the attic and basement to see if anyone has been messing around."

"Someone had to be in here; someone lit that fire."

"Yeah, you're right."

"I didn't even think that old stone hearth worked anymore. It was one of the first things I planned to tear out."

The thought of her tearing out that gorgeous hearth hit like a physical blow. "That old stone hearth is a heritage focal point in this house. It just needs to be rebuilt, not demolished." He opened his mouth to say more, wanting her to see what he saw, but then closed it again, thankful for the female voice calling up to them from the downstairs main entrance.

"Hello. Sam, are you here?"

"Who's that?" Lex asked.

Sam jumped from the bed and grabbed his shorts. "It sounds like Tabby Taylor. Or rather, Tabby McGrath now that she's married to Reece."

"How did she get in?"

"The door was unlocked, so I let myself in," Tabby called out.

"How did the door get unlocked?"

Sam shook his head. "Another unexplained mystery."

Eyes wide, Alexis drew the sheet up to cover herself. "And doesn't anyone knock around here?"

Sam laughed. "You're in Whispering Cove, Alexis. Get used to it." He tossed her his T-shirt. "You stay here. I'll go talk to her."

He hurried from the room, and found Tabby waiting at the foot of the stairs. He dropped a kiss onto her cheek and asked, "What brings you here so early?"

She looked at her watch and frowned. "It's after lunch, Sam."

"Oh, I didn't realize. It was a late night."

She rubbed her very big stomach and looked past his shoulders. "Everything okay?"

"Just some late-night noises that kept us up."

"More screams from the bedroom?"

Oh yeah...

Wait!

He cocked his head. "How did you know about that?"

"I ran in to Errol at the Seafarer, and he said something about a ghost and that you were staying here to check it out. I thought I'd stop by to see if everything was okay."

"Actually, Alexis had all her clothes go missing last night. Do you think you'd be able to help her out?"

Tabby laughed, and a strange knowing look came over her face, much like the one he'd spotted on Sheriff McGrath's face last night. "I have a whole wardrobe that I can't fit into anymore." She turned toward the door. "Let me go grab some things and I'll be right back."

As Sam watched her go, he couldn't help but think that not only were there strange things going on in the house, there were also strange things going on with the people he'd grown up with.

$$29$$

Dressed in Sam's T-shirt Lex paced the floor, waiting for Tabby to return with some clothes. She caught a whiff of Sam's scent on the shirt as it brushed over her skin and drew his aroma into her lungs. As it overwhelmed her and once again stirred all her senses, she bit down on her bottom lip to stifle a groan.

It doesn't have to be a one-time thing.

Good Lord, she could hardly believe what he'd suggested. Of course, it wasn't like she hadn't thought of it, but to hear him say it, to know he wanted to do this with her while he was home on vacation excited her beyond anything she'd ever known. The truth was most men paid little attention to her, not only because her brothers continually scared them off, but because she always dressed down and was easy to overlook. But Sam didn't overlook anything. Nope. There wasn't one inch of her body that he failed to touch.

A shiver moved through her as she reminisced about the way he used his tongue to pleasure her, and this time there was nothing she could do to smother the groan of desire rumbling up from her throat.

She took a moment to recall the distracted, almost nervous look on his face earlier, when she'd awoken and met his glance. She'd pegged him a playboy, one who did this kind of thing often, and because she didn't want to hear him say that last night was simply casual sex to him, she jumped on it first. She wanted to let him know where she stood, and that she didn't expect anything more. She was intelligent enough to understand that she could easily fall for him, but she was also wise enough to know she would never be enough to keep a guy like him around. All the more reason to keep her emotions out of this and enjoy the sex for what it was—sex.

"Everything okay?" Sam asked, coming back in her room. She looked at the T-shirt he was tugging on and read the print, YOLO.

It was true—you only live once—which was why she was going to keep her emotions out of it and make the best of her time in Whispering Cove.

Redirecting the conversation, she said, "Nice shirt."

He smiled. "Did you want to borrow it?"

"I think I'll wait to see what Tabby brings first."

Sam scrubbed his hand over his chin, and looking thoughtful for a moment he opened his mouth like he wanted to say something, then shut it again. He walked to her window and ran his fingers over the wavy glass. She watched him, taking in the quiet side to the flirty guy with the smart-assed comebacks.

She was about to ask if he was okay, when Tabby called from the front entrance. "Is it okay if I come up?"

With his smile back in place, Sam turned. "Sure," he called out, then grinned wickedly as he looked over Alexis. "Alexis is decent, but I'm not."

"Sam..." Tabby warned. "You'd better be dressed."

"Ignore him," Lex called out, and rolled her eyes at Sam.

Tabby looked a bit breathless when she appeared at her

door with a bag full of clothes. She frowned when she saw the way Lex was dressed. "These should get you started, and I'd be happy to take you shopping for more."

Lex took the bag from her, and dumped the pile on the cot. She almost grimaced when she saw all the pretty floral girly clothes and dresses.

Tabby rubbed her huge belly. "Before this I was about the same size as you. Just a bit taller, but that shouldn't matter too much with the shorts and dresses."

"I appreciate this, Tabby. Thank you."

Tabby crinkled her nose. "So you have no idea what happened to all your stuff?"

Lex shook her head. "No. They just disappeared."

"That's strange."

"There are a lot of strange things going on," Sam said. He looked at Lex. "Will you be okay here by yourself for a while? I want to go track down the sheriff."

"I'll stay with her," Tabby said.

"You don't have to do that," Lex jumped in, her heart warming a little at how sweet Tabby was being to her. Even the townsfolk really seemed to care about her well-being, especially crazy old Errol. "Besides, I have a meeting with Devon today."

Tabby's eyes lit. "Since he is my brother, I can go with you, and afterward we could go shopping. Once you're finished reviving this old place you're going to want to stage it and I've been dying to take on a house like this. It will be great for my portfolio."

"In case you didn't know, Tabby's an interior designer," Sam piped in. "She works with her brother, Devon, and her husband, Reece."

"Oh," Lex said. "I didn't realize that."

Sam stepped up to Lex, his gait relaxed, his demeanor carefree as he leaned into her and dipped his head. "I'll meet you back here later. Be sure to lock up, okay? Have fun and don't worry, you're in good hands with Tabby." He dropped a tender kiss onto Lex's mouth, and then pulled back abruptly, like it suddenly occurred to him what he'd done.

Their eyes met and locked. A strange moment of silence lingered as Lex considered the easy, comfortable kiss he'd given her—not at all unlike a warm, familiar kiss long-time lovers gave one other when they departed for the day.

As if oblivious to what had just transpired between the two, Tabby broke the quiet and said, "So let's try on a few of these clothes to see how they fit."

Lex turned her attention to Tabby and before Sam disappeared out the bedroom door, she said, "There's an extra key on the kitchen counter." Once he disappeared, she tried to focus on the clothes, she really did, but her thoughts were preoccupied with Sam.

God, she needed to stop thinking about last night and get her head on straight. Working to focus her thoughts, she chose a plain T-shirt and pair of mid-thigh shorts. She quickly dressed and made her way outdoors with Tabby. After a very disappointing meeting with Devon, and learning that the company was already overbooked, they spent the afternoon shopping. Lex bought some clothes and restocked her intimate apparel. Then they picked out pieces of furniture and accessories that Lex loved and Tabby thought she could use to stage the house when completed. Even though Lex couldn't afford to stage a house after she paid her construction crew—if she ever found one—she still pointed out all the things she'd like and would buy for the house if she had the funds. Then they visited a shop on the waterfront and Tabby fawned over all the gorgeous glass pieces made by the talented Skylar Wellington.

After shopping, Tabby took her to the Seafarer for dinner, and when they were joined by Katy, Josie, Lila, Vic, Carmen and a few other women, along with all their kids, the conversation turned to Tabby's upcoming baby shower that Josie was hosting, and how Lex most definitely needed to attend.

Throughout the day Lex had checked her phone repeatedly, hoping to hear from the restoration committee. When nighttime approached and she made her way back to the house after a wonderful day with her new friend, she knew it was after hours and she wasn't going to hear from anyone today.

As she approached her front steps, her pulse kicked up and she suddenly found herself looking forward to seeing Sam. She felt a little thrill inside to know he'd be there waiting for her. She fished her key from her purse and opened the door. With night upon her, she flicked on the lights and called out to him. When her words were met with silence she made her way into the kitchen, and that's when she realized he wasn't there.

With the heat of the day getting to her, she tried to fight down the sense of longing that was enveloping her. She was missing Sam far more than she should. Not wanting to dwell on her feelings, she dropped her bags onto the counter and opened the door to her veranda to allow a breeze to rush in. Her heart did a little flip when she spotted Sam on the beach, waving his arms at her.

"Hey, Alexis," he called out. "Come for a swim."

"I don't have a suit," she called back.

She couldn't see his expression, but she could just imagine the mischievous grin on his face when he said, "You don't need one."

Her glance went to her bags, and she thought about the sexy underwear she'd purchased earlier that day, knowing they could easily pass as a bikini. She considered it a moment longer, and then remembered the saying on Sam's T-shirt. YOLO.

"I'll be right there," she called out, and hurried to the bathroom to change. A few minutes later she found herself walking the beach, squishing the warm sand between her toes as she walked by his towel and backpack. When she reached Sam, he scooped her up and carried her into the cold water.

She squealed, his skin wet and cold against her own. She protested, even though she loved being in his arms. "Put me down."

"Okay," he said, dipping her into the water before letting her go.

"You're going to pay for that," she said, the frigid water enveloping her.

"Can't wait," he responded, then disappeared under the water. He surfaced a few feet out. "Come on. Let's swim."

She dove under and met up with him in the surf and they spent the next half hour just swimming, and enjoying the star-filled night. The exercise relaxed her, helped her forget about her troubles for a while. But when Sam swam to the shore and she caught the way his swim trunks rode low on his hard body, her thoughts went off in another direction.

He dropped onto his towel and patted it. Lex followed his footsteps in the sand, and sank down next to him on the beach towel. He rolled to his side and pulled her in close. When she relaxed into him, soaking in his warmth, he propped himself up on his elbow and brushed her hair from her face.

Once again he went quiet, like he was deep in thought. After a long moment he said, "You mentioned you had brothers."

"Four, to be exact."

He ran his fingers along her neck, then down her arm, like he needed to be touching her at all times. "Four? That must have been fun."

She frowned. "Not when you're the youngest girl."

"Pretty protective?"

"Overbearing is the word I like to use." When Sam laughed, she went on to explain, "They scared off every guy I ever liked, and they treat me like I'm breakable...or incapable." She went quiet for a moment, then wasn't sure what compelled her to say it. Maybe it was the closeness she felt with Sam, or the way the stars were shining just right, but she suddenly found herself confessing, "That's why I'm here. That's why I bought the house. I needed to do something drastic to prove to them, and to my father, that I have what it takes to work in their all-boy construction company."

"Ah, I see."

She shivered as Sam ran his fingers over the inside of her wrist. "They don't know I'm here. I told them I was visiting with an old school friend in Rhode Island. I was hoping to restore it without them knowing, so I could show them I have what it takes."

"Their approval is important to you?"

"I guess...I don't know. It's a family business and I just want to be a part of it." *Part of something...*

"Is that why you dress like a tomboy, to fit in with their all-boys club?"

"Yeah."

"What about your mom, does she work in their business?"

"No. She's not a part of our lives. She left when I was little."

"I'm sorry."

"It's not your fault."

His glance moved over her face, like he could read her innermost thoughts. "But you think it's yours somehow don't you?"

She shrugged and mumbled under her breath, "I wish there was something I could have done to make her stay."

He brushed her hair from her face, his eyes dark, solemn.

"You were a child, Alexis. What could you have possibly done?" When she didn't answer he said, "My guess is she wasn't in her right mind."

"What do you mean?"

"What I mean is no one in their right mind would ever walk away from an amazing girl like you."

"Sam..."

"I mean it. Look at you. Smart, confident, beautiful." He smiled and added, "And I've never met a more determined woman." He gestured toward the house. "You're the kind of girl who goes after what she wants and lets nothing or no one stand in the way."

Surprised at the way he saw her and wanting to talk about something else she said, "It's just really important that I get the house flipped." She caught conflicting emotions in Sam's dark eyes before he rolled onto his back. "But between Errol's ghost, the restoration committee, and the townsfolk's resistance, I've been meeting with roadblocks at every turn." She closed her mouth, deciding to stop talking before she blurted out her financial situation. This was her problem, not Sam's, and he didn't need to know how heavily she invested. Or that if she didn't soon get the work done and turn a profit, she'd have to default on her loans and lose everything.

Directing the conversation his way, and wanting to lighten things up, she asked, "Do you have any siblings?

"No, but I never felt like I missed out because Jon was like a brother to me, and Errol like another grandfather."

"Errol treats everyone like they're family."

"Whispering Cove is kind of like that. One big happy family."

"So you like it here?"

"Yeah."

"Why did you leave?"

"Because I have a talent most don't, and there was a team

of ghost hunters forming in New Mexico looking for a fifth member." He shrugged easily, but she sensed he wasn't telling her everything. "So I went."

"Sam?" she began, wanting to ask the question that had been plaguing her since they first met.

"Yeah?"

"Do you really believe in ghosts?"

"Yeah."

"You can see them?"

"I can."

"Do they scare you?"

"Not really. Most are harmless. Just lost and confused." He scoffed, then added, "It's the living that can hurt you the most."

She sat up, drew her knees to her chest, and glanced up at the beautiful house overlooking the water. "My house isn't haunted, right?"

"No."

"And you talked to the sheriff again?"

"He's looking in to it, but doesn't think anyone is trying to drive you out."

"That's good I guess." She paused then asked, "And you checked the attic and basement."

He nodded. "It looks like there was a stack of boxes placed over the closet hatch, which is why we couldn't open it."

She frowned. "I was shifting things around but I don't remember putting any boxes over the hatch."

"I checked the attic door leading to the roof. It was locked so no one can get in or out unless they have a key." He captured her elbow and drew her back to him. She settled in beside him, and he touched her chin and turned her face his way. "Don't worry. Until I get to the bottom of matters, I'll stay close."

She wet her lips, the air between them charging. With her mind racing and her body warming all over, she searched for something intelligent to say, only to come out with, "So you really can see things others can't?"

"Yeah, I really can," he murmured, his voice lower and deeper. "And you know what else I can see?"

"What?"

He pressed against her and she could feel his erection on her leg. "I can see that underneath this lace, your nipples are hard."

She gulped, the hunger in his eyes making her feel so desirable, pretty even...*wanted*.

"I can also see how much they need me, Alexis."

Sam craved the taste of her, hadn't been able to get her off his mind all day, and he couldn't wait one more second to touch her, kiss her, carry her to her bedroom and make her scream for him again. But when she writhed beneath him, her body so hot and needy for his, he knew he'd never be able to make the short trek to the house without losing it. He glanced at his backpack and grinned. The hell with taking her to her bedroom. He had everything he needed to make her scream for him right here on the beach.

He grabbed her hands and pinned them above her head and closed his lips over hers. As he savored the sweetness of her mouth, he slipped a knee between her legs to widen them. She moaned beneath him, her tongue tangling with his in the most mind-fucking ways.

"Alexis," he murmured, drawing a quick breath to center himself. "I've wanted to do this all day."

"Mmm, me too," she responded between heated kisses, her nipples pressing into his flesh.

Sam slid lower, and released one of her hands so he could

caress her pebbled nipple through her lacy bra. "You look so sexy in this." He shot her a glance and they exchanged a long, heated look. "Does wearing this make you feel sexy, sweetheart?"

"You make me feel sexy," she admitted.

"You're way too beautiful to keep yourself covered up in oversized coveralls," he murmured. "Your family should take you seriously because you're smart and driven, not because you dress like a boy," he added before drawing her nipple into his mouth. She moaned, and it urged him on. Waves lapped gently against the shore a few feet away, and the briny scent of salty air washed over them. Sam tuned everything out except this woman, and the hunger she roused in him. Her hand raked through his hair, holding him to her, and he sucked harder, twirling his tongue over her marbled tip.

"That feels so good," she whispered.

As much as he liked pleasuring her orally, tonight he needed to be inside her, needed to finish what they started before he burst into flames.

He skated his hands over her curves, loving the warmth of her skin and the desire he could feel mounting in her body. His hand settled between her legs and slipped inside her damp panties. Her legs automatically widened for him, and when he found her clit wet and hard, lust swamped him.

Her nails scratched along his back, her soft mewling sounds catching on a breeze. "Sam," she murmured.

A tremor raced through him, the urgency in her voice letting him know she needed this every bit as much as he did. His body grew shaky, his cock swollen to the point of pain inside his suddenly too tight swim trunks.

He climbed back up her body, and put his mouth close to hers. "I want to be inside you."

"But we don't—"

He gestured toward his backpack. "I came prepared, sweetheart. Like I said, I've been thinking about you all day."

Her smile warmed him from the inside out and when she lifted herself and planted a gentle kiss on his mouth, one that was full of passion and pleasure, it was all he could do to keep his shit together.

He exhaled a shallow breath, and moved between her legs. She propped herself up on her elbow, dark lashes blinking rapidly over eager eyes as he went back on his heels to look at her. He stroked her pussy through her panties, all smooth and silky and wet, then eased the lace from her hips. He tossed them to the side, then climbed to his feet to remove his trunks.

Her glance went to his cock as it thickened, clamoring for her attention. But he knew if she touched him, put her mouth around his girth, he'd go off like a Roman candle and never get inside her, where he most desperately needed to be.

She crooked her finger. "You're too far away, and I need to touch you."

His heart pinched, loving the way she wanted him, the way her body beckoned his touch. He grabbed a condom from his backpack and quickly sheathed himself before dropping back to his knees. He breathed a kiss over her pussy, and even though she was more than ready for him, he wet her with his tongue before settling on top of her.

His cock throbbed between her legs as he surfed his mouth over her eyelids, her cheek, her mouth. Jesus, she was so sweet, so intoxicating, the depth of his desire for her was almost beyond his comprehension.

He shifted, his crown breaching her opening, and when he felt her body relaxing for him, welcoming him inside, he offered her an inch. Her pussy gripped him hard and tension coiled through him, tightening his every muscle and feeding the intensity of his arousal.

She tossed her head to the side, and tried to move her hips, to force him in deeper. But he kept her pinned, immobilized, because if he entered her hard and fast, he'd lose it harder and faster. And he didn't want to lose it with her, because he didn't ever want this moment to end. Christ, never had a woman made him feel so crazed and out of control before.

He groaned, his mouth coming down hard over hers to muffle her cries of protest. He kissed her, tasted her, enjoying her flavor on the tip of his tongue, and even though he was touching her all over, he still wasn't able to get enough of her as his cock burrowed deeper. She moaned and palmed his muscles as blood pounded through his veins.

His balls tightened against his body as her warm heat cocooned him, squeezing and massaging his cock as he went deeper still. Her heat seared him, and his mind practically shut down when he finally buried every inch of his throbbing cock inside her deliciously tight pussy.

His mouth moved to her neck, and he savored the taste of her damp skin as he began to move his hips. He slid in and out of her tight sheath, picking up the pace and rhythm until they were both delirious with pleasure.

"Sam, oh God, Sam. It feels so good," she murmured, her voice a strange, strangled whisper in the dark, moonlit night.

He gripped her hair when she wrapped her legs around his waist, pulling him in impossibly deeper, he growled loud, sure everyone in town could hear him. As she fueled his lust, deepening his need, blood rushed to his cock. He bit down on the inside of his cheek to hang on. Jesus, it was near impossible, but her pleasures were paramount, and he'd never take without giving first.

She gyrated, her hard nipples scraping over his chest in the most provocative way. Her body grew hotter and he could feel her muscles grow tight, a clear indication that she was right there, hovering on the precipice of ecstasy. *Thank Christ!* She began panting, her eyes moving over his face, seeking, searching. Jesus, she was so beautiful. Sam shifted on top of her and slipped a hand between them to stroke her sensitive cleft, and when her mouth opened, but no words came, he couldn't help but feel a sense of male pride to know he could do this to her.

"That's it, sweetheart. Come for me."

"Sam," she whispered as her muscles clenched around his cock. Fire burned through him, his senses exploding in a kaleidoscope of color, the last of his control unraveling like an old frayed fishing net. The second he felt her hot cream coat his cock, he pitched forward, reaching the point of no return. He buried himself inside her as he succumbed to the blinding pressure racing through him.

His body convulsed, and he sucked in a breath and held it as he released inside her. Her palm brushed gently over his face as his fingers bit into her hips, bruising her delicate skin before he collapsed on top of her.

He stayed there, buried inside her for a long time. As he relaxed on top of her body, she stroked her fingers over his back, eliciting a shiver from him. A long time later he lifted himself up and shifted his weight to the side. When he found her smiling at him, contentment written all over her face, he knew he had to have her again. But he also suspected that no matter how many times he fucked her, how many times he was inside her, he'd never be able to sate the need she pulled from him.

He brushed her hair from her face, and she sputtered when he got sand in her mouth.

"Sorry," he said, as they both laughed. "I guess we'd better get back in the water and get washed up."

Noises at the other end of the beach reached their ears.

She pulled a worried face and said, "I think maybe we should get inside."

His cock began to harden all over again. "Inside?" he asked, as he pulled her to her feet and wrapped her in the towel. He bent forward, dropped a soft kiss onto her mouth and whispered, "I think getting *inside* is a very good idea."

30

After spending a week trying to extend her loans at the bank, and trying to get approval from the restoration committee, Lex stood on her veranda, looked out over the ocean and took a deep, fortifying breath. Even though the week hadn't been all bad, Sam spent every night in her bed and the noises in the house had subsided, she'd yet to get the permits she needed to move forward with her restoration.

"Everything okay?" Sam asked, coming up behind her and wrapping his hands around her waist in a familiar way that always warmed her from the inside out.

She blew a strand of hair from her face as one of the button-down, pretty floral dresses Tabby had lent her ruffled around her thighs in the late morning breeze. "The clock is ticking, and I really need to get this place renovated. But no one at the restoration committee will answer me and even though I keep leaving messages, no one will call me back."

Sam's arms moved to her shoulders and he turned her around. His dark eyes moved over her face. He exhaled slowly then said, "They're never going to approve your plans, Alexis. Not unless you change them. You do realize that, right?"

She threw her hands up in the air. "What's wrong with modernizing this place?"

"Everything," he said simply, and went quiet for a moment, looking past her shoulders like he was remembering something very important from the past. Then he glanced at his watch and redirected the conversation. "You'd better get going, otherwise you're going to be late." He grabbed her hand. "Come on, I'll walk you. The guys and I are going out on Braydon's boat for the day, and Josie's place is on the way to the dock."

Lex bit her bottom lip, wondering if she really should be going to Tabby's baby shower at her friend Josie's house. Sure she liked Tabby, as well as the rest of the women in this town, and while they all made her feel welcome, she knew they were only being polite by extending an invitation. They were a tight-knit group and she really wasn't a part of it, didn't really belong.

They stepped into the kitchen and she looked at the shiny gift bag on the counter. "Maybe I shouldn't go."

Sam gave a casual shrug, one that said no matter where he went or who he was with, he always fit in. "Why not?"

She took in his laid-back look. "Is everything always so easy for you?"

Something moved over his eyes, some deeper emotion that she'd never before seen on his face. As she tried to puzzle it out, it disappeared as quickly as it appeared, and he gave her one of his infamous grins. "Yeah, it is," he said. "Now come on, let's go."

Twenty minutes later, Lex sat on the sofa next to Katy and played a game of peek-a-boo with her sweet daughter, Katherine. All around her kids played together and women chatted about their work, their families and the bountiful fishing season they were having in Whispering Cove while they partook in silly shower games.

On the other side of her she half-heartedly listened to a conversation between Lila and the bikini-clad girl with the chocolate lab, who happened to be Lila's sister visiting from Chicago. Apparently Lila's sister Eden had been flirting with Sam during the beach party in an effort to get Jacob to see her as something more than a fellow dog walker. Unfortunately, her efforts proved futile.

A door opened and Lex glanced up in time to see Josie stepping into the room with Tabby, whose cheeks were glowing with happiness. After all the Braxton Hicks Tabby had been experiencing recently it was easy to tell how ready she was to be done with her pregnancy and get on to mothering.

"Okay, time to open the presents, then we can eat," Josie said, rubbing her little baby bump as she quieted the crowd down. "Katy made her famous lemon chiffon cake, and I know we're all dying to dig in."

Laughter broke out and then they spent the next hour unwrapping presents. As Lex watched Tabby showcase the new baby clothes, a strange sensation began growing in her stomach. She'd never thought about having kids before, never thought about settling down and raising a family. But seeing how happy these women were and watching their kids play seemed to have flicked a maternal switch in her.

The women all oohed and aahed over the tiny clothes and gifts and even though Lex was sure she'd feel like an outcast, like she didn't belong at this gathering, she couldn't deny that everyone here made her feel welcome. It was the first time in her life she had a sense of belonging. No, she corrected herself. It was the second time. The first was with Sam.

An uneasy feeling curled through her. Oh, boy. Maybe agreeing to this affair wasn't her smartest move. Then again, she hadn't been making a lot of great decisions lately, considering she bought a heritage home that was going to end up bankrupting her, and make her the laughingstock of her family.

Tabby squealed when she opened Lex's gift, and as everyone's eyes lit with excitement, Lex exchanged a private smile with Skylar. After visiting her shop with Tabby last week and catching the way Tabby admired all the pieces, Lex had commissioned Sky to create a one-of-a-kind multi-colored glass mobile for the baby's nursery. She couldn't be happier with how beautiful it turned out.

As the gorgeous piece played Brahms's "Lullaby", Tabby thanked her profusely. After a long time she set it aside and turned her attention to the other parcels. Once all the gifts were open everyone made their way to the spacious dining room, with the long antique table, gorgeous wainscoting and tray ceiling. As they feasted on finger food, veggies and dips, the women laughed and joked. Lex joined in, temporarily forgetting her worries as she became a part of this womanhood.

She helped herself to a piece of cake and as she bit into it, she ran her hand along the cream-colored panels, admiring the craftsmanship.

"Isn't this place gorgeous?" Lila asked, coming up beside her.

She glanced at the pretty brunette with the long dark curls. "It is," Lex said, then she cocked her head and asked, "You run the bed and breakfast, right?"

Lila's eyes lit. "I do."

"I'm curious. Did you renovate it when you took it over?" Lex asked, wondering if she too had faced roadblocks with the restoration committee.

Lila nodded, traced a longing finger over the rail and said, "Yeah. I love how it turned out but I sure wish Sam had been around. He has an ability to see things others can't."

"What do you mean? Like ghosts?" Good Lord, did crazy old Errol think Lila's place was haunted too?

Lila grinned. "Well yeah, but I'm talking about his work, and his attention to the ornamental detailing. He can envision things the rest of us can't."

"I know. I wish he worked with me," Tabby said, stepping up to the two.

Lex's focus went from Lila to Tabby back to Lila again. "You two lost me."

"Just look around," Tabby said, then she called out to Josie. "Hey, Josie, is it okay if I give Lex a tour?"

"You bet," Josie said. "Be sure to show her the gorgeous, carved handrail leading upstairs. It's the original."

"Come on," Tabby said, and both she and Lila followed her into the den, where Tabby began pointing out all the trims, the detailing and the old-time craftsmanship that Sam had respected and adhered to when refinishing the house. Then she showed her the old rolled glass window, much like the ones in Lex's place.

"Wait," Lex said, shaking her head. "Are you telling me Sam did this?" She spun around the room. "He restored this den."

Tabby shook her head. "No, I'm telling you he restored the house."

Lex's jaw fell slack. "Sam did all this?"

"You mean you didn't know?" Lila asked.

She gave a bewildered shake of her head. "I had no idea." She took a moment to think back and remembered his reactions when she talked about changing the windows, tearing out the hearth, refinishing the place from the ground up. He'd looked physically ill. "Sam never mentioned any of this to me."

Tabby nodded her head, like she knew something Lex didn't, but instead of explaining she said, "Well if I were you and had Sam staying with me, I'd be sure to pick his brain. With his help, you could have the most beautiful heritage house in all of Whispering Cove."

"He really understands and appreciates craftsmanship reflective of the period, that's for sure," Lila added.

Dumbfounded, Lex followed the two women around the house as they showed her the features. Sam was right when he said he had a talent most didn't, and it wasn't just in seeing the supernatural...or in the bedroom. The place was absolutely gorgeous, and to think he'd restored this by himself was beyond impressive. It did, however make her wonder more about him, and why, after sleeping with her for a week, he kept this side of his life private when she'd spilled so much about herself.

After the shower, she made her way along the bustling streets. She breathed in the smells of the ocean and raw seafood as she watched the fishermen bring in their catches and sell it at the outdoor market. She found herself smiling. This really was a quaint old town, and the people in it were so different from the city where she lived.

As she passed by Hauk's bar, she caught a glimpse of Errol, Harold and Byron making their way inside. She couldn't hear what they were saying but she did hear something about a month's worth of rum. She also saw Errol swinging his cane, walking like he didn't need it at all.

She hurried home, and when she stepped inside the old Victorian home, she just stood there for a moment. As she looked around, taking in the grand front entrance, she suddenly began seeing the rundown place with its paint-chipped walls and battered floors in a new light. She made her way from room to room and considered the drastic changes she'd put in her report and sent to the restoration committee. Changes that didn't adhere to their code. She truly loved the work Sam had done on Josie's home and wondered how he might envision this house, if she was keeping with old-style tradition. There was no denying that the man had talent. So why did he leave Whispering Cove some ten years ago to become a ghost hunter in New Mexico when the people here clearly loved his work? He definitely had a future in the renovation industry.

She ran her hands along the crumbling hearth, and when footsteps heralded someone's approach she spun around. Her heart did a weird little leap when she caught Sam standing there watching her, a small smile on his face.

"How was the baby shower?"

"It was great." She looked at his tanned face. "How was sailing?"

He took a predatory step toward her. "Fun, but not as fun as hanging out with you. It's all I could think about all day."

She swallowed at the heat she spotted in his eyes. "Sam?" she asked.

His steps slowed and he gave her a curious look. "Yeah?"

She waved her hand around the empty living room. "If you were to renovate this room, what would you do?"

Conflicting emotions moved over his face, and he jammed his hands in his pockets and went quiet for a moment. Then, tone sober, he finally asked, "Why do you want to know?"

"I saw your work at Josie's place today." She gave a slow shake of her head. "I had no idea you knew how to do any of this."

He shrugged like it was nothing, but there was a hint of sadness in his eyes when he said, "That was a long time ago."

"I know, but I'm still curious to know what you'd do with this place if given the chance."

Sam walked over to the hearth. He ran his hands over the rough stone, and went quiet for a long time.

"Sam?" she asked.

"First I'd bring this back to life, and give it the proper care it deserves." He looked thoughtful for a moment, then smiled and said, "Can you imagine all the families that lived in this house, all the kids who sat on this wooden floor and huddled around this hearth on a cold winter night?"

Lex smiled as she pictured it, and then something lit in Sam's eyes when he moved to the window to examine the trim. Once he started talking, he couldn't seem to stop, and Lex just stood there in amazement listing to his ideas, shocked and a little impressed at how deep and profound this laid-back playboy really was.

He moved around the house, and she followed, listening quietly and intently as he spoke. Even though his ideas completely conflicted with what she wanted, she couldn't deny that the man had a rare talent. He clearly loved restoration work more than anyone she knew. Which once again had her wondering why he'd run off to New Mexico.

"Look at this dark wood trim, Alexis." He grabbed her hand and took her into the front entranceway. "Touch this."

She ran her hand down the oak railing. "Can you imagine how many kids slid down this?" He gave a slow shake of his head and said, "The stories this house could tell." His fingers closed over hers, his grip warm and strong as he led her outside. He took her to the side of the house where he touched the bright red, paint-chipped cedar shingles, and she felt excitement bubbling up inside him. "Over two centuries ago, this house was painted red to help the captain who lived here find his way home after being out to sea."

"You know a lot about this house."

"I know a lot about Whispering Cove, and every house has a similar story." He backed her up a bit and pointed to the widow's peak. "Over the centuries many women sat in that widow's peak, waiting for their loved ones to return. My mother, my grandmother, my great-grandmother spent a great many hours in theirs as well."

Loving this enthusiastic side of Sam, she couldn't help but feel something stir inside her too. She loved his zest for life, and that he could see beauty in everything around him, even when it was crumbling before their eyes.

"Don't you see, Alexis?" he said, passion and excitement in his eyes. "This is what the house was meant to be." He gave her a sexy, bad-boy grin that made her pussy clench with want as he led her back inside the house and up the wide staircase. "Maybe that's why the spirits are upset with you," he teased with a wink.

When they reached her brightly lit bedroom and found her suitcase lying wide open on the floor, exactly where it had been before it went missing a week ago, they both stopped midstride.

"What the heck?" Lex asked, bending down to grab her coveralls from the pile. She blinked up at Sam. "When? How?"

"I have no idea," Sam said, his voice lower, his eyes darker as they moved over the short dress she was wearing, a dress that she'd never be caught dead in before Whispering Cove. "Maybe there really are ghosts at play here, and maybe they are trying to tell us something."

"Like what?" she asked, her voice a little higher than normal as Sam visually undressed her with his eyes.

"Well," he began as he slowly backed her up toward the cot, passion backlighting his eyes. "Maybe they're trying to tell you that instead of making the house into something it's not, you're supposed to embrace the beauty of it just the way it is." As she acknowledged the flare of desire between her legs, he took the coveralls from her and tossed them aside. He trailed a finger over her mouth and her neck, going lower until he reached the button on her dress. His eyes locked on hers and he softened his words when he added, "And maybe they took all your boy clothes because they are trying to tell you that *you* are the way you're meant to be too. That you should stop trying to be something you're not." He toyed with the button and fingered the floral dress, rubbing the material between his thumb and index finger in a way that had her hormones firing and her brain cells melting.

Heat rose in her, and her fingers curled in his T-shirt as sexual energy arced between them. God, everything in the way he looked at her made her feel so beautiful, like she was one half of something very special. But she was here in this coastal town to prove herself, not to fall in love with the town, the people in it, and more importantly, Sam Doherty, a man who, she was coming to learn, was so much more than he appeared.

All thoughts fled when he released the first button on her dress, then the second and third, exposing the pretty black bra she'd bought last week. When his eyes widened in delight, taking pleasure in the lace material and the way it hugged her breasts, it occurred to her that she liked wearing sexy under-things. Maybe sexy outer things too. They made her feel feminine and sexy and girlie. *Sam* made her feel feminine and sexy and girlie. Yet even in her coveralls, she hadn't gone unnoticed by him. He was definitely a man who could see things others couldn't.

With exquisite gentleness, he slipped her dress from her shoulders, letting it fall to the floor. He cupped her breasts, and leaned forward to kiss her nipples through the lace. His hair brushed over her flesh, and she pulled in the salty tang of his skin.

Hunger whispered through her blood, and her body rippled, craving this man's touch in ways that could prove dangerous—to her head and her heart.

With a great deal of tenderness on his face, he picked her

up and spread her out on the sheets. His glance moved over her half-naked body as he removed his clothes and pulled a condom from his pocket.

As he climbed over her, her hands skimmed his sinewy muscles. She loved the feel of him on top of her, and more importantly, the weight of his body pinning her to the cot. His mouth took possession of hers and in no time at all she became lost in the moment, the sensations...this man. Everything in the way he touched her, kissed her, felt more intimate than the last time they made love, taking their relationship to a whole new level.

"I can't get enough of you," he murmured into her mouth, as her nipples hardened and her body quivered with want.

She grew slick between her legs as he shifted his weight, his fingers dipping beneath her damp panties. "Jesus," he groaned. "I love how you're always so ready for me." He stroked her just right, a soft caress that showed her how aware he was of her body, her needs.

"Sam, please," she begged, although she wasn't quite sure what she was begging for.

He inched her panties from her hips and tossed them aside. His eyes flared hot when they met hers, yet the gentleness and warmth lingering in their stormy depths covered her like a soft, protective blanket.

Chaos erupted inside her, her emotions in turmoil as he sheathed himself and entered her, slowly, methodically, giving her only an inch at a time as he drew out his very powerful seduction.

An erotic whimper bubbled in her throat as his strong arms circled her, holding her tight against him as he buried his mouth in her neck and pushed deep inside. Her pussy muscles gripped him hard, and heat poured from her body to his and back again. Pressure began brewing deep in her core, and she couldn't believe how close she felt to Sam, the emotions he so easily roused in her.

"You feel so fucking good," he whispered into her ear, and she could hear the need and impatience in his voice.

She moved with him, meeting and welcoming each stroke as his mouth found hers and his hands roamed her body. While his caresses were softer, like he was taking his time to really get to know her body, and his kisses were gentler, this coupling was by no means less powerful than the last. In fact, the intimacy in the slow, easy way he was making love was much more profound, touching her in the deepest of places.

Moisture sealed their bodies together as he sank all the way into her and joined them as one. Her heart swelled and she had a sense that something else was happening between them, and that this union, this sense of belonging she was feeling, went well beyond sex.

With unhurried movements he built her orgasm, taking her higher and higher until pleasure zinged through her and completely overcame her.

"Sam," she murmured, wrapping her arms around his back to hold him tight. "Oh, God, Sam."

"I know, sweetheart. I know," he whispered as their bodies began to ripple, both succumbing to the ecstasy and emotions swirling around them.

As she rode out the waves, their moans of bliss merged, and they both held on to each other like their lives depended on it. His hair brushed over her shoulders as he kissed her neck, his breath hot on her skin. She savored the taste of him on her tongue, and pulled his scent deep into her lungs. God, she loved everything about this man, and the way he made her feel so cherished—like this was where she'd always belonged.

When her body stopped spasming, she lay there beneath him, contentment moving through her veins. She looked past his shoulders, her mind sorting things through as she perused the room, and listened to the waves crash against the sandy shore outside.

"I want to do it," she said.

Sam pulled out of her, removed the condom, and shifted to face her, a grin curling his lips. His look was playful when he said, "Ah, we just did it sweetheart, but hey, I'm all for doing it again."

She laughed and whacked him, taking note of this new comfort between them as he rolled onto his back. "I'm talking about the house. I want to restore it using your ideas. Instead of fighting the heritage committee, I want to preserve the features in this home." She leaned into him and rested her head on his chest. "You were right, you know," she said as she trailed her fingers over his chest. "You opened my eyes and helped me see that this is what the house was meant to be." And maybe, just maybe it was time for her to be what she was meant to be, and who she was meant to be too.

When he went quiet, she lifted her chin to see him. Dark eyes regarded her warily, torment on his face. "What?" she asked.

"What about proving yourself to your brothers? Isn't that what this is all about?"

"It might have started out that way, but I think my priorities are changing."

Sam opened his mouth like he wanted to ask her something but then he shut it again.

"What?" she asked.

"Nothing. It's just...you're beautiful, is all."

Her heart skipped a beat, because as he stared down at her, there was no denying that she was falling for him. Not only did he make her feel important and sexy, he also made her feel like she belonged, and he saw things in her no one else ever had. But when his vacation was over, and she wanted more, would he simply pack up and leave town?

Or would she be enough to keep an amazing guy like him around?

Sam was in so much fucking trouble it wasn't even funny.

After spending the entire week detailing every room in depth with Alexis, and helping her revise her restoration plans and submit them to the committee, he knew he was getting in too deep. Which meant he needed to pull back and enjoy the physical aspects of their relationship only. She'd told him her priorities were changing, but he was sure she had no intention of staying in Whispering Cove. The last thing he wanted was to fall for the sweet yet sexy girl who could undoubtedly break his heart when she walked out of this town.

With Alexis out shopping with Tabby, he glanced at his watch and cut through the town square, needing to pick up his suit for tomorrow's wedding. From the corner of his eye he spotted the Whispering Salon and raked his hands through his hair.

Deciding it was time for a cut, he hurried across the street. A bell overhead dinged as he entered the busy salon and was greeted with a big hug from Vic.

"Sam," she said. "What brings you in here today?" She frowned, looked at his long hair and said, "Clearly you've been avoiding any establishment with a pair of scissors."

He laughed and rubbed his scalp. "I think maybe it's time for a trim."

"Sit," she said, pointing to her chair. "And if it's okay with you, I'd like to do more than a trim."

Sam dropped down into her cushiony chair, and before she put a cape over him, she said, "Nice shirt."

In the mirror facing his chair, Sam took note of his T-shirt with the picture of the camel on it and the saying, "Happy Hump Day". Okay, okay, so it was a bit juvenile—and it had holes—but it was worn and comfortable and in his profession he had no need to dress up. Besides, he had no one to impress.

Vic ran a comb through his disheveled hair, and all around him women chatted, or rather gossiped. He listened in, not at all opposed to hearing the latest news, but soon enough all eyes turned to him.

"So Sam, are you back for good?" Vic asked.

"Nope, I'm heading back to New Mexico at the first of next month."

"Oh," Hannah McGrath, Reece's mother, piped in from the chair beside him. "Errol said you were back for good."

Sam frowned. "Why would he say that?"

"I have no idea," she said.

"He also said you were helping Lex renovate the place because you both planned to live there," Errol's better half, Delilah Kean, added.

Sam shook his head. "I think someone needs to cut off Errol's rum supply."

"So it's not true? You're not back for good?" Annette Wilson, Katy's mother, asked from a few chairs over.

"No—"

"But you helped her design new plans for the house didn't you?" Vic asked, as she met his glance in the mirror and made quick work of his hair.

"Yes, but—" he began, but was quickly cut off.

Mrs. McGrath pursed her lips. "I heard the restoration committee just approved them."

Sam opened his mouth to try again. "Really? When—"

"Yeah, I was talking to your grandfather earlier, Sam," Ms. Kean said. "He said the board sat today and approved Lex's plans. He also said the house design had your signature all over it. They'll be sending out her letter and permits next week."

Braydon's mother, Ruth Mitchell, nodded her head. "Your granddad is proud of your work."

"But he hates that you ran off to New Mexico...after, well you know," Ms. Kean said.

Mrs. Mitchell clapped her hands. "Lex is going to have the nicest house in Whispering Cove."

Mrs. McGrath gave a slow shake of her head. "If she can ever get it done."

"What do you mean?" Vic asked.

"Didn't you hear?" Mrs. McGrath's eyes went wide. "My son's construction company is the only one in town that is a licensed preservation contractor, and he's currently tied up, so without a qualified contractor overseeing the work, she won't get it done for months."

"Sam could do the work, though," Ms. Kean said. "He's qualified. Aren't you, Sam?"

Mrs. Wilson nodded her head in agreement. "Maybe you should consider staying. I'd love to hire you to redo my house."

"Come to think of it, mine needs an update too," Mrs. Kean added.

Vic clipped away at his hair and said, "I know Tabby would love to have your insight in the early stages of designing a place."

Conversation continued around him, and he opened his mouth numerous times, but couldn't manage to get a word out. By the time Vic finished his hair and removed his cape his head was spinning, trying to sort through all the information that had come his way.

After he left the salon, he made his way across town. He picked up his suit from the tailors, then caught his reflection in the mirror outside Delmart's department store. He frowned when he saw the holes in his old, worn T-shirt. Maybe it was time to pick up a few new dress shirts to go with the new haircut. He ducked inside and walked through the men's department. As he strolled, trying to convince himself he was shopping for new clothes because everything he owned was old and ratty, he knew the real reason was Alexis and that he wanted to look nice for her.

After making a few purchases, he made his way back to the house, wondering if the salon's gossip had reached her ears. When he walked in the door, he overhead Alexis on her phone in the kitchen, pleading with her bank to extend her loan. She was explaining that she'd run into a few roadblocks and was working hard to iron them out. As he listened, he knew she had no idea her plans had been approved.

He also knew he was going to do it.

Even though he'd walked away from the business and swore he'd never restore an old house for a woman who'd only end up leaving when all was said and done, he was damn well going to go against his own best interests, call in a few favors and personally oversee Alexis's restoration project, even if it ended up being the death of him.

31

As Sky and Leo exchanged vows in the town's century-old church, a beautifully restored lighthouse, Lex couldn't help but look at the man seated beside her. Stunning was the only word she could find to describe him. With his hair cut short, and a suit that fit his gorgeous body to perfection, Sam looked like he'd stepped straight out of *GQ*. But not only did he look different, he seemed different. Even though he was still easygoing and laid back, there was a new seriousness about him.

Needing something to do with her hands, she smoothed down the bodice of the dress she'd bought yesterday, having asked Tabby to take her shopping to pick out a few new dresses that she knew Sam would like. She'd paid a little more than she would have liked, considering she was flat broke, but Sam's reaction when he saw her was well worth it.

After the wedding, they all attended the reception and as she sipped champagne and spoke to the women, she could feel Sam's eyes on her. She met his glance from across the yard, and when warmth moved through her, she wondered how she'd ever be able to be with another man after him.

He cut through the throngs of people and slipped in beside her. His strong arm curled around her waist and she leaned in to him, never having felt such an easy intimacy with anyone.

"Want to get out of here?" he whispered into her ear.

As much as she was enjoying herself, Sam would be leaving town in a couple of weeks and she wanted to enjoy every minute with him that she could. She could hear speculative whispers from the women as Sam whisked her away and back to her house, but she didn't care. All she cared about was spending every minute she could with this man.

Without speaking, he took her straight to the bedroom and closed the door behind him. Dark eyes met hers, and she was sure she'd never seen him look so intense, so serious. "You look beautiful in this dress," he said, taking a small step toward her. "But I seriously can't wait to get you out of it."

He slipped his hand around her back and drew down the zipper. His mouth found hers as the dress slid to the floor. He groaned, and murmured into her mouth, "Why is it I can't get enough of you?"

Before she could answer he gathered her into his arms and took her to the cot. He made quick work of his clothes, sheathed himself, and a few minutes later he was inside her, pumping hard and taking her higher than she'd ever been before. There was no denying their sex was amazing the first time, but the more they got to know each other outside the bedroom, the better and better things got between the sheets.

"Sam," she whimpered into his ear as her orgasm approached. "I can't get enough of you either."

As soon as the words left her mouth she climaxed and when her pussy squeezed his cock, he threw his head back and stilled, releasing high inside her.

After he discarded the condom, they held each other tight

until they both dozed off, only to wake again in the wee hours of the night to make love again.

Soon enough Lex woke to the sound of voices inside her house. Many, many voices, to be precise. Both male and female. She pulled the sheet up and looked at Sam, who was propped up on his elbow and watching her carefully.

"What's going on? Is there someone in the house again?"

He gave her a lopsided grin. "Oh, did I forget to tell you?"

"Forget to tell me what?"

"Your plans were approved and I gathered everyone who was available to help get this place done by your deadline."

"You…you did what?" she asked around the lump forming in her throat. She climbed from her cot and put her hand on her chest when she caught the crowd milling around outside and examining the exterior. "The whole town is practically here."

"It's the only way we can get it done on time."

"But the work has to be overseen by a licensed preservation contractor."

"I've got it covered."

Sam climbed from the mattress and pulled on his jeans. He dropped a soft kiss onto her mouth and there was such warmth in his eyes when they met hers that a surge of love rushed to her heart. "You might want to get dressed. It's going to be a crazy week."

And a crazy week it was.

Lex was run ragged, helping out wherever she could and getting to work closely with Sam to refurbish the gorgeous, ornate handrail that he took such painstaking care to restore to its natural state. Once they finished it, he slid down it with childlike exuberance and wouldn't let up until she did the same.

She loved watching him work, loved the concentration on his face. To know she was a part of restoring something special, something that meant so much to him, filled her with a sense of pride. By the time the next Saturday rolled around, with a huge crew working hard all week, the house was practically finished.

She crept from the bed early, letting Sam get a few more hours' sleep before the crowd gathered once again to add the final touches. She walked through the house, admiring the gorgeous restored hearth, the polished plank floors, the wainscoting, the tray ceilings, and the new bathtub with the gorgeous clawfoot legs. She was so glad she listened to Sam, because the house was beautiful, the way it was meant to be. Even though it went against what her brothers did, modernization would have been a colossal mistake. She stepped outside and when she breathed in the salt air, and looked at the freshly painted cedar shingle exterior, tears pooled in her eyes.

She could hardly believe the town had come together like this to help her, that Sam, a man she'd fallen hard for and would likely never set eyes on again after this month, had arranged it all.

She exchanged a smile with young Jake as he worked with landscaper Ryan Alden and planted shrubs and flowers around the place. She moved past Devon, who had a scowl on his face. In fact he'd been scowling all week, every since he'd found out Sahara Caan had plans to construct a huge resort. In fact the whole town was in an uproar over her proposed plans. Lex cringed, because she definitely understood what that was like to be on the receiving end.

She was about to go talk to Errol, who was giving orders and poking everyone with his cane, when the sound of a loud vehicle pulling into her long driveway gained her attention.

Lex made her way toward it, and when Tabby climbed from the passenger seat and moved to the back of the truck,

Lex followed her. She gave her friend a perplexed frown and asked, "What's going on?"

The driver met her at the back, flipped open the latch and the door made a grinding sound as he pushed it up and out of the way. Lex gasped when she saw all the furniture and accessories inside, things that she and Tabby had picked out for the place a couple weeks back. Then she spotted a few of the old antique pieces she'd taken to the pawn shop. Pieces she now knew would look spectacular in the place.

"Tabby," she said, shaking her head. "I can't afford this."

Tabby gave an easy roll of her shoulder. "Sure you can."

"But—"

"Hey, when the labor is free, you can spend your money elsewhere."

Lex's eyes went wide, wondering what she was talking about. "The labor isn't free."

"Sure it is. Didn't Sam tell you?"

"No." Her stomach tightened. "I don't understand. How could it be free?"

"Everyone is pitching in because they want to, not because they're getting paid."

Her heart turned over in her chest and she fought back the tears. "Why would you all do this...for me?"

Tabby smiled. "Because we like you, Lex. Whether you realize it or not, you're one of us now." She laughed and added, "And because Sam asked us to. He's a pretty persuasive guy."

She thought back to when he asked her to have an affair with him and how she agreed, even though deep in her heart she knew it was a bad idea. "Oh, I know."

Just then Jake, Vic, Sophie, Carmen, Andie and Dani along with a few other women she'd met showed up with buckets and soap and mops. Katy and Josie came up behind them with enough sandwiches and drinks to feed a town, which, she supposed, they were.

"Now come on, let's get the guys to help lift the furniture and put it in place, so we can clean and then eat. The baby is starving."

As she watched Tabby step up to her friends and divvy up chores, Lex's heart went to her throat. It baffled her the way this town came together...for her. How on earth could she ever walk away from these people?

From Sam?

Night had fallen by the time everyone left, exhausted after a long day and even longer week. Sam dipped his toes in the water and turned to see Alexis, who was shedding her clothes. His heart thundered as he watched her, his body needed her all over again.

"Hurry up," he growled.

"I'm coming, I'm coming," she said, her voice lighter than he'd ever heard it. A lump formed in his throat as she approached, her beautiful refurbished house providing a backdrop. He stole a quick glance at it and while he was happy that he could do this for her, and get her back on track with her loans, it damn near killed him to see the For Sale sign go up.

When she reached him, he pushed his worries aside, wanting to enjoy these last few days, maybe even only a few minutes, he'd have with her before she skipped town. He kissed her hard, then hand in hand they waded out into the water. They swam to a ledge below Dresden's Bluff, and he lifted her onto the rocks with him.

Their feet dangled in the water and she shimmied close. When he felt her body quiver, he pulled her in tight, noticing that she was unusually quiet. Sam took a moment to sort through everything that had happened between them the last week, and how maybe it was time to settle down in Whispering Cove. Only problem was, there was only one girl he wanted to settle down with and her life was in Portland.

"Sam," she said, breaking the quiet.

He lightly trailed his finger up and down her arm. "Yeah."

"Can I ask you something?"

"Sure."

"Why did you leave Whispering Cove?"

"I told you I had a talent most don't."

She touched his chin and angled his face her way. When he caught the emotion in her eyes his heart tightened. "You're right. You do. And that talent is in restoring houses. Why did you stop?"

He exhaled slowly. "It was a long time ago. I was young and in love," he said, holding her tighter and realizing for the first time that while he cared for his ex very much, what he felt for Alexis went much deeper. "Or at least I thought I was."

"And..."

"And I secretly restored a house for her and asked her to marry me. She turned me down and, because she wanted a house that was shiny and new, left town with another guy who could give it to her. I swore I'd never restore another house again—especially for another woman—and walked away from it all."

Her voice was soft, barely audible, when she stated, "Yet you did it for me."

"Yeah, Alexis," he said softly. "I did it for you."

"You're a licensed preservation contractor, aren't you? You're the one who signed off on all the work right?"

"Yeah."

Lex pursed her lips, like she was deep in thought, then said, "Maybe it's time to stop letting other people dictate what you do." He gave her a sideways look and she poked him in the chest, throwing his words back at him. "Maybe it's time to be who you really are, and stop trying to be something you're not."

As they exchanged a long, thoughtful look, he considered what she was saying. Maybe she was right. Maybe it was time to grow up, put the past behind him, and stop letting it haunt him.

He jumped back into the water and dragged her in with him. "Come on."

"Where?" she asked, her teeth shivering as the cold waves enveloped them.

"Your bedroom has a brand new king-sized bed, and I believe I need to toss you on it and have my wicked way with you before you leave town."

Sadness moved over her face, but then was quickly replaced by desire. "I don't believe we should be sleeping in furniture that I'll be selling with the house."

He gave her a lopsided grin. "I never said anything about sleeping."

32

Lex stretched out and reached across the mattress, her body warm and content after last night's all-night lovemaking session on a big, *comfortable* bed. When her hand came up empty, she sat up and glanced around the room in search of Sam.

When he was nowhere to be found, she drew a breath and fought down the anxiety worming its way through her blood. Honestly, when she agreed to this affair, she knew what she was getting into and had gone so far to warn herself not to fall for an immature guy who hunted ghosts on the other side of the country.

Sure she'd learned more about Sam since making that decision, and had come to understand that while he chased ghosts, the truth was he had a few demons of his own, which was why he'd never told her he was a licensed preservation contractor. He'd been reluctant to do any work on her place all along, because he refused to restore a house for another woman he cared for only for her to up and leave his life.

He did it anyway—risking his heart because there was no doubt he cared for her. But after hearing him say he wanted to christen her bed before she left town, he clearly never expected her to stay.

She sat there and mulled over her time in Whispering Cove, specifically her time with Sam. Her priorities had shifted, and she now knew what was important to her, and what wasn't. Lex was a girl who'd grown up with four brothers, and anything and everything she'd ever wanted she had to fight for. And the truth was, she wasn't a child anymore, one who could do nothing but sit by helplessly while someone she loved walked out of her life. She was all grown up now, so was she really just going to sit here and feel sorry for herself while someone else she loved skipped town? Or was she going to fight for the man who'd come to mean so much to her? After all, wasn't she a girl who went after what she wanted, letting nothing or no one stand in her way?

With renewed purpose she climbed from the bed and pulled on a sundress. She had no idea where Sam had run off to but she was damn well going to track him down and use Errol's cane to pound some sense into him if she had to. They were good together—great together—and he knew it every bit as much as she did.

He'd taught her to be who she really was, taught her to understand what was important, and it was time for her to teach him the same.

A loud sound coming from downstairs startled her, and when she realized it was someone knocking on her front door, she rushed down the steps and gasped when she saw her four overbearing, overprotective brothers standing there.

She pulled open the door. "What...what are you guys doing here?"

Her oldest brother Donnie stepped forward. "More like what are *you* doing here?" he asked, looking past her shoulders into the house.

"How did you find me?"

"You said you were visiting Charlotte in Rhode Island, but she called the other day, so we tracked you down through the bank."

She held her ground and asked, "So you all decided to drive down from Portland to see what I was up to?" Damn, she really should have called Charlotte to fill her in on her plan, but they hadn't spoken in so long she never expected her to call the house.

"Yeah, something like that," Donnie said.

"What's going on here, Lex?" Scott, her youngest brother, asked.

She inhaled, and pointed behind her. "I came here to restore this house to prove to you guys that I have what it takes to be a part of your business."

"Fine," Donnie blurted out hastily, as his shrewd eyes took in the work done on the house. "You can be a part of the business. Just get in the truck and come home where you belong."

Belong...

"You're only saying that because you want me to come home so you can watch over me," she said.

"So you really did all this, Lex?" her second-youngest brother Drake asked.

"With a little help from my friends." Warmth moved through her, because she knew deep in her heart she'd finally found a place where she belonged and that was Whispering Cove.

Scott jerked his thumb toward the truck. "Okay, so you proved yourself. Now we can go."

"I'm not going." She rooted her feet, and as her brothers examined the front foyer, she suddenly, inexplicably, no longer cared if her renovations met their standards or not. She only cared what Sam thought, because keeping with heritage was important to him, which meant it was important to her.

"What are you wearing?" her second-oldest brother Keevan asked, pulling a face as his glance moved over her girlie dress.

"Look…" she began, ready to tell them that she didn't need their protection or approval and that she wanted to stay in Whispering Cove, even though she didn't yet have a place to live.

Someone from behind her brothers cleared their throat. They all turned and formed a protective wall around Lex. She went up on her tiptoes to see who was there, but from his familiar scent alone she knew it was Sam.

"Who are you?" Donnie asked.

"The name's Sam. Who are you?"

Donnie widened his stance. "Who we are doesn't matter."

"What are you doing with that For Sale sign?" Keevan asked. He snickered and jabbed Drake. "I think he plans to use that as some kind of weapon against us."

"Good luck with that," Drake said.

"Actually, I took it down because I want to buy this place."

Lex squeaked and tried to push past her brothers. Her attempts proved futile.

"Do you think you could move out of the way?" Sam asked. "I need to talk to Alexis."

Donnie stepped forward. "The only way you're getting to her is through us."

"Well if that's the way it has to be," Sam said.

"Donnie, stop it," Lex said. "So help me if you lay a hand on him…"

She heard the For Sale sign fall to the floor as she pounded on Keevan's back, trying to get around him.

"Shit, I just bought this shirt, and now I'm going to get

blood all over it. You wouldn't at least let me change would you?" Sam asked.

Donnie growled.

"Guess not." Sam sighed. "Alexis?"

"Yeah?"

"When this fight is over, I might not be able to talk so I want to ask you something now while I still have teeth."

Her heart raced, her stomach sick with worry as her brothers bullied the man she loved, a man who didn't seem at all afraid to stand up to them, which, while stupid, warmed her heart immensely. "Okay."

"I want you to stay here in Whispering Cove, with me." He got quiet for a moment, and she didn't miss the worry in his voice when he whispered, "Please say yes."

She clapped her hands together and did a little jump, her heart soaring. It was a good thing he only wanted a one-word answer because "Yes" was all she could manage around the lump in her throat.

"I want to live in this house with you, have babies with you and watch them grow up and slide down the rail we refinished together." She swiped the tears in her eyes, unable to find her voice. "And Alexis?"

"Yeah."

"Even in coveralls, you're the smartest, most beautiful restoration specialist I know. I want to spend the rest of my life working together to restore old houses with you."

"I don't need the coveralls, Sam. You taught me to be who I really am and I can be feminine and still be taken seriously in this industry."

"Okay, enough of this sappy shit," Donnie said, grabbing Sam by the shirt.

Before he could throw a punch, he let out a loud oomph and sank to his knees. Over his drooping head Lex spotted Errol removing his cane from her brother's gut. She pushed past Donnie and ran into Sam's arms. He placed a soft, loving kiss onto her mouth before pulling her in tight.

"What's going on here, boys?" Errol questioned. "You got a problem with my Sam and Alexis?"

"She's not your Alexis, she's our Lex," Scott said, jamming his thumb into his own chest as he took a predatory step forward.

Errol held up his cane in warning. "Not anymore she's not." He grinned and gave Sam a nudge with the cane. "How many men do you know who would stand up and take a beating from you four just to be with your sister?"

The four guys all started mumbling under their breath.

"Yeah, that's right," Errol said. "So doesn't that tell you boys that she's his, not yours?"

"Lex," Donnie began when he finally managed to climb to his feet. "What the hell is going on here?"

Sam positioned Alexis behind him and stepped forward. "I love her," he stated. "And I only want what's best for her. She's in good hands with me and I will never, ever hurt her. You have my word on that."

"You think you're what's best for her?" Donnie asked.

Sam stepped back beside her. "Why don't you ask her?"

Donnie turned to her. "Lex?"

She smiled up at Sam. "There are no other hands I'd rather be in."

When Donnie's shoulders sagged, Sam turned toward her and when he drew her in tight, she saw love shining in his eyes. "I love you, Alexis."

She was about to tell him she loved him too, when Errol held his hands up palms out. "Do you feel that?"

Oh, good God no. "Errol, the place isn't haunted."

"That's what I'm trying to tell you, lassie," he said with a mischievous grin on his face that had her wondering if he was behind the strange goings on in the house all along. "Not a cold spot to be found. Ol' Lady Landry is now resting nicely."

"There never were any ghosts," Sam said.

As her four brothers stood there dumbfounded, like they had no idea what crazy old Errol was going on about, he continued with, "Sure there were. Your gizmos just weren't working."

"My gizmos were working just fine, but now that my priorities have changed, I think I'll be packing them away for good."

She leaned into him, and when she felt a hard ridge in the vicinity of his zipper she whispered playfully, "Hopefully not every gizmo."

"No, Alexis," he said laughing as he picked her up and spun her around. "Not every gizmo."

A warm summer breeze blew over Errol's face as he picked up a candy wrapper and tossed it into the trash. Town square was quiet now that the parade had passed through and families were gathered for their annual barbeques. He couldn't help but smile as he, Byron and Harold walked around the gazebo, admiring the work Carmen and Ryan had revealed during the Fourth of July parade. He might not have won the bet this time around, but it didn't matter. He was just happy to have Sam back in his life, and hitched to sweet little Alexis. He just knew they were going to fill that house with love and babies.

He turned to Harold and nudged him with his cane. "We did good, ol' buddy."

Harold furrowed his bushy brows. "Was worried for a bit there. Things got mighty tricky with Devon and Sahara, but in the end love won out."

Byron gave a low, slow whistle, and rubbed his arthritic hands together. "You think you had it tough. That Carmen is one strong-willed girl."

When Byron frowned, Errol poked him with his cane.

"What have you got to be upset about, you barnacle-plucking ol' goat? Ryan had the biggest declaration of love, in front of the whole dang town, which means you won the bet and Harold and I are out a month's worth of rum?"

Harold guffawed. "Not that we don't plan to help you drink it."

Byron stepped away from the gazebo and looked around the town, taking in all the folks making their way to their backyard to prepare for family, fun and good food. "It's getting mighty hard to keep meddling, though. The whole town is on to us," Byron explained.

Errol nodded. "Yeah, it makes it a bit tricky doesn't it?"

They left the gazebo and made their way across the town square toward Byron's place, to where they'd get in a couple card games and a few shots of rum before joining their families. Jacob Collins, one of the town's veterinarians, who was out for a run with his dog Charlie, ran through the park, giving the three a wave.

Errol's mind started racing...scheming. "Maybe we're going to have to shake things up a bit."

"You've got something in mind?" Byron asked.

"He'd have to have a mind first," Harold piped in.

"Why, you old bloated—" he began, but his words fell off when he spotted Lila and Eden, along with Eden's big Labrador retriever, coming from Sleepy Cove B&B.

Instead of turning right when they reached the sidewalk, Errol went left. "Where you going?" Harold asked, nodding toward Byron's house. "The rum's that way."

Byron narrowed his beady eyes. "Wait, why are you grinning like the village idiot?"

"'Cause I'm going to get my dog, that's why."

"Dang, Errol, you losin' it? You ain't got no dang dog," Byron said, shaking his head.

Harold's glance went from Jacob to sweet and *single* Eden

Sheppard back to Errol. "Why, you sneaky ol' puffer fish. Think you're gonna get the jump on us, do ya?"

"Yeah, well, before we know it, another opportunity to meddle will be on us, so if you two want to stand a chance against me, you'd better get scheming!"

AFTERWORD

Thank You!

Thank you so much for reading WET, BRAZEN, SILK, and FLIRTY, in my Whispering Cove series. I hope you enjoyed the stories as much as I loved writing them. Please keep reading for an excerpt of Yours To Take.

Interested in leaving a review? Please do! Reviews help readers connect with books that work for them. I appreciate all reviews, whether positive or negative.

Happy Reading,
Cathryn

"Please tell me you're not serious?"

Jaw slack, and hands planted on the small round table, Rebecca Andrews stared at her three best friends, hardly able to believe what they were suggesting.

Lilliana James closed her palm over Rebecca's hand and gave a reassuring squeeze. Even though the lights had been dimmed in their favorite New York piano bar, a place where they all convened after a challenging day in the courtroom, Rebecca didn't miss the sympathy in her friend's big brown eyes when she said, "Come on, Becs, you know as well as I do that you need a vacation."

"It's not a vacation she needs," Melanie Collins piped in, running her fingers up and down the crystal stemware in a highly suggestive manner that had Rebecca's thoughts careening in an erotic direction. She smirked and added, "What she needs is to get laid. Plain and simple."

"Good, God," Rebecca murmured under her breath, hoping like hell no one in the near vicinity could hear her tell-it-like-it-is friend.

"Don't even try to deny it," Melanie challenged playfully, her eyes gleaming with mischief.

As their conversation headed south—literally—Rebecca fished her olive out of the martini glass and gestured the bartender for another, having decided then and there that this was the perfect occasion to overturn her two two-drink rule. Hell, who could blame her for wanting to consume copious amounts of alcohol after discovering her well-meaning friends wanted to send her to some sort of sex club on a private island off the coast of Nova Scotia?

She chewed on her olive as her glance went to the tickets on the table—one for a resort called Freedom, the other for the private charter that was scheduled to fly her there first thing tomorrow. Groaning, she took in the other patrons seated around them, many of whom were colleagues, their identities masked by the lounge's dark lighting and intimate seating. She leaned forward, desperate to keep this embarrassing conversation private, and arched an accusing brow. "How long have you three been scheming this up, anyway?"

"Just a few weeks now," Melanie answered.

Rebecca did the mental math, her thoughts rewinding to three weeks ago, then shook her head, suddenly understanding what this was really all about. "Look, Jon didn't break up with me. I broke up with him." When her rebuttal was met with silence, she desperately searched for an alliance in the group. Her glance met Sophie's and she cast her a pleading look.

But Sophie simply shrugged and said, "Just like you broke up with Justin, Matthew, Phillip..."

"And we know, we know," Melanie said, rolling her eyes. "You just weren't compatible."

Rebecca held her hands up, palms out. "Okay, fine. I get it. You're saying I'm too picky." She frowned, and added, "It's just that...well, we weren't...they weren't," she paused, unable to put in to words what she truly felt. How could she explain what was missing from those relationships, when she couldn't identify it herself?

She took a moment to consider the men from her past. Not only were they successful, kind and generous, they were also deeply considerate lovers. A woman in her right mind would jump at the chance to date any one of those men. She sighed inwardly. Okay, perhaps the problem really did lie with her, and *she* was the one who wasn't in her right mind. But she just couldn't seem to find a man that suited her.

If only she could figure out what it was that was lacking...

Oddly enough her thoughts drifted back to last year's trial against Montgomery Charters, specifically to Quinn Montgomery, owner of the airline, and one of the world's youngest, self-made millionaires. Rebecca always prided herself on being calm, cool and collected, inside the courtroom and out, but there was just something about that man's steely command that threw her off her game. Whenever she met those intense black eyes from across the table, eyes that looked like they could see into the depth of her soul, something always compelled her to shy away. She wasn't sure what it was about the powerful tycoon that had her reacting in such a peculiar way, she only knew that he had the ability to rattle her hard-earned control, and because of it, she needed to keep her distance.

The bartender stepped up to the table with fresh drinks, and as his presence pulled her thoughts back to the conversation at hand, Rebecca shook her head, wondering why she was thinking of the powerful and enigmatic Quinn Montgomery after all this time.

Perhaps it was the fact that her friends had booked her flight through his airline...or perhaps it was something else entirely. Either way, he was a man she never wanted to come up against again, because the next time she wasn't so sure she could keep her composure.

"It's just a weekend away to relax, let you hair down." Melanie waved a dismissive hand like what they were suggesting was nothing more than an innocent day at the spa. Except what they wanted her to do had sex, sin and seduction written all over it. "Maybe at Freedom you'll learn to relax and stop trying to be in control of everything all the time."

Rebecca squared her shoulders and tucked a long, loose strand of hair back into the bun piled at the top of her head. "Hey, I don't always have to be in control of everything."

Her rebuttal was met with laughter. Okay, so maybe it was true, but it wasn't her fault. She'd come from nothing and had to work hard to get where she was, and it wasn't easy to loosen up and let go. Controlling every aspect of her life was how she got to where she was today.

And where is that, some inner voice asked, only to answer with, *alone every night, with nothing but a battery-operated friend to keep you warm.*

Sophie squeezed her hand and Rebecca looked up to meet a pair of big blue eyes full of genuine concern. "You've been so uptight that we just thought you could use a bit of time to yourself."

Melanie bobbed her head. "And you never know, while you're away maybe you'll figure out what it is you're looking for in a man."

"At a sex resort?"

"It's not a sex resort," Lilliana reassured her. "It's just a place where single people go to meet others."

Slipping into lawyer mode, Rebecca challenged, "But when you say *others*, you mean the opposite sex right? So in my book that's a sex resort." Rebecca picked up the ticket and turned it over in her hand, but as she thought about it, really, really thought about what her friend's were offering her, her body began warming in the most intimate places. She wet her suddenly dry lips, her nipples tightening as she envisioned the salacious activities that undoubtedly took place on the exclusive island.

A strange garbled noise caught in her throat and she shook her head to clear it. God, she must be crazy—and the jury was still out on that—because for a moment there she actually found herself considering their ludicrous offer.

Rebecca squinted to read the fine print. "Is this place even legal?"

"Of course it is, and you leave first thing in the morning." Melanie snatched the ticket and shoved it into Rebecca's purse; her way of saying the topic was no longer up for debate.

Rebecca stiffened. "I don't think—"

"Which is why we're doing the thinking for you," Lillian countered.

"If you're not at the airport by nine sharp, I'll personally drag you from your bed and take you there." Melanie finished her drink, and grinned. "And don't come back until you've had at least a dozen orgasms."

"And we don't want to hear a peep from you until Monday morning, when we'll meet you at the office to hear all the juicy details," Lilliana said. "If you call before then, we won't answer."

"That's right," Sophie added, pointing to Rebecca's purse. "You've just been gifted with a ticked to Freedom. So go. Be free."

———

Quinn Montgomery took one look at the flight manifest and felt his cock swell with an excitement he hadn't felt in a long time. As the Dom in him stirred to life, he carefully set the paper on his desk and took two measured steps to his office window. He adjusted his tie and blinked against the bright morning rays glistening on the wings of the Cessna idling quietly on the tarmac below. He turned his attention to his ground crew, who were performing maintenance checks before today's scheduled flights, but his thoughts were too preoccupied with the names on his manifest, one name in particular, to follow their progress.

Rebecca Andrews.

Now what were the odds that the lawyer who'd cost his company hundreds of thousands of dollars had booked a charter on one of his crafts? A charter to a hedonistic resort, nonetheless.

His mind raced back to last year's trial, and to the lawsuit Ms. Andrews' client never should have won. How it was his company's fault that Ms. Andrews' client had booked a package though a shady travel agent, only to find herself alone and stranded on Nantucket Island during one of the year's worst storm was beyond him. Yet in the end, his company had to go good for the damages, as well as the mental stress and loss of wages that the woman had allegedly suffered.

Quinn's mouth twitched and he scrubbed his hand over his chin as he rolled back and forth on the balls of his feet. While the money was only a drop in the bucket for his company, the tricks the lawyer had used to get what she wanted from him, left him wanting to use a few tricks of his own—to get what he wanted from her.

Oh yeah, watching her from the hot seat during his trial, watching that sharp tongue of hers in action, had him wanting to find other ways to put that smart mouth of hers to work. Heat prowled through his body as he thought about how Ms. Andrews kept her control close, kept her body poised and her head held high. But during the proceeding, every time her glance had landed on him and she lowered her gaze in a submissive move, he knew she was in denial. Damned if he didn't want to be the one to open her eyes and her body, and put her in touch with her deeper needs.

Even though they'd never crossed paths since the trial, she'd consumed his thoughts for well over a year now. He'd spent many nights thinking about the ways he'd like to strip her bare and give her ass a good hard paddling for wrongfully stealing money from his company. But the truth was, what he wanted had little to do with revenge, and more to do with showing the woman who dressed in prim and proper business suits that real control came in the form of surrender.

With his cock throbbing, and heat coursing through him, he moved back to his desk to look over the day's schedule a second time. He glanced at her name again, and his entire body came alive, because there was no denying that he'd just been gifted the perfect opportunity to help her free her submissive side. Of course, given that he'd only have one weekend, he'd have no choice but to push her limits and resort to some stronger methods to seduce the submission out of her. His fingers itched as he thought about that lush heart-shaped ass of hers and how much it needed his attention.

He inspected the itinerary closer and discovered that Jack Armstrong, a pilot that had been with the company since its early days was scheduled to depart for Freedom at nine sharp —Ms. Andrews the only passenger on board. Quinn considered her final destination. Not only had his company taken guests to the private island numerous time, he personally knew the resort well, having played there a time or two. Although this time he suspected the plane wasn't going to make it to the well-known island nestled in the Atlantic Ocean, especially if he was the one in the pilot seat.

He picked up the paper, and traced his finger over her

name as a devious plan began to formulate in his mind. As he sorted through all the naughty details, all the tricks he was going to use on her, he checked his watch then picked up his phone to call his personal assistant. After giving her a list of things he needed before takeoff, he dialed a friend and called in a favor. Once all the pieces were in place, and the discreet information he needed was on its way, he crossed Jack's name off the manifesto, shrugged out of his dress jacket and grabbed his flight suit. Ms. Andrews might be looking for a little adventure at Freedom, but he'd be damned if he wasn't going to be the guy to give her what she really wanted, yet had no idea how much she needed.

Confessions of a Bad Boy CEO

Hands On

Hands On

Body Contact

Full Exposure

Dossier

Private Reserve

House Rules

Under Pressure

Big Catch

Brazilian Fantasy

Improper Proposal

Boys of Beachville

Good at Being Bad

Igniting the Bad Boy

Bad Girl Therapy

Stone Cliff Series:

Crashing Down

Wasted Summer

Love Lessons

Wrapped Up

Eternal Pleasure Series

Instinctive

Impulsive

Indulgent

Sun Stroked Series

Seaside Seduction

Deep Desire

Private Pleasure

Captured and Claimed Series:

Yours to Take

Yours to Teach

Yours to Keep

Firefighter Heat Series

Fever

Siren

Flash Fire

Playing For Keeps Series

Slow Ride

Wild Ride

Sweet Ride

Breaking the Rules:

Hold Me Down Hard

Pin Me Up Proper

Tie Me Down Tight

Stand Alone Title:

Hands on with the CEO

Torn Between Two Brothers

Holiday Spirit

Unleashed

Knocking on Demon's Door

Web of Desire

Pinterest http://www.pinterest.com/catkalen/